UNDER ATTACK

Tremors shook the ground, creating more of the cracks that already covered it. A few more seconds passed, and then all went still.

"An earthquake?" I asked uncertainly.

"No," said Volusian. He was in his solid, two-legged form, staring around with narrowed eyes. It was a little disconcerting that he didn't seem to know precisely what the problem was.

"Then what are we—"

The ground below us suddenly split open. With only the light of the fire, my vision was bad, but I thought I saw what looked kind of like a serpentine shape emerge from the earth. No, it was *exactly* like a serpentine shape because a moment later, a giant snake shot up from the earth and landed neatly in a perfect coil. Its head towering over Kiyo and me as it regarded us with glowing green eyes. The light from them illuminated a flicking, forked tongue, and the loud hissing that followed was kind of a given.

Beside me, Kiyo was shifting into fox form, and I decided a gun was probably going to get me farther here than the athame's small blade. A drop of venom fell from the snake's mouth and sizzled when it hit the ground in front of me. . . .

Books by Richelle Mead

The Georgina Kincaid Series

SUCCUBUS BLUES

SUCCUBUS ON TOP

SUCCUBUS DREAMS

SUCCUBUS HEAT

SUCCUBUS SHADOWS

The Eugenie Markham/Dark Swan Series

STORM BORN

THORN QUEEN

IRON CROWNED

Published by Kensington Publishing Corporation

Iron Crowned

RICHELLE MEAD

ZEBRA BOOKS
KENSINGTON PUBLISHING CORP.
http://www.kensingtonbooks.com

ZEBRA BOOKS are published by

Kensington Publishing Corp.
119 West 40th Street
New York, NY 10018

All Kensington titles, imprints, and distributed lines are available at special quantity discounts for bulk purchases for sales promotion, premiums, fund-raising, educational, or institutional use.

Special book excerpts or customized printings can also be created to fit specific needs. For details, write or phone the office of the Kensington Special Sales Manager: Attn. Special Sales Department. Kensington Publishing Corp., 119 West 40th Street, New York, NY 10018. Phone: 1-800-221-2647.

Zebra and the Z logo Reg. U.S. Pat. & TM Off.

ISBN-13: 978-1-4201-1179-8
ISBN-10: 1-4201-1179-5

First Printing: March 2011
10 9 8 7 6 5 4 3 2 1

Printed in the United States of America

For David, my first reader

Acknowledgments

Many thanks to the friends and family who always support me through my writing—especially as life gets more and more hectic! Thanks also to editor John Scognamiglio and agent Jim McCarthy, for making sure these books keep getting written. A shout-out also goes to my doctor, for letting me abuse her for research. And finally, I can't express enough gratitude to the Eugenie fans who have been so, so patient in waiting for this next installment. Thank you for hanging in there!

Chapter 1

Don't confuse fairy queens with fairy princesses. Where I come from, girls who want to be fairy princesses usually dream about gossamer wings and frilly dresses. Pink dresses, at that. I'm pretty sure rhinestones are part of being a fairy princess too, as are cute wands with stars on top that grant wishes. Fairy princesses expect lovely lives of luxury and lounging, ones that involve small woodland creatures waiting on their every need.

As a fairy queen, I can admit that there *is* a bit more involvement with woodland creatures than one might expect. But the rest? A total joke. Fairies—the kind I deal with, at least—rarely have wings. My wand is made of rough gemstones bound together, and I use it to blast Otherworldly creatures out of existence. I've also whacked a few people in the head with it. My life is dirty, harsh, and deadly, the kind of life no frilly dress could withstand. I wear jeans. Most important, I look horrible in pink.

I'm also pretty sure that fairy princesses don't

have to deal with this kind of shit first thing in the morning.

"I have killed . . . Eugenie Markham."

The words rang out loud and clear through a dining room filled with about thirty people eating at round wooden tables. The ceilings were vaulted, and the rough stone walls made it look like part of a medieval castle because . . . well, it kind of was. Most of the morning diners were soldiers and guards, but a few were officials and high-ranking servants who lived and worked within the castle.

Dorian, King of the Oak Land and my bondage-loving Otherworldly boyfriend, sat at the head table and looked up from his breakfast to see who had made such a bold statement. "I'm sorry, did you say something?"

The speaker, standing on the other side of the table, turned as red as the uniform he wore. He looked about twenty-something in human years, meaning he was probably a hundred or so in fairy—or gentry, the name I preferred—years. The guy bit his lip and straightened his posture, making another attempt at dignity as he glared at Dorian.

"I *said* I killed Eugenie Markham." The man—a soldier, it appeared—looked around at the faces, no doubt hoping his message would inspire horrified reactions. Mostly his words brought about good-natured confusion, largely because half of the people gathered in the room could see me standing in the hall outside. "I have killed your queen, and now your armies will crumble.

Surrender immediately, and Her Royal Majesty, Queen Katrice of the Rowan Land, will be merciful."

Dorian didn't answer right away and didn't look very concerned. He delicately patted his mouth with a brocade napkin and then returned it to his lap. "Dead? Are you sure?" He glanced over at a dark-haired woman sitting beside him. "Shaya, didn't we just see her yesterday?"

"Yes, sire," replied Shaya, pouring cream into her tea.

Dorian brushed autumn-red hair out of his face and returned to cutting up the sugary, almond-coated pastry that was serving as his most important meal of the day. "Well, there you have it. She can't be dead."

The Rowan soldier stared in disbelief, growing more and more incredulous as people continued to either regard him curiously or simply ignore him altogether. The only person who seemed mildly concerned was an elderly gentry woman sitting on the other side of Dorian. Her name was Ranelle, and she was an ambassador from the Linden Land. She'd only arrived yesterday and clearly wasn't used to the wacky mishaps around here.

The soldier turned his attention back to Dorian. "Are you as insane as they say you are? I killed the Thorn Queen! Look." He threw down a silver and moonstone necklace. It clattered against the hard, tiled floor, and the pale, iridescent stones just barely picked up some of the morning light. "I cut this off of her corpse. *Now* do you believe me?"

That brought some silence to the room, and

even Dorian paused. It was indeed my necklace, and seeing it made me absentmindedly touch the bare spot on my throat. Dorian wore his perpetually bored expression, but I knew him well enough to guess at the maelstrom of thoughts swirling behind his green eyes.

"If that's true," Dorian replied at last, "then why didn't you actually bring us her corpse?"

"It's with my queen," said the soldier smugly, thinking he'd finally gained ground. "She kept it as a trophy. If you cooperate, she *might* release it to you."

"I don't believe it." Dorian peered down the table. "Rurik, will you pass the salt? Ah, thank you."

"King Dorian," said Ranelle uneasily, "perhaps you should pay more attention to what this man has to say. If the queen is dead—"

"She's not," said Dorian bluntly. "And this sauce is delicious."

"Why don't you believe me?" exclaimed the soldier, sounding oddly childlike. "Did you think she was invincible? Did you think no one could kill her?"

"No," admitted Dorian. "I just don't think *you* could kill her."

Ranelle tried again. "My lord, how do you know that the queen isn't—"

"Because she's standing right there. Will you all shut up now so I can eat in peace?"

The interruption—and end to this farce—came from Jasmine, my teenage sister. Like me, she was half-human. Unlike me, she was totally unstable and was consequently eating her breakfast while wearing loose but magic-stunting handcuffs. She also had headphones on, and the breakfast debate must have been overpowering her current playlist.

Thirty faces turned toward where I stood near the doorway, and there was a mad scramble as almost everyone shoved back their chairs and tried to rise for a hasty bow. I sighed. I'd been comfortable leaning against the wall, resting from a hard night's journey as I watched this absurdity unfolding in my Otherworldly home. The gig was up now. I threw back my shoulders and strode into the dining room, putting on all the queenly airs I could.

"The reports of my death have been greatly exaggerated," I announced. I had a feeling I'd messed up the Mark Twain quote, but in this crowd, nobody knew the reference anyway. Most thought I was simply stating the facts. Which, really, I was.

The Rowan soldier's flushed face suddenly turned white, his eyes bugging out. He took a few steps backward and glanced uneasily around. There was really nowhere else he could go.

I gestured for those who were standing and bowing to sit down as I walked up to my necklace. Picking it up from the floor, I eyed it critically. "You broke the clasp." I studied it for a few more moments and then turned my glare on him. "You broke it when you ripped it off my neck while we were fighting—*not* when you killed me. Obviously." I just barely recalled grappling with this guy last night. He'd been one among many. I'd lost him in the midst of the chaos, but apparently, Katrice had decided to send him here with a story after he'd captured this "evidence."

"You look amazing for being dead, my dear," called Dorian. "You should really come join us and try this sauce that Ranelle brought."

I ignored Dorian, both because he expected me to and because I knew I didn't look so amazing. My clothes were ripped and dirty, and I'd accrued a few cuts in last night's battle. Judging from the haze of red I kept seeing out of the corners of my eyes, I had a feeling my hair was frizzy and sticking up in about a hundred different directions. It was already turning into a hot day, and my stuffy castle was making me sweat profusely.

"No," gasped the Rowan soldier. "You can't be alive. Balor swore he saw you fall—he told the queen—"

"Will you guys stop this already?" I demanded, leaning in close to his face. This made a few of my own guards step nearer, but I wasn't worried. This loser wouldn't try anything, and besides, I could defend myself. "When is your fucking queen going to stop turning every rumor about Dorian or me dying into some huge proclamation? Haven't you ever heard of *habeas corpus?* Never mind. Of course you haven't."

"Actually," piped in Dorian. "I know Latin."

"It won't work anyway," I growled to the Rowan guy. "Even if I were dead, it's not going to stop our kingdoms from trampling yours."

That pulled him out of his stupefied state. Fury lit his features—fury spiked with a little bit of insane zeal. "You half-breed bitch! *You're* the one who's going to be blighted from existence! You, the Oak King, and everyone else who lives in your cursed lands. Our queen is mighty and great! Already she's in negotiations with the Aspen and Willow Lands to unite against you! She will grind you with her foot and take this land, take it and—"

"Can I kill him? Please?" This was Jasmine. Her gray eyes looked at me pleadingly, and she'd taken the headphones off. What should have been teenage sarcasm was actually deadly seriousness. It was days like these I regretted keeping her in the Otherworld, rather than sending her back to live with humans. Surely it wasn't too late for reform school. "I haven't killed any of your people, Eugenie. You know I haven't. Let me do something to him. Please."

"He's under a truce flag," replied Shaya automatically. Protocol was her specialty.

Dorian turned toward her. "Blast it, woman! I've told you to stop letting them in with immunity. Wartime rules be damned." Shaya only smiled, unconcerned by his mock outrage.

"But he *is* protected," I said, suddenly feeling exhausted. Last's night battle—more of a skirmish, really—had ended in a draw between my armies and Katrice's. It was incredibly frustrating, making the loss of life on both sides seem totally pointless. I beckoned some of my guards forward. "Get him out of here. Put him on a horse, and don't send him with any water. Let's hope the roads are kind to him today."

The guards bowed obediently, and I turned back to Katrice's man.

"And you can let Katrice know that she's wasting her time, no matter how often she wants to claim she's killed me—or even if she manages it. We're still going to see this war through, and she's the one who's going to lose. She's outnumbered and out-resourced. She started this over a personal fight, and no one else is going to help her with it. Tell her that if *she* surrenders immediately, then maybe we'll be merciful."

The Rowan soldier glared at me, his malice palpable, but offered no response. The best he could manage was to spit on the ground before the guards dragged him off. With another sigh, I turned away and looked at the breakfast table. They'd already brought up a chair for me.

"Is there any toast?" I asked, sitting down wearily.

Toast was not a common item on the gentry menu, but the servants here had gotten used to my human preferences. They still couldn't make decent tequila, and Pop-Tarts were totally out of the question. But toast? Toast was within their skill set. Someone handed a basket of it to me, and everyone continued eating peacefully. Well, almost everyone. Ranelle was staring at all of us like we were crazy, which I could understand.

"How can you be so calm?" she exclaimed. "After that man just—just—and you . . ." She looked me over in amazement. "Forgive me, Your Majesty, but your attire . . . You've clearly been in battle. Yet, here you are, sitting as though this is all perfectly ordinary."

I gave her a cheerful look, not wanting to offend our guest or project a weak image. I'd just arrogantly told the Rowan soldier that his queen would never gain any allies, but his comment about her negotiating with the Aspen and Willow Lands hadn't been lost on me. Katrice and I were both scrambling for allies in this war. Dorian was mine, giving me the edge in numbers right now, and I didn't want to risk any chance of that changing.

Dorian caught my eye and gave me one of his small, laconic smiles. It warmed me up, easing a little of the frustration I felt. Some days, I felt like he was all that was going to get me through this war I'd inadvertently stumbled into. I'd never wanted it. I'd never wanted to be queen of a fey kingdom either, forcing me to split my time between here and my human life in Tucson. I certainly hadn't wanted to be at the center of a prophecy that claimed I'd give birth to humanity's conqueror, a prophecy that had driven Katrice's son to rape me. Dorian had killed him for it, something I still didn't regret, even though I hated every day of the war that had followed in the killing's wake.

I couldn't tell Ranelle any of that, of course. I wanted to send her back to her land with an image of confidence and power, so that her king would think allying with us was a smart move. A brilliant move, even. I couldn't tell Ranelle my fears. I couldn't tell her how much it hurt me to see refugees showing up at my castle, poor petitioners whose homes had been destroyed by the war. I couldn't tell her that Dorian and I took turns visiting the armies and fighting with them—and how on those nights, the one who wasn't fighting never got any sleep. Despite his flippancy, I knew Dorian had felt a spark of fear at the Rowan soldier's initial claim. Katrice was always trying to demoralize us. Both Dorian and I feared that someday, one of her heralds would show up telling the truth. It made me want to run away with him right now, run away from all of this and just wrap myself up in his arms.

But again, I reminded myself that I had to brush those thoughts away. Leaning over, I gave Dorian a soft kiss on his cheek. The smile I offered Ranelle was as winning and upbeat as one he might produce. "Actually," I told her. "This *is* a pretty ordinary day for us."

The sad part? It was true.

Chapter 2

I retreated to my bedroom as soon as etiquette allowed, collapsing onto the bed the moment I entered. Dorian had followed me in, and I tossed an arm over my eyes, groaning.

"Do you think that display helped win us over with Ranelle or scared her off?"

I felt Dorian sit on the bed beside me. "Hard to say. At the very least, I don't think it'll turn her king against us. We're too terrifying and unstable."

I smiled and uncovered my face, looking into those green and gold eyes. "If only that reputation would spread to everyone else. I heard a rumor the Honeysuckle Land might join with Katrice. Honestly, how anyone could call their kingdom that and keep a straight face is beyond me."

Dorian leaned over me, lightly brushing hair from my face and trailing his fingers along my cheekbone. "It's quite lovely, actually. Almost tropical. I mean, it's no barren wasteland of a desert kingdom, but it's not half-bad."

I was so used to his jibes about my kingdom that there was almost something comforting about them. His fingers ran down to my neck and were soon replaced by his lips. "Honestly, I'm not worried about this Honeysuckle place. It's other potential allies worrying me. Hey, stop." His lips had moved down to my collarbone, and his hand was starting to lift my shirt. I wriggled away. "I don't have time."

His lifted his head, arching an eyebrow in surprise. "You have some place to be?"

"Yeah, actually." I sighed. "I have a job back in Tucson. Besides, I'm filthy."

Dorian was undeterred and returned to trying to get my shirt off. "I'll help bathe you."

I swatted his hand away but then pulled him over so that I could put my arms around him and hold him against me. I knew he wanted more than cuddling, but I didn't have the energy. Considering his fastidious nature, I was surprised he consented to resting his head on my chest, seeing as how dirty and ragged the shirt was.

"No offense, but I'll take human showers any day over some servant lugging water up to a tub."

"You can't leave without talking to Ranelle," he pointed out. "And you can't see her like this."

I grimaced and ran my hand over his brilliant hair. "Damn it." He was right. I was still bad at this queen thing, but I knew enough about gentry customs to know that if I really did want the Linden King's help, I would need to look and sound good. So much to do. Never enough time. All so wearying.

Dorian lifted his head and looked back down at me. "Was it bad?"

He was referring to last night's battle. "It's always bad. I'm still not okay with people fighting and dying for me. Especially over one insult." The living suffered from this war too. I often had refugees coming to me for food and shelter.

"Their kingdom's at stake," he said. "Their homes. And that was more than an insult. Letting it pass would make the Thorn Land look weak— like prey. It would make you open to invasion, which is the same as surrendering to Katrice. Your people don't want that. They *have* to fight."

"But why do yours fight?"

Dorian looked at me like that was a crazy question. "Because I tell them to."

I left the conversation at that and called for a servant to fill the bathtub in the chamber adjacent to my bedroom. It was a tedious task I hated making them do, though Dorian would no doubt argue it was their duty too. The magic I'd inherited from my tyrant father gave me control over storm elements, so I could have summoned water straight to the tub, rather than making my servants haul it up one bucket at a time. The Thorn Land was so dry, however, that pulling that much water magically would both dry out the castle's air even more and possibly kill surrounding vegetation.

The servants had their own entrance to the bath chamber, and as soon as we heard them hauling and pouring water, Dorian grinned and pulled me back to the bed. "See?" he said. "Now we have time."

I stopped protesting. And as our clothes came off and I felt the heat of his lips, I had to admit to myself that I wasn't averse to sex, not really. This war really did put our lives constantly at risk, and he had worried about me. Having me here, merging physically, seemed to reassure him that I truly was all right. And I took comfort in it too, being with this man I'd fallen in love with against all reason. I'd once feared and hated the gentry—and it had taken me a long time to trust Dorian.

Sex was surprisingly tame for us this time. Usually, we found ourselves caught up in bad, kinky sex, sex that was a game of power and control I both loved and felt dirty about. Now, I sat on top of him, wrapping my legs around his hips as I drew him inside me. A sigh of bliss escaped his lips, his eyes closing as I began to slowly move my body and ride him. A moment later, his eyes opened and held mine with an expression of such affection and lust that a chill ran through me.

It always amazed me that he found me so desirable. I'd seen his past lovers—sexy, voluptuous women with curves and cleavage reminiscent of classic Hollywood starlets. My body's build was lean and athletic from all the activity I did, my breasts pretty nicely shaped—though hardly porn star quality. Yet, since we'd officially become a couple these last few months, he had never looked at another woman. It was me he watched, his gaze hungry even at the most unromantic times.

I increased my pace, tilting forward and rocking us so that more of my body rubbed against his, bringing me closer to orgasm. I came shortly thereafter, my lips parting without a sound as a sweet ecstasy wracked my body, and every nerve in my skin seemed to ignite. I leaned forward, kissing him, letting his tongue explore my mouth as his fingers stroked my nipples.

The door to the bath chamber suddenly opened, and I jerked my head up as a servant peered in. "Your Majesty? The bath is ready." Her words were bland, and she disappeared as quickly as she'd come. My being naked on top of Dorian hadn't seemed like any big deal to her—and probably, it wasn't. The gentry had much looser sexual mores than humans, public displays being very common. It probably would have been weirder for her if she *hadn't* found her monarchs immediately going at it upon my return.

This sexual ease wasn't something I'd picked up, and Dorian knew it. "No, no," he said, feeling me slow down in my shock. The hands cupping my breasts moved down to my hips. "Let's finish this."

Dragging my eyes from the door, I turned my attention back to him and found my arousal returning. He rolled me over, not holding anything back now that I'd come. He pushed his body into mine, thrusting as hard and fast as he could. Moments later, his body shuddered, his fingers digging in where he gripped my arms. I loved watching it happen, loved watching this smug, confident king lose his control between my thighs. When he finished, I gave him another long, lingering kiss and then slid over to lie beside him.

He exhaled in contentment, regarding me again with that mix of hunger and love. He wouldn't say it, but I knew he always secretly hoped that somehow, some way, our lovemaking would result in me getting pregnant. I had explained to him a hundred times how birth control pills worked, but the gentry had difficulty with conception, making them obsessed with having children. Dorian claimed he wanted a child just for the sake of having one with me, but the prophecy about my firstborn son conquering humanity had always been alluring. Obviously, I wasn't in favor of that idea—hence my emphasis on contraceptives. Dorian had ostensibly let go of that dream for my sake, but there were days I suspected he wouldn't mind fathering such a conqueror. As it was, our alliance already made us dangerous. He loved me, I was certain, but he also craved power. Our united kingdoms put us in a good position to conquer others, if we chose.

It was difficult leaving him, but there was too much to be done. I retreated to the bath, washing both sex and battle off of me. Life and death. The tub was only big enough for one, but Dorian seemed perfectly happy watching me and lounging in the afterglow. He was less excited about my wardrobe choice. As queen, I had a closet filled with elaborate dresses, dresses he loved seeing me in. As a human shaman, I'd also made sure it was stocked with human clothes. He looked at my jeans and tank top with dismay.

"Ranelle would be more impressed with a dress," he said. "Especially one that showed your lovely cleavage."

I rolled my eyes. We were back in my bedroom, and I was loading myself up with weapons: charmed jewelry and an iron athame, along with a satchel containing a gun, a wand, and a silver athame. "You'd be more impressed with that. And anyway, it'd be a waste now."

"Not true." He got up from the bed, still naked, and gently pushed me against the wall, cautious of the athame's sharp blade. "I'm ready again."

I could see that he was, and honestly, I probably could have gone back to bed too. Whether that was from lust or a reluctance to fulfill my impending tasks, it was hard to say.

"Later," I told him, brushing a kiss against his lips.

He regarded me suspiciously. "Later means a lot of things with you. An hour. A day."

I smiled and kissed him again. "Not more than a day." I reconsidered. "Maybe two." I laughed at the face this earned me. "I'll see what I can do. Now get some clothes on before the women around here are driven into a frenzy."

He gave me a mournful look. "I'm afraid that'll happen with or without clothes, my dear."

When we finally managed to part, I headed off toward Ranelle's room, my post-sex good humor fading. A little air magic left me with only semi-wet hair by the time I reached her. Once admitted, I found her writing a letter at her room's desk. Seeing me, she leapt up and curtsied.

"Your Majesty."

I motioned her down and took a nearby chair. "No need. I just wanted to have a quick chat before I returned to the human world." Her face twitched a little at this, but ambassador training quickly moved her past how strange she probably found that. The ease with which I jumped worlds wasn't normal for gentry. "I'm sorry for the grisly display this morning. And that I haven't been around much during your visit."

"You're at war, Your Majesty. These things happen. Besides, King Dorian has been quite hospitable in your absence."

I hid a smile. Ranelle was hardly in a frenzy, but it was clear Dorian had charmed her, as he did so many women. "I'm glad. Were you writing your king?"

She nodded. "I wanted to send him my report right away, although I'll be leaving later today."

Magic filled the Otherworld and the gentry, and there were those among them with the power to expedite messages. A magical e-mail, of sorts. It allowed gossip to spread fast and meant her letter would get back to her homeland before she did. I eyed it on the desk.

"What will you tell him?"

She hesitated. "May I be blunt, Your Majesty?"

"Of course," I said, smiling. "I'm human. Er, half-human."

"I empathize with you. I understand your grievance and know King Damos will too." She was carefully skirting the explicit details of Leith raping me. "But tragic as your situation is . . . well, it is *your* situation. I don't believe it's one we should risk the lives of our people for—begging your pardon, Your Majesty." Delivering bad news obviously made her uneasy. My father, honorifically referred to as Storm King, had been known for his power and cruelty. I wasn't as ruthless, but I'd had my share of frightening shows of power as well.

"No offense taken," I assured her. "But . . . if I may also be blunt, your king is in a precarious situation. He's growing old. His power will eventually fade. Your kingdom will be open for others to move in on."

Ranelle went perfectly still. The lands of the Otherworld bound themselves to those with enough power to claim them. "Are you threatening us, Your Majesty?" she asked quietly.

"No. I have no interest in another kingdom—especially one so far away." Distance was relative in the Otherworld, but the Linden Land did take a bit longer to get to compared to some of the kingdoms nearer to me, like the Rowan Land and Dorian's Oak Land.

"Perhaps not," she said uncertainly. "But it's no secret King Dorian has wanted to expand his territory. That's why he took you as a consort, right?"

Now I stiffened. "No. That's not it at all. Neither of us have interest in your land. But your neighbors—or people within the land itself—probably do. From what I've heard, Damos would like his daughter to inherit."

Ranelle nodded slowly. Inheritance was by power here, not by blood—but most monarchs still longed for family succession, if they were lucky enough to have children at all. I gave Ranelle a knowing smile.

"Her control of the land depends on her own power, of course. But if Damos helped us now, we could certainly help later against any . . . usurpers hoping to claim the Linden Land."

Assassination, outright war. The methods were less important than my meaning. Ranelle stayed silent, no doubt turning this over in her mind. Was a promise like that worth committing their armies to? Unclear. But it was certainly worth bringing to her king.

"And," I added casually, shifting us from that dangerous topic, "I'd be happy to negotiate very favorable trade agreements with your king."

By which I meant my staff would negotiate it. I *hated* economics and the politics of trade. But, my kingdom had literally and figuratively become a hot commodity. My shaping it in Arizona's image had created harsh conditions—but also brought along tons of copper deposits. Copper was the chief metal in a world that couldn't work with iron.

Ranelle nodded again. "I understand. I'll bring this to his attention."

"Good." I rose from my chair. "I'm sorry I have to go now, but definitely let anyone here know if you need anything else. And send my greetings to Damos."

Ranelle told me she would, and I left her, feeling rather pleased with myself. I disliked these sort of diplomatic talks almost as much as economic ones, mostly because I didn't think I was very adept. But that one had gone well, and even if the Linden Land didn't join us, I felt certain Dorian had been right: they wouldn't fight against us either.

I was walking toward the castle's exit, intending to go to the nearest gate back to the human world, when I passed a certain hallway. I hesitated, staring down it as I waged a mental war. Then, grimacing, I altered my destination and turned the corner. The room I sought was easy to find because two guards stood outside of it. Both were Dorian's soldiers, chosen because if anyone was going to father the heir to Storm King's legacy, they wanted it to be their own lord. And everyone knew *I* was the mother he wanted, not the room's occupant.

One of the guards knocked and then opened the door slightly. "The queen is here."

I didn't need permission to enter any room in my own castle but still waited for a response. "Come in."

I entered and found Jasmine sitting cross-legged on her bed, attempting some kind of embroidery. Seeing me, she irritably tossed it aside. "This is the stupidest thing ever. I wish the shining ones had more fun things to do. I wish I could go horseback riding."

That last part was spoken with a knowing tone, and I ignored it. Jasmine was under house arrest, and I wasn't about to allow an activity that might let her slip her guards. I picked up the green velvet she'd been working on and studied her stitches.

"Goldfish?" I asked.

"Daffodils!" she exclaimed.

I hastily set it down. Really, considering the loose iron chains she wore on her wrists to stunt magic use, it was impressive that she could sew at all.

"I'm going back to Tucson," I said. "I wanted to check on you."

She shrugged. "I'm fine."

Despite her young age, Jasmine had wanted—and still did want, I suspected—to be the mother of Storm King's heir. The prophecy hadn't been specific. It simply said his daughter's first son would be the conqueror. That made it a race between the two of us—except I wasn't playing. Her forced stay here ensured she wasn't either. She'd hated me for this initially but had grown more civil after the war started. She considered Leith's actions an insult to our family. It was bizarre logic, but seeing as it had stopped her temper tantrums, I welcomed it.

"Do you . . . need anything?" I asked. A stupid question to ask someone who wanted freedom.

She pointed to the iPod lying beside her. "It needs charging again." It always needed charging. Normal battery life aside, the Otherworld interfered with electronics. "Books or magazines or something. I'd kill for a TV."

I smiled. That one was out of my reach. "Sometimes I would too when I'm here."

"How'd it go with that Linden lady? Is she going to help us beat up Katrice?" Jasmine's moping face suddenly turned fierce. She had powers similar to mine, and while not as strong, they could still cause a lot of damage. If I'd let her loose, Jasmine would probably march right over to the Rowan Land and try to bring the castle down.

"I don't know. I'm not getting my hopes up."

Jasmine's gray eyes turned calculating, making her seem wiser than her fifteen years should be capable of. "As long as you and Dorian stay together, you're the badasses around here—especially you." Surprisingly, there was no sneer as she said this. "But you've gotta make sure Maiwenn doesn't join Katrice. You know she's thinking about it."

Yes, despite her often pouty and childish attitude, Jasmine was smart. "You're right," I said. "But thinking and doing are two different things. You said it yourself: Dorian and I are badasses. I don't think she's going to want to mess with us."

There was something comfortable about being able to have a discussion with someone not using the gentry's formal language construction.

"Probably not. But she's scared to death you're going to have our father's heir." Jasmine eyed me carefully. "You haven't changed your mind, have you? You and Dorian certainly do it enough."

"That's none of your business," I said, wondering if that servant had already talked about what she'd seen in bed.

"Tell that to Dorian. He brags about it all the time."

I groaned, knowing it was true. "Well, regardless, I'm not having kids anytime soon."

"You should," Jasmine said. "Or let me. Katrice would totally back off."

"And then Maiwenn really would come after us." Maiwenn ruled the Willow Land and was very much against Storm King's prophecy coming true. She also had a few other reasons for not liking my alliance with Dorian—or rather, her associates did.

"Yeah," said Jasmine. "But you could still kick her ass."

I rose and scooped up the iPod, putting it in my satchel. "Let's stick to one ass-kicking at a time."

An awkward silence fell. How odd that we'd just had a civil conversation. I'd grown up an only child, sometimes wishing I had a sister. The one I'd ended up with was hardly what I'd expected, but maybe I should be grateful for even this.

"Well," I said at last. "I'll see you soon."

She nodded and picked up the velvet, scowling at it as though it had given her personal offense. I was almost at the door when she suddenly said, "Eugenie?"

I glanced back. "Yeah?"

"Will you bring me some Twinkies?"

I smiled. "Sure."

She didn't look up from her embroidery, but I was almost certain she smiled too.

Chapter 3

I might have come to accept being queen of the Thorn Land, and it was hard not to grow attached to a place you had a spiritual connection to. Nonetheless, nothing the Otherworld offered would ever take the place of my home in Tucson. It was a small house, but in a nice neighborhood, near the Catalina Mountains north of the city. Gateways between the worlds existed all over, facilitating travel, but I had an "anchor" in my home, meaning once I shifted out of the Thorn Land's gate, I was able to materialize directly in my bedroom. An anchor could be any object tied to your essence.

My roommate Tim, who hadn't seen me in a few days, was understandably shocked when I came strolling into the kitchen.

"Jesus Christ, Eug!" he exclaimed. He'd been flipping pancakes at the stove. "We've got to put a bell around your neck or something."

I grinned and had an inexplicable urge to hug him—though I knew that would freak him out even more. After all the craziness in the Otherworld, his normality was a welcome sight. Well, "normality" might have been an exaggeration. Tim—with his tall, dark, and handsome looks—had taken to impersonating Native Americans (badly) in order to score chicks and make money selling his awful poetry. He rotated through various tribes, and last I knew, he'd been passing himself off as Tlingit, seeing as the locals got a little less pissed off by him donning the clothes of a tribe living hundreds of miles away. He lived in my house rent-free in exchange for cooking and housework, and I was glad to see him dressed in an ordinary jeans and T-shirt ensemble today.

"Are you making enough for two?" I asked, heading straight for the full coffee pot.

"I always make enough for two. But most of it goes to waste." That last part came out as a grumble. He'd once complained about being my "slave" but missed my being around now.

"Messages?"

"Usual place."

When in the Otherworld, I left my cell phone with Tim. It forced him to play secretary, something he resented since I actually already employed one. Indeed, most of the messages he'd scrawled on the refrigerator's white board were from her.

Tue.—11 AM—Lara: two job offers
Tue.—2:30 PM—Lara: one possible client needs
  ASAP help
Tue.—5:15 PM—Lara: still wants to talk to you

*Tue.—5:20 PM—Lara: needs you to finish tax
  paperwork*
Tue.—10:30 PM—Lara: won't stop calling
Wed.—8 AM—Lara: who calls this early?
Wed.—11:15 AM—Bitch
*Wed.—11:30 AM—Sam's Home Improvement:
  interested in vinyl siding?*

I admired his detailed message taking—frustration with Lara aside—but my heart sank when I saw who was conspicuously missing. Every time I came home, I secretly hoped I'd see their names up there. Sometimes, on the sly, my mom would check on me. But my stepdad, Roland? He never called anymore, not after finding out about my allegiance to the Otherworld.

Tim, preoccupied with his cooking, didn't see my face. "I don't get why she keeps calling. She knows you can't get any of her messages. Why does she need more than one? It's not like a billion of them are magically going to get through to you."

"It's just her way," I said. "She's efficient."

"That's not efficient," he declared. "It's borderline neurotic."

I sighed, wondering not for the first time if I should just let messages go to voice mail. Despite having never met, Tim and Lara were mortal phone enemies. Hearing them bitch about each other was wearying. Nonetheless, staring at her string of calls already made me feel tired. I'd once had a brisk trade as a freelance shaman, kicking out ghosts and other annoying supernatural creatures who harassed humans. Now that I moonlighted as a fairy queen, I'd had to become much more selective with clientele. I could no longer keep up with the demand around here and felt bad about that. I suspected Roland was picking up my slack but didn't know for sure.

I waited until after breakfast before dealing with Lara. Pancakes, sausage, and coffee gave me the strength to deal with this latest batch of requests. Undoubtedly seeing my number on her caller ID, Lara didn't bother with formalities when I finally called.

"About time," she exclaimed. "Has he been giving you my messages?"

"He just did. I've been gone for three days. You know you don't need to keep bugging him about it."

"I want to make sure he tells you I called."

"He writes them down, every one. Besides, my phone's log also tells me you've called . . . a lot."

"Hmphf." She let it go. "Well, you're getting a lot of requests lately. I've thinned them out, but you've still got to choose."

It was almost February. We weren't near any major sabbats, when paranormal activity always increased. Sometimes, though, it happened for no reason. It figured now would be one of those times—right while I was in the middle of a war. Or, I realized, it might be happening *because* of that. My identities as queen and shaman were both well-known among many creatures. Maybe they hoped they could get away with more while I was distracted. Half seemed to show up for selfish purposes in our world; the other half hoped to forcibly father Storm King's heir on me.

"Okay," I said. "Let's hear the priorities."

"We need to finish your taxes."

"That's not a priority. Keep going."

"Single woman, stalked by a fetch."

"That's serious. I'll have to get on that one."

"Tree elemental. In your neighborhood."

"Yeah, that one's here for me. He won't hurt anyone else."

"Phantom-infested subdivision."

"On a graveyard?"

"Yup."

"Schedule it, and make sure the builder's charged double. Their own stupid fault."

"Will do. Then you've got the usual weirdness. Lights in the sky. Possible UFO."

"Was that Wil again?"

"Yes."

"Damn it! Did you tell him it's just the military?"

"Yes. He also said there's been some Bigfoot sightings—"

I froze. "Bigfoot? Where?"

"I didn't get the details. I thought it was his usual craziness. And didn't you say they don't live in Arizona?"

"They don't. Has there been anything weird in the news? Deaths?"

There was a pause, and I heard the rustling of papers. "Two hikers died over in Coronado, near the Rappel Rock trail. The report's that they fell.

Took a couple days to find their bodies. Nasty stuff. Some animals got to them."

I was up and out of my chair in a flash, making the dishes on the kitchen table rattle. Tim, leafing through a magazine, looked up in alarm.

"Call Wil," I told her, trying to tug on one of my boots while balancing the phone. "Find out where he heard about these Bigfoot sightings. If it's not Coronado, give me a call back. If it is, no need to call." Wil was Jasmine's half-brother, and I avoided speaking to him when I could. One reason was that he always asked me about her. The other was that he was a crazy, paranoid conspiracy theorist. This time, he might be on to something.

Lara was understandably startled. "But you said Bigfoot—"

"It's not Bigfoot."

"Don't forget your other job tonight!"

"I won't."

I disconnected and managed to get on the other boot. Tim regarded me warily. "I don't like it when you get that look."

"That makes two of us."

He watched as I went to our hallway closet and produced a little-worn leather coat. "You're going to Coronado?"

"Yup."

"High?"

"Yup."

He sighed and gestured to where we hung our keys near the door. "Take my car. It'll handle better if you run into snow."

I slung my satchel over my shoulder and

flashed him a grateful smile. He warned me to be careful, but I was already out the door with the keys, heading for his Subaru.

My eyes barely saw the road as I drove toward Coronado State Park. Bigfoot. No, you wouldn't find Bigfoot out here, not even in the Catalinas. Now, tell me there'd been a sighting in the Pacific Northwest? Or anywhere in Canada? Yeah, it'd be Bigfoot hunting time. But it wouldn't be a priority. They were generally harmless.

Here? When you got a Bigfoot sighting in Tucson, it was a demon bear. Yeah—I know. It was a ridiculous name, but it got the point across—and really, there was nothing funny about them. They came from the Underworld and were utterly lethal. With their tall and furry appearance, it was easy to understand why the untrained eye would mistake them for popular images of Bigfoot. Demon bears didn't fuck around either. If only two people were dead, then this one hadn't been in the area long. We were lucky—even if the hikers weren't. No rodents or foxes had fed on those bodies.

In Tucson proper, we were enjoying our typically mild winter weather—mid-seventies today, if I had to guess. As I drove higher into the mountains, the temperature dropped rapidly. I soon saw snow on the ground and signs for Mt. Lemmon's ski resorts. Other signs directed me toward popular hiking and climbing areas—including Rappel Rock. In and of itself, it was a popular area for outdoorsmen. With its proximity to the ski areas, the demon bear's presence was doubly dangerous this time of year.

I finally reached the trailhead and parked in a gravel lot. Only a couple other cars were there, which was a small blessing. I stepped out of the Subaru, shocked by the blast of cold air that hit me. I was *not* used to these temperatures. I hadn't been bred for them. Give me monsters and ghosts? No problem. But cold weather? That was a weakness. I could've used magic to adjust the air but needed to conserve my power. Instead, as I stuffed my arsenal into my belt—not comfortable but ready for easy access—I used my magic for a summoning. I spoke the ritual words, and a few moments later, a small imp-like creature appeared before me. He had pointed ears, smooth night-black skin, and red slits for eyes.

"My mistress calls," he said in a flat voice, "and I answer, no doubt for some mundane task."

"We're going after a demon bear," I said, moving briskly toward the trail and trying my best to ignore the cold. My jacket wasn't suited for this weather at all, but it was the best I had.

"A more challenging task than most," he observed.

I ignored his condescension as I stopped before the sign indicating the various routes and levels of difficulty for these climbs and hikes. Volusian was a cursed spirit I'd subdued and enslaved. His power made him a useful asset—and a risky one. He hated me and spent a good deal of his time planning how to kill me, should I ever lose the control needed to bind him.

I closed my eyes, attempting to become one with the air rather than its victim. The world was silent here, save for the rustling of wind in the pines and chatter of birds and small animals. I spread my senses out, seeking something out of place. My abilities weren't perfect, but I could often sense a presence not from our world.

"There." I opened my eyes abruptly and pointed near a trail marked "moderately difficult." "Do you feel anything?"

Volusian studied the area, using his senses as well. "Yes. But more there." He pointed not at the trail itself but more toward its left, off into the woods. I grimaced but knew his senses were slightly better than mine.

"Off-roading. Lovely."

We set out in that direction. Volusian shifted to a more ghostly form that floated along with me, rather than treading through the underbrush like I had to. It wasn't anything I couldn't handle, but it made for slow going. Yet, as I traveled farther and farther, that magical feel increased.

"It will sense you too, mistress," said Volusian, in a rare show of unsolicited commentary.

I didn't doubt it. "Will it come after me? Or will it run?"

"Run? No. Hide? Perhaps." There was a calculated pause. "It won't try to force itself sexually on you, however. The blood of the shining ones is too alluring. It will simply try to eat you."

"How reassuring," I muttered. "I'll do the banishing. You distract it."

Soon, I needed no special senses to know we'd

reached our goal. The forest had grown deadly silent. No more birds or other signs of life. A strong sense of . . . wrongness filled the air. The worlds were stacked: human, Otherworld, Underworld. With our proximity, Otherworldly creatures could sometimes move throughout this world without me feeling anything. Something from the Underworld was too foreign. It stuck out.

"We're close," I murmured. "We're practically—oomphf!"

A massive arm swung out from a cluster of trees and hit me in the stomach, knocking me painfully backward. There was nothing I could do to prevent my fall onto the forest floor of sharp sticks and rocks, but I did manage to grab hold of my wand as I went down.

A giant form loomed in front of me, almost eight-feet tall. Long-limbed, with clawed feet and hands, its muscled body could easily be mistaken for that of a Bigfoot. Its ears—while definitely bearlike—were flattened against its head, adding to the humanoid appearance. It roared, showing a mouthful of sharp teeth. Black eyes, filled with nothing but mindless rage, peered down at me.

Volusian, compelled by my orders, threw himself against the bear. The power radiating around Volusian's body had the substantiality of a ton of bricks. The creature staggered backward, eyes shifting angrily to my minion. The fact that Volusian hadn't knocked it to the ground was concerning. They were either well-matched, or the demon was even more powerful than Volusian. The latter would be problematic, seeing as I wasn't strong enough to banish Volusian.

Well, that is, I wasn't strong enough to banish him *and* fight him. If someone else subdued him, I could have sent Volusian on. If this demon bear had the means to defeat Volusian, then I'd be cake. Hopefully, like me, the demon bear couldn't obliterate Volusian while distracted by something else—me. I scrambled to my feet, holding my wand out as I prepared to open a door to the Underworld. Volusian and the demon battled it out, neither capable of killing each other.

I gathered my will, channeling the power of my soul to spread past this world and the Otherworld, on to the Underworld. On my arm, a tattoo of a black and white butterfly sacred to Persephone began to burn as I touched her domain. The air near the demon dematerialized, forming an opening to the Underworld. Grabbing my silver athame with my free hand, I approached the battle, cautious of both the combatants and the forming gate.

Volusian hovered over the demon, keeping its eyes directed high. I sneaked up unnoticed. With well-practiced speed, I snaked out with the athame, drawing an arcane symbol on the demon's chest. Usually, banishing a demon back to its domain kept it from returning. A binding mark like this ensured it. I didn't want to take any chances.

The demon's roar of rage echoed through the woods, and it turned toward me. I'd anticipated this and had already scrambled away, keeping out of its reach. Really, I'd been lucky the first time it hit me. It had the strength to kill me with one blow. Volusian came forward again to pull the demon's attention back—only, it didn't work. The demon recognized the threat I was and could feel the opening of the gate. Volusian, attacking and attacking, was a nuisance—a painful one—but one the demon could apparently ignore as it came toward me.

"Shit," I said. I backed further and further away, but the demon was quickly closing the distance. Its massive feet could trample the underbrush that slowed me so much. I worked hard to ignore just how dire my situation had become and instead concentrated on the gateway. That door grew more substantial, and soon, its power began calling to its own—sucking the demon back. The creature paused in its attack. The problem was, the gate wanted to pull Volusian too. Orders or not, he moved out of range for self-preservation, which I didn't exactly blame him for. Only, without my minion to beat on the demon, it now had just enough strength to fight the gate and keep coming toward me. It had to know that if it could take me out, the gate would go away too.

Suddenly, I heard something coming toward us, sticks and leaves crackling under strong feet—or, to be more precise, paws. A red fox—much larger than a normal one—sprang out onto the demon's back, sinking its teeth into the furry brown hide. This brought another shriek from the demon—and gave me a moment's respite. I threw all my power into the gate and jerked the demon toward it. The demon flailed, unable to fight being sent back to its own world. The fox had the sense to get out of the way, its services no longer needed. The demon gave one last mournful cry and then faded from our sight. I stretched the wand toward where the demon had disappeared, sending my energy through the wand's gems to banish the gate as well and reseal this world.

Silence followed, except for my own rapid breathing. Slowly, birds began to sing again, and the forest's natural state returned. I leaned against a tall, leafless oak in relief. The banishing hadn't been as easy as I expected, but it certainly could have ended worse—like, with my death.

"We didn't need your help," I said. "We were doing just fine."

The fox was no longer there, as I'd already known. It had transformed into a tall, muscled man, with deep, golden-brown skin and black hair that barely touched his shoulders. He was a kitsune, a shape-shifting Japanese fox from the Otherworld. Actually, he was half-kitsune. His mother had been the kitsune; his father a mortal from Arizona. Power-wise, it made little difference.

"Yeah," said Kiyo, crossing his arms over his chest. He needed no coat and simply wore a burgundy T-shirt. "You seemed to have it all under control."

"We were about to," I retorted.

"Actually, mistress," said Volusian, deadpan, "your death was probably imminent."

"Oh shut up," I snapped. "You're dismissed. Go back to the Otherworld." Volusian vanished.

I turned back to Kiyo. "What are you doing out here anyway?"

He shrugged, and I worked hard to ignore the effect his physical appearance always had on me. "Same thing as you. I'm on Wil's mailing list. When I heard about the Bigfoot sightings . . ."

I sighed and turned back the way we'd come. "I don't need your help."

"I wasn't coming to help you." He caught up with me easily. "I was coming to kill a demon bear. You just happened to be here first."

Considering the trouble Volusian and I had had, I doubted Kiyo could have taken out the demon through brute force. Kiyo was strong, yeah, but hardly all-powerful. Unfortunately, he was all-bravery. He rushed into impossible situations, ready to defend others—even at cost to himself. He'd always been reckless that way—except for once.

And that was the core of our problems.

Kiyo and I used to date, wrapped in a deeply romantic and physical relationship. His continual disapproval of my Otherworldly relations had begun to fracture things between us. The final break had occurred after Leith had raped me. Kiyo had come to rescue me but had refused to punish Leith. Kiyo had advised a tamer course of action: letting Otherworldly justice take its course. Dorian, however, had opted for on-the-spot justice: he'd run Leith through with a sword. Kiyo and I had broken up shortly after that.

"You were outclassed," I told Kiyo. "There are a

billion other creatures running loose right now. If you want to help, go after them."

"Ah, yes. I forgot," he said. "Tucson's former caretaker is too busy playing queen."

I came to a halt and glared. "I'm not playing at anything! Controlling the Thorn Land wasn't my choice, and you know it."

"That's true. It was Dorian's choice—one he tricked you into. Yet, somehow that doesn't matter, and now it's okay for you to shack up with him and wage war."

I started moving again, marching through the woods in a haze of anger. When we'd broken up, Kiyo had been sad and withdrawn. Over time, he'd gotten his spunk back and now—whenever we ran into each other—didn't hesitate to express his opinion of Dorian, the war, or anything else Otherworldly I was involved in.

"The war wasn't my choice either," I said at last, after refusing to respond for several minutes.

"Stopping it wasn't exactly out of your control either."

"So what are you saying? That I should just stop now and surrender?"

"No." His calmness was annoying. "But there must be a peaceful way to end it. To negotiate something."

"Don't you think we've tried?" I exclaimed. "How bloodthirsty do you think I am? Every diplomat we send is either given unreasonable demands or met with death threats."

"I like the use of 'we.' I wonder how seriously Dorian is taking the peace process."

I could see the parking lot through the trees ahead. Good. I needed to be away from Kiyo. His presence was stifling. It stirred up too many feelings, too many feelings I didn't want to deal with.

"Dorian isn't running this by himself. We're in it together, and *we* have tried to settle with Katrice."

"And as that's failed, you're now going to march in with your allies and take her land with overwhelming force, expanding your empire."

We reached the gravel lot, and I turned on Kiyo in full anger, hands on my hips. "We don't have any allies. And I don't want another kingdom! I sure as hell don't want an empire!"

He shrugged. "Say whatever you want, but everyone knows you're looking for people to join up with you."

"And Katrice is doing the same," I said smoothly. "I hear she's visited the Willow Land quite a bit."

Ah, that broke him. Kiyo's smug, cool façade faltered. "Nothing's decided," he said stiffly.

"But your girlfriend's no fan of Dorian and me. She's afraid of us. How long, Kiyo? How long until she—and you—fight against us?" I was gaining ground; he was on the defensive. He and Maiwenn the Willow Queen had once been lovers; they'd even had a daughter together. I'd never believed their "just friends" claims since our break-up.

Kiyo took a step forward, leaning toward me and fixing me with that dark, dark gaze. "She's not my girlfriend. And we're staying neutral."

I gave a shrug as masterfully casual as the one

he'd given me earlier. "If you say so. And I like *your* use of 'we.' Except, you don't really have an equal share in it, do you? You just run along and follow her orders."

"Damn it, Eugenie!" He clenched his fists. "Why do you have to be so—"

He couldn't finish, and as we stood there, so close, I became aware once more of his body and the memories of our time together. I remembered what that body could do in bed. I remembered the way we'd laughed, how easily we'd connected. The Otherworld consumed so much of my time lately, but I was still half-human. The human part of me called to other humans.

And as he looked down at me, the anger softening a little, I had a feeling he was thinking the same thing. If he had any lingering attraction, the animal attributes in him would make this doubly awkward. My physical appearance would trigger sexual attraction that much more quickly. Even my scent could arouse him.

He looked away. "Well. None of that matters. You should go home. You're freezing."

"I'm fine," I said automatically, like I wasn't shivering and covered in goosebumps.

"Of course you are." He glanced back at me, a small, wry smile on his face. "Be careful, Eugenie."

"With what exactly?" I asked.

"Everything."

With that, he shape-shifted back into a fox— a smaller, normal one—and scampered off through the trees. Naturally, he was too hardcore to have driven up here. Suddenly feeling weary, I got out

Tim's keys and turned toward the car. I'd done what I needed to, that was what counted. I didn't want to think about Kiyo or war or anything like that. I wanted to go home and rest before the next job.

A tingling along my spine made me drop the keys as I felt an Otherworldly presence appear behind me. I spun around, pulling my wand back out as I did. There, before me, was a ghost. It was female, looking like she'd died in her mid-thirties. Her translucent form washed out any color, but her hair was curly and shoulder-length, her clothing casual. Seeing a ghost outdoors was rare; they tended to be attracted to material things. Still, location didn't matter. They were dangerous. I pointed my wand at her, banishing words upon my lips.

"Wait, don't!" she cried, holding up her hands.

Pleading ghosts weren't uncommon. "Sorry. This isn't your world. You need to move on. It's for the best."

"Please. Not yet. I need to talk to you, Eugenie Markham."

I frowned, wand still poised and ready. "How do you know my name?"

"Because I've come to ask for your help. I need you to find out who killed me."

Chapter 4

Distracting your enemies by saying shocking things is a classic way to get an attack in. If this ghost had wanted to catch me off guard and move in, this would have been her chance. Instead, she just hung there in the air, staring at me. I forced my jaw closed and kind of wished Kiyo had stuck around to hear this bizarre development.

Finally, I said, "That's not what I do. And anyway . . . I mean, wouldn't you kind of know? Wouldn't you have seen it?"

"No," she said mournfully. "Whoever did it shot me in the head before I could see. They made it look like a suicide."

I grimaced. Weak ghosts often appeared in their final state, as they'd looked at the time of death. This one was strong and able to appear as she remembered herself, for which I was grateful. I wouldn't have wanted to see her after that gunshot.

"Well, I'm sorry for your . . . loss," I told her, wondering why I hadn't already banished her. "But private detective work isn't my thing."

"I can't go to one!" she cried. "Or the police. Only you can see me. All the other ghosts said you were the one to go to."

"All the other—what, do you guys have a country club or something?"

"Please, Miss Markham," she begged. Her eyes were so, so sad. "I have to find out. If someone dangerous is walking around, I have to know. My *family* has to know."

From what I knew, family was usually behind most homicides. "Look, you're obviously strong. You have to be in order to move around like you do and come outside. It makes sense. If you're this upset about what happened, then you're bound strongly to this world while the, um, murder's unsettled. So, the odds are, you probably could appear to someone else. Wouldn't work on most humans, but you might get someone close to you to see you and hear you."

"But would they *believe* me?" she asked bitterly. "They'd think they were imagining things. You're the only one who knows this is real."

I shook my head. "Sorry. I don't investigate this stuff. Certainly not for ghosts. You're getting my best offer here. Otherwise . . ." I held up the wand. "You move on to peace."

She scowled and disappeared. Yes, a very strong ghost, one who should have already been in the Underworld right then and there. I shouldn't have stopped to talk.

But what was one more ghost when I was already letting so many slide by? Kiyo's accusatory words came back to me. I felt like I was doing a half-ass job in both worlds, too divided to give either my full attention.

Nonetheless, I made the most of my day in Tucson. I knocked off three more jobs for Lara, much to her relief. Jobs meant money, meaning both of us got paid. She'd hinted in the past that our drop in work was creating financial problems, enough that she might need a second job. That made me uneasy because a second job could easily turn into her only job. Finding an administrative assistant who could schedule and bill supernatural appointments wasn't that easy.

I came home at last to an empty house, with a note scrawled from Tim saying he had "a gig" tonight and that there was fettuccine alfredo in the refrigerator if I wanted it. Eating in front of the TV, I selfishly felt resentful that he'd go out on one of the few nights I was home. But why wouldn't he? He certainly had a life, one I was hardly in. What really brought me down was that on a night like this, I once would have been over at my mom's eating dinner. For a second, I stared at my phone and considered taking the plunge. But, no. If she wanted to get in touch clandestinely, she would. Calling now would risk me getting Roland, who would hang up on me. Or most likely not answer.

Frustrated, I decided I didn't want to stay here anymore. It was weird, especially since I'd wanted to come home so badly earlier. Yet, I felt like I wasn't welcome in my own house. I showered off the day's fights—no gentry baths for me—and headed right back to the Otherworld. I almost never came and went the same day, but suddenly, my kingdom seemed like the only place I had friends at the moment.

They were surprised to see me back so soon. I found Shaya and Rurik playing chess in a formal sitting room, leaning together and laughing as she planned her next move. Both jumped when they saw me.

"Your Majesty," said Shaya. They'd instantly gone from casual to formal mode.

"Sit, both of you. You should know better." I sat as well, sinking into a down-filled loveseat that I'd inherited from the castle's previous owner.

Shaya and Rurik returned to their seats, relaxing somewhat. "We didn't think you'd be back for a while," said Rurik, ever blunt.

Shaya looked twitchy, like she wanted to get up, despite what I'd said. "Should I have the kitchen start preparing dinner?"

"No, no, don't bother." It was common among gentry monarchs for every meal to be a full-fledged banquet, particularly dinner, hosting the full court. With my schedule and the fact that I didn't even keep a full court—just the essentials— that was not the case around here. My kitchen staff had it easy, and I certainly didn't want them to get in a sudden panic over a meal they would have normally started on hours ago, had they known I'd be there.

I stared off at the empty fireplace, which had been unused since I'd taken over. Had the Thorn Land shifted into winter, we might have needed it. A kingdom's seasons bent to its monarch's will, and although Tucson was in winter right now, my subconscious apparently thought summer was the proper state.

Shaya and Rurik regarded me patiently, wondering what it was I wanted, if not dinner. I wasn't sure myself. I fumbled for something to say. "News or messages on the war front?"

"No," said Rurik. Not surprising. Ranelle had probably only just gotten home. She was likely feasting with the Linden King right now.

I met Shaya's eyes. "It's probably dinnertime at Dorian's, huh? Or close to it."

She tilted her head thoughtfully. There were no clocks in the Otherworld, but she had a good sense of the time. "I would imagine so, Your Majesty."

"Do you think he'd mind unscheduled visitors?"

"You?" Shaya laughed. "Hardly."

I glanced between the two of them, feeling a smile creep onto my lips. "What do you say? Should we go crash his party?"

"Party crashing" might not be a colloquialism among the gentry, but it didn't take Shaya or Rurik long to figure out what I meant. Both sprang to action. I couldn't travel alone during wartime, so Rurik had to assemble a military escort for us. Shaya left to alert the civilians who'd go with us and make herself ready for a royal visit. Both of them were excited, I could tell. Humans and gentry weren't so different, in a lot of ways. Once at Dorian's, Shaya and Rurik would have few official duties. This was the equivalent of an Otherworldly night on the town.

In my rooms, I found my handmaiden Nia anxiously awaiting me. Gentry magical skills ranged greatly. I controlled weather. Dorian could rip apart the earth. And Nia? Her talent was in beautifying others, in hair and clothing. Like those of my cooks, her skills were often underutilized.

"Let's get ready," I told her.

Her face lit up, and she practically ran to the wardrobe. "Which would you like, Your Majesty?" Her hand hovered near a black cocktail dress from the human world, then moved to a gauzy blue sundress. Then, she hesitated altogether and glanced at me questioningly. It wouldn't have been out of character for me to show up at a state function in the jeans I already wore.

After my earlier loneliness, I was excited to see Dorian—almost desperately so. He seemed like my only connection right now, and I suddenly liked the idea of surprising him. "The peach one," I said.

Nia nodded, her fingers skimming the dresses. Finding no peach, she frowned and rechecked them. Then, her gaze went to the other half of my wardrobe, where the gentry dresses she and others had had made for me hung. Her eyes widened as she pulled out a peach silk dress she'd probably never thought would see the light of day.

"Your Majesty!" was all she could gasp. It was like Christmas morning for her.

With coppery hair, I had to be careful with what colors I wore, but this was a warm enough shade of peach that it worked. The fabric was shining and fluid, like some living thing. The dress was one long piece, clinging around the torso and then flaring and falling like water from the waist to the floor. Gold ribbons laced up the back, decorated with aquamarines. Straps, also made from strings of aquamarines, hung loosely off my shoulders around my upper arm, trailing more streams of silk beneath my arm and giving the illusion of sleeves. For all intents and purposes, it was a strapless dress, leaving my arms, shoulders, and a healthy amount of cleavage exposed.

"I think I need a bra," I said, eyeing the way the thin silk wrapped around my chest.

"But that's how it's worn!" said Nia. Gentry, in fashion and other ways, didn't always share the same taste as humans. Nia knew this, and I could see in her face she was terrified I'd do something *human* to ruin this dream-come-true of finally dressing me properly.

"Fine," I said. "But keep my hair down." Hopefully it would give me some coverage. Lack of a haircut had my ends just barely touching my shoulder blades lately.

Nia took this as an acceptable compromise, going over every lock of my hair so that it was smooth and slightly curled at the ends. Aquamarine barrettes (the gentry loved jewels too) were placed strategically throughout my hair, and she forced more jewelry on me in the same color scheme. After a bit of cosmetics, Nia deemed me fit to be a queen. I planned on bringing her to Dorian's and was about to tell her we should go when a strange and unexpected thought came to me.

"Nia . . . can you get my sister ready too?"

"Your . . . your sister, Your Majesty?" She was equally surprised. "Is she coming?"

I thought about it, wondering the same thing. I never let Jasmine leave the castle and its grounds, for everyone's safety. Yet, I couldn't shake the thought of how bored and lonely she seemed. Plus, I'd forgotten her Twinkies.

"Yes," I decided. "She's coming. Be fast." Nia nodded and headed toward my door, off to whatever closet she always produced endless stores of dresses and jewelry from. Jasmine had once been the mistress of this castle's former king; for all I knew, her wardrobe was still here. "Nia?" I called. The gentry girl paused. "Long sleeves."

Nia nodded again, catching my meaning. It was no secret among the gentry that the Thorn Queen kept her sister a prisoner. That didn't mean I wanted her chains flaunted, however. And when my whole entourage met up to leave, I could see that Nia really was magically gifted with beauty. Jasmine—who looked utterly stunned by this unexpected field trip—wore a dress made of pale green velvet. It was floor-length like mine but had long bell sleeves that did a good job of hiding the chains. The dress was more modest than mine too, but I had a feeling Nia hadn't done it to protect Jasmine's fifteen-year-old modesty. Most likely, Nia didn't want the queen's sister to draw more attention than the queen herself. The minimal jewels on Jasmine proved as much, and the looks from my own people showed that I was definitely attention-getting. I doubted they'd ever seen me dressed up like a full-fledged gentry woman.

Riding a horse in that dress was a pain in the ass. It wasn't the first time I'd done so, and I was glad the skirt wasn't as snug as the top. I was also glad our route was short tonight. The Otherworld folded in upon itself, taking travelers through ways that seemed impossible but which often proved the most direct path. These paths also cut through other kingdoms—often my neighbors'. Knowing this, our party was on high alert as we rode, everyone tense. To my relief, the road didn't take us through the Rowan Land—as it frequently did. The only transition between my land and the Oak Land was a brief stint in the Willow Land. Not comforting, but safer than enemy territory.

Once Dorian's castle was in sight, my group's mood lifted, and the party-crashing spirit returned. His home was exactly what you expected from a castle, multi-turreted and made of heavy dark stones, with stained glass windows. As always, it was autumn in the Oak Land, and although night prevented me from seeing the orange-leaved trees, the smell of harvest and touch of fall chill on my skin reaffirmed for me what season it was. Scattered on the castle grounds, I spotted small clusters of peasants around campfires, watching us curiously. Like me, Dorian had war refugees seeking aid from their monarch. The sight of their faces twisted my stomach, and I forced myself to look away.

Servants took our horses, people scrambling at our unexpected arrival. Guests dropped in all the time for dinner—especially at Dorian's—but we were VIPs. I walked briskly toward the banquet hall while groveling stewards scurried at my side, promising proper accommodations for my companions and checking on anything else we might need. I came to a halt when I reached the banquet doors. Even I with my bad human etiquette knew I had to be announced first.

A herald swung open the door, revealing light, color, and noise. Dorian had about a hundred people in there tonight, gathered around various tables on chairs and couches. Most were gentry nobility. Some were his soldiers. Others were creatures of the Otherworld, types I fought when they crossed to the human world. As I'd guessed, dinner was already being served, with servants scurrying around and the guests chatting and eating.

That all came to a halt when the herald's voice rang out: "Her Royal Majesty, Queen Eugenie Markham, Called Odile Dark Swan, Daughter of Tirigan the Storm King, Protector of the Thorn Land, Beloved of the Triple Moon Goddess."

I would never get used to all those titles. Conversation dropped, and then there was the usual screeching of chair legs as people hastily stood up. Once I would have cringed from this, but I knew what was expected now. I began to stride forward but stopped after two steps. Most of my soldiers had stayed at the doors, and none of the rest of my retinue would be announced since I had no high-ranking nobility with me. Almost. I glanced at the herald.

"My sister, announce my sister."

His eyes bugged, and I could guess his confusion. Not only was that kind of a weird request coming from me, it was also hard for him to manage since Jasmine didn't have any official titles. The guy was fast on his feet, though. That was his job.

"The Lady Jasmine Delaney, Daughter of Tirigan the Storm King, Sister of Eugenie the Thorn Queen."

That got a few surprised glances. I smiled at the herald. "Thank you," I said softly. "Only next time, announce my name before our father's."

He blanched. "Y-yes, Your Majesty."

I entered the room at the head of my party, startled I'd said that to the herald. Where had that come from? A need to diminish Storm King? A desire to tout my own importance? Whatever the reason, I already regretted the words.

A long walkway stretched through the room, and halfway down it, Dorian emerged from the crowd and stood to meet me. I reached him, and he took my hand, giving it a long and languid kiss. Among the gentry, that kiss was perfectly acceptable for receiving one's lover or a visiting monarch.

"My dear," he said, lifting his eyes. They swept over me in that clever, efficient way of his. To all those watching, he was as calm and in control as always, his lips curved into the devil-may-care smile normal for him. Still, I could imagine his surprise. He hadn't expected to see me this soon. He certainly hadn't expected to see me in full queenly glory. I might have been Christmas morning for Nia, but for Dorian, I was dessert being served before dinner. "You and yours are very welcome."

It was a formality, one that returned the guests to their seats and declared my party was under Dorian's hospitality, meaning no one here could do us any harm and vice versa.

"I guess 'soon' does mean all sorts of things," he murmured. He glanced toward my cleavage. "*All* sorts of things."

"Hey." I kept my voice as low as his. "Are you looking down my dress?"

"My dear, I want to do much more than look down it. Much, much more. And I want to do it *now*. I don't suppose," he added, "that your transformation came along with an embracing of many of our other superior customs?"

He was referring, of course, to couples scattered about the room who had promptly returned to amorous activities after I was announced. People made out, took off clothing, and even had sex with ease in public. Some guests watched, but most went on with their meal as though nothing out of the ordinary were happening.

"No," I said firmly.

"Are you sure?" he asked, leaning closer. "No one would take it amiss. Indeed, many would find it reassuring to see their king and queen consummating their relationship. It's a sign of dominance and power."

"I'm here for dinner," I said sweetly. Underneath my prim attitude, his words and his body language were already getting to me. You would have thought we'd last had sex a year ago, not this morning. I might not consent to his exhibitionism, but if I said I wanted to go to his bedroom right now, he'd immediately turn around and walk out with me.

"Dinner, it is," he said regretfully. "Perhaps I'll serve you something special. And I'm sure you'll enjoy our guests tonight."

He began steering me toward the hall's front. His throne sat on a high pedestal, and below that was the head table where he'd been dining. My eyes fell on the aforementioned guests, and I nearly stopped walking. Instead, I glanced behind me and called, "Rurik?"

I'd given instructions for Shaya and Rurik (and a handful of guards) not to leave Jasmine's side. They were seeking out their own table, and even though they were halfway across the room, Rurik heard me and turned. With a sharp head nod, I gestured for him to join us. He crossed the room swiftly, arching an eyebrow when he saw the dinner guests and understanding why I'd want one of my own people around.

There, sitting at the head table and watching me with cold blue eyes was Ysabel—Dorian's former lover.

Chapter 5

"Damn it," I muttered to Dorian.

He simply squeezed my hand tighter, his smile growing bigger. I wasn't afraid of Ysabel, not at all. I didn't think for an instant she could hook Dorian back in, and magic-wise, she was no match for me. She'd actually helped teach me control of air and wind—her specialty—and I'd quickly surpassed her. Nonetheless, she was sharp-tongued; I was certain dinner with her would be an onslaught of snide and passive aggressive remarks. Rurik's blunt nature made him good at throwing out barbs of his own, so I was hoping he might assist me.

Once we sat down, though, I soon learned Ysabel wasn't the only one I had to worry about. Other nobles of no consequence were there, but a new face took precedence. Her name was Edria—and she was Ysabel's mother. She had an attractive, matronly look about her, though her hair and eyes were dark. Ysabel was blue-eyed with rich auburn hair that made her stunning. Ysabel's body went a long way to contribute to her allure as well. What the two women definitely had in common was a crafty, sly demeanor that told me both had few scruples when it came to furthering their own interests. And it was clear that my being with Dorian was not in their interests.

In public, gentry etiquette dominated, and Edria was the picture of politeness. "Your Majesty, it is an honor."

"Thank you," I said, settling next to Dorian on a very cozy and ornate loveseat. It squeezed us together, something I knew he didn't mind as his eyes continued to rake over my body. Our legs were so near each other's that I made the concession of letting mine drape slightly over his. Our seat was pulled up close to the table, so the long, heavy tablecloth hid this boldness on my part—as well as the hand he rested on my thigh.

"I'm surprised to see you here, Your Majesty," said Ysabel demurely. With the way her breasts practically spilled out of her dress, I wondered how I could have felt self-conscious about my tight bodice. "I thought you were busy managing your land and your . . . human matters."

"It's not surprising at all," remarked Rurik, just before reaching for a giant drumstick. He took a huge, savage bite, but waited until he swallowed before continuing with the next remark. It was an improvement on past manners. "She and my lord can hardly stay away from each other." I smiled at the use of "my lord." Even after Dorian had sent Rurik to serve me, the soldier still thought of Dorian as his master.

"Of course," said Edria, rushing in when Ysabel's expression turned frosty. "It's just, from what we've heard, you aren't interested in these types of functions. Indeed, I hadn't expected to meet you in such . . . lovely attire."

"Very lovely," said Dorian. He'd dragged his eyes from me at last and gestured for a refill on his wine.

I didn't necessarily like having my appearance discussed—even if the discussion was positive—but praising me gave me a boost in status. "I'm surprised *you* were surprised," said Rurik, this time speaking with his mouth full. Well, we could only expect so much progress. "Everyone's heard how beautiful my lady is. Men far and wide want her, but of course, she would only accept the best for her consort. As would my lord."

From Rurik, this was almost charming, but not to the mother and daughter duo. "My understanding," said Edria delicately, "is that more than your, eh, looks add to your appeal. You and your lady sister are both valued for your future children. I can already see she has a number of suitors."

I glanced across the room at Jasmine, sitting by Shaya. Jasmine had a genuine smile on her face, but whether it was from being out and about or because of the men who had gathered and seemed to be paying her compliments, I couldn't say. I forced away a frown.

"My sister and I have no intention of having children," I said, turning back to my companions.

"How unfortunate," said Edria. Her eyes darted

ever so slightly toward Dorian. "How unfortunate for everyone."

"Your Majesty," said Ysabel, "have you met *my* children?"

I flinched in surprise. I'd forgotten she had kids. Mother and daughter might insinuate that the prophecy was half of my attractiveness, but I knew that Ysabel, after losing her husband, had come to Dorian's court seeking a powerful man through the use of both her beauty and her fertility.

I followed her gaze toward a small table by the fireplace. Most of its occupants were young. It was like a kids' table at Thanksgiving. I'd hadn't seen many gentry children and could make a good guess at Ysabel's progeny based on their red hair. She confirmed as much.

"That's my daughter, Ansonia." In human years, I would have pegged Ansonia to be about ten or eleven. Her brilliant hair was piled in braids on her head, and she was giggling at a puppy that kept nudging her feet, undoubtedly seeking handouts. "Beside her is my son, Pagiel."

He was a serious-looking young man, contrasting sharply with his laughing sister. Relatively speaking, he looked a little older than Jasmine. His red hair was darker than Ansonia's, more like Ysabel's, and his blue-gray eyes regarded the puppy's antics critically, as though deciding if he approved. At last, a tiny smile appeared on his face, transforming him and making a couple of nearby girls his age sigh adoringly.

Ysabel had clearly pointed her children out as a slam against me, yet I caught sincere affection in her eyes as she regarded the two. I'd always thought her coming to court to push herself off on some guy was bordering on prostitution, but there was more to the story. Her husband had died, leaving her family in financial trouble. It made her actions more understandable, though I still thought she was a bitch.

"Children are such a joy," said Edria, looking at Dorian again.

I looked at him too as he gazed at Ansonia and Pagiel. Long study had taught me that his eyes held the secrets to his true feelings whenever he wore that lazy, mysterious expression of his. And now, hidden in those green depths, I could see the glint of admiration and longing. A strange feeling welled up in my stomach, and for the first time, I could honestly believe Dorian wanted kids with me just for the sake of parenthood and no other agenda. I felt unexpected guilt over this.

As though reading my thoughts, he turned his attention on me. His smile warmed me, and whatever wistfulness his eyes had betrayed was replaced now with love—love quickly mingling with lust as he took in my appearance again. In fact, his desire seemed even stronger than it had been when I first entered, and I suddenly wondered if he'd make a serious attempt at exhibitionism after all. But no, with a deep breath that seemed to summon his control, he respectfully looked back at his guests.

Yet, under the table, I felt the hand on my thigh tighten, his fingers sliding over the smooth silk of the dress. Chills ran over my flesh, but I also politely kept my attention on the others.

"It was amazing how easily Ysabel conceived her children," Edria continued. "If poor Mareth had lived, I have no doubt they'd have a dozen by now."

I considered pointing out that if Ysabel was so fertile, then she would have surely gotten pregnant when she and Dorian were lovers. It seemed in bad taste to me, so I said nothing. Such topics weren't out of line for gentry, however, and Rurik again jumped in to defend my honor and point out exactly what I'd been thinking.

"But you've been with others since then," he said. "And you haven't had any more children."

Dorian's hand began skillfully gathering the fabric of my dress's skirt so that it rose up my leg, soon bunching up and exposing my thigh altogether so that his fingers now touched bare skin. I had a feeling he wasn't paying much attention to the conversation anymore, despite a very convincing look of interest as he kept his eyes on everyone except me.

Ysabel glared at Rurik. "I haven't had *that* many lovers." Promiscuity wasn't an insult among gentry, but in this case, playing down her sex life was intended to explain why she had no other children.

Meanwhile, Dorian's hand had moved to my inner thigh, slowly and carefully moving up so that he betrayed nothing to the others. When he reached my underwear, his fingers stopped, as though pondering this obstacle. I'd picked something thin and lacy, mostly to be alluring for later bedroom activities, but it apparently proved convenient now. He gripped the edges, braced a moment, and then jerked so hard that the fabric ripped. In the noisy room, no one heard, and I just barely swallowed a gasp. I gave him a small glare that he either ignored or didn't see. I suspected the former.

"Sometimes the gods simply wait for the right opportunity—or rather, the right man." Edria's eyes darted to Dorian who smiled at her winningly. His chin rested in the hand not under the table, his elbow propped up. "Clearly, Mareth was the right union then, and I'm sure the gods will smile approvingly on Ysabel's next husband." Her tone and look left no question about who *that* would be.

Rurik snorted in disgust. "I believe the gods have their hands in our affairs, but they're not interested in every detail—certainly not what goes on between the sheets."

Or under the table, apparently. Dorian's fingers, now with free access, slid all the way up between my legs. Whatever disapproval I wanted to convey was contradicted by how wet he found me. The inane smile he was giving Edria changed to something a bit more smug. With well-practiced skill, one of his fingers began stroking me, immediately finding the spot that ignited me and burned with pleasure. My heart rate sped up, both from arousal and from anxiety that someone would notice.

Then, as though wanting to flaunt his audacity, he actually managed perfect conversation while still working to get me off. "Well, if Ysabel wants a new husband, we can certainly arrange that. I have a number of nobles who'd be happy to take her as a wife—or even a consort if she didn't wish to be tied down yet."

The teasing fingers between my legs had now set the rest of my body on fire. I felt my nipples hardening and regretted the thin silk of the dress. Fortunately, no one seemed to be paying attention to me, though that might change, seeing how quickly I was building to orgasm.

Dorian's suggestion wasn't what Edria had wanted to hear, and the grateful expression she put on was clearly forced. "You're too kind, Your Majesty. But it would be so wasteful to give such a fertile woman to some minor lord. Surely a gift like Ysabel's deserves . . . royalty."

The aching, tingling ecstasy created by his touch was ready to explode. And to my chagrin, I wanted it to. It was a need I had to have fulfilled. Completed. So, it was a shock when his finger moved down from my clit, sliding into me instead. It created a different kind of pleasure, but the move was frustrating considering how close I'd been. I spread my legs slightly, giving permission for him to return, but he continued thrusting his finger into me. His motions grew harder and faster, but only the slightest movement of his body gave any sign of what he was doing, and no one seemed to pick up on it. There was something thrilling, something dangerously erotic about knowing he was doing this to me with so many potential witnesses.

"You're right," Dorian said, face turning serious,

as though he was truly considering Edria's words. "And I know a couple of kings who might be interested. Rurik, do you remember . . . does the Lotus King have a consort?"

"I'm not sure," said Rurik, clearly enjoying Dorian's game. "He's the one who has the gray streak down the middle of his beard, right? And the slightly pointed ears?"

"That's the one," replied Dorian.

And then, without warning, Dorian's finger—so, so wet now—slid out and returned to my clit with such fierce rubbing that I came almost instantly. I'd been ready and aching, and that touch was all it took to push me over. My body twitched as waves of bliss radiated through me, and Dorian continued to stroke me, long after it was needed. At last, he pulled away and even went so far as to neatly pull my skirt back before returning his hand to his own lap.

A very pleased smile tugged at his lips, though his attention was all on Ysabel. "Would you like me to make an introduction?"

Her expression was cold, her response stiff. "You're too kind, Your Majesty. I'd hate to inconvenience you." I hadn't paid much attention to her but realized now that she'd been paying attention to *me*. I was pretty sure she was the only one at the table who realized what had happened—and she wasn't happy about it.

"No inconvenience at all," he said. "I'll see what I can arrange."

Edria went out of her way to move conversation away from her daughter being hooked up with someone who wasn't Dorian. I barely heard any of it, and when dinner finally ended, I returned with Dorian to his room. My post-orgasm languor gave way to anger almost the moment he shut the door behind us.

"What the hell do you think you were doing?" I exclaimed. "You had no right to do that!"

Dorian made a scoffing noise as he carefully removed and folded his heavy cloak. "You didn't seem to mind. Besides, you're lucky that's all I did, what with you showing up without warning in that dress."

"Hey, I don't have to consult you on my fashion choices."

"No, but you should expect consequences." He moved swiftly toward me, hands moving to my waist. "It was only out of respect for your silly human prudishness that I didn't just take you openly. Really, you should be grateful."

"Grateful?" I exclaimed. I sounded outraged, but in truth, the closeness of his body was arousing me again. Jesus. It was like I was always in heat.

"Grateful," he said, a glint of fierceness in his eyes. "*Especially* after the favor I did you. A favor you now need to repay."

The hold on my waist went tight, and he pushed me down onto the bed. I could easily have resisted—we both knew who'd win in a hand-to-hand fight—but I was more than willing to play this game, particularly when he swiftly pulled off his pants and showed the long, hard erection that had undoubtedly been ready to burst the moment he saw me in the dress.

I was still wet from earlier and desperately wanted to feel him in me, thrusting as hard as he had with his finger. But to my surprise, it wasn't my legs he went for. Instead he came forward and knelt, one leg on each side of my head, and pushed himself between my lips. I made a sound of surprise at this, a sound muffled as he filled my mouth and began sliding in and out.

He was so big, I could barely contain him. He knew and seemed to exalt in it, his eyes holding mine as he forced my mouth to pleasure him. "You can take it," he said, pumping steadily. "You *will* take it. I told you: you owe me."

It was rough and fierce, but we both knew I didn't mind when Dorian played dominant. Besides, this change in our sex life was kind of a turn on. Gentry, while not opposed to oral sex, almost always preferred intercourse because of their obsession with children. Somehow, the thought of him exploding in my mouth, on my lips, drove me wild.

I could feel him swelling, see the lines of tension as his climax grew closer. His lips parted slightly, a small moan escaping. Then, just as I was certain he would come, he pulled out and shifted his body down and deftly pulled off my dress. With a tight grip on my legs, he pushed my thighs apart and thrust into me with a hardness that made me cry out and arch my body. It was only a few seconds, hard and fast, and then he came, his whole body spasming as he released himself into me, proving he still had the usual gentry urges.

When he was finally spent, he collapsed beside

me, sweating and panting. I found his hand, my own body exhausted for different reasons than his. I rolled against him, kissing his chest and tasting the salt of his skin.

"I thought for sure you'd come in my mouth," I murmured, letting my tongue dance with his nipple.

"Wasteful," he murmured, running a hand over my hair.

"Is it?" I pushed myself up, looking down into his eyes. I kept my voice low and dangerous. "Are you saying you wouldn't like that? Letting yourself come in my mouth, filling it up, forcing me to taste you . . . swallow you? Or maybe you want to come on me? Spread yourself all over me?"

There was a slight widening of his eyes, a rekindling of his desire. He gave me an enigmatic smile. "Maybe. Maybe next time."

I gave him a playful push. "Tease."

He yawned and took off his shirt. "It'll give you something to wonder about and look forward to, something more cheerful than the battle's outcome."

"What battle?" I asked. I'd been feeling tired too, but his words jolted me to alertness.

"Tomorrow," he said. He shifted me off of him so that he could pull the covers over us and then took me back into his arms. "I received word earlier about some Rowan movement tonight. I've sent an army to meet them, and I'll join them myself in the morning. It's near my villages at the river's bend. I think Katrice hoped to take them by surprise, but a spy tipped me off."

"Which army did you send?" We had them divided into units.

"The first and third."

"Both?" I exclaimed. "That's huge."

He shrugged. "So is hers. We have to answer in kind. Besides, those villages are crucial. They supply a lot of food—to both of us."

I repressed a shiver. Those villages were full of civilians as well. Dorian's civilians, farmers and fishermen who could have been looted and killed if he hadn't gotten the warning. He and I were allies, but again, I couldn't shake the guilt of my own people being in danger over this dispute—let alone his.

"I should go too," I murmured. "I should help."

Dorian stroked my hair. "No need to put us both at risk. Besides, don't you have more mundane human tasks?"

Yes, I'd promised Lara more jobs tomorrow. "They're not as important—not like this."

"Only one of us is needed," he said firmly. "Honestly, probably not even that. We have good leaders, but the fact that one of us always shows up boosts our armies' confidence—and demoralizes hers. She won't set one dainty foot near the battlefield. So stop fretting. We'll take them. We have greater numbers."

He kissed the top of my head and took my silence as acquiescence. Soon, I felt him sleep, with that ease so many men possessed after sex. Not me. I was a long time insomniac, and this was the kind of thing that could keep me up all night. I was tired of the armies endangering themselves. I was tired of Dorian endangering himself. I wanted the killing to stop. Kiyo had acted like it was so easy. If only that were true.

After a while, I gave up on sleep altogether. I slid out of Dorian's arms and got up from the bed. Knowing my party would stay overnight, I'd packed casual clothes but nothing more. Searching through his wardrobe—twice the size of mine—I found a thick green satin robe. It was way too big but served fine as a cover-up. I left the room, needing to walk off my thoughts.

The castle halls were silent now, all the revelers having gone to bed. I walked barefoot along the stone floor, trying not to trip over the too-long hem. A few stationed guards nodded as I passed, murmuring, "Your Majesty." I'd long ago learned that while some of my human behaviors would always baffle the gentry, most of a monarch's actions—no matter how bizarre—weren't questioned. No one thought much of me wandering around in Dorian's robe.

I reached a set of glass doors that led out to one of Dorian's exquisite courtyards. I knew it'd be chilly there, but sitting outside suddenly seemed like a good idea. Another guard stood there watchfully and opened the door at my approach. I knew this courtyard and knew where a gorgeously colored mosaic-tiled table stood in the corner. It was dull in the night, but as I sat in a chair, the spot gave me a good view of the garden and the thick stars above. Flickering torches set on poles were scattered around, just enough for guidance but not enough to ruin the night's charm.

The beauty and peacefulness soothed me a little but couldn't shake away my worries about the war. I'd spent so much of my life fighting that I'd thought I was immune to blood and killing. I now knew there was a very big difference between an individual kill and death en masse. One—usually—had a point. An individual kill punished the guilty party. Armies dead on the battlefield punished no one except the innocent.

"My lady Thorn Queen?"

I jumped at the hissing voice that spoke to me from the darkness. At first I saw nothing and wondered if I had a ghost on hand. Then, a dark shape materialized from between some trees. It came closer, revealing a wizened gentry woman. She was small, shorter than Jasmine, but her white hair was thick and lustrous, her clothing rich. She came to a halt before me.

"Who-who are you?" I asked. My words came out harsh, mostly because of my surprise.

She took no offense. Again, a queen's behaviors weren't questioned. "My name is Masthera."

I shivered, not from the night's chill. There was something unsettling about her. "What are you doing out here?"

"I've come to speak with you, Your Majesty. You're worried about the war. You want to end it."

"How do you know that?"

She spread her hands out. "I am a seeress. I sense things that are, sometimes things to come. I also offer advice."

This chased a little of my fear away. "Seeress" was a fancy way of saying "psychic," as far as I was concerned. When you dealt with the supernatural as often as I did, you ran into a lot of so-called psychics. Most were frauds, and I suspected that was as true among gentry as humans.

"Have you come to offer me advice?" I asked wryly.

Masthera nodded, face grave. "Yes, Your Majesty. I've come to tell you how to end your war—without any more bloodshed."

Chapter 6

I glanced around uneasily. I knew there had to be guards on watch in the garden and wondered what it would take for them to come tackle a crazy old woman. Unless she openly jumped me or something, I had a feeling I was on my own.

"Unless your power extends to some kind of mind control over Katrice, I don't see how that's going to happen," I said finally.

She crooked me a grin. "No, that's not a gift the gods have chosen to bestow on any of the shining ones. Even they know the limits of mortals."

I pulled the robe more tightly around me. Seeing as I couldn't sleep, I might as well humor her. "Then what's your plan?"

"You need to find the Iron Crown."

"The what?"

"The Iron Crown."

She said it in a grand, ominous way . . . one that really deserved an echo chamber to give it its full effect.

"Okay," I said. "I'll bite. What's the Iron Crown?"

"An ancient artifact. One worn by the greatest, most powerful leaders in the shining ones' history. Leaders feared by all, who ruled many kingdoms."

"I have a crown. A few of them." Only one was my official "crown of state," but designers had crafted me others to coordinate with my outfits.

"Not like this one," she said.

"Let me guess. It's made of iron."

She nodded and looked like she was waiting for me to be impressed.

"Sorry. Like I said, short of mind control power, I'm not going on some magic object quest. My life is already like a *Dungeons and Dragons* campaign."

Masthera frowned. "Dragons haven't lived in the Otherworld in centuries."

"Forget it. Thanks for the, er, advice, but I'm not interested." I shifted uncomfortably. "I should really get to bed."

Masthera leaned forward, undaunted. "You don't understand, Thorn Queen," she hissed. "Only a few are capable of completing the tasks required to gain the crown. Most would not even be able to wear it."

That was easy to figure out. "Right. Because it's made of iron. I don't think an ability everyone already knows I have from being human would be that impressive."

"Queen Katrice would think so. Many of her people would too. Her armies might revolt. She herself would be afraid and back off."

"All because of the reputation of a crown that doesn't have any power?" I asked skeptically. "Where is it?"

"Far away, in a place unknown."

"Oh good grief. If no one knows where it is, then how am I supposed to get it?"

"That's part of the challenge. Find it, and you end the war."

I eyed her carefully. "If this is such a great idea, why not bring it to Dorian? Your king?"

"He knows of it," she agreed. "He's old enough to remember the legends. But he couldn't wear it. Only you." Now she eyed me carefully. "Your father sought it—and failed."

I stiffened, my voice turning to ice. "Is this part of the prophecy? Some way of marking me as the conqueror's mother? Is it something I'm supposed to give to my hypothetical son?"

"No," she said. Her demeanor turned humble, but those eyes still looked shrewd. "It is merely a means to help you end your war."

"I've heard enough of this ridiculousness." I stood up. "I'm going to bed."

Masthera started to call after me as I strode away but then bit off her words. I wondered if she had accepted my refusal or simply feared the guards' responding to continual harassment of me.

I returned to Dorian's room and slipped back into bed with him. His arm unconsciously wrapped around me, and although it took a while, my troubled mind finally calmed enough to allow me some brief sleep. It was his movements that woke me a few hours later. I sat up in bed, watching as he dressed. Through the windows, the sky was barely a pinkish purple.

"You're going to meet the armies already?" I asked quietly.

From a chaise, he lifted a breastplate made of fine copper chain. Normally, he had attendants dressing him, and I knew he was doing it alone so that a group of people traipsing through his room wouldn't wake me. Watching him fumble at fastening it, I hurried over to help.

"Katrice's forces will attack as soon as they have enough light. They may have already. It's only the unfamiliar terrain that stopped them from doing it overnight."

I finished hooking the chainmail, trying not to think about how rare it was for him to wear any sort of armor. It was a sign of the danger he walked into, even if he avoided the front lines.

"I wish you weren't going."

He gave me that easy smile and rested his hands on my bare hips. "Me too. I'd much rather be back in bed with you. Stay a couple hours. I'm sure I'll be right back."

That brought a smile to my lips, though I felt no humor. "Yes, I'm sure that's all it'll take."

He released me and turned to a cabinet on the wall. Opening it, he revealed a number of weapons. One of them was an exquisitely made copper sword, crafted by a metalsmith in my employ named Girard. Dorian touched it reverently, then slipped it into a scabbard he fastened around his waist. While dangerous in and of itself, the sword possessed an extra threat because of Dorian's connection to the earth and its elements. He could infuse it with power.

"Dorian . . ." I hesitated, afraid to ask my next question. "Have you ever heard of the Iron Crown?"

"Of course." He finished fastening the scabbard and glanced back up at me. "Why?"

"I ran into a woman named Masthera last night, who told me about it."

"Ah, Masthera," he said fondly. "Every court should have a seeress. Her predictions are right about half the time—which is quite remarkable. You should see the farce of a seer they've got over in the Maple Land. I'd be humiliated to keep someone like that around."

"Hey, focus," I chastised. "This Iron Crown. Masthera claims it could end the war. That by winning it and proving our—er, my—power, I could make Katrice back down."

The smile faded as Dorian frowned, looking deep in thought. "That's a very real possibility. And you could wear it, couldn't you?" A sense of wonder lit his words. "The iron wouldn't bother you. In legends, some shining ones could wear it through strength and force of will. But you'd need none of that. It'd just be in your nature."

I could hardly believe he was speaking about this seriously. "And you think she's right? This crown—with no power except a reputation— could end the war?"

"Well, it's not the crown's reputation, exactly," he said. "It's the reputation *you* gain by fighting the many obstacles to get it. Show you can do it, and you show your power." It was similar to what Masthera had said.

"If others have possessed it—"

"Not for ages," he interrupted.

"Okay, even if it hasn't been for ages . . . why would I have to quest for it? Wouldn't the last owner have just kept it around? Passed it through the family?"

His smile came back. "It doesn't work that way. The crown won't stay with anyone unworthy. Once its owner passes, it returns to its home—a home that kills many who seek it."

"You didn't answer the earlier question," I pointed out. "Could it end the war? Peacefully?"

He sighed. "I don't know. Maybe. But as much as you fear me going out today . . . I'd worry more about you going after this trinket."

I caught hold of his hand. "You wouldn't help?" I teased, though I still wasn't buying any of it.

His free hand cupped my face. "I would if I could. And maybe I could. If the legends are true, you pass through iron fields to get to it. Hardly any of the shining ones could do that. I might be able to, with my abilities. . . . I'd stand a better chance than most."

I didn't like the tone of his voice. It sounded as though he was actually considering this. He might connect with the elements of the earth, but iron was still beyond him.

"I could bring Volusian," I said, wanting to distract him. "If something happens to him, no harm done, eh?"

Dorian's face stayed serious. "No, the legends are quite clear. The Iron Crown's lair is blocked to the dead."

"Well, none of it matters," I said. "The whole idea is ridiculous."

His face lightened, and he pressed a soft kiss to my lips. "Which is why I leave now."

My heart sank, knowing the inevitable had arrived. I hurriedly put on my jeans and shirt so that I could see him and the accompanying soldiers off. I knew the armies they would join were massive, but as he rode off toward the rising sun, his group seemed so frighteningly small. When he was out of my sight, I went to summon the rest of my own party. It was time for us to go home.

Most had enjoyed their "night out," but my mood that morning soon set the tone for our journey back. The one small comfort to my dark morning was that Jasmine hadn't gotten impregnated. Shaya assured me that my sister had never left her sight throughout the night and that Jasmine hadn't actually even tried anything sinister. She had simply been content to be away from my castle. Eyeing her tight iron cuffs and the chains that connected them, I felt a small pang of guilt. I quickly banished it. Those constraints had to stay.

After that, it was time for another Tucson jump. I first summoned Volusian and sent him to Dorian's side, both for backup and later reports. I knew Dorian wouldn't welcome my minion, but his having a fighter that couldn't be killed would certainly make me feel better. Once that and other household affairs were settled, I went back to join humanity.

The scene at my house was nearly the same as yesterday. A quiet morning, with Tim cooking in the kitchen. Only, today he was dolled up in full costume.

"You're Lakota," I said, once he'd recovered from the shock of my abrupt arrival. "What happened to Tlingit?"

He shrugged. "The Tlingit are cool, but your average stereotype-loving tourist expects this." He wore tassled buckskin pants and a long feathered headdress. His bare tanned chest looked like it had been oiled, and it had beaded necklaces hanging on it. Studying him, I reconsidered. He wasn't true Lakota either. Just some amalgamation of stereotypes, like he'd said.

"Why are you dressed up so early? Morning commuters aren't going to stop for poetry slams."

"It's Saturday, Eug."

"Is it?" I asked, startled. My timing was all awry with my double life.

"There's a cultural fest out by the university, just begging to hear my beautiful insights on nature." He flipped some sunny-side up eggs onto a plate with a flourish.

"A cultural—?" I groaned. "Tim, the local tribes will be there. You know they'll try to beat you up again."

He flashed me a grin. "Be a pal. Come protect me."

"Can't. Too much stuff to do."

A knock at the back door astonished us both. We didn't get a lot of visitors. Hoping it wasn't a missionary, I opened the door and gaped at what I found. I couldn't have been more surprised if Katrice had come calling. It was Lara. She smiled at my shock. I almost never saw her in the flesh. She worked out of a home office, most of our correspondence being handled by phone and e-mail.

"Come in," I said, still amazed. She stepped into the kitchen, just as tiny, blond, and cute as I remembered. A big stack of papers was in her arms. "I don't like the looks of that."

"It's your—"

Lara came to a halt when she saw Tim. Her eyes widened. He flipped his last egg onto a plate and glanced up at her. His eyes registered equal amazement. And in that charming, con-artist way of his, he instantly slipped into character.

"A beautiful blossom has joined us, her petals brilliant and unfurled in the morning sun." He was using his awful 'How, white man' voice. Hastily, he pulled out a chair at the kitchen table. "Join us. We'll feast and enjoy Mother Earth's bounty together."

Dazed, Lara walked over to the table and sat down, unable to take her eyes off of him—his chest in particular. "Thank you."

"It is my honor to—shit! The cinnamon rolls!"

Tim dove backwards, grabbing a mitt and opening the oven, from which smoke was pouring out. Lara turned to me conspiratorially as he groaned about the state of his baked goods.

"Eugenie, why is there a hot Native American chief cooking in your kitchen?" she whispered.

"Well," I said, suddenly realizing the two had never actually met. "He's neither a chief nor Native American. That's Tim."

"That's what—?" Her baby blue eyes opened even wider. "Are you sure?"

"Positive."

Tim meanwhile was scraping blackened bottoms off of his cinnamon rolls. He held one up for my inspection.

"It's fine," I said.

He turned to Lara, putting his smile back on. "I beg your pardon a thousand times for this unworthy feast I must set before you. Such a delicate, beautiful creature like you deserves—"

"Oh for God's sake," I exclaimed. "Will you cut the bullshit, Tim? This is Lara."

"This is . . ." The cinnamon roll dropped off his spatula, back onto the pan. "Are you sure?"

I sighed.

Both seemed at a loss for what to say. Lara's mouth moved, no words coming out for several moments. Finally, she blurted out, "I brought tax paperwork."

Tim swallowed. "I . . . That's pretty cool."

I moved past sighing or groaning. Now, I was fighting hitting my head against the table. "No, it's not. Can we get on with breakfast?"

"I . . ." Tim finally recovered himself. "Sure. Of course." He looked at Lara. "Do you like eggs and cinnamon rolls?"

"I *love* eggs and cinnamon rolls."

He promptly built her a plate and handed it over.

"Hey!" I said.

He shot me a glare. "Be patient a sec. We have a guest. You should be more polite—especially since she went to the trouble of doing your taxes."

"I pay her to do my taxes."

Lara bit into a cinnamon roll. In his daze, Tim had forgotten to cut off the bottom. "This is the best thing I've ever tasted. How is this even possible?" She gave him a shy smile. "Good looks *and* cooking skills."

He smiled back, nearly dropping the plate he handed to me. "I have all sorts of skills."

"Oh my God," I said. Until this moment, I'd thought nothing was more annoying than their phone bickering. I suddenly wished they'd get into an argument now.

"Besides," he added, joining us with his own food. "You've got mad tax skills. I could never do that."

"That's because you don't have an income or actually file taxes," I said.

"Hey," he shot back. "Don't judge. You obviously can't do your own."

"I don't have to! That's why I pay someone."

With great effort, Lara managed to drag her eyes over to me and remember her job. "They're all done. I just need you to sign them. I wasn't sure you'd 'get around to it' if I mailed them."

I nodded. As far as the federal government and state of Arizona were concerned, I was a self-employed contractor who did assorted home repairs. Which wasn't *that* far from the truth.

"That was really nice of you," said Tim. "Taking time out of your Saturday for that."

"I take my job seriously," she replied. "Besides, I didn't have any other plans."

"Really?" He leaned forward. "Do you want to

go over to the university's cultural festival with me? I'll be reading poetry there."

She gasped. "I would love that. I bet your people have some really amazing insights on the world."

"He's not—" I began.

Lara turned back to me, her business face on. "Make sure you sign these while we're gone. And you know your schedule today, right? Three jobs?"

"Yes, yes. While you guys are out slumming with college kids, I'll be fighting for my life."

Tim stood up and set his barely touched plate on the counter. "We can go whenever you're ready."

She handed him her equally untouched plate. "I'm ready now. Just let me run to the bathroom first."

The instant she was gone, Tim turned on me. "Why didn't you tell me she was so nice? All this time, you've let me think she was a total bitch."

"I've told you a hundred times she wasn't a bitch! You're the one who decided that, after talking to her on the phone. You only think she's nice now because you've seen her and want to get her into bed!"

Tim gave me a grave look. "Eugenie, that is not the kind of woman you have a one-night stand with. She's a goddess among women."

"Unbelievable," I said.

When Lara returned, I noticed she was wearing lipstick and had neatened her hair. "All set."

I scowled at the dirty plates Tim had left on the

counter. "Don't forget to do the dishes when you get back!" I called as they headed out the door.

"Don't forget to earn a living while we're gone!" he called back. "This mortgage doesn't pay itself."

"Neither do you," I muttered. But they were already gone, lost in the throes of infatuation. Considering all the things that had happened in my life, you'd think nothing could surprise me anymore. Clearly, I was wrong.

Turning around, I set to washing the dishes myself, deciding that kicking some supernatural ass was exactly what I needed.

Chapter 7

I signed the tax return and left a check before heading out. It figured: I owed. Self-employed people always owe. It was a credit to Lara that she'd managed my books well enough that the amount was low, but after seeing her run off with my roommate, I decided it was a good thing our working relationship didn't include performance reviews.

She'd also left me a jam-packed day, which turned out to be beneficial. A busy schedule kept my mind off Dorian (mostly) and what was transpiring in the Otherworld. I fought with ferocity, as though each ghost or monster I battled was Katrice herself. It was the drives in between that were the roughest on me. There was no action then. Just my own thoughts.

My last job of the day was the most difficult, undoubtedly scheduled that way on purpose so that I didn't walk into the little ones tired and injured. True, I was feeling weary, but concern for Dorian kept a spike of adrenaline burning through me, one that I knew would get me through this last job. Yet, walking up to the client's house, I couldn't stop asking the same questions in my mind. *Why hasn't Volusian reported to me yet? Isn't the fight over?*

A nervous-looking young woman answered the door, introducing herself as Jenna. She was the one who had made the call, though it wasn't exactly on her own behalf.

"She's in the living room," Jenna whispered to me, letting me inside the foyer. Her eyes were wide with fear. "Just sitting there. Staring."

"Does she speak?" I asked. "Does she answer your questions?"

"Yes . . . but . . . it's not her. I know that doesn't make sense, but it's not. The people at work think she's just gone crazy. I'm pretty much the only one who still talks to her. She's about to lose her job, but . . ." Jenna shook her head. "I swear, it's just not her."

"You're right." I held my wand in my left hand and my silver athame in the right.

"Is she . . ." Jenna's voice dropped even lower. "Is she possessed?"

"Not exactly." Lara had warned me about this one. It had initially sounded like possession, but further data suggested otherwise, unfortunately. A possession would have been easier. "It's a fetch. It's like . . . I don't know. Her double. Kind of."

"Then . . . what happened to Regan?"

I hesitated. "I don't know." I didn't want to tell Jenna there was a strong possibility that Regan was dead. That was the usual fate for a fetch's victim. Of course, fetches usually left once they'd sucked all the energy and goodness from someone's life. If this one was still here, the odds of Regan still being alive were marginally higher. "If . . . er, when we find her, she may be in bad shape."

I stared off down the hallway, where I could hear the sound of a TV in the living room. I shifted my grip on my weapons and prepared myself.

"What should I do?" asked Jenna.

"Wait outside. Don't come back inside until I tell you to—no matter what."

Once she was safely away, I set off down the hall. There, in the living room, I found a woman sitting perfectly straight on the couch, her hands folded neatly upon her lap as she stared at the TV. There was a blankness in her brown eyes that told me she wasn't really watching. She didn't even acknowledge my arrival. Glancing around the living room, I took in its space and features, assessing them for a fight. I also noticed a couple pictures on the wall, group shots with Jenna and a smiling brunette who looked exactly like the woman on the couch. Yet, glancing between them, I knew Jenna was right. This wasn't Regan.

"Where's Regan?" I asked.

The fetch didn't look at me. "I am Regan."

"Where's Regan?" I repeated harshly. "What have you done with her?" *Please, please let her be alive.*

This time, the fetch turned her head, those cold eyes taking me and my weapons in. "I told you. I am Regan."

I had a moment's debate on what to do. Killing the fetch without learning Regan's location would make the next part of this job even more difficult. Yet, as the fetch continued staring at me, I knew she'd recognized what I was and what threat I represented. I had to take her out now, banking on the fact that fetches usually kept their victims close.

I held out my wand and began chanting the words that would drive this creature back to the Otherworld. It was where fetches came from, and a forceful enough banishing was usually enough to deter them from returning. I'd only have to get the Underworld involved if she decided to—

She attacked.

The fetch didn't transform into her true shape as she sprang at me. Rather, she turned into something in the middle. She still wore Regan's face, but it had a sickly green hue. Her eyes were bigger and darker and looked like they'd been stretched out. Her hands and feet were bigger too—and clawed.

She came at me with her full strength, knocking me into a wall mercifully free of furniture. I kneed her in the stomach, needing to get distance between me and the claws trying to rake my face and neck. She fell back a little, not much, but enough to give me more maneuvering room. I swung out with the silver blade, and she recoiled. Iron could inflict lethal blows on the gentry, but silver was the metal of choice for almost any other creature.

"Tell me where Regan is," I said, advancing forward. "Tell me, and I'll simply banish you back to the Otherworld. Make this difficult, and you die."

I was managing that balance I always did: weapon ready to attack while part of my mind focused on a connection to the Otherworld. Hecate's tattoo, a snake on my upper arm, began to tingle.

The fetch decided I wasn't a full threat yet and rushed me again. I dodged this time, anticipating her movements based on the last attack. A fetch might be able to replicate someone, but their fighting style was mostly brute force. My athame caught her arm as I moved, and she snarled in pain, showing fangs that dripped with green saliva. It hurt her but didn't slow her down as she lunged back at me. I sidestepped her again but overlooked what was behind me, hitting painfully against a cabinet.

I winced, and she pressed her advantage, swinging those claws at me. I barely escaped them, managing to squirm away and hurry to the other side of the room. A banishing, I decided. I'd just keep my distance and do a banishing. I just needed a couple minutes—and to stay alive. I began chanting words to send her from this world, words that didn't have to follow any ancient form so long as my power and intent were clear. She paused briefly, realizing what I was doing, and seemed to consider her options.

A circle. I should have put a circle of protection around the house. There was a very real possibility she might try to flee. That and killing me were pretty much her only options. The former would probably be easier for her—and would release Regan. But I didn't want this fetch freely walking the world. I needed to send her on.

Power surged in me and through me, out to the wand and toward her. This was her last chance to run—or, as it turned out, throw a coffee table at me.

I admit, I didn't see that coming—literally or figuratively. I should have, though. Furniture, props, whatever . . . they were all fair game in a fight. The fetch had no reason to rely simply on hand to hand combat, and my athame gave her good reason to attack from a distance. The coffee table was a simple one, a smooth circle of glass on iron legs. A wood framed one would have been better. The frame would have slowed the spread of glass. This table had nothing to stop it, except me. I tried to jump out of its way, saving my head and face. I wasn't far enough away when it hit the wall and shattered, though. Stinging, burning pain went through my back and left arm as glass scraped and—no doubt—embedded itself in my flesh.

My sense of self-preservation kept me moving through the pain, but my connection to the Otherworld had shattered with the glass. The fetch knew this and leaped forward, risking the athame in the hope I was too addled and injured from the glass to stop her.

I wasn't. I had never let go of my weapons, and my athame was ready and waiting when she came. I plunged it into her heart and started the banishing again. Over the years, as I'd grown in power and spent so much time in the Otherworld myself, these banishings had become easier. Not easy, but easier. There was a time when I couldn't have held a fetch off with my athame while simultaneously attempting a quick banishing.

But now, the power flowed through me as the fetch pulled herself off my blade. She had no time to react, attack, or flee. The magic seized her, and she disappeared before my eyes, fading into sparkles and then nothing. I didn't know the extent of the athame's damage. I might have just sent her back to die. Or, she might survive and come after me in the Otherworld as some creatures tried. I wasn't worried. My abilities stayed consistent in both worlds, but my magic was a bit stronger over there—especially in the Thorn Land.

I took a deep breath of relief and stuck the weapons back in my belt as I hurried toward the front door. Jenna was sitting on the lawn, face pale with worry. She sprang up when she saw me.

"What happened? Is she okay?"

"I'm not sure," I said, wiping sweat off my brow. My hand came away red with blood. "We have to find her. Does she have a basement?"

"No." Jenna followed me inside and then halted. "Oh my God . . . your back . . ."

"It's nothing. I'll deal with it later."

"At least—" She reached toward a spot between my upper arm and shoulder blade, wincing as she did. I yelped in pain and watched as she pulled away a huge piece of jagged glass. "That's bleeding . . . really bad . . ."

"I'm in better shape than Regan," I said brusquely, trying to ignore both pain and the sight of my blood all over the shard she'd taken. "No basement. Closets? Attic?"

"Both."

We checked the closets with no luck, and Jenna stuck her head in the attic's tiny space. Still nothing.

"Shit," I said. I shouldn't have let the fetch go without getting Regan's location. What if Regan wasn't nearby? What if the fetch had broken habit and hidden her victim far from home?

Jenna looked as defeated as I felt, then her head shot up. "The shed. There's a shed out back."

We were out the back door in a flash, jerking open the door to a little garden shed that was mercifully unlocked. There, curled up on the ground in a fetal position, was Regan. Jenna let out a strangled cry, and we both dropped to the ground. Jenna propped Regan up while I gently shook her.

"Regan, Regan. Wake up. Please wake up."

For a few moments, I feared the worst. Then, Regan's eyes fluttered open, her expression frightened and confused. Her breathing came in short rasps, and she futilely tried to sit up on her own. Her failure didn't surprise me. When a fetch took over someone's life, it put its double into a sort of magic coma. It required no ropes or gags, simply leaving behind a silent and immobile victim. Regan's ability to wake up verified that the fetch was gone, but the woman had spent days without food, water, or using her muscles.

"She's dehydrated," I said. Studying Regan's state, I knew this was beyond a few glasses of water. "Let's get her to the hospital."

Jenna drove, with Regan laid out carefully across the backseat. She said little, only making the occasional moan. Meanwhile, in the passenger seat, I attempted to clean myself off with baby wipes and to pull glass bits out of my back. The blood on my face was cleaned off when we reached the ER, as was most from my body, but I didn't want to answer questions about what had happened to me. I borrowed Jenna's jean jacket, figuring the few scratches on my face weren't enough to attract attention.

We told the staff that Regan had been depressed and starving herself. We went on about how we hadn't seen her for days and had only just found her tonight. Since there was no ostensible bruising or signs of binding, they took us at our word and hurried to hook her up to fluids. We'd also probably landed her in therapy, but that was of little concern now.

I waited with Jenna just outside Regan's room as a nurse finished attaching the appropriate tubes and a doctor performed further examination. When they were done, they told us we could go in and that Regan would recover once her body had sustenance again. I had no intention of going with Jenna. Now that Regan was safe, my plan was to get a taxi back to my car and go home to clean up before an Otherworldly jump. Lara could bill these women later.

"Wait," said Jenna, as the doctor and nurse were about to leave. "My friend's hurt. She broke a window to get in Regan's house and got cut."

I shook my head. "No, really, I'm fine—"

I shut my mouth when I followed everyone's gaze. Even I could see that the left sleeve of the jacket was soaked with blood. There was little argument to make after that. Jenna stayed with Regan, and I was ushered off to a cubicle in the ER. The nurse shut the curtain, and I took off my shirt. The doctor's eyebrows rose.

"You broke a window? With what, your entire body?" He called for another nurse, who began assisting the other with glass removal and sanitizing.

"I threw a rock," I said. "It didn't make a very big hole, but I didn't have time to make it bigger. I just had to get to Regan."

"Noble," said the doctor, whose attention was on the larger shoulder gash. "If stupid."

Someone with a better understanding of physics might have realized my injuries didn't quite line up with what I'd get crawling through a jagged hole in a window. Fortunately, this group's talents were elsewhere. The myriad scratches and cuts were dealt with by bandages and painful antiseptics. The big cut required a fair number of stitches.

I was restless the whole time, wanting only to get back and see what had happened to Dorian. The medical staff was thorough in its work, however. I decided I should just be grateful that they were letting me go and not forcing a longer stay. I was the walking wounded, in bad shape but not in life-threatening danger.

"Here," said the doctor, just before letting me go. He scrawled out a prescription and handed it to me, along with reams of paper on wound care and cleaning. "Antibiotics. Get it filled tonight."

"I will," I said glibly.

He gave me a warning look. "I mean it. I know your type. You think you're invincible, but any of that could get infected. Get the prescription. Clean and change the bandages on the cuts."

He was right that I thought I was invincible. I'd had stitches and wounds before, my gentry blood usually expediting the healing. But I nodded meekly, promising I'd obey.

"Good," he said, following me out to the waiting room. "Follow up with your family doctor in a week. I think your ride's over there."

"My ride . . . ?"

I stared around the room, freezing when I saw a familiar face. "Mom?"

She'd been leaning against a wall, eyes anxiously studying everyone in the room. Spotting me, she practically ran over, staring at my bandages in alarm. I had no coat, and the tank top showed my battle wounds. "Eugenie! Are you okay? What have you done now?"

For some reason, that made the doctor snort a laugh before walking away. "I'm fine," I told her automatically. "What are you doing here?"

"I'm your emergency contact. And that is *not* fine."

I was still stunned to see her. It felt like it had been so long. Ages. "It is now," I said dazedly. "All patched up. And I've got all this . . . stuff." I waved my stack of paper around.

She brushed dark hair from her face, her expression both weary and distraught as we headed for her car. "It never gets easier. Not with you, not with him."

I gave her a sidelong look. "Does he know you're here?"

"No," she said, getting out her keys. "Not that it

would matter if he did. Nothing could have stopped me from coming when they called me. I thought . . . Well, I never know what to think. . . ."

I couldn't look at her as I sat gingerly in the car. My eyes were filling with tears. I'd missed her so much. I'd missed her, well, *momness*. Lots of people cared about me, but it wasn't the same. Plus, I felt horrible, horrible that I made her worry. And because of me, Roland was out endangering himself again too.

I hastily ran a hand over my eyes and turned to her as we pulled out of the parking lot. "When did you get glasses?" I asked in surprise. Delicate wire frames rested on a face very similar to mine. It was our coloring that was different. My red hair and violet eyes had come from Storm King.

"A few weeks ago. They're just for night driving."

I looked away, fearing the tears would return. Glasses. Such a stupid thing. There was a time, though, when I would have known every little detail of her life. There was so much distance between us now. My churning, guilty thoughts only came to a standstill when she turned into a pharmacy a few blocks from the hospital.

"Mom, no! I have to get back to my car and—"

"You can go back to endangering your life again soon enough. Here, let me see those."

"It's not my usual pharmacy," I said petulantly.

She was skimming the wound care instructions. "Yes, well, I'm sure this one still has a couple bandages stashed away somewhere."

"You're such a mom."

She glanced up, a small twinkle in her eyes that

reminded me of how things used to be between us. "I'm *your* mom."

I followed her sullenly as we waited for the prescription, and she forced me to get a basketful of gauze, bandages, and other first aid supplies. I already owned a lot of them, but she wouldn't rest easy until she actually saw them in my hands.

"I really appreciate you coming," I admitted as we waited. "It . . . it's good to see you."

Her expression softened. "It's good to see you too, baby. I've missed you."

"I don't suppose Roland's forgiven me?"

"It's more complicated than that," she told me. "He still loves you. Really. But he's worried. And he doesn't like you being over . . . *there*. Neither do I."

I averted my eyes again. I knew she didn't—and she had good reason. My conception was the result of her captivity and rape in the Otherworld. She'd spent years keeping that knowledge from me, hoping to protect me from both my heritage and the agony she believed that place caused.

"Well, that's complicated too. I have to be there, Mom. I know you guys don't approve, but there are people counting on me. They're not all like you think. I can't let them down. They're . . . they're dying because of me."

"Is there a man involved?"

I considered a flippant remark, then chose honesty. "Yes."

"The obvious problem aside . . . would I like him?"

I tried to picture my mom meeting Dorian and couldn't stop a small smile. "Probably not."

"Do you ever talk to Kiyo anymore?"

I looked up sharply, my smile fading. "It's over with us. He let me down. You know that. This other guy . . . he won't."

I was saved from further conversation when my name was finally called. I added the prescription to my portable hospital bag and felt grateful that my mom didn't pursue the topic of my love life anymore. I was equally grateful when she drove me back to Regan's house. It wouldn't have surprised me if she'd left me carless in Tim's care.

Leaving my mom stirred conflicting feelings in me. After missing her so much, part of me just wanted to stay and gaze at her, to drink in those features I loved so much. I wanted her to hold me, to be my mom and take care of everything. And yet . . . always, always, the Otherworld was pressing on me. I didn't have the luxury of being a little girl right now. I didn't have the luxury of being her daughter.

"Thank you," I said, giving her as careful a hug as we could manage. "Thank you for . . . I don't know. Everything."

She held me for a few moments and then pressed a kiss to my forehead. "There's nothing to thank me for. Just be careful." She broke from the embrace. "Do what the doctor says. And for God's sake, don't end up there again. I don't want another call."

"I'll try," I said. This made us both smile, largely because we knew my trying to stay out of harm's way was pretty futile. "And tell Roland . . ." I couldn't finish, but she nodded.

"I know."

I left her then, loading my loot into my own car and driving home. Regan didn't live too far from me, only about ten minutes. The time flew by. I had so many things to think about that when I arrived at my house, I hardly knew how I'd gotten there. Tim's car was parked out front—as was Lara's. I dragged myself out of my own self-pitying miasma, uneasily wondering what I'd find inside. Seeing the two of them naked on my kitchen table would *not* be cool.

Instead, they were cuddled up on the living room couch, watching a movie. All seemed innocent, but some vibe made me suspect they hadn't been actually *watching* too much of it. I shook my head in exasperation.

"How is this my life?" I muttered, setting my bag on the counter.

"Did you say something?" called Tim. The living room and kitchen were mostly open to each other. He muted the film.

"Nothing important."

"We figured you'd be out for the night," he said. I was pretty sure there was an accusatory tone in his voice.

I opened the cupboards, rummaging for food. I was suddenly starving. "Well, rest easy. I'll be gone soon enough, right after I get dinner."

Lara turned and peered over the couch's back. "Pop-Tarts aren't—oh my God! What happened to you?" Tim noticed my bandages now too. He didn't look as shocked as her—he saw me come home after fights a lot—but worry had replaced his snark.

"What have you been doing?"

"Earning the mortgage." I put two blueberry Pop-Tarts in the toaster. "Isn't that what you told me to do?"

"Jesus, Eug. I didn't—"

"Forget it," I told him. "Everything's fine. But you're going to have to send a bill to Jenna Benson, Lara. I wasn't able to collect."

Lara nodded without a word, still aghast at seeing what my real life looked like. I poured some water and choked down one of the antibiotics while waiting for the Pop-Tarts. As soon as they were done, I retreated to my room, eating quickly as I threw together an overnight bag. While I was packing, my eyes lingered on a half-finished puzzle on my desk. I sighed. How long ago had I started that one? A month ago? I loved jigsaw puzzles. I used to do one a night.

I was almost finished packing—I even included the first aid supplies, thanks to some residual mom-guilt—when the temperature dropped. An unsettling yet familiar presence filled the room, and soon Volusian appeared before me. I nearly dropped the bag.

"Mistress," he said with a mock bow. "I've come to report on the battle."

Chapter 8

There was a long pause as I waited expectantly. Volusian was enjoying this, I realized. He wasn't going to elaborate until I asked because he wanted to draw out the agony.

"Damn it! Tell me what happened!"

Volusian got this pleased look on his face that I suspected was the closest he ever came to smiling. "The Oak King is . . ." I held my breath. ". . . alive."

"Thank God." Of course, thinking of my own wounds, 'alive' might not mean much. "Is he hurt?"

"He is well and uninjured."

I sank gratefully onto my bed, knowing I wore my emotions all over my face. I hated to ever show anything like that in front of Volusian. I wanted to maintain an image of power. This situation was too important, though. Fear and worry for Dorian and the battle had been a knot within me, one I only just now dared to loosen.

"What about the others? Who won?"

"Your forces, mistress."

Again, relief flooded through me. We had won. Dorian was okay. "Casualties?"

"Inevitable, of course." Volusian didn't seem particularly concerned, but then, he was never concerned about much. "Death and injury on both sides. The Oak King's lands and towns remained untouched."

That last part was good news. But death and injury? No, I didn't like that. I wanted to know numbers, but for now, that was irrelevant. One death was too much. I'd get all the stats I needed from Dorian soon enough. I started to thank Volusian, but that wasn't the way our relationship worked.

"Go back to the Oak Land. Tell Dorian I'll be there shortly."

Volusian gave a small nod of acknowledgment. I expected him to vanish instantly, but he paused, eyes narrowing slightly. "My mistress has also been in a battle tonight."

I shifted slightly, becoming aware of the bandages covering my shoulder and back. "Yeah, I fought a fetch."

"Who inflicted great injury."

"It would appear so, wouldn't it?"

"But not enough to kill you."

The look I gave him was answer enough.

"Pity," he said. He vanished.

"Damn it," I muttered. I stayed where I was, staring off into space. I needed to cross to Dorian's land soon, but for now, I allowed the news to percolate in my head for a few moments more. Only, a new distraction presented itself.

Otherworldly magic washed over me seconds before a voice spoke. "You could end it easily, you know."

I jumped up from my bed as the ghost from the mountains appeared before me. Silently, I cursed myself for having packed up my weapons. Since my queenhood, attacks at home had dropped off, lulling me into a false sense of security. It was lazy of me. Foolish. With no care for the other carefully packed items, I upended my bag, dumping everything out. I grabbed my wand, expecting the ghost to attack.

Instead, she just hung in the air, face blank. "You shouldn't have come back," I said, wand ready and pointed. Weary as I was, banishing magic tingled within me. "You should have stayed away."

She stayed motionless, uncaring of the threat I presented. "I told you. I can't. I need your help."

"And I told you, I can't help you."

"I can help *you*," she said. "I can help you find the Iron Crown."

The magic welling within me paused and then I dropped it altogether. I eyed her warily. "How do you know about that?"

She gave a weak shrug. "I've been following you."

I began the banishing again, quickly working out her words. Of course she could follow me. She was a strong ghost, one who could likely flit between this and the Otherworld as easily as I saw her move around here. The magic of the Otherworld, which concealed so many spirits, would make her harder to detect there. Following—and spying—would be easy.

"We're done with this," I said. Power coursed into the wand. Still, she didn't flinch.

"The Iron Crown," she repeated. "I know where it is. I can lead you."

Again, I paused the banishing and recalled something Dorian had said. "The way is blocked to spirits."

"Yes," she agreed. "But I know the starting point. You don't even know that. I can take you there, and you can go the rest of the way on your own."

"I don't believe you. I have no reason to. You could just get me mucked up in your little investigation and then disappear."

This finally brought about emotion. Anger flickered in those pale eyes. "'Little investigation?' This is my family! Their lives! They mean everything to me."

"Meant," I corrected. "You need to cut your ties to this world."

Her lips flattened into a straight line, as though she fought to control her temper. "I'll take you there first. After you have the crown, you'll help me. I'll be the one taking you at *your* word. You have nothing to lose."

"Nothing except my life," I muttered. "A crown that does nothing except lead me on some lethal journey is a big gamble. I don't even believe Masthera's crazy logic."

"Other spirits say it can do what she says," the ghost said. "They're old. They remember it."

Well, that at least answered one of my questions. The dubious nature of the crown aside, I understood how a ghost like this would know about something so ancient. The grief that bound her to this world might make her strong, but she struck me as a new ghost, one that would hardly know about some legendary artifact.

"It's all ridiculous," I said. "It's time for you to go."

"It is," she agreed. "Think about my offer. Summon me when you're ready. My name is Deanna."

And as easily as she'd come, she disappeared, beating my banishing. Admittedly, it had less to do with my skill than with my own doubt. Her words had struck something in me. A tiny spark of wonder, wonder that maybe there was some wacky way to end this war. If the legends were true. If Deanna wasn't lying. If I didn't die setting out alone on a treacherous journey.

Shaking my head, I once more chastised myself for letting her go. Next time. Next time I'd banish her to the Underworld as soon as I saw her face. For now, I had to go to Dorian. I'd wasted too much time. Hastily, I repacked my bag and went on my way.

Tim and Lara still sat in the living room. Recognizing what the bag meant, Tim again muted the TV, an uncharacteristic look of concern on his face.

"Eug . . . don't you think going over to Never Never Land is a bad idea after getting your ass kicked tonight?"

"You should see the other guy." I shifted the

bag, careful to keep it on my good shoulder and away from my back. "Besides, sad as it is, I think I'm safer there than here."

He sighed, and I couldn't help a smile. I glanced at Lara. "I'll be back as soon as I can."

Her face was as grave as Tim's. "I don't think we're charging enough."

I laughed. "Probably not."

I left them for a gateway that opened up near Dorian's. I had an anchor in his castle too, and crossing over nearby pulled me to it. I appeared in a small, empty chamber that he reserved purely for the anchor. Even injured, I'd had no difficulty making the transition. A long time ago, I couldn't even cross in human form. I'd come over as my spirit's totem: a dark swan. Now, coming here was as easy as stepping through a door. My power had indeed grown, something that Kiyo and my parents feared.

I didn't get very far down the adjacent hall before I was spotted by a servant. "Your Majesty!" he sputtered, managing a clumsy bow. "The king has been expecting you."

"Then take me to him," I said.

Dinner had long since ended, and Dorian was in one of his posh sitting rooms, surrounded by a handful of counselors and generals. To my surprise, Masthera sat there too, off in a corner where she observed rather than participated in the meeting. Dorian's face was calm and collected as he spoke to the others, but his expression broke a little when he saw me.

"Eugenie!"

In a few strides, he was across the room. Something cracked inside of me too, something that was so, so glad to see him alive and well. Despite Volusian's report, I'd needed to see Dorian alive for myself. My heart swelled, and I let go of my aversion to gentry customs. I dropped the bag and wrapped my arms around his neck, seeking his lips before he could hardly even get his hands on me. His hands went to my hips as we kissed, the power of that kiss sweeping my body and filling it with heat as I pressed against him. It was suddenly easy to understand why gentry sometimes felt the need to have sex in public.

No such option was given to me because Dorian's hands slid up my waist, freezing when he touched the bandages. He pulled away abruptly, studying me with astonishment. I still wore my tank top, giving a full view of the hospital's handiwork.

"Good grief, woman," he exclaimed. "What happened?"

I gave as unconcerned a shrug as he might. "I got in a fight. With a fetch."

He stared.

"She threw a table at me."

Dorian peered beyond me, over at the servant who'd escorted me to the room. "Get a healer."

"No, don't," I said. The guy hesitated, glancing between us, torn between two commands. "You need your healers for the armies. This looks worse than it is." That wasn't entirely true. The painkillers I'd been given were wearing off, making the scratches itchy and sore. Yet, I couldn't shake Volusian's words about death and injury. I wouldn't take any healers away from the armies. I gave Dorian a warning look. "It's *fine*."

He returned my look, locking us in a brief battle of wills. "Fine," he repeated. He glanced over at the servant. "She says it's fine. Far be it from me to question my lady. Come join us, dear. I assume your despicable little pet gave you the essentials?"

A chair was quickly brought over to me, and I joined the meeting. The details of it were a blur. I was no strategist, not for this kind of war. One-on-one fights were my thing. Mostly I listened to the group, not always understanding, as they studied maps and discussed army movement and strategic targets. Borders and areas with resources—like my copper mines—seemed to be a protective priority, which was about the only part I truly understood.

The part that really stuck with me was the recap of this battle. It had been long, even though our superior numbers had ensured victory almost from the beginning. The towns and our food were safe. The number of casualties were recounted briefly. Dorian and his advisors seemed pleased by them, considering them low. I supposed, as far as percentages went in the army, they were. Still . . . people had died. Gentry or not, it didn't matter. They had families, people who loved them. People who would mourn. I felt sick to my stomach.

The meeting closed with plans for our next move, plans I agreed to automatically when consulted.

Everyone left, off for bed, except me, Dorian, and Masthera. The pleased, laconic look Dorian had worn for his team vanished once the last person was out of our sight. He turned on me, outrage in those beautiful eyes.

"What were you thinking? *I* was the one who was supposed to be facing an army today. Not you."

"I didn't," I countered. "It was just a fetch. Did I mention the table?"

"You're making a joke out of this."

"No more than what you usually do." I frowned. "And this is nothing . . . nothing compared to what you and the others faced."

His blasé expression returned. "We had a great victory."

"We have different ideas of victory," I said sadly. My eyes landed on Masthera, who watched us intently. "What are you doing here?"

She seemed to read my question as an invitation and moved to a nearer chair. "Waiting for you, Your Majesty. I sensed that you would come."

I scoffed. "Volusian came and said I was coming."

The comment didn't bother her. "You've come to discuss the Iron Crown."

"Hardly." Yet, I found myself frowning as crazy thoughts swirled in my head. Dorian arched an eyebrow of surprise.

"Is that true? You made your feelings clear on that last time."

"They haven't really changed," I admitted. "I still don't see it as a convenient end to all of this. Except . . . well, a ghost came to me today."

"Ghosts are always coming to you."

"Yeah, yeah. But this one claimed she could lead me to the crown. Or rather, the place surrounding it. She needs a favor and offered this in return."

Masthera's eyes widened, and she leaned forward. "This is it! What I've seen. This will bring you to the crown."

"Presuming this ghost isn't part of some elaborate plan to kill me," I said. "Wouldn't be the first time."

"No, no," she said. "This is real. I feel it. I've had a vision of you crowned."

Dorian gave her a sharp look. "Enough. It doesn't matter if this ghost is telling the truth. I'm not sending Eugenie off into a nightmarish landscape."

"Hey, *you* don't send me anywhere," I retorted.

He rolled his eyes. "Please. Don't start with the mock wounded pride over your capabilities. You're a great warrior; I accept that. You defeat fetches and tables and all other sorts of fiends. But this . . . no. The risk is too great, and I couldn't help you."

"But Your Majesty!" exclaimed Masthera. "You see the opportunity. An end to the war. The power. The fear this would inspire among others."

"My own fear is more than enough, thank you," he said dryly.

An end to the war. An astonishing thought struck me. "Gentry would suffer in the iron fields . . . but I'm not the only half-human. I could take Jasmine with me." Jasmine was almost as unaffected by iron as I was. Touching it caused her no pain, and it was only her cuffs' tight binding that stunted her magic. Otherwise, to my knowledge, simply being near iron wasn't enough to dim her power.

"No," said Dorian swiftly. "Absolutely not. I wouldn't have your unstable sister go anywhere near that crown."

"The queen is right, though," said Masthera. "Storm King's younger daughter might be protected by her human blood."

I expected another refusal from Dorian, but he remained silent. He was actually considering this, I realized. Jasmine would be a safe companion— or not.

"No," he repeated at last. "If she somehow returned in control of the crown . . . Well, I wouldn't want to see that. She craves power too much."

"I thought the crown didn't have power in and of itself," I said suspiciously.

"It doesn't—but if she possessed it, others would believe she was the daughter to fear. Right now, you carry that honor. I'd like to keep it that way. You can't go with such a dangerous companion."

"Your Majesty—" attempted Masthera again.

"Enough," said Dorian, standing up. "It's late. The discussion is over, and I want to go to bed. You're dismissed."

Masthera looked upset but didn't contradict her lord. After a brief curtsey to each of us, she scurried away. We left as well, staying silent as we walked through the halls, past stationed guards.

As soon as we were alone in Dorian's room, I turned on him.

"You have a lot of fucking nerve! Don't ever talk to me like that in front of someone—like you've got the power around here. We're equals in this, remember?"

He smiled and took off his cloak and shirt. "Of course we are. And equals sometimes trade power. When it comes to you making foolish choices, *I* wield the power."

"When it comes to making foolish choices, I— never mind. Look, if there's a chance to end this with as little bloodshed as possible, I want it."

"As do I." He stood before me and ran a gentle finger along the side of my neck. "But not at the cost of your life or reputation. Find a better option, and you can go." He moved his hands down and caught the edges of my shirt, carefully lifting it over my head without disturbing the bandages.

"There you go again," I growled. "Acting like you control this."

"I do. Just as I control this." He grabbed hold of my waist and jerked me to him, his lips crushing mine in a fierce kiss, one that left me gasping when I managed to pull back.

"You don't control anything," I said. Yet, that kiss and his closeness made me ache with arousal. Maybe it was my anger or the residual adrenaline from all my fights today. Maybe it was just relief at seeing him, no matter how much he annoyed me now. Whenever I returned from battle, sex was his way of truly confirming I was alive and safe. Today,

I shared that. He was alive. I wanted him, and he knew it.

"You see?" His lips moved to my neck, and I felt the edge of his teeth. "I've got the power here . . . and you like that . . ."

"I . . . that is . . ." Forming coherent words was difficult for obvious reasons. His mouth was too distracting, as was the rest of his touch.

He moved his lips up near my ear, his hands cupping my breasts. I pushed down his pants, feeling how hard he was as my hands slid over him. "I know you, Eugenie. I know what you want . . . and here? You want me in control. Really, those wounds you insist on keeping are all that are stopping me from throwing you against the wall or the bed."

The rest of our clothes fell off, piece by piece, while we still attempted some sort of debate. "Guess you're not as in control as you think," I said. We were pressed together, bare skin against bare skin. We managed to stay wrapped up with each other as we moved toward the bed.

His hands slid up over my breasts, lingering briefly on my nipples. Then—again avoiding any wounded areas—he gripped my shoulders, and I expected him to throw me onto the bed anyway. Instead, he pushed me down onto my knees, so that my back was barely an inch from the bed, and he stood right in front of me. The tip of his huge swelling erection was right against my lips, just like the last time we'd been together, save that I'd been on my back then.

"I still have the control. I can make you do all

sorts of things," he murmured. "Now, are you going to do this on your own? Or will I have to make you?"

There was no coercion needed. I parted my lips and took him into my mouth. Just like the last time we'd had sex, he felt so large and long that I could barely fit him as I sucked and slid my lips along that shaft. He realized I was holding back and tsked disapproval.

"You can do better than that." His hands were tangled in my hair, and he pulled my head closer, forcing more of him into me, more than I thought I could take as I felt him touch the back of my throat. "More . . ." he breathed. "Take more . . . or I'll make you. . . ."

I increased my speed and intensity as I took him into my mouth over and over. It was as much as I could do, and he knew it, but that didn't matter. This was a game, a game of power. Deciding where I went and who I fought? No. He couldn't do that. But here? He could play master.

"Still not good enough," he said. He took over from me, and just as he had last time, he thrust into my mouth as steadily and hard as he might have my thighs. His hold on my hair tipped my face up and made me look into his eyes, just as I was forced to take as much of him into my mouth as he chose.

"I wish we'd done this downstairs. Should have taken you . . . the instant you walked into the room . . ." He still had that smooth, controlling tone to his voice, but it was cracking a little as the pleasure of this began to take over. "I wish the whole court could see this. You're so beautiful . . . so beautiful with your mouth full of me . . . more beautiful still when I pour my seed into you . . ."

I shivered, making a small groan of desire. He was pumping harder now, almost uncomfortably so for me, yet it was giving me a thrill of my own.

"That was . . . what you . . . wanted, wasn't it? Last time?" His voice was low and strained, his whole body suddenly tensing. "This?"

He came, and warm liquid exploded in my mouth. Although he slowed, he still continued sliding in and out as he released himself into me. Then, he pulled out, finishing his orgasm and spilling onto my lips and breasts. I coughed slightly, and he slid a finger across my lips.

"Swallow," he hissed. "Swallow it all."

I did, surprised that he'd been able to come so much both in my mouth and on me. The finger toying with my lip slid along my face and down to my breasts, rubbing in his semen. When his finger returned to my lips, I knew what he wanted. I took it into my mouth and licked his finger, sucking on it until there was nothing left.

Smiling he helped me up to the bed and laid me down on my side, where he continued massaging my sticky breasts.

"Wasteful," he said at last. I knew what a big concession it was for him to forego intercourse. "Wasteful, but enjoyable."

"Seeing as this was what I wanted, maybe I had the power here after all," I teased.

"Hush, woman," he chastised good-naturedly. He shifted me again, so that my head rested on his chest. His hand slid down my body, his fingers moving between my thighs as deftly as they had under the table. He groaned when he felt how wet I was. "Wasteful, I say."

I laughed, shifting up to kiss him. "I've told you before, it doesn't—ah . . ."

Taunting thoughts faded away, and soon all that consumed me was his fingers stroking me harder and faster. He brought his lips back to mine so that we were locked in a kiss when I came. Agonizing pleasure radiated through my body at his touch, and my cries were swallowed into that kiss. He released me only when my shaking stopped and breathing calmed, again letting me rest against his chest. One hand stroked my hair while the one that had just got me off moved to rest on my bare lower back.

We both sighed in contentment, and I closed my eyes, exhaustion from the day's battles finally catching up with me. I was nearly asleep—and thought he was too—when quiet words brought me back to consciousness.

"Masthera *is* right. The crown could solve a lot of problems."

Yes, I was definitely awake now. "I thought you didn't believe that."

"Oh, no. I believe it could end this war. I believe it would make Katrice cower in fear." He sighed. "I just don't want to risk you. I couldn't cope with losing you."

My heart tightened at his words. I didn't know what to say and simply brushed my lips against his chest.

"And you're both right," he continued. "That if I can't . . . if I can't go with you, then a half-human companion is the ideal choice."

Now I was really surprised. I lifted my head, hardly believing what I'd heard. "So, what are you saying? I should take Jasmine after all?"

"No. That's still a horrible idea. But not *quite* as horrible as this one." He gave another sigh, one that seemed to cause him pain. "You should bring the kitsune."

Chapter 9

I propped myself up so that I could look Dorian in the face. Even in dim lighting, I could see he was serious.

"Who, Kiyo?" I asked in astonishment.

"No, the other annoying kitsune in your life."

"Why would you . . . why would you suggest something like that?"

"Excellent question," he murmured. His brow furrowed in thought, then relaxed into resignation. "Because his human blood would protect him and—my personal opinions of him aside—he *is* a good asset in a fight. Most importantly, he would have no interest in the crown. Nor would it be of any use to him."

Every one of those things was true. But there was one obvious problem. "Kiyo wouldn't help me. Not anymore. Jasmine would be more willing— if only for a chance to escape." The argument that Kiyo and I had had in the mountains was still fresh in my head.

This brought a smile to Dorian's lips, and he

trailed his fingertips down my arm. "You doubt your own charms. The kitsune will help you, if you ask him nicely. He's not over you as much as you think. And he too would jump at the chance at some foolhardy way to end this war."

"Foolhardy . . . You've gone back and forth on the usefulness of the crown yourself. And now you're willing to—" I almost said 'allow' but recalled my earlier words. Dorian didn't dictate my life. "—accept me going off with my ex-boyfriend?"

"This is an acceptable solution. Still dangerous . . . but I believe you two could manage it. And I trust you," Dorian said simply. "As you trust me."

I stared down into his eyes, dark in the flickering torchlight, though the striking shape of his face and fair skin glowed like a masterpiece in marble. "I do trust you."

He smiled again. "Good. We'll make plans in the morning. But for now . . ." The smile gave way to a yawn. "I need sleep. This has been a long day."

It was true. He'd been part of an epic battle and then made love—or whatever you wanted to classify that kinky shit as—like a pro. My day had been pretty busy too, to say the least. I put my head down, wrapping back against him, and soon slept in spite of the shocking suggestion he'd just made.

When we woke, however, the crown became our immediate breakfast topic. We'd opted for private dining at a small table in the sitting room adjacent to his bedroom. After hearing about my traipsing about in his too-long robe, he'd had my own made for these slumber parties: white velvet with gold embroidery. It was a bit more elaborate than I would have preferred but felt nice against my bare skin. The wounds certainly appreciated loose clothing too.

"Invite him to your castle," said Dorian. Fully rested, he'd shifted completely into cunning mode, barely touching the elaborate spread of pastries and meats his servants had set before us. "The gods know he won't come here."

"Or Tucson," I suggested after swallowing a gentry version of a cinnamon roll. Maybe I could get Tim the recipe. "He'd probably come to my house there."

Dorian considered. "No. Get him to this world, to your domain, so that you can leave as soon as possible. Above all, you must not—under any circumstances—allow him to go back to Maiwenn and consult her on this."

I swallowed another bite and smiled. "You think she'd be jealous?"

"That's the least of our reasons." He ticked them off on his fingers. "Remember—she fears you. Us. She wouldn't see this as an end to the war. She'd see it as you scrambling for power. And, who knows? The kitsune might have no use for the crown himself, but she could coax him into bringing it to her."

"She's not vying for power, last I knew. Besides— it's winning the crown that's the big deal, right? If it was just given to her, no one would respect her for it. If it can even be given . . . I thought it returns home when it's away from its victor."

Dorian didn't respond right away. "True. But

then that would still keep the crown from you. And we mustn't forget she might simply talk him out of it because of simple concern for his life." Dorian's tone implied this was a petty concern. "No, don't give him a chance to talk to her. Invite him to you and ask—beg, if need be—for his help. Stress whatever urgent reason will work. A need to end the war. Make up some ultimatum from the ghost."

I set the roll down and tapped my water glass absentmindedly. This was all starting to make me feel strange. "There's a lot of conniving here."

"There always is in politics. In war. In love, even. But this can help us—more than you can imagine. We must put our faith in the old adage that the ends justify the means."

I sighed. "Okay, then. I'll do it. When?"

"As soon as possible. Katrice is regrouping. We can take advantage of that." That smooth, calculating air faded. "Though I hate to lose you."

"Hey." I reached across the table and laid my hand over his. "Don't think of it as 'losing' me. It's just like I'm going to Tucson for a few days."

He grimaced. "Except your petty human job doesn't carry such risks. Fetches aside. I *do* wish you'd let my healers take care of those wounds before you go."

The stitched up cut itched, though the rest weren't bothering me. I tested the range of motion on my left arm. It was stiff but moved. "Let your healers keep working here. Maybe I'll have Shaya fix it up." She didn't possess the skill of a bona fide healer but could do some quick patches.

Dorian didn't like that but let the matter go. We finished breakfast, rehashing what little he knew about the path to the Iron Crown. I shed my robe for my normal clothes, after first having one of his servants clean and re-bandage my back. My mother would be proud, seeing me follow doctor's orders.

We didn't know where Kiyo was exactly, here or the human world, but Dorian sent a messenger to Maiwenn's court, inviting him to mine. No one from our lands would be welcomed with open arms in her territory, but she'd allow a messenger through and hopefully let us know if he wasn't currently in the Otherworld. I also sent Volusian to Tim and Lara, warning I'd be gone for a while and to cancel all my appointments. Lara wouldn't like that, but I had a feeling it would be the least of her worries when faced with Volusian for the first time.

When the time for me to leave came, Dorian couldn't hide his conflicted feelings. The part of him always striving for advantage and control wanted that crown. The part of him that loved me worried about what I was walking into.

"It'll be okay," I said, wrapping my arms around him. "I'm Storm King's daughter, remember? This'll be cake. And hey, if that ghost's lying, I'll be back tonight."

"I don't know if I'd prefer that or not," he mused. He rested his hand behind my neck and gave me a long, lingering kiss. "Be careful, Eugenie. Fight hard, but be careful. And take this."

From a hidden pocket in his cloak, he produced something glittering and handed it to me.

I held it up. It was a ring, hanging on a fine chain. Both were made of gold. A diamond flanked by sapphires sat prominently on the ring, which was fashioned to look like a circle of leaves.

"Is this magic?" I asked.

He shook his head. "Just something to remember me by. Just something to think about."

I eyed him carefully. Marriage happened among the gentry, though not as often as among humans. Considering our divorce rate, maybe that was smart. They didn't give engagement rings like humans did, but he'd know my world's custom. This ring suddenly made me uneasy.

"It's a thing of beauty," he said, seeing my reaction. "For someone beautiful. I knew you wouldn't wear it on your finger, so keep it on the chain."

I nodded. Sometimes a gift was just a gift—particularly when someone was afraid his beloved might get killed soon. I kissed him again. "Thank you."

I'd come alone via the human world, so he sent an escort back to the Thorn Land with me. No one except Dorian and Masthera knew what I was going to do, but the group could sense something big was about to go down. Tension crackled around us as we traveled. Like so many, these soldiers considered Dorian and me a power-house. They could hardly wait to see what would happen next.

Kiyo wasn't waiting for me in the Thorn Land, not that I'd expected results that quickly.

No refusal had come from Maiwenn either, which I took as a good sign.

"What are you and my lord planning?" asked Rurik when he saw me. "You've got *that look*."

"What look is that?" I asked curiously. He reminded me of Tim.

"The look that says you're planning something."

I rolled my eyes. "Eloquent as ever, Rurik."

"Should I assemble fighters?" he asked, shrugging off my comment. Shaya joined us then, scrolls in her arms.

"No. I do this alone. Well, not exactly. Kiyo's coming with me. I hope. He should be showing up here today." I spoke more confidently than I felt. Despite Dorian's certainties, I still wasn't sure whether Kiyo would help or not. Rurik and Shaya exchanged glances. "Stop that," I told them. "It's perfectly platonic. Dorian suggested it."

Rurik looked like he still had a few things to say about it, but Shaya interrupted. "The Linden King wrote back. He won't join with us—but he also won't fight against us."

"Not the best news, not the worst. We'll see if he comes crawling when his power's in dispute." The words came out with more venom than I expected. Rurik seemed to approve. Shaya leafed through more papers.

"Caria, the Laurel Queen, would like to meet with you and discuss the war, however."

I knew nothing about that land. "Have we even contacted her?"

"No," said Shaya, giving me a meaningful look. "But her kingdom borders the Linden Land."

"Ah." I smiled. My comment to Ranelle that others would be eyeing her king's land as his power faded was true. In refusing my offer to defend against that, they'd allowed someone else to solicit me for the other side of that future dispute. "He'll regret his neutrality later. See if Caria'll meet with Dorian while I'm gone." Dorian would understand the situation perfectly.

I figured this was it and started to leave. "There's one more thing," added Shaya, twisting a black braid in that nervous habit of hers. "Girard would like to see you."

Her unease had made me think something bad was coming, but Girard was one of the few people who rarely delivered bad news. If anything, he usually delivered gifts, always coming up with some marvelous new piece of craftsmanship. Some pieces—like Dorian's sword and Jasmine's chains—I'd commissioned specifically. Sometimes, however, inspiration struck the artist, and he'd present some intricately worked necklace or diadem that I felt certain was beyond human skill. He could even touch iron in very small amounts.

"I'm sure he's made something great, but I'm not in the mood today," I told her. "I want to see Jasmine."

"He's not here to display work. He wants to introduce you to his sister." She looked at me expectantly and seemed surprised by my lack of reaction. "You've never heard of her? Imanuelle de la Colline?"

I shook my head. "Should I have?"

Shaya shrugged. "Maybe not. But I think you'll find her . . . interesting. It'll only take a minute."

It was true I was in a hurry, but Shaya's attitude intrigued me. We went to Girard's workshop, rooms I'd given to him on the castle's outer edge in case his work ever set something on fire. He was bent over a table, fingers magically working a bundle of metal and jewels.

"Another crown?" I asked with amusement. They seemed to be his favorite thing to make.

Girard looked up, startled, and bowed. "No, Your Majesty. It's something Lord Rurik has requested. If you'd like another crown—"

I waved him silent. "No, no. God knows I have plenty. Hardly seems like Rurik's style, though."

Girard didn't comment. Client confidentiality, I supposed. Turning, he pointed off toward the side of his workshop, and I gaped. A woman stood there, and somehow I hadn't noticed her upon entering—which seemed impossible. She and her brother shared the same dark skin and black hair, as well as a taste for bright clothing. The dress she wore was a stunning teal silk, cut shorter than most gentry dresses. Something about it gave me the impression she wore it for utility, not sexiness.

"Your Majesty," she said, sweeping me a curtsey. Also like Girard, a faintly French-sounding accent laced her words.

"This is my sister, Imanuelle," he said. Like Shaya, he seemed to expect me to know who his sister was.

"It's nice to meet you," I told her. When no one

said anything, I shifted restlessly, impatient to go. Seeing this, Imanuelle strode forward, her steps graceful and liquid.

"Your Majesty," she said. "I've come to offer my services to you, should you like to hire me."

I glanced at the other faces, seeking more information, but received none. "What do you do?" I asked. "Do you work metal like Girard?"

A mischievous smile crossed Imanuelle's face. She had caught on that I really didn't know who she was and appeared to enjoy that. "No. My talents are of . . . a different nature."

I saw a slight gesture of her hand, and then suddenly, the teal silk dress turned yellow. A moment later, it changed form altogether, turning into a flowing velvet gown. Then, she wasn't Imanuelle at all. A clone of Shaya stood before me. After letting that sink in, Imanuelle returned to her original form. She bowed, as though having just performed a stage show.

"I'm an illusionist," she said. "I can make people see things that aren't there. Most importantly, I can make myself look like anything I choose."

It was one of the cooler gentry powers, but I didn't entirely see how it'd be useful for me. "So I can finally be in two places at once?" I joked.

That brought another smile. "I suppose . . . but I've honed other skills to accompany these. Ones many monarchs find useful. I . . . get rid of problems."

Apparently guessing my confusion, Shaya sighed and dropped her usual formality. "You're better off not dancing around the subject. My queen prefers directness." She turned to me. "Imanuelle is an assassin, Your Majesty."

Imanuelle's smile tightened a little. I think she preferred her more flowery description. "That's an ugly word for a formidable skill set."

It took me a moment to catch on. "So, you're here to—Wait. You think I'm going to hire you to, what, assassinate Katrice?"

Imanuelle shrugged eloquently, and her brother spoke up for her. "Some might see that as a quick way to end the war, if I may be so bold." Girard had picked up that I didn't like this idea at all and was understandably nervous. He valued his position with me.

"It's a dirty, sneaky way to end a war!" I exclaimed. "It'd make me no better than Katrice and her bastard son."

"It would eliminate Katrice directly," said Imanuelle. "Since she *is* the source of your problems. I could disguise myself as someone in her castle. Quick, easy. No other innocents need be hurt."

For a heartbeat, her words almost made sense. Then I shook my head emphatically. "No. I'm not going to stoop to that level."

Some of Imanuelle's pleasant demeanor faded. "There are monarchs who would give half their kingdoms for my services! I'm very selective. I'm doing you a great honor."

I narrowed my eyes. "*You're* doing *me* an honor?"

She hesitated, realizing she was addressing one of the most formidable queens in the Otherworld. Again, Girard jumped in to save her.

"Forgive our presumption, Your Majesty. We only wanted to offer it as an option."

"It's been offered," I said bluntly. "And refused. Thank you for the 'honor.' You're welcome to visit your brother, of course, but I'd prefer that you stay here no longer than absolutely necessary."

I turned dramatically away from them, just catching the outrage on Imanuelle's face, and strode out. Shaya hurried by my side.

"Spoken like a queen," she said.

"Do I need to worry about that woman killing me now?" I asked. "Is she going to change into you and pull a knife on me?"

"I'm sure you'd respond as efficiently as you do to the other attacks on you," said Shaya dryly. "Her illusions aren't foolproof to everyone. I'm guessing Volusian could see through them if he were around. But, honestly . . . although her pride has been hurt—she does have quite the reputation—I suspect she'll simply stalk off and leave you be, if only for her brother's sake."

"Well, that's nice. One less person trying to kill me." I raked my hand through my hair. "Anything else I need to deal with?"

That was a loaded question, of course. Shaya had a few more business matters for me to look over before I could finally see Jasmine. I hadn't talked to her after the dinner at Dorian's and felt she'd be a good distraction as I waited to see if Kiyo would come. I found her outside in one of the gardens, sitting in the shade of a mesquite tree as the sun grew higher and the heat increased. Her guards stood stoically nearby, and her fine chains glittered in the light. At my approach, she glanced up from a book. Petulant, power-hungry teen that she might be, she was also an avid reader, using fantasy to escape her mundane existence when she'd still lived among humans. This book was one I'd brought her recently, the first in a trendy series.

"Is it good?" I asked, sitting down opposite her.

"Not bad," she said, playing cool. A moment later, she gave herself away. "Are there more out in the series?"

"Three more, I think."

She said nothing but smiled as she set the book beside her.

"Did you have fun at Dorian's?" I asked.

"Yeah. It was nice to be out." Her eyes gazed off, not really focusing on anything. "I think the best part was watching Shaya scare off all the guys hitting on me." She turned back to me. "Is that what it's like for you all the time?"

"Not since I got together with Dorian. They've slacked off—and Shaya doesn't scare them away. She abandons me."

Jasmine smiled again. "Dorian's crazy about you. Obsessed."

"That's kind of an extreme observation."

"It's true." She brushed hair out of her eyes. The sunlight was turning it to gold, making me a little envious; I'd gotten true red from our father, rather than strawberry blond. She could wear pink. "It's good," she continued. "His obsession.

That bitch Ysabel wants him, you know. And she hates you. So does her mom."

"Yeah, I kind of figured that out."

She shrugged. "Well, then, keep Dorian close."

"I'm not worried."

"Ysabel's got kids, and you won't give him any."

I was so sick of hearing about me and procreation. "Lots of gentry women have kids. Are you saying I should worry about all of them, Little Miss Love Guru?"

"Not all of them look like you. I mean, not exactly like you . . . but I think Dorian gets off on redheads. Maybe he figures he'll have red-haired kids that way. I don't know. But, whatever. I'm just saying she's waiting there for you to slip up with Dorian. And he's already gone for her before. She's got a bigger chest than you, too."

"Hey," I said indignantly. "That's irrelevant. Besides, he went for her—and she annoyed him. And I'm not going to 'slip up.' He's not going anywhere." I frowned, surprised by my next words, that I'd actually say them to her. "It's Kiyo I've got to pull in."

Jasmine's gray eyes widened in shock. "Him? He's no use to you . . . unless, oh Jesus. You guys aren't planning some three-way, are you? I mean, I know you and Dorian get into some—"

"No!" I exclaimed. "It's nothing like that. I need a favor from Kiyo, that's all. A big one. A dangerous one. I'm not sure what'll convince him." I smiled weakly, remembering Dorian's expression when I'd showed up in the tight gentry dress. "I'd know what to do if it was Dorian."

Jasmine scoffed and gave me a scathing look. "How stupid are you? Even *I* know what to do if you want to suck in Kiyo. Look human."

"I *am* human. Who's stupid now?" Good grief. We'd advanced to snippy quarrelling. We were becoming real sisters more and more each day.

"You're half-human. Dorian likes that because he thinks he can knock you up . . . but the rest? He wants you to be a queen. One of the shining ones. Kiyo doesn't. He hates all of that. He doesn't want you anywhere near it. You hooked up before you were into all the Otherworld stuff. Be like that."

I stared at her, startled because she had an excellent point. "Do I look human now?"

Jasmine studied me critically. I had jeans and a T-shirt on, my hair pulled sloppily into a ponytail. My boots were sturdy, made for hiking. Plain. "Yeah," she said, sounding surprised. "Scruffy and human. He'll be into that. Except for the ring. It's from Dorian, right? Put it under your shirt."

I touched the ring hanging on my chest, having forgotten about it. "How'd you know it was from him?"

"Because you wouldn't get it for yourself, and no one else would either. It's also got oak leaves."

I peered down at it. Sure enough. I hadn't identified the leaves earlier. I followed her advice, concealing it under the shirt. She watched with approval, then seemed to really notice my shirt.

"Who's Mötley Crüe?"

I was saved from lecturing her on classic rock when a servant scurried up to us, telling me Kiyo was here. The ease I'd felt with Jasmine vanished. I stood up, forcing calm, half-wondering if I should take her after all. No. Kiyo was the right choice.

"Good luck," Jasmine said, picking up her book. "And remember: be human."

I followed the servant away, embarrassed that I was taking advice from an insane fifteen-year-old. Except . . . I knew she was right. I made sure my gait was casual, nothing regal. Then, I sent the servant away, deciding it'd be best to come to Kiyo on my own, rather than approaching with an escort, no matter how insignificant.

He was waiting inside a parlor, pacing restlessly. I knew how uneasy I made him, and this invitation had no doubt put him on guard. I watched him unnoticed for a moment, admiring that muscled body while knowing it was wrong to do so. Sneaking up on him was impossible, though. He could smell me. My sweat and skin alone would have given me away, let alone the vanilla sunscreen and violet perfume I also wore.

"Eugenie," he said, turning around. "Nice to see you." He seemed impassive, but his eyes made me think he really did like seeing me—physically at least.

"Sorry for the abrupt request," I said. "You were probably visiting Luisa, huh?"

The mention of his daughter softened his expression a tiny, tiny bit. "Yeah, she's . . . she grows every day. It's amazing." He flipped back to alert mode. "But that's not why you asked me here."

"No." I settled into one of the chairs, crossing my legs and hoping I looked casual and unassuming. "I need your help."

He continued standing. "That's unexpected."

"Well, I got an unexpected offer. Do you still want me to get out of this war?"

"Of course." He made a face. "Oh, Eug. Please tell me you don't want me to negotiate or something."

I smiled, both at the suggestion and his use of the nickname. "No, I need you for something that's more your specialty. I don't suppose you've ever heard of the Iron Crown?"

Kiyo hadn't. I provided a brief rundown, explaining how the person who fought through and won it could allegedly inspire fear and awe.

"And that's enough to make Katrice back off?" he asked skeptically.

"So they say." I shrugged. "It's weird to me too, but everyone I've talked to claims it'll intimidate Katrice and her armies." Best not to mention that 'everyone' was Dorian, a ghost, and a crazy seeress. "It'll prove what a badass I am. And if that forces her into peace talks . . ." I let him draw his own conclusions.

"It's a gamble," Kiyo said. He still sounded doubtful, but there was a crack there. He wanted the war over. He wanted me out of it. "But why ask me? Why not Dorian?"

"Because he couldn't survive the quest. The way's lined with iron. It would take an insanely strong gentry—or people with human blood, like you and me. Plus, I trust you."

I didn't know if the human solidarity had gotten me anywhere, but he was definitely considering this more and more. I also wondered if admitting trust in him did anything. Part of what had driven us apart was my accusation that he didn't care enough about me to punish Leith.

"I'd like to help you," Kiyo said finally. "It's crazy—but no crazier than half the stuff around here. I should talk to Maiwenn first, though."

You must not—under any circumstances—allow him to go back to Maiwenn and consult her on this.

"There's no time," I said, hastily running through Dorian's laundry list of excuses. "We have to go now. The ghost who's going to help me threatened to back out if I didn't act soon. And we're currently on hold with Katrice. If I could return with the crown before the next battle, it would be . . . well, it'd be amazing. No more bloodshed."

I could see him wavering, but he wasn't quite convinced. Really, I didn't blame him. If I had an ally who could advise me on some bizarre quest, I'd want to talk to her too before jumping in.

"You can talk to her if you want," I said. "But I've got to leave now. I can't stand waiting. I'll just go by myself."

That drove the dagger in. No matter how sketchy the logic, no matter how smart it would be to get Maiwenn's advice . . . the fear of my running off into unknown dangers was too great. He stared at me for several heavy moments, his expression unreadable. Finally, he sighed.

"Right now?" he asked.

"Right now," I said.

"Then let's go."

Chapter 10

Deanna came easily when I summoned her, making me wonder if she'd been hanging around invisibly since our last chat. Regardless, she didn't mention the fake ultimatum, thus letting Kiyo continue to believe we were in a time crunch. I called Volusian as well, figuring it couldn't hurt to have his protection while traveling to the ghost cutoff point. The two spirits didn't interact as we traveled, no surprise seeing as they had little in common. Deanna was tied to the living because of unfinished business and love for others. Volusian's soul was damned for eternity, forced to wander for his crimes—unless I ever sent him to the Underworld.

Deanna hadn't been able to give us a time estimate on how long it would take to reach the crown's lair (as I was beginning to refer to it). The Otherworld's twisted terrain always made travel hard to gauge, plus spirits could move faster than we could. I wouldn't have minded walking, but the unknown variables made me ride horseback.

Kiyo did the same out of courtesy for me, though he could have tirelessly covered miles and miles in fox form. The only thing I really knew for sure was that this wouldn't be a day trip.

Kiyo and I were as silent as the ghosts, though once we crossed out of the lands adjacent to mine, he would occasionally tell me where we were. I'd never ventured this far into the Otherworld, and it made me uneasy, though knowing we were clear of the Rowan Land was a relief. Even Kiyo, neutral as he claimed, had tensed in Katrice's territory.

"This is the Honeysuckle Land," he said, when the road led us to a hot, riotously colored landscape. Flowers grew everywhere, and even the trees were covered in blossoms. Arizona was notorious for all its hummingbirds, but here, they swarmed like flies.

"Dorian was right," I mused. "It is beautiful." It was hard to imagine this place mustering up a military. This seemed more like a world where people frolicked in scanty clothing, beating drums and engaging in free love. Well, since they were gentry, free love would have been a given.

"Dorian would know," said Kiyo stiffly, eyes focused straight ahead. "I'm surprised he let you come with me."

"Dorian doesn't say what I can or can't do," I snapped. "If you're going to just keep doing this the whole time, I'll—"

"You'll what?" asked Kiyo with amusement, when I didn't continue. "Send me back? Face death-threatening situations alone?"

"I would gladly escort you back, if that is what you choose," Volusian told Kiyo.

I sighed. "Please. Just don't get on Dorian the whole time, okay? He wants this over. It was his idea to get your help. He's worried, believe me."

"That," said Kiyo gravely, "I can believe. I don't trust him. I don't believe his alliance with you is as straightforward as it seems. But I *do* believe he cares about you." The landscape suddenly shifted around us, becoming a rolling desert of white sand. It stretched out under a blazing sun, reflecting back at us in a way that was hard on the eyes.

"Ugh," I said, focusing down on the road. "What's this?"

"The Myrrh Land," said Kiyo. Even with my eyes averted, I knew he was smiling. "Figured you'd like this place. You should go make friends with its king. They've got some badass fighters."

"Big difference between this and the Sonora Desert," I said.

Although harsh and scalding, the desert I'd grown up with was full of life. This place was desolate and dead. Mercifully, we soon passed out of it into sweeping moors, covered in snow. I took my leather jacket out of my pack. I'd brought it knowing we might travel through lands that were in winter. It still wasn't much protection, and I realized I could have easily gotten one of my servants to whip up something more suitable. No doubt it would've been gentry-style, probably a cloak. *Look human*, Jasmine had said. Mostly I looked cold. Kiyo identified this place as the Birch Land.

We crossed into the Honeysuckle Land again,

which was typical of the Otherworld. Other places repeated as well. When the road took us through a landscape that reminded me of northern Texas, Kiyo had nothing to say.

"What's this?" I asked.

"I don't know," he admitted.

"The Pecan Land," said Volusian.

"Sounds delicious," I teased. We'd had few stops and mostly eaten travel rations. "I could go for a pecan pie right now."

Kiyo didn't respond. He seemed lost in thought, his expression growing darker as we passed through more and more terrain he didn't know. He seemed to know the names, though, and didn't like them.

"You're taking us to the Unclaimed Lands," he said to Deanna. It was near the end of our day, the sky burning red.

"I don't know," she said simply. "I'm only going where I was shown."

"Volusian?" I asked.

"Of course we're going to the Unclaimed Lands," he said, sounding mildly annoyed by my stupidity. "We're nearly upon them. Where else would you expect a coveted object to be hidden?"

I glanced at Kiyo. "I'm going to go out on a limb here and guess these are kingdoms no one controls?"

"'Kingdoms' isn't even the right word," he said. "No one lives here."

"Why not?" I asked.

The scenery changed again. The texture of the ground was like recently dried mud, covered in a pattern of cracks that reminded me of one of my jigsaw puzzles. Odd holes were scattered here and there. This eerie landscape stretched far, far ahead, no end in sight. Not far from us—ten miles at most—the land rose sharply along the sides of the cracked road, forming high, rocky cliffs that curled in at their tops like jaws. Erratic gusts of wind blew through the tunnel they formed. The setting sun made everything bloodred.

"Guess," said Kiyo. "Because we're here."

I peered around, studying the depressing landscape. Its superficial appearance meant little, really. Any gentry seizing control of it could shape the land to his or her will, instantly beautifying it. Then, a strange feeling settled in me. I couldn't quite define it. It didn't make me ill or disoriented. It just didn't feel right. I squinted at the cliffs, taking in their striation. Through the red haze, I could see many of the loose rocks were a dull gray, streaked with orange. Oxidized metal.

"Iron," I realized. "We're surrounded in iron. We're not even in the crown's lair yet. We can't get to the lair without passing through iron."

"Can you feel it?" asked Kiyo.

"Yes . . ." That was the odd feeling in the pit of my stomach.

"That's the gentry in you. Even with your human blood, you can't help but be affected. There's a lot of iron here."

"I don't feel weak," I said, astonished the iron would affect me at all. "Or sick or in pain." I'd seen gentry scream just from the smallest touch of iron. I summoned the magic within me, letting it reach out to the air and unseen moisture, though I didn't actively use it. "I don't think it's hurting my magic either."

"Good," said Kiyo. "You're strong, so I'm not surprised. You may just have a simple awareness of it."

I thought about this for a moment and came to another realization. "You're not affected at all, are you?"

He shook his head. "Nope."

I always thought of Kiyo and me as being alike, children born of both worlds. That part was true, as was our half-human heritage. But my Otherworldly blood came from the gentry. Only gentry were affected by iron, and kitsunes had no fairy connection. As with the demon bear and the fetch, a kitsune's bane would be silver. At least, a full-blooded kitsune's would be. I'd seen Kiyo handle silver objects; his human blood protected him as mine did me. The bottom line was that he was a more useful companion here than I'd realized. I wondered if Dorian had made the connection.

"We will cross through no other lands until you turn back, mistress," said Volusian.

"So this is the world's end. The Otherworld's end, at least." I turned to Deanna, hovering along-side us. "Will we reach the entrance before night?"

She thought about it, and I braced myself for another vague response. "No. If you don't stop, you'll reach it in the morning."

Kiyo and I exchanged looks, both of us thinking

the same thing. Get to the crown sooner or camp
and be rested?

I looked over at Volusian. "You said there are
no other lands. But will the terrain in this one
change?"

"No."

"What do you think?" I asked Kiyo. "I don't
want to be tired when we face whatever's guarding
the crown, but this isn't great camping territory."

"No," he agreed. His eyes scanned around us,
able to see more than mine in the waning light.
He pointed. "There. There's a small outcrop
that'll block most of the wind. Enough to keep a
fire going. I hope."

I couldn't see the spot but trusted him. "Camping it is."

When we reached it, I saw the site was indeed
sheltered. I tethered the horses while Kiyo built
up a fire. We watched it warily as the wind
abruptly came and went. The fire flickered and
waved but appeared capable of lasting the night.

"I could hold off the wind a little," I said.

"Don't bother," said Kiyo, settling down beside
the blaze. "Save your magic. This'll hold."

I wondered if he really was concerned about
me conserving my strength or just wanted me to
avoid my magic altogether. He'd never liked it. I
didn't question him, though, and sat down as well,
mostly because the cold was finally starting to get
to me. I buttoned up the leather jacket, achieving
little. Our dinner consisted of more travel food:
jerky, granola, and some bread that would probably be stale tomorrow.

"I don't suppose you can use your wilderness skills to go hunt us something fresh?" I asked.

He smiled, the campfire casting strange shadows on his face, now that night had fully come. "I would if there was anything alive out here. It's just us." He eyed me, taking in my shivering. "Don't you own a warmer coat?"

"Where am I going to get a down coat in Tucson?" I demanded.

"This time of year? Any sporting goods store. For the skiers. Lara could order you one if you can't be troubled."

"I think Lara and Tim are in love," I said abruptly, remembering that bizarre development.

"What?" asked Kiyo, as astonished as I had been. "Are you sure?"

"Well, they're in infatuation, at least. Volusian, were they together when you went back?"

My minion was off in the shadows, only his red eyes visible. "Yes, mistress. They were in bed, their bodies naked and—"

"Okay, okay, stop," I exclaimed. "I don't need to hear anymore."

"Well, I'll be damned," said Kiyo. While we'd dated, he'd been witness to their phone battles. "But I guess stranger things have happened."

"Yeah," I agreed. "Look at us. We're sitting in an iron landscape, being led by a ghost to a mythical object, which—if it even exists—may or may not make me scary enough to end a war."

"Fair point," said Kiyo, his smile returning. We sat in companionable silence. It was a nice change from the animosity and tension that had surrounded us for so long. I'd missed him, I realized. "Eugenie?"

"Hmm?" I glanced up, feeling embarrassed by my thoughts.

"Why didn't you bring Roland with you? He could've fought unaffected. And God knows he doesn't want gentry power."

I looked away from those dark eyes, down at the fire's blue heart. "He doesn't want me to have gentry power either."

"Yeah, but he'd put that aside if he knew you were walking into—"

"He doesn't know anything," I said bluntly. My voice then grew soft. "We aren't speaking anymore."

"How . . ." Kiyo paused, no doubt trying to wrap his mind around this. "How is this possible?"

I shrugged. "He cut me off. When he found out I'd been keeping the truth from him, about the Thorn Land and everything else . . . Well, ever since what happened with Leith, he's refused to speak to or acknowledge me."

"But your mom . . ."

"Talks to me occasionally. She's caught in the middle, and I don't want to make it harder on her than it already is. She shouldn't have to go against her husband."

Kiyo's confusion was becoming anger. "Yeah, but you're her daughter! She should be able to—"

"Just forget it, okay?" I drew my knees up to me and wrapped my arms around them to draw in more warmth. "I don't want to talk about it."

"Eug, I'm sorry."

I kept quiet. There was nothing to say.

He cleared his throat. "I don't suppose you brought anything else to keep you warm? Blankets? Camping supplies?"

"I didn't think about the possible overnight part," I said, grateful for the subject shift. "I've got a change of clothes like these, food, weapons, and first aid supplies."

"You brought first aid stuff?" He sounded impressed. "It's not like you to think ahead. Er, I mean, you don't usually worry about—"

"I know what you mean," I said with a weary smile. "And don't worry, the universe is the same. I didn't plan ahead. It's for current injuries."

"Current?"

"I got hit by a table."

There might be a million reasons that Kiyo and I were wrong for each other, but one nice thing was that when I made a statement like that, he just didn't question it.

I was still freezing when it came time to sleep, forcing Kiyo into a bold suggestion. "Come sleep over here, between me and the fire. The cold doesn't bug me as much, and I can block the wind."

"Kiyo—"

"Yeah, yeah. I know. Dorian. But if he wanted me here to protect you, then here's the perfect chance. Besides, we all know you can kick my ass if I try anything."

I said and did nothing. When this continued for about a minute, he sighed and lay down on his side, back to the wind. I attempted the same, after ordering Volusian to stay on watch, but even with the fire's warmth, I was still cold. *I'm tough, I'm tough.* I played those words over and over through my head, not wanting to admit weakness. After about fifteen minutes, I gave in and crawled over to Kiyo's side of the fire.

There was no "I told you so." He simply made room but was surprised when I positioned myself to face him.

"I thought you'd want your back to me."

"Can't," I said. "That's where the injuries are."

"From the table."

"Right."

He could have attempted propriety by turning over so his back faced me, but that would have put his face to the wind. He didn't deserve that. I wiggled myself closer, curling myself against his body, and resting my head against his chest. He was big enough that he did almost completely shield me. His whole body stood still as I made myself comfortable, either from his astonishment or for my ease. Once I was settled, he relaxed slightly and tried to put his arms around me. He suddenly fumbled and pulled them away, grazing my breast as he did. I don't know if he noticed. I certainly did.

"Wait. Where are you hurt?"

"Back. Left shoulder."

Tentatively, he reached out again and wrapped his arms around my waist. "This okay?"

"Mmm-hmm."

Holding me, he shifted closer so that our bodies pressed together, holding in the warmth. "This?"

"Fine."

He relaxed again and exhaled. Tucked against him, I couldn't see his face but had the sneaking suspicion that I wouldn't be getting much sleep tonight. Survival-wise, this plan was sound. I was warm(ish) now, protected and heated by him. But I was also pressed up against a body that I knew intimately, one that used to move in mine with a possessive fierceness. Dorian claimed me with mind games and exquisite acts of dominance. Kiyo had always done it through strength and ferocity, an animal taking his mate.

I bit my lip and closed my eyes, hoping I'd fall asleep if I mentally enumerated the reasons we'd broken up. But mostly, I kept remembering how his hand had lightly rubbed my breast. Sleep finally took me, but it was a long time in coming. As I drifted off, I wondered how he was coping. This probably didn't affect him at all. If he really wasn't sleeping with Maiwenn again, then he was probably out picking up women all the time. Kitsunes had kind of a supernatural allure, and God knew he'd been pretty persuasive the night we'd met.

I awoke a couple hours before dawn—and not by choice. Volusian's warning came only seconds before the surface below us began to tremble. I was up in a flash, but unsurprisingly, Kiyo had already beaten me. I'd gone to sleep with weapons, uncomfortable though it was. I hadn't known what I'd need out here, except that I wouldn't need the iron athame since this was a gentry free zone. I had my gun (safety on) and the silver athame. Both were out as Kiyo and I stood back to back, staring around us.

The tremors shook the ground, forcing some fancy footwork, and creating more of the cracks that already covered the ground. A few more seconds passed, and then all went still.

"An earthquake?" I asked uncertainly.

"No," said Volusian. He was in his solid, two-legged form, staring around with narrowed eyes. It was a little disconcerting that he didn't seem to know precisely what the problem was.

"Then what are we—"

The ground below us suddenly split open. With only the light of the fire, my vision was bad, but I thought I saw what looked kind of like a serpentine shape emerge from the earth. No, it was *exactly* like a serpentine shape because a moment later, a giant fucking snake shot up from the earth and landed neatly in a perfect coil, its head towering over Kiyo and me as it regarded us with glowing green eyes. The light from them illuminated a flicking, forked tongue, and the loud hissing that followed was kind of a given.

"Volusian!" I yelled. My minion sprang into action. The deadly touch of his hands made the snake jerk in surprise. Beside me, Kiyo was shifting into fox form, and I decided a gun was probably going to get me farther here than the athame's small blade. A drop of venom fell from the snake's mouth, and it sizzled when it hit the ground in front of me. Lovely. Still, I felt confident the three of us could take this thing.

At least until the ground shook again, and

another snake popped up. It was soon followed by a third.

"Son of a bitch." I deliberated, wondering if mass force on one snake at a time was the way to go. No. I'd leave Kiyo and Volusian to the first. I yelled a warning to Kiyo that the snake was poisonous, but it was hard to say if he understood.

I turned on the two new snakes. Even with part of their bodies coiled, their heads stood a good ten feet above mine. More venom dropped before me. Deciding not to play favorites, I aimed the gun and quickly fired off a couple of rounds into each. I'd had the foresight to load up silver bullets, but it didn't look like the gun was going to kill the snakes anytime soon—at least not without fifty more shots. Mostly, the bullets seemed to piss them off more.

Still, I kept firing since that seemed to make the snakes keep their distance. It proved to be a short-term solution, seeing as my bullets soon ran out. I reached for another clip. I could reload a gun quickly, but that pause gave one of the snakes an opening. Its head—no pun intended—snaked toward me, giving me a close-up view of large fangs. I'd been on guard for such an attack and jumped out of its way, only to be struck by the other's tail. It knocked me several feet away, causing me to loose my grip on the new cartridge. The cartridge disappeared into the night, and I landed hard on the ground. My back and shoulder screamed in agony, but I had no time to baby them. There were two other clips in my belt, but as one of the snakes came for me again, my hand went to the athame after all.

The snake that had hit me leaned down, its face and dripping jaw inches from me. Rather than run again, I leaped forward and plunged the blade into its eye. It cried out in pain, suffering from the silver, just as any Otherworldy creature would. Well, actually, any creature with a knife in its eye would probably suffer, magical or not.

I had the sense to jerk my athame out, having no desire either to lose the blade or get pulled along as the snake reared back up. The suffering of its pal made the other hold off. In those moments, I shoved the athame back into my belt, yelping in surprise. Apparently, the snake's eye was poisonous too, and whatever liquid had come away with the blade ate through my jeans and burned my skin. Nonetheless, I managed to get another cartridge loaded. Without hesitation, I turned and emptied the entire gun into the snake's head. I wasn't precise enough to hit the eye, but all those bullets took their toll. The snake wavered in the air, blood mixing with venom on its skin, and with a last hiss of pain, it fell over and slammed into the ground.

Wondering why the other snake hadn't come for me, I spun around and saw Volusian and Kiyo attacking it. I took it on faith that the first one was dead and loaded the gun with my last cartridge. Volusian's touch was searing the snake's skin, and Kiyo was simply ripping into it with his teeth. Opting for what seemed tried and true, I fired into the snake's head again. Between the three of us, we soon literally took the snake down.

I stood there tense and ready, empty gun in one hand and athame in the other. The world was silent except for the wind and the occasional twitching of the third snake as it died. Moments later, Kiyo morphed out of the fox shape, giving me a better view of any injuries now that he wasn't covered in fur. He grimaced and spit on the ground a few times, but biting the snake apparently hadn't destroyed his mouth or face. A couple red spots on his arms made me think he too had been splattered with the venom. Otherwise, he looked unharmed.

He sighed and raked a hand through his black hair, which was curling slightly from sweat.

"You know," he said. "I don't think I'll ever be able to bring myself to watch *Dune* again."

Chapter 11

"Cute," I said.

Kiyo turned to me, giving me the same assessment I'd just given him. "You okay?"

"A little venom and probably some bruising tomorrow."

He nodded, relieved, and then did a double take. "You're bleeding."

"Am I?" I asked, almost as surprised as he was.

He hurried over to me. "Your shoulder."

"Oh, shit," I said, craning my neck to look back. "That's the table injury."

"Take off your shirt. And don't even start with some ridiculous modesty spiel," he added, seeing me start to protest. I knew he was right and gingerly lifted off the Mötley Crüe shirt. He helped me part of the way, saving me from raising my arms too far. Examining the shirt, I saw blood soaked in it.

"Bad?" I asked.

"I'll know once I take the bandages off. Please

tell me you have more and that we don't have to reuse these."

"I've got more. I told you I brought supplies."

Carefully, he peeled off the gash's cloth coverings and tossed them to the ground. In the firelight and dim glow of sunrise, I could see the fabric was completely red with blood.

"You broke some stitches," he said wearily. "I don't have the tools to fix it." I'd once been kind of freaked out that he used his veterinarian skills to patch battle wounds, but now I kind of took it in stride.

"Pain aside, is that going to matter?" I asked.

"You'll bleed more, though I'll wrap it as much as I can. You'll risk a scar too if you don't get it stitched again. Once we finish this craziness up, I can do it for you back in Tucson if you don't want to explain it to your doctor."

"My regular one's kind of used to this," I said.

He snorted. "I imagine so."

I fetched my pack, and we both sat on the ground. The light was increasing, making it easier for him to work as he tidied up my back. The old bandages were tossed away, and I winced as he swabbed everything with antiseptic wipes.

"I thought the danger didn't start until we were in the crown's cave," I muttered.

"As often happens, mistress, you've made an incorrect assumption," said Volusian. "The legends say the path to the crown is perilous. We are on the path. Your testing has begun."

"Fantastic. Ow!"

"I'm saving you from infection," chastised Kiyo.

That seemed to be the last of the sanitizing, thankfully, and from there he began layering gauze and tape. What he did was far from erotic, but it amazed me how gentle and steady his hands could be after seeing him savagely fight and rip things apart.

I glanced over at Deanna, who had simply observed the fight. She'd said nothing, but I thought I caught a glimpse of relief on her face. My death would have put a serious hitch in our bargain.

"How long until the entrance? When we lose you guys?" I asked. Annoying or not, Volusian would be missed—especially if these snakes were just the warm-up act.

"A few hours," said Deanna.

I frowned, unsure if I should dread it or not. We'd lose our backup but be that much closer to finishing this anti-vacation.

"I suppose it'd be too much to hope you've brought any painkillers?" asked Kiyo, still layering me up. I felt like I had a quilt on my back.

"Vicodin probably isn't the best asset for impending battle."

"I was thinking more like aspirin."

"Nope." But it did remind me I was due for another antibiotic dose. I'd arrogantly thought I didn't need them but now was glad for my mom's vigilance. Not that I wanted to admit any of this to Kiyo. The thing about dating a doctor was that he'd always been on me about taking better care of myself. I didn't want to hear any I-told-you-so's now. And unsurprisingly, there was more advice to come.

He finished the last of the tape and helped me put on the clean shirt I'd packed. "Eugenie, wrapping this is a nuisance, but any gentry healer could have fixed this up in their sleep. Dorian's got great healers. Why didn't he have one of them take care of this? He should know better."

I shifted around so I faced him. "How on earth did this suddenly become Dorian's fault? Why is he responsible for everything evil? Of course he offered to get a healer. I refused because I figured other people needed it more." I'd also totally forgotten to ask Shaya.

Kiyo's expression relaxed and actually grew apologetic. He looked away. "Of course you did. I'm sorry."

"Sorry for accusing Dorian or for forgetting I'd be foolishly altruistic?"

Kiyo turned back, a small smile on his lips. "What do you think? There's very little I feel apologetic for when it comes to Dorian, especially when I'm still convinced he wants to father Storm King's heir."

I smiled back. "I'm sure he does too. But it's a moot point. I've still got birth control pills. I still don't want any kids. My life's stressful enough." Belatedly, I recalled his adoration of Luisa. "No offense."

"None taken," he said, still smiling. "Really . . . I should be better about trusting you. I just keep thinking . . ." The smile dimmed a little.

"Thinking what?"

"I don't know. That one day this will all get to you. And I don't mean about Storm King. I mean just . . . everything. You'll totally give yourself over to this world. I'll lose the Eugenie I know."

I grabbed his hand without thinking and squeezed it. "Hey, stop that. You said it yourself: trust me. I'm the same Eugenie. Still split between identities . . . but nothing can change that."

"I know." He continued holding my hand. The touch of his fingers, which had been so objectively medical minutes ago, now took on another feel . . . something warmer. Something that made my body feel strange, as those dark eyes stayed fixed on me. I found myself falling into them like I used to, into those sexy, smoky depths. . . .

I abruptly stood up, breaking that dangerous touch. "Well," I said awkwardly, "seeing as it's already light out and we're up, we might as well get going. Breakfast in the saddle?"

Kiyo rose too, looking troubled. "Sure. The sooner we're moving, the sooner we're past any snake threats."

As we packed up and got back on the horses, I wondered if we were riding toward something much worse than snakes. Don't get me wrong: they'd been bad. But I fought supernatural creatures all the time. There'd been so much hype about the crown. Was it simply going to involve a monster buffet?

I kept those thoughts to myself as we traveled, having plenty of other things to preoccupy me. My meager breakfast. Kiyo's presence. The pain in my back. The meaning behind the scattered holes in the terrain.

On the road went, just as it would through any

part of the Otherworld. I wondered how far it went. To infinity? Or would a traveler simply fall off the edge, like on those maps made back when people believed the world was flat?

"This is it."

Deanna's voice, though soft, seemed harsh in the emptiness around us. We came to a halt, and I glanced around, searching for what she'd found. At last, I spotted a small, dark opening tucked in one of the iron mountains.

"That's it? It seems so . . . small."

"Out here it does," said Kiyo. "We don't know what's inside . . . except that it's going to completely enclose us in iron. Remember—that'd kill most gentry. It's a test you're lucky enough to skip. Hopefully."

"True," I murmured. I still felt no ostensible effects from this land, but what would happen inside the mountain?

"I can't go inside," said Deanna. "I'll just wait here for you to come out."

"I too shall wait," said Volusian, "in the hopes that you meet your death and that it is your spirit that emerges, so that I may torment it for all eternity."

I pushed away the desire to order him away. Even if he couldn't follow us, I'd feel better having him right here for defense when we came out. And we would come out, I decided fiercely. There was no *if* here.

I left my bag and gun outside, seeing as I had no ammunition left. Fucking snakes. Surveying the rest of my arsenal, I left the iron athame in my belt, putting the silver athame in my right hand and the wand in my left. I glanced at Kiyo.

"Ready?"

He nodded. "I'll go first."

It was a very manly thing to do. I let him lead and faintly heard Deanna wishing us luck. The cave we entered was pitch black and cramped. I could just barely get through without ducking and knew Kiyo had to walk slightly hunched. We followed the twists and turns, scraping against the close, rough walls. We spoke occasionally to check location, and I'd sometimes touch his back as well. The deeper we went, the more I could feel the iron around us. Again, I had no indications of weakness . . . just an awareness.

"Light," said Kiyo suddenly.

I blinked. He was right. I saw no light source, but something farther ahead was casting light down the tunnel. It started as only faint illumination, just giving me a glimpse of his silhouette. Soon, the light increased . . . as did the heat. A roaring sound came to my ears.

"I have a bad feeling about this," I said.

We rounded a corner, and my jaw nearly dropped. The path ahead was blocked by fire. To be precise, it was blocked by sheets of very neatly contained fire, giving the impression of giant blades—particularly since they swung from the ceiling. Magically flattened into sheets or not, the flames burned intensely, and the heat radiating through the corridor left no doubt that these bastards would incinerate us.

"I think I saw this in a video game," I muttered.

Kiyo's gaze was fixed unwaveringly on the fire blades. There were five of them. His face was blank, but the concentration in his eyes told me what he was doing. He was timing them, studying their patterns.

"They're staggered in a way that would let us get through," he said. "We just have to watch the timing."

"*You* can get through. I don't know about me." I wasn't being defeatist; I was just stating the truth. Kiyo possessed reflexes I didn't have. I could sit here for hours and probably not learn their patterns like he could.

He frowned. "Maybe I can just hold your hand. Or put you on my back."

"What? No. That's ridiculous. It'd affect your speed—throw you off." I studied the flames, hypnotized by the swinging patterns. There were spaces between each sheet. "Maybe I can wing it, take them one at a time."

"Now *that's* a ridiculous idea." Frustration lined his brow.

"And to think, I would have given anything for heat last night. We should have camped in here. . . ." My joke trailed off as an idea came to me. "I'll just walk through."

The look he gave me required no words to convey his opinion.

"Seriously," I said. I put my weapons away and drew on the magic within me. The iron wasn't affecting me. I toyed with the elements of air and water, testing and weaving them like a scarf. Kiyo could feel the shift in temperature near us.

"What are you thinking?"

"I can protect myself," I said. "The cave's damp enough—aside from here—for me to draw water. I'll make a shield for me and use air to blow out against the fire."

"The air could feed the flames."

"Not if I do it right."

Our eyes met. He didn't like this idea, not at all. "This'll work," I told him. "I know for a fact it will."

"For a fact, huh? I still think I should carry you."

"And I still think that's idiotic. You've gotta trust me, Kiyo. I can do this. I can *feel* it."

He didn't answer immediately, but I knew I had him. "If I watch you get burned alive, I'm not going to be happy."

"Volusian'll be happy," I said. "At least someone comes out on top."

"Eugenie!"

"Sorry." I gave Kiyo what I hoped was a reassuring smile. "This'll work. You go first."

He hesitated a few moments more and then transformed into a fox. For fighting, he often chose a powerful, larger than life one. Now, he was small and quick like any ordinary red fox. He turned toward the flames, the human part—and probably animal too—again gauging timing. Then—he sprang forward.

I'd piled assurances on him, but it was my own breath that caught while watching him. He ran without stopping, stride smooth and consistent as he flawlessly ran through empty space caused by the flames' swinging to the opposite side of the cave. In seconds, he reached the end, on the other side of the fifth sheet. I exhaled. He transformed back to Kiyo and peered at me through the sporadic gaps, worry all over him.

I gave him another confident smile, hoping my earlier argument would hold true. I stared at the flames, not to time them but simply to muster my own courage. Magic welled up within me as I pulled moisture around my body, creating a spinning, almost cyclone-like cocoon—that instantly soaked me. That was the least of my worries. Then, I called on the air, drawing it to me and forcing it to blast away from my body.

As I stepped forward, my mind suddenly ran through a hundred other scenarios. Maybe I could have just sucked out the oxygen here and killed the fire. Of course, that'd likely render me unconscious. And would ordinary physics even work against magic fire? That question came to me too late, along with the realization that magic fire might similarly be immune to air and water.

Woosh!

I lacked Kiyo's timing. The first fiery sheet flew at me—and went around me. My fan-effect blew it away and the scalding heat that would have still reached me was mitigated by the water. I picked up my pace, walking through the second one in a similar way. Lucky timing made me miss the third altogether. The fourth nailed me—or would have—and then I just barely sidestepped the fifth.

I reached Kiyo's side and dropped the magic. "Three out of five ain't bad," I said cheerfully. To my surprise he hugged me, in spite of my dripping clothes and hair.

"Jesus Christ that was scary, Eug. When I saw you walk through that first wall . . ."

". . . you thought it was pretty cool?"

He pulled back and shook his head, watching as I wrung water from my shirt. "You sure are making an awful lot of jokes about some pretty serious stuff."

"Hey, you're the one who made the *Dune* reference." I sighed and let my hands fall to my sides. "Besides, if I wasn't making jokes, I'd probably come to my senses and be running straight back to the Thorn Land." I drew air to me, taking along some of the heat, to sort of blow-dry me off. I stopped when I was semi-dry, not wanting to use up the magic.

"I understand," he said. He gently touched my arm, smiled weakly, and then tilted his head toward the darkness ahead. "Ready for more?"

I nodded, following him once again. We walked farther and farther from the flames, losing the light as we did. A strange flashback came to me, a trip to the Underworld where I'd walked through similar caves and faced tests to bring back Kiyo's soul. How could I have nearly forgotten about that? I'd loved him so much, I'd faced Death herself. How did love like that change?

More tunnel crawling followed, and I wondered if perhaps this was a test for claustrophobic gentry. Gradually, though, the tunnel began to expand and expand until it suddenly dead-ended into a large cavernous room. Much like the tunnel, everything here was simply rough rock with occasional glimpses of iron. A few torches lit the chamber, revealing its centerpiece: an elegant marble pedestal with an iron crown sitting on it.

"Seriously?" I said.

Kiyo and I hovered near the room's opening, wary of entering. Yet, as I stared at the crown, it wasn't any potential trap that sent a chill down my spine. Another test in my trip to the Underworld replayed in my mind: I'd been forced to wear my father's crown, despite my protests. That crown had been platinum, but it and the one before me both had a similar silvery sheen. Both were adorned with purple jewels. Both had a harsh, martial feel to them. The one in the vision had been a little more delicate, though, with a bit more artistic flair. Designer planning had also clearly gone into this one, with its circle of jeweled spikes alternating in size, but my feel was that it was meant to be impressive, not pretty.

"It's an illusion," I said to Kiyo. "We can't have reached it already. We've hardly done anything."

He didn't take his eyes off the crown as he spoke. "Snakes and walking through fire are nothing?"

"Well, no. But I expected more, considering all the hype."

"The iron," Kiyo reminded me. "You used magic to get through the fire. Most gentry would too—but imagine what it would be like for them in all this iron. If they even got this far. You're . . . not cheating, exactly, but you're bypassing a lot of the challenges here."

"If it's meant to be for gentry, then maybe the crown is too. Maybe I'm too human and won't be able to claim it." Man, that would suck.

"One way to find out."

I stared at the crown, noticing how little light reflected off it. Was this it? Did I really just go up and claim it? Time to find out. I took a few steps forward . . . and the room abruptly became cold. A dark feeling, a feeling of power and pure evil filled the small space. What does evil feel like? You just know. I hastily returned to Kiyo's side, but it was too late.

A male figure materialized before us, clad in beautiful purple velvet robes, embroidered and tailored in a way Dorian might have envied. This guy's hair was nearly as beautiful, a pale white blond that shone in the torchlight and grazed his shoulders. Yes, definitely an impressively attired figure. The only thing that really detracted from it all was that he was a skeleton.

"Oh, fuck," I said.

"What is it?" asked Kiyo, moving close to me.

"A lich. Like a . . . I don't know. An undead necromancer or magic user." My mind was frantically spinning. Liches used magic before their deaths to purposely keep themselves from the Underworld. It made them very hard to banish, according to Roland. I'd only ever heard of them in stories.

"Like a zombie?"

"No. Smarter. And they can also do—duck!"

Kiyo, always a hair faster than me had already dropped down and taken me with him as the lich hurled a ball of blue fire at us. It hit the wall above us, dispersing and blasting us with heat but otherwise doing no harm. More of that fire was already forming in its skeletal hand, and I knew it would aim low.

Kiyo transformed to his largest fox form and leapt at the lich, attacking the best way he knew how. His jaws started to close around the lich's robe-enclosed leg, but a small gesture from the lich sent Kiyo flying. He hit a wall, shook it off, and growled, pacing and planning what to do next in light of this new development.

During their split second encounter, I had just enough time to send my senses out through the wand. I touched the Underworld and attempted to form a connection. The butterfly on my arm burned like the snake's venom, but I couldn't open the way. It was like beating on a heavy locked door. More effort might have helped me break through, but I had no chance to try before another fireball came toward me. I dodged and rolled away. Seeing the lich deflect Kiyo again made me think an athame attack wasn't going to be much help either.

The lich seemed to recognize my problems and laughed, a low, guttural sound that echoed unnaturally in the chamber. "You will not wear the Iron Crown. You do not possess the power to wear the Iron Crown."

I was ready to evade another fireball, but a flick of the lich's hand threw me back against the wall. I didn't even have time to process the agony that caused to my wounds because the unseen force that pinned me there hurt too much. It was like a million invisible needles were piercing my skin, going straight through me, and lodging in the stone to hold me in place. I screamed at the pain, and Kiyo instantly raced toward the lich again. The larger the fox form, the more animal he was, and I had a feeling this was just a gut reaction at seeing me attacked.

The lich threw him off again with that invisible force—only harder this time. Kiyo slammed against the wall, slumping down to the cave's floor. Weakly, he tried to stand up on all four legs but was too disoriented and injured. The lich turned back to me, and I saw death in his eyes. Had I really joked about this being easy? The only one this had been easy for was the lich. He'd taken us out with just a few spells, and now I would die. This was why those who wore the Iron Crown were feared. If you could survive this, you could survive anything.

"You will not wear the Iron Crown," he repeated, lifting his hands for the final spell. "You are not worthy."

I summoned my magic, despite the pain. A gale force wind blasted into him, making him stagger back. So. He wasn't totally impervious to physical force. Calling the magic was difficult, but when Dorian had first trained me, we'd practiced casting spells in a number of uncomfortable positions. I increased the force of the wind, pushing the lich back a couple more steps. The Iron Crown didn't budge, but the wind had pinned Kiyo up against the wall, almost making him go flat. I nearly hesitated, fearing I'd hurt him. He was still alive from the last hit. Surely he could handle this.

And that added force was a good call. It distracted the lich so that when I mentally pushed back against his spell, he couldn't hold it. The invisible pins vanished, and I slid to the floor, landing shakily but upright. I still hurt and already felt worn out but held strong to my magic. It kept the lich away, but it also didn't knock him into the walls the way he could us. His skull-face wore a perpetual grin, making this all that much more annoying.

"You don't have the power," he said, seeing I couldn't do much more with the wind. "You are not worthy of the crown."

White light began glowing between his hands. No fireballs this time. It was lightning. It flew from his hands with incredible speed—say, like, the speed of light—but I evaded it, with almost no thought. Lightning was in my skill set. My body was attuned to it, able to anticipate and avoid it even with its speed.

Nonetheless, the lightning blasted away half of the cave wall and the thunder that accompanied the bolt nearly left me deaf. Rocks and debris from the shattered stone were swept up in my windstorm, flying around the room like shrapnel. A few of them hit me. One cut my arm. In spite of it all, I laughed, sounding slightly crazy even to myself.

"You're going to fight me with lightning?" I yelled above the raging wind, which I had managed to kick up a notch after all. "Do you know who I am?"

"I know you will never have the crown," the lich replied, summoning more lightning.

His words dug into me, and not just because my life was on the line here. It was the meaning behind them. *You are not worthy.* A dismissal of me. Of my power. He really didn't know who he was dealing with, though. He had no idea of the power I could wield, even in this iron dungeon. No one would say it directly, but I was beginning to suspect I was the most powerful magic user since my father. This bastard lich was about to find that out. He'd see my power. I'd destroy him and take his fucking crown.

"You call that lightning?" I yelled, after dodging the next bolt. My magical senses touched the molecules in the room, the positive and negative charges. The scent of ozone was everywhere. "*This* is lightning."

I didn't need my hands. I could create lightning from the air. It blasted into the lich and should have disintegrated him. He stayed intact, unfortunately, but the way he wobbled and didn't instantly go for another bolt told me I'd made progress.

The magic burned within me, filling every ounce of my being as I held onto the surrounding air. The wind still blew, the ions stayed readied. In the center of it all was the crown, the crown I was going to walk out of here with. I would stop this war and show Katrice and everyone else not to screw with me.

But first, I needed to finish this. I considered continually blasting the lich with bolts, but another idea came to mind. It would bring all of this to an end quickly. Scientists have long debated the existence of ball lightning, but I knew it was real. I'd never really used it in a serious way but had experimented. Some of the principles of its formation were like those of "regular" lightning, but a few quirks were what made it unique—and so hard to study.

I knew how to summon it. I knew what it could do in here. Whereas the magically created bolts the lich and I had wielded had been shaped and controlled, ball lightning was huge and radiating. It would fill this cave, incinerating the lich. I wouldn't be surprised if it melted the walls. And the crown? The crown would survive—as would I, being the magic's mistress.

The power blasted out of me, lightning forming an orb in the cave that exploded outward, blinding even my eyes. The walls shook, heat washed over me, and a roaring filled my ears. I heard the lich scream, a horrible, raspy sound. I didn't let go of the spell until his cry faded to silence. The ball lightning disappeared instantly, almost startlingly so. My own control of such power surprised me a little.

My ears rang in the silence. The crown stood unharmed, as expected. The pile of bones I'd expected was not there, however. Instead, a small, wizened man stood before me, dressed in the same purple robes. I reached out and readied my magic for this new threat. He didn't move, though. To my astonishment, he smiled and gave me a small bow.

"Congratulations," he said. He gestured to the crown. "You are worthy—if you can wear it, of course. And something tells me you can, if you've survived this much iron."

I glanced back and forth between him and the crown, unbelieving. "I did it. . . . I won through. Won the crown. I defeated the lich . . . er, you . . . or whatever."

"Certainly the lich was part of the test. It takes great magic to defeat one. But the test was about more than your power," said the old man slyly. "It was about your determination. Your will. Your ruthlessness to get to the crown, no matter the cost."

He stepped aside, waving his hand over at the cave's side. I gasped. Kiyo—in human form—lay against the wall. His dark eyes were open, and I saw no obvious injuries. He was simply watching the interaction. I flew to his side, kneeling down.

"Oh my God. Are you okay?" I asked, helping him sit up. His breathing was even, though he looked a little addled. "Please . . . talk to me. Kiyo. Are you okay?"

"Yeah, yeah . . ." He lightly touched his forehead and winced. "Hell of a headache."

I could scarcely breathe. I felt numb all over. "You shouldn't be alive," I whispered. "You should have died."

That ball lightning had eradiated the room. That had been my plan, after all. Destroy everything except me and the crown—and everything would have included Kiyo. In the moment, I had forgotten. I had forgotten all about him. I'd been too fixated on the crown, on proving to the lich who the real badass around here was. Kiyo hadn't mattered in that moment, and it had nothing to do with our rocky relationship. I had the horrible, terrifying feeling that it wouldn't have mattered who was in the room.

"Oh, God," I said again, pulling his head against my chest. Tears stung my eyes. "Oh God oh God. I'm so sorry. I'm so, so sorry. I don't know what . . . I don't what I was thinking. . . ." A nasty voice spoke inside my head. *Didn't you?*

"Hey, Eug, calm down," said Kiyo, patting the back of my head. "I'm okay, don't worry. You did it. You defeated it."

He didn't get it. He didn't get what I'd done—or nearly done. Clearly, whatever crazy, powerful magic was involved here had protected him for the sake of the test. But if it hadn't . . .

"Seriously," said Kiyo, still not understanding my distress. "I'm fine. Just got tossed around too much. Now go get the crown. He said it's yours." I pulled away and looked into Kiyo's eyes, eyes full of fondness and pride. I didn't deserve that look, but we needed the crown, and we needed to get out of here.

I rose unsteadily and walked over to the pedestal. The crown sat there ominously, and I glanced at the old man. He nodded encouragingly. *If you can wear it.* I supposed there was one more test, one I might fail. When my fingers touched the crown, I felt nothing, only cold metal. I lifted it gingerly, almost afraid of what I did. It was heavy—far heavier than my crown of state or fashionable ones. Yet, it fit my head perfectly, which was weird. When I'd first seen it, I'd been overwhelmed by its size. I'd been certain it would fall right off.

The old man beamed and bowed again. "And now it is yours. Its powers are yours. You can make armies tremble. You can rip away lands and subdue them. The world can be yours."

Hoping I'd proven myself, I removed the crown. "I just hope I can end a war."

Kiyo rose shakily to his feet. He no longer smiled. "What do you mean she can rip away lands?"

The old man spread his hands out wide. "That is the crown's power."

"The crown has no power," I said, frowning. "It's a prize, a status symbol for enduring all this."

"A *prize*?" The old man's eyebrows rose, and he gave a great belly laugh. "Do you believe all of that was just for a prize? For some bauble?"

Kiyo and I exchanged uneasy looks. "Then what does it do?" I asked.

"The Iron Crown allows you to break the bond between a monarch and his or her kingdom, thus freeing it. If you have the strength, you can then claim it." The old man shrugged. "Why, with enough power, you could control half the kingdoms in this world."

Chapter 12

There was a moment of stunned silence.

"That's impossible," said Kiyo at last. "Unless you're saying she should kill all those monarchs?"

"No need," the old man replied.

"Even I know how it works," I argued. "The only way to claim a land is if its previous monarch dies or grows too weak to hold it. Otherwise, they're bound together. The monarch and the land are one."

"Aren't you listening?" he asked. "The crown changes that. The crown breaks that bond. Doesn't matter how strong they are. No killing—unless you want to. The land is freed up, allowing you to seize it if you're strong and ambitious enough, which, of course, you have to be even to possess the crown."

Ambitious enough.

His words reminded me of our fight, when I'd nearly killed Kiyo in my rage. I stared down at the crown in disgust. "I don't want it. I don't want that kind of power. That was never my intention."

The crown's keeper now looked as baffled as Kiyo and I had been moments ago. "Then why did you come for it?"

"Eugenie," said Kiyo uneasily. "I don't think you should leave it. Regardless of what it truly does . . . well, the original plan still holds. You don't actually have to use it. Just having it may still be enough to scare Katrice into peace—especially if she knows its true power."

I lifted my eyes from the crown, staring off absentmindedly at the cave's scorched walls. "Of course she knows. And so does Dorian. He's known all along."

It was a sign of Kiyo's tact and self-control that he made no scathing remarks about Dorian.

"You have to take it," exclaimed the old man, glancing back and forth between our faces. He seemed shocked and even offended that I was seriously considering leaving it. "You passed the test. No one who has done that has ever refused the crown."

The sick feeling in my stomach grew. *He knew. Dorian knew.*

"You don't have to use it," reiterated Kiyo. "But Katrice won't know that."

"I was an idiot," I murmured. "An idiot to think it was just a war prize. If I accept it . . . what happens if someone else takes it? If it's stolen?" After experiencing so many attempts at rape, I was well aware of the extent of Otherworldly ambition.

"The crown will only work for its current owner," said the caretaker. "It will only stay with the worthy. If it's taken—or if you die—it will return here, and we will wait for the next challenger."

"Hold on," said Kiyo. "You just wait here all the time? How old are you?"

I didn't wait for a response. I felt dizzy on my feet and so, so tired, both mentally and physically. I wanted to get out of this place. "Let's go," I said. "We'll take the crown."

The old man beamed. "Excellent. I look forward to hearing of your victories."

I scowled and moved for the exit. This was hardly the situation for warm and fuzzy good-byes, so Kiyo and I simply left without any more conversation, though I could feel the caretaker's gaze burning into my back. The trek out of the mountain was quiet as well and seemed to go much more quickly. The fire barriers were gone.

When we finally emerged, the light and air of that barren landscape seemed like the sweetest, most refreshing thing ever. Volusian and Deanna were exactly where we left them. Deanna's expression lit up. Volusian's didn't ostensibly change, but I sensed definite dismay.

"You did it!" exclaimed Deanna. "Now you can help me and find out—"

"No," I interrupted, heading straight to my horse. "Not now. We're not dealing with that yet."

Her pale eyes widened. "But you promised to—"

"*Not yet*," I growled.

Something about my tone and look must have been pretty intimidating because she vanished without comment. I knew she'd be back, though.

I glanced at Kiyo, who was already on his horse, face troubled.

"Think those snakes are regular residents or just part of the test?" I asked.

He glanced around, taking in the scattered holes in the ground. "I don't think we can assume they're gone."

I made sure my pack was secure, the crown inside it. "Then let's get out of here. We're not stopping until we're out of the unclaimed lands."

Kiyo's face was lined with worry. "Eugenie—"

But I was already urging my horse down the road, back in the direction we'd come. Our initial ride had been brisk but still energy conserving. Now, I held nothing back. I let the horse run as fast as she could, half-suspecting she wanted out of this cursed place as much as I did. The speed and rush of air was almost enough to distract me from what had just happened and what was to come. Almost.

Kiyo easily kept up with my hard pace, and the speed made any conversation difficult. I lost track of time but had the sense of riding for hours as the sun moved across the sky. I fell into such a lull surrounded by the dreary landscape that crossing back into the Otherworld's claimed regions was like a splash of water in the face. We'd emerged into the Honeysuckle Land and were suddenly surrounded by heat and color.

Kiyo slowed his horse down. "Eugenie, we have to stop." When I didn't react, he yelled more harshly, "Eugenie!"

It snapped me from my haze, and I slowed too,

eventually bringing my horse to a halt. His trotted up to us.

"Eugenie, it's almost night. We have to make camp here. We'll be safe now that we're out of that place."

"Safe? I'm a war leader. This place isn't on our side yet. They could have a lot of leverage if they found and captured me."

"That's just an excuse," he said. "It won't happen, and you can't keep up this pace without rest. The horses certainly can't either."

I didn't know much about animals, but Kiyo did. These two didn't seem ostensibly exhausted, but they were breathing a bit more heavily than when we'd left. I petted the head of mine in apology. I didn't want to stop, but Kiyo was right.

The lush and beautiful land provided any number of camping spots. The trick was finding a concealed one that kept us near the road. If we strayed too far, the Otherworld's nature could very well shift us away to another location. And, despite his confident words, I think Kiyo did worry a little bit about the Thorn Queen being discovered in this kingdom. At least we had Volusian to keep watch.

We finally settled for a small glade that was almost impossible to see through the trees until you were right inside it. Not far away was a small lagoon edged in stones. I was filthy from the fight but didn't have the energy to bathe fully and settled for washing my hands and face. Nonetheless, back in our camp—which really was just a place to sleep since we needed no fire here—Kiyo insisted on changing my bandages again.

"You tore more stitches in the lich fight," he said with dismay. "We can keep the blood loss down, but you have to get this treated soon."

I nodded without hearing him, my mind still wrapped around what I'd learned. Once he'd pulled my shirt back down, I turned and faced him. "Dorian knew, Kiyo. Dorian knew what this crown could do. That's why he wanted it. I wouldn't be surprised . . ." It killed me to say the next words. "I wouldn't be surprised if he set it up from the beginning with Masthera."

I again expected mockery from Kiyo, but his dark eyes were serious and full of sympathy. "I wouldn't be surprised either. I'm sorry."

It was true what I'd said in the cave: I was such an idiot. I should have listened to my initial instincts, the ones that said a battle prize wasn't enough to end a war. A prize that could strip Katrice's kingdom from her? Yeah. That would end a war, true, but Dorian should have told me. He should have told me what the crown's real threat was.

And then you wouldn't have done it, a voice in my head pointed out. I knew it was the truth. I wouldn't have risked my life—or Kiyo's—to come after some artifact that put me one step closer to being the conqueror everyone expected me to be.

"Dorian knew," I repeated. "Dorian let me risk my life for this."

Kiyo stayed silent for a few moments, staring off into the rapidly darkening trees around us. "You said he resisted at first, though. Until he realized I could go."

"Was that an act, though?" I rested my forehead in my hands, doubting everything I'd come to believe about Dorian. I'd so, so wanted to trust him. "Did he pretend to be hesitant, knowing I'd be suspicious if he was aggressive?"

"For all his faults . . . I don't know. He does care about you, Eugenie. I don't think he'd carelessly throw you into danger. He might have seriously waited until he knew you could go in with backup."

I sighed and lifted my head back up. "You're giving an awful lot of credit to someone you hate."

A small smile crossed Kiyo's lips. "I don't hate him, not exactly. I don't trust him. I don't like him. And . . . well, I certainly carry a grudge for his taking you from me."

I narrowed my eyes, a spark of anger flaring up in me. "No one 'took' me. I'm not something you guys can just pass around!"

"Sorry, sorry," he said hastily. "I didn't mean it like that. I just mean that after we split up, it's been hard seeing you with him. That's petty jealousy, I admit it. But I also hate that his grand, brash action won you over and drove the final stake in our relationship."

"His 'grand, brash action?' Do you mean killing Leith? I'll never regret him doing that," I said fiercely.

Despite how dark it was growing out here, I could see Kiyo's eyes boring into me. "Do you mean that, Eugenie? Was your personal vengeance worth all the people who've died since then?"

I looked away. "He deserved it. You don't understand."

"I understand perfectly well what he did. And if I could have? I would have done a lot more than run a sword through him. Really, that was almost merciful compared to what he deserved. But the fallout . . ."

"I know." I sighed again. "I know what I've caused, all the upheaval in this world." A sudden odd thought occurred to me. "Maiwenn . . ."

Kiyo tensed, not following my jump in thoughts. "What about her?"

"Dorian knew that too! She knows what the crown does; I'm certain of it. That's why he kept telling me not to let you talk to her!" I shot up, full of fury now. "Goddamnit! He played me. He's always played me! It doesn't matter if he loves me. It's his nature. He can't love without using it to his advantage. *Goddamnit!*" My cry rang out into the empty night as I paced irritably.

In seconds, Kiyo was up too, gripping me by my arms. "Hey, hey. Calm down. He may have tricked you, but he can't make you do anything you don't want to with the crown. You're in control. No harm's done."

"No harm?" I exclaimed. "Kiyo, I almost killed you! Do you understand? Do you understand what I almost did? I lost control! How am I supposed to forgive myself for that?"

He drew me into his arms. "*I* forgive you for

that, and that's all you need to worry about. Don't beat yourself up with the guilt."

I clenched my fists. "The craziest part is that the fake-lich whatever guy thought what I did was a good thing. Me shoving my friends aside for power. That's what the crown represents. That's what I'll become."

"I won't let you," said Kiyo fiercely.

"It's in my blood," I said weakly. "I realize that now."

"Maybe. I don't know. I used to think . . . well, I used to think it was all just some easy decision you could make. 'Do this, don't do this.' That was stupid of me. It's more than that, this conflict in you. And I didn't help—not in the way you needed. I will now—if you'll let me."

I peered up at him in confusion. "Why? After everything I've done?"

"Because I—" Kiyo cut himself off. I could hardly see him now, but the feel of his hands was warm on my skin. "Because it doesn't matter. Because I screwed up. Because we never should have split up. I've been wanting to tell you something for a while. We should have—"

I broke away and stalked off across the glade. I couldn't hear this. I couldn't hear some proclamation of love, not when my heart was still broken over Dorian's betrayal. I'd trusted him. I'd trusted him, despite all the evidence that he would go to great extremes for power. I'd thought love for me would be stronger than that ambition. I'd been wrong. Even if he loved me, his heart would always be split between me and his craving for power. It was his nature, just as my own nature was divided between human and gentry ways.

"I need to sleep, Kiyo," I said roughly. "I can't hear this right now."

"But Eugenie—"

"Good *night*." I turned my back to him—I knew he could see in the darkness—and curled up on the grass. It was hardly a comfortable bed, but compared to last night's discomfort, this felt like heaven.

Kiyo said no more, and I eventually heard him settle down. Volusian had been put on watch, meaning neither Kiyo nor I had to stay awake. In my case, it didn't matter. Sleep wouldn't come no matter how much I willed it to. I stayed up most of the night, staring up at the clear sky and its glitter of stars. The Otherworld had the same constellations as the human world, which surely presented some sort of physics quandary, one I didn't have time to think much about right now.

Dorian knew.

That crown. That fucking crown. Part of me wanted to go over to my bag, grab the crown, and throw it off into night, never to be seen again. What had the old man said? It'd return to its home? No harm done. No harm except the loss of my potential to steal Katrice's land from her— hers and anyone else's who opposed me.

Was that what Dorian had wanted? Would he have tried to convince me that it was the only way to win the war? And would I have believed it? Maybe. I'd been willing to risk a lot for peace by coming after the crown at all. Maybe that had just been the "gateway drug" in Dorian's eventual plan for conquest.

In the end, it didn't matter what his plan was. What mattered was that he'd betrayed me. I'd opened myself to him, loved him. That was over now.

It was that thought, that thought and the anger burning within me, that got me up and around early when dawn broke. Kiyo—who apparently had slept—instantly woke when he heard me stirring.

"Let me guess," he said. "You didn't sleep."

"Nope."

I took out some of the travel food from my bag, cringing when my fingers brushed against the crown. Kiyo stood up and stretched, then wandered off into the foliage. He returned several minutes later with some mangos in his arms.

"Supplement your breakfast," he said, tossing me one. He leaned against a tree and bit into one of his own.

I nodded my thanks, but the fruit's sweetness was lost on me. Nothing had any taste. I was distantly aware of Kiyo's eyes on me but ignored them.

"What are you thinking?" he asked at last.

"How much I hate Dorian."

"What are you going to do?"

This was something I'd thought about for a while, so I had a solid answer. "Go to him. Call him out. Pass him a note in class. Tell him it's over—everything. Us. Our alliance."

Kiyo's eyebrows rose. "You might not want to be so hasty on that last one."

"How can I be in a partnership with someone like that?" I exclaimed.

"You can be in business with people you don't like. I wouldn't throw away his military support in the middle of this mess."

"I don't need his help," I said obstinately. "Especially if Katrice *does* call a truce over the crown."

"And if she doesn't?"

"I don't know." I stood up and rubbed my sticky hands on my jeans. Kiyo was the last person I expected to be having this discussion with. "What are you getting at? Should I forgive him? Let it all go and jump back into bed?"

"No. Absolutely not." Kiyo walked over to me, almost mirroring our positions from last night when he'd been on the verge of telling me something romantic. Only, I'd since had more time to come to terms with my anger and could actually focus now on Kiyo, the concern in his eyes and the way his body always made mine feel. "But I don't think Dorian will leave the war, no matter what else happens between you. And you should take that help."

"I'm afraid . . ." Until those words came out of my mouth, I didn't realize I meant them. "I'm afraid when I see him, when I talk to him . . . he'll do it again. He'll convince me of, I don't know. Whatever his plan is. He'll justify it and lure me back in."

Kiyo cupped my face between his hands. "You don't have to do anything you don't want to. You're strong. And I'll go with you, if you want."

I looked up into Kiyo's eyes, feeling lost in their

depths and confused by what I saw in them. "I do want you to."

Leaning down, he pulled me close and kissed me almost before I realized what had happened. There was heat in his lips, heat and hunger and that raw, animal passion that so defined him. My body pressed against his, and I was startled at the arousal that kiss ignited within me, me who twenty-four hours ago had been sworn and sealed to Dorian. Now, the desire within me was all for Kiyo, a desire that was probably equal parts revenge against Dorian, a resurgence of my feelings for Kiyo, and the simple lust triggered by being with anyone I found so attractive.

I pulled away from him, and it wasn't easy. That kiss had consumed me, taken over my reasoning. I had a feeling I was seconds away from ripping his clothes off and throwing myself at him. Some annoyingly rational part of me kept saying I shouldn't do that until I knew for sure if it'd be because I still cared about Kiyo or because I wanted to get back at Dorian.

"No, don't. I can't," I said, taking a few steps away. "I'm not . . . I'm not ready. . . ."

I knew he could tell that wasn't exactly true. He'd be able to smell the desire on me, the pheromones and other physical signs that said I wanted him. But my head and heart? No, I wasn't sure about that.

"Eugenie . . ." His voice was husky, every ounce of him radiating that dark, primal sexuality that had always drawn me in.

"I can't," I repeated. "Please . . . don't do that again. . . ."

I hurried off blindly, into the forest, ignoring the branches and leaves whipping against me. I didn't have to go very far because something told me Kiyo wouldn't follow. He'd leave me alone for now. I sank to the ground, leaning my head back against the smooth bark of a tree I didn't recognize. My heart pounded in my chest, in turmoil from Kiyo's advances.

I'd suspected he still cared, especially seeing as the breakup had been more my idea than his. He'd conceded its wisdom, true, but I'd always known he'd wished things could have been different. Hell, that made two of us. I exhaled and closed my eyes. What did I do with this? What did I do with Kiyo's feelings? What did I do with my own feelings?

Because at the core of it all, my heart was still raging over Dorian. I'd meant what I said to Kiyo: I was indeed going to go back and tell Dorian we were over. I'd been disappointed in Kiyo—still was, a little—over his not taking direct action against Leith. Yet, as much as that had hurt me, Kiyo had been blunt and open about his reasons for it. That was better than someone telling you pretty lies. Pretty lies. Dorian was full of them—and not just about the crown. Suddenly, I found myself questioning why he'd even suggested Kiyo come along on this quest, rather than Jasmine. Maybe Dorian had thought this would be a convenient way to get rid of someone he'd always seen as a potential rival.

I didn't know. The only thing I was certain of was that I was getting more and more worked up as I sat there. A faint splash startled me out of my emotional maelstrom, and I opened my eyes. No cry of alarm had come from Volusian back at camp, and a moment later, I realized what was going on. Rising, I headed over toward the pool in the glade's heart.

Sure enough, I found Kiyo swimming laps back and forth. The lagoon was crystal clear, sparkling in the morning sunlight, and it sang to my magical senses. I wondered if he was there to clean off yesterday's battle or to work out his frustration over me. Judging from the lines on his face— maybe both. I watched him for a minute, knowing opportunities to catch him unaware were rare. The water and his mood had distracted him; he normally would have smelled and heard an observer. After a little while longer, I made my decision. I began taking off my clothes. Kiyo turned and noticed me just as I slipped into the water, easing myself down the stone edge.

"Eugenie . . . what are you doing? You're soaking your bandages."

I swam over to him, on the pool's far side. "I'm here naked with you, and that's your biggest concern?"

He eyed me carefully. "Well, that was our last batch of them."

I put my hands on his chest. "We'll be home soon."

When I brought my lips to his, joining us in a deep kiss, I felt the same response as earlier. He answered me hungrily, arms wrapping around my waist as we pressed together. Now, however, it was Kiyo who broke us apart—despite the arousal in his eyes. I had a feeling there was a human versus animal war going on within him.

"Wait," he said. "Earlier . . . you told me you couldn't . . ."

"I changed my mind. I can do *this*," I said. "Does it need to be more than that right now?" I was still going to tell Dorian I was done with him, but I didn't need to for this. I had mentally broken up with him. I was free to do whatever I wanted. I moved toward Kiyo again, slowly walking us toward the water's edge. Our top halves emerged, the morning air slightly chill against my wet skin.

"I don't trust why you're doing this," said Kiyo. But when I drew him closer, he didn't pull back. "I think you're getting back at Dorian."

I kissed him hard, cutting off whatever logical arguments he might attempt. "Maybe I am," I said at last. He was gasping, a little surprised at the intensity. I felt empowered, filled with lust for Kiyo and—yes—anger at Dorian. "But you're the one I'm doing it with. Doesn't that mean something?"

There was a pause as Kiyo's dark, smoky eyes studied me intensely. "Yes." With one swift motion, he turned me around, pushing his body against mine. "It does. This is how it should have been anyway." I caught my breath as he kissed my neck, teeth grazing my skin. "And I'll take back what's mine."

My body burned, both at his touch and the dangerous tone in his voice. Then, the full meaning of his words hit me. I started to turn around but his hands were on me, pinning me against the ledge surrounding the water. "Hey, I'm not yours," I growled. "I thought I made that clear."

"You're right," he said. "But you're not his either. Not anymore. You never should have been. We never should have been apart. And if you want this—if you want to do this—you have to tell me you feel *something* for me. I can't believe this is just simple revenge sex."

"Kiyo—"

The hands that held me slid forward to my breasts, the roughness of his touch sending shock-waves through my body. "Tell me," he breathed against my ear, his hands sliding along my stomach and down between my thighs. "Tell me you still feel something for me."

His body closed the miniscule space left between us, pushing me right to stone. I felt him hard and ready. "I . . ." I closed my eyes, lost in the way his hands touched me and stoked the sexual tension that had been building between us for days. What did I feel? For a moment, I was conflicted. Maybe this wasn't right. Maybe I did need to end things formally with Dorian before letting my emotions run away with me. "I . . ."

"Yes?"

He bent me over, hands gripping my waist, and suddenly, he was sliding into me, a low groan escaping his lips as he filled me up. I gave a small cry at the unexpected act, one that turned into a moan of pleasure as he began to move in and out of me.

"Tell me there's still something, anything . . ." he grunted. "If not, I'll stop and let this go. Just say it."

"I . . ."

Again, I couldn't summon the words. This time, it was simply because I was too lost in how he felt. I'd forgotten what it was like with him, the way he'd always loved to take me from behind, driven by the animal instinct within him. There was more than that to him, though. Images flashed through me, the way he'd fought by my side, the compassion when he'd seen how hurt I was over Dorian's deception.

"Tell me," he said again, a savage and hungry note in his voice. "Tell me you want me; tell me there's still something between us. That you don't want me to stop."

He felt so good, so strong and hard. "No . . ."

"No what?"

"No . . . don't stop . . . there is . . . of course there's still something. . . ."

I meant it. And with that, the animal within him was unleashed. I screamed as he gave me the full force of his body, my arms pushing hard to keep me from being shoved against the ledge. The sound of our bodies slapping together echoed around us as he thrust tirelessly, taking me over and over as he reclaimed my body.

"I've missed you, Eug," he managed to say. "Missed having sex with you. Missed making love to you. But especially . . . especially missed fucking you."

His words were punctuated with a particularly sharp thrust, one that took me hard and deep as he bent me over more. I screamed again, but it was out of ecstasy, not pain. Kiyo had always been able to make me come this way, and now was no exception. I felt the nerves of my body explode, every part of me shaking. Still he kept moving in me with that primal need, pushing me into sensory overload. He'd given up on words, simply making small grunts as our bodies connected.

At last his body reached its breaking point, giving me the hardest thrusts he was capable of as his climax hit. He held me tight, my body there to fulfill his need as he came in me, groaning and spasming until he'd finally given me all he had.

He pulled out, and I turned around, my own breath shallow and rapid. "That . . . maybe we shouldn't have done that . . ."

Kiyo put an arm around my waist and pulled me to him. His lips grazed mine. "You sound like a guy the morning after. You're the one who attacked me, remember?"

"True," I admitted. With my lust sated, I was feeling slightly more coherent. But only barely. His naked body was still right against mine, and that was distracting.

"Give me a few more minutes," he murmured. "A few more minutes and we can do it again . . ."

"We're probably just creating more problems."

He kissed my neck. "What's one more problem among all the others we have? One more time, Eugenie. I've missed you so much. Let's do this just one more time."

I could feel that he was indeed almost ready again. I lifted one of my legs up, half-wrapping it around him as my body decided it was ready again too. "And then what?"

"Then?" Kiyo's mouth moved toward mine. "Then we go see Dorian."

Chapter 13

The journey back was uneventful, the most notable thing being the afterglow that now burned between Kiyo and me—something I now questioned the wisdom of. My words had been true: I'd never stopped caring about him. But he'd been right too: what had happened between us back in the glade had come from my own outrage and need to get back at Dorian. That wasn't really a good reason to start a relationship. It wasn't even a really good reason for casual sex, and honestly, I wasn't sure what my status was with Kiyo at the moment.

Deanna reappeared and followed along so quietly and obediently that I finally broke the silence to reassure her I'd keep my part of the bargain. Her drab face lit up, and I had to give her credit for not pushing the matter until I settled my other business.

Kiyo and I went straight to Dorian's, once we'd crossed back into more familiar territory. My plan was to deal with him first and then jump to the human world. I thought it would be safer to have the crown there. Dorian's guards met me with pleased grins, and while they were surprised to see Kiyo, most seemed to know I'd been off on some secret mission. Coming back alive was a good sign.

As soon as we entered the castle, I ordered a messenger to go to Katrice and inform her that I now possessed the Iron Crown and that if she wanted to talk surrender, I was all ears. As Dorian's consort, I had the power to order around his staff—but I had a feeling that would end soon.

Kiyo and I were admitted into Dorian's exalted presence out in a courtyard, where he was making a long-tormented courtier named Muran play the harp. I knew for a fact that Muran had had exactly one lesson, and Dorian seemed quite amused watching the guy struggle through. This kind of thing was one of Dorian's greatest pastimes, and usually, even though I felt bad for Muran, it provided me with a little amusement. Today I felt none.

When we entered the courtyard, Dorian took one look at our faces and promptly ordered everyone away—even his guards. He still wore that small, carefree smile, but I'd seen a subtle shift in the lines of his face. He knew something was up. His astuteness was what made him such a good ruler.

"Well, here you are," he said, sitting back in the gentry equivalent of a lawn chair. Except, of course, I'd never seen Home Depot sell anything so ornate and gilded. Normally when I arrived, Dorian kissed me, but his wariness must have held him back. "As beautiful as ever, my dear, if a little beat up around the edges. I suppose this means you either succeeded or just barely escaped with your life?"

"We succeeded," I said. "I've got the crown."

Again—that smile didn't change, but an eager light flickered in Dorian's eyes. He leaned forward. "I knew it. I knew you could do it." He studied me up and down, his gaze finally resting on the bag over my shoulder. "May I see it?"

"No," I said bluntly. "No one's going to see it. It's going to be hidden away where it can't be used to start eating up people's lands."

Dorian's eyebrows rose, and he began to speak. I could already imagine a hundred variations of what was going to come out of his mouth, something along the lines of, *"Whatever are you talking about, my dear?"*

I stepped forward, my control snapping as I cut him off. "Don't start! Don't even start with some sugar-coated denial. You've known all along what the crown could do! You knew it'd scare Katrice because it meant I—and by default *you*—could take over her kingdom!"

Dorian hesitated, and again, I could guess at the thoughts spinning in his head. Denial or backpedaling? He finally went with the latter.

"And what better way to push her into peace?" he said at last. "The point of a war like this is to eventually march over and subdue someone anyway. Isn't it much simpler and faster to achieve that same end through another way?"

"A way that rips her land from her!" I exclaimed. "And sticks me with another fucking kingdom!" I stepped forward and had to forcibly keep myself from getting closer. I was so, so angry. So angry that this man I cared about could do this to me. I was almost angrier at him than Katrice at the moment. From her, at least, I expected betrayal. "And that's what you would have wanted to do—not just scare her. You would have found some way, some justification for taking that drastic step, just like you got me to go after this in the first place."

Much of the humor had faded from Dorian's face now. "And would you have gone after it if you'd known?"

"No."

He shrugged. "Well, there you have it."

I was aghast. "That's it? How the hell can you be so lax about this? How can you act like it's okay to have tricked me from the beginning—you and that hag? How can you claim to love me and lie to me?"

"I do love you," he said. "More than you know. I did this for your own good."

"You did it for *your* own good," I snapped. "I can't believe I fell for it again. You've done this before, and now I'm done. Done with you. Done with all of this. I don't need your help anymore. I'll finish this fucking war on my own."

"Eugenie," warned Kiyo softly. He didn't contradict me, not in front of Dorian, but I understood the subtext. It was the point he'd made before: not to spurn Dorian's military help.

Dorian scoffed, sharing that sentiment. "Of course you need me. If you can get past your hurt pride, you'll see that we're in this together. Use the crown however you want, but be reasonable so that the two of us can finally end this war."

My voice was low and dangerous when I spoke. I was furious that he could be so condescending, that he assumed he could just smooth this all over. "There is no more us."

"Now you're just overreacting," he said. "We need to finish this war together, and *we* need to be together, period. We're meant to be."

"No," I said. "We're done. It's over."

I could see from his face that he didn't take that seriously either. He didn't get it. His ego wouldn't allow him to. Before he could respond, Kiyo lightly touched my arm. "Be careful. Look what you're doing."

I glanced around. The wind was rising and falling, making the apple trees sway back and forth. Dark clouds began to gather above. It wasn't uncommon for my emotions to unconsciously affect the weather, but the fact that I could do it in a land under someone else's control was a sign of how much my power had grown. If Dorian had wanted sunny weather, it should have stayed that way. The realization of what I could do was heady. Nonetheless, I pushed back, calming the air and dissipating the storm clouds.

But Dorian wasn't concerned about any of that. His attention had snapped to one small gesture: Kiyo's touch on my arm. I'm not sure how Dorian knew—maybe just the way Kiyo and I stood near each other—but in that moment, Dorian realized what had happened between Kiyo and me. And that, more than any of the arguments here, was what finally broke that laid-back attitude. His face turned to stone.

"Oh," he said to Kiyo, voice completely devoid of emotion. "I see. It's your turn again." Outrage filled me at the insinuation that I could be passed around—a sentiment not unlike what Kiyo himself had expressed. Dorian allowed me no chance to counter. "Well, if that's how it's going to be, then that's how it's going to be. You may be right that there's no *us*, but we are still in this war together. My armies are too enmeshed, and I can hardly let Katrice think I'm backing down. Dareth!"

Dorian's voice rang out, loudly enough that one of the guards behind the glass doors heard. He swiftly opened the doors and stepped outside.

"Your Majesty?"

"Please escort the Thorn Queen and her pet from the premises. They are denied hospitality. Do not admit them again. Should any of her household come, they may be allowed into my presence." His eyes flicked to me. "Send Rurik as your proxy for all military matters. He was doing all the work anyway." Dorian's attention went back to his guard. "You have your orders."

Dareth had trouble keeping the shock off his face. I had become a fixture around here, treated nearly the same as Dorian. After a few moments, Dareth composed his features, his loyalty to his king overriding any disbelief he might feel. He turned to me, expression formal. He gestured inside.

"Your Majesty."

The respect was there, but the message was clear. I was being thrown out and could see Dareth practically praying I wouldn't resist. I didn't, and while a dozen parting retorts to Dorian filled my head, I shoved them aside. He thrived on that kind of attention. It would only make him feel more important, and I wanted it made clear that I really was done with him—even though the cold reality of what was happening made my heart break.

Kiyo and I began to follow Dareth without comment, but then I paused. Reaching toward my neck, I ripped off the necklace I wore, the one with Dorian's ring. I tossed it at his feet, meeting his gaze with a message I hoped he understood. He did. His answered mine with green fury.

"I said get out of here."

I turned away, letting Dareth take us to the castle's front doors. As soon as we were outside, I heard him giving instructions about the revoking of our hospitality. I imagined the other guards shared his shock, but I walked on without looking back. Once Kiyo and I had traveled far enough that the land shifted and put us in Maiwenn's kingdom, he turned to look at me.

"Are you okay?" he asked, worry in those dark eyes.

"Fine," I said flatly. I was confident my anger was justified . . . but leaving Dorian still hurt. He'd dismissed me so easily, once he'd realized I'd slept with Kiyo. I'd expected something . . . something more emotional, I guess. Some sign that I'd meant more to him than a useful consort.

I should have known better. "Let's go back to Tucson."

I'd kept Volusian and Deanna away while we'd met with Dorian but brought them both back now. I told Deanna to come to my home tomorrow and that we'd start working on her problem then. To Volusian, I gave orders to return to the Thorn Land. He would tell Rurik to go to Dorian and then wait until word came back from Katrice. I had no doubt that word of my being banned from Dorian's would spread around quickly enough; I didn't want to see the reactions of my people when that happened.

Kiyo and I crossed back to Arizona at a nearby gateway, going to his place instead of mine so that he could redo my stitches. He was as good as any 'real' doctor, and I didn't want to have to explain my new cuts and bruises to someone else. A slew of cats and dogs greeted me when I entered his apartment, making me feel oddly nostalgic.

"Are you *sure* you're okay?" Kiyo asked later. I was lying stomach-down on his bed while his needle went to work on the cut.

My cheek rested on a pillow, my only view being his dresser as I tried to stay still. "Fine."

"You keep saying that, but what went down was pretty serious." I could imagine the frown on his face. "I didn't expect him to pull hospitality."

"He knows we slept together," I said. "Guys get upset when their girlfriends do that." I'd broken up with Dorian in my head the instant I found out about the deception, but as far as he was concerned, I'd cheated on him. Maybe I had. But betraying someone who'd deceived you didn't seem like that much of a betrayal.

"Yes," said Kiyo. "Yes, they do." He tied off his thread and re-bandaged it all. "Please, please do not pull these out again. The fact that this isn't infected is a miracle."

"I won't," I said, sitting up and carefully putting my shirt back on. "I don't plan on getting in any fights for a while. I'm staying out of the Otherworld until they really need me, and investigating Deanna's murder should only involve questions. Actually, I'm hoping to pass it off on someone else."

"She won't like that," he said.

"It'll get it done," I said. "And she'll like that. Probably even faster than if I did it."

I started to stand, but Kiyo caught hold of my hand and kept me down. His expression turned sly. "You want to stay for a while?"

I shook my head, smiling faintly. "I've got some things to do. Besides, just because we did what we did doesn't mean . . . well, it doesn't mean things are the same again."

His mischievous smile faded. "You're right. A lot kind of got rushed. I suppose we should . . . I don't know. Do you want to go on a date?"

"A date?" I laughed in spite of myself. It seemed so out of place after what we'd been through these last few days. Too ordinary. "Dinner and a movie?"

"Something like that. I could pick you up later, after your errands are done. Or tomorrow if you need a little more time."

A little more time? Maybe I needed a lot more time. I really didn't know. I might have jumped into bed—figuratively speaking—right after my relationship with Dorian had crumbled, but as I'd said, that didn't mean I was ready to establish something committed with Kiyo again. I'd had sex with Kiyo in the throes of my anger; I had more to think about now that I'd cooled down—and seen Dorian's face. My head told me we were through, but my heart already missed him.

"Tomorrow," I said.

Kiyo nodded. "Fair enough. I should probably check in at the clinic anyway."

I honestly didn't understand the terms of Kiyo's employment. With his constant visits to the Other-world, he didn't seem to have any regular schedule with the emergency vet clinic he worked at. He just seemed to show up whenever he wanted. It was more convenient than my own job for maintaining a dual existence between worlds.

Confused feelings or not, I let him kiss me good-bye before I left. There was a part of me that wished I could just stay with him, hiding out in his bed and avoiding the rest of the world. Worlds, even. But I had too much to do.

The first thing was to get home and change into clean clothes. I arrived to what initially appeared to be an empty house, but the cars in the driveway tipped me off. Sure enough, a minute or so after I walked inside, I heard Tim's bedroom door open. He emerged, wearing only jeans, his black hair standing in all directions.

"Hey, Eug. Didn't expect to see you back."

"Apparently not. I take it Lara's in there?"

He had the grace to look sheepish. "Ah, well—"

"Hi Eugenie." Lara appeared in the kitchen beside him, her hair as messed up as his. Her clothes—including Tim's "West Coast Powwow 2002" T-shirt—showed signs of hasty assembly. She was blushing, but her embarrassment turned to surprise as she eyed my appearance. She still wasn't used to seeing me in real life. "Rough day?"

"Days," I said.

"Oh . . . I don't suppose . . . I don't suppose you'd be interested in hearing about some job offers?" It was the first time she'd been hesitant to bring up work. I think she was finally starting to understand the grueling nature of my life and that back-to-back jobs weren't as easy as checking items off a list.

"Not really. Not for a few days."

"A few—" She bit off her protest and meekly nodded.

I walked around them, heading for my room. "I've got things to do," I called back to them. "So you can go back to . . . whatever it is you were doing."

Truthfully, I didn't want to do the task hanging before me. I wanted to find whatever baked goods Tim had squirreled away in the kitchen and then take that nap I'd longed for at Kiyo's. But, no. I'd made a promise to Deanna, one I had to honor, no matter how messed up the rest of my life was. So, after cleaning up and changing, I sat on the edge of my bed and picked up my cell phone. I stared at for a long time, running my fingers along its edges as I procrastinated. Finally, I dialed a memorized number and waited.

There was a good chance that no one would answer. I was calling my mom's cell phone, though, which gave me better odds than if I'd called her house number. I knew Roland had asked her to keep her distance from me, but after seeing me at the hospital, my mom would likely resist any directives like that—if only out of fear that I'd lost a limb or something.

"Hello?"

My breath caught, and I almost couldn't speak. Just that one word . . . the sound of her voice. It sent a flood of emotions through me, and I forced myself to remember my mission here.

"Mom?"

"Genie? Are you okay?" she asked promptly. As suspected, she feared limb loss.

"Yeah, yeah, fine. How are you?"

"Fine. Worried about you—like always."

"I'm okay," I said. "Really. But I need . . . I, um, need to talk to Roland."

Long silence.

"Eugenie—"

"I know, I know. But I need his help with something. It won't take long. Just one question. Please."

She sighed. "Oh, baby. I wish I could, but he's made it clear . . . You know how he feels about everything. . . ."

"It's a human thing," I said, only partially lying. "A job in this world. Please, Mom. Just ask him if he'll talk to me for a minute?"

More silence, then another sigh. "Hang on."

I waited, nervously twisting the fabric of my bed's duvet. What would happen? The two most likely options were that either my mom would relay his refusal or they would simply hang up on me. But, no. It was Roland's voice I heard next.

"Yes?" Cold. Wary.

After everything that had just happened to me in the Otherworld, hearing his voice nearly broke me. I wanted to sob and beg him to forgive me. Beg him to love me again. My mom had undoubtedly done a fair share of that already, though. She'd clearly had no luck. I had no reason to believe I'd fare any better, so I made my tone match his as I swallowed back tears. Just business here.

"I need a referral," I said brusquely. "To a private investigator. One who isn't going to be freaked out by the stuff we deal with. I figured you must know someone."

"You need a P.I. to deal with some monster?" he asked harshly.

"No, no. It actually should be pretty mundane—all human stuff. But considering what we do . . . Well, I thought I should have someone prepared in case things get weird." I didn't have any reason for Deanna to interact directly with a P.I.—or for me even to mention her—but I wanted to be safe.

"Well," said Roland. "Let's make it clear: 'we' don't do the same kinds of things."

With great effort, I bit off the retorts that wanted to burst out of me. I wanted to explain for the hundredth time that I'd never expected—or wanted—to reach this level of involvement in the Otherworld. Again, I opted for directness.

"Please, Roland," I said simply. "This is for a human family. Just forget about me for a minute."

When he didn't respond, I thought for sure the anticipated hang-up would come. "Enrique Valdez," he said at last. "You should be able to look up his number. I'll call too and give him a heads-up."

"Oh, Roland. Thank you so—"

Click.

There it was. I pulled the phone away and held it in front of me again, staring at it as though it were to blame for all my problems. A few moments later, I tossed it on the floor. Anger surged through me, quickly fading into sadness. My eyes fell on my travel pack in the corner, the pack containing the Iron Crown. That—and all it represented—was the source of my problems.

I fell back onto my bed, staring up at the glow-in-the-dark stars stuck on my ceiling. Roland, Dorian . . . I was losing the men in my life. Why, why had Dorian done that? Why had he let me fall in love with him, only to play me? Was that what love meant to him? Was that how all his relationships worked? He'd hurt me, hurt me so terribly, and the petty, dark voice that lived inside me said that if sleeping with Kiyo had hurt Dorian in return, it was no more than he deserved.

Kiyo.

Kiyo was all I had left now, and I didn't know if I could trust him either. Before I could ruminate very much on that particular woe, a cold presence filled the room. I sat up quickly, putting aside all my self-pity as Volusian materialized before me.

"Mistress," he said.

"Volusian," I replied. "What's going on?"

"I've come with a message, as you requested." As always, his words were emotionless, yet he somehow conveyed the feeling that he resented every one of them. "Queen Katrice has responded to your news of the Iron Crown."

That was fast, even for the Otherworld. "And?"

"And, she has agreed to a temporary truce."

I shot up from the bed. "You have got to be kidding."

Volusian didn't respond. I'd long since learned that any comment I made about him joking or kidding was treated rhetorically. Volusian did not joke or kid.

"It worked," I murmured, more to myself than him. "I can't believe it. Dorian was right."

"Indeed. But I assume my mistress will not resume carnal relations with him."

I made a face. If there was anyone I hated discussing my sex life with more than Jasmine, it was Volusian. "No. It doesn't matter if he was right. He lied to me to make it happen. He should have told me the whole story. He used half-truth means to achieve his ends."

Volusian nodded solemnly. "I told you that long ago, that the Oak King's own agenda will always come first. As will the kitsune's. But, unsurprisingly, my mistress chooses to ignore the only sound advice given to her and instead listens to those who use affection for their own purposes." The word 'affection' was spoken with particular venom.

"Kiyo and Dorian don't—Look. Stay out of this, okay? I never asked for your 'sound' advice. Get back to Katrice. How does this truce work exactly?"

"Hostilities will cease until all parties are able to discuss the current situation. How said discussion proceeds will be settled beforehand by messengers. You and the Oak King may meet with her directly, or you may have representatives do the negotiating."

I tried to picture myself in a room with Dorian and Katrice. Lovely. "And where would this happen? I'm sure as hell not going to the Rowan Land."

"That too will be negotiated during this truce," he said. "A neutral kingdom is the most likely choice. Shaya would like to discuss that with you at your earliest convenience."

"I'm sure she would. Go back and tell her I trust her to set up whatever arrangements need to be made. If I have to go myself . . . well, then I go. I'll check in with her soon, but come back if anything happens in the meantime." Volusian waited, and I gestured him away. "Go."

He vanished, and I sank onto my bed. My eyes fell on the concealed Iron Crown once again, and I dared to wonder if maybe some good had come out of this whole mess.

Chapter 14

"This isn't what I had in mind when I said we should go out on a date."

It took me a few days to get in to see Enrique Valdez, and Kiyo had decided to accompany me. While waiting for my appointment, I'd checked in once with the Thorn Land, only to find the whole experience frustrating. Though no one openly said it—well, except for Jasmine—they all thought me breaking up with Dorian was the worst idea ever. I also learned from Shaya that arrangements for a war meeting were getting bogged down. Dorian insisted all three monarchs meet in person. Katrice wanted to send her nephew. There was also the matter of which kingdom would host because several others wanted to, most likely in the hopes of getting in good with one or all of us. I told Shaya I didn't care about the details and to simply do whatever it took to finish this war quickly.

When Kiyo and I reached Enrique's address, we found it was in a small, sad-looking office building in one of the more rundown areas of downtown Tucson. I eyed it askance as we stood outside and waited for him to buzz us up.

"I don't get why it took us three days to get in," I said. "It doesn't really seem like he's got that much business."

The door buzzed, and Kiyo opened it. "Maybe it's a cover," he said. We walked up to the second floor, where Enrique's office was located. "Maybe he wants to hide how successful he is."

"That's ridiculous—"

I stopped when the office door opened before we knocked. Even with Enrique standing in the doorway, I could see beautiful, expensive furnishings.

"Well, I'll be damned," I muttered, entering at Enrique's gesture.

He was shorter than me, with deeply tanned skin and black hair starting to gray. I put him somewhere in his mid to late forties. His attire didn't quite match the office's opulence. In fact, it looked like stereotypical P.I. clothing from some old detective noir film, complete with a fedora.

"Markham's girl, huh?" he asked, voice laced with a faint Spanish accent. His eyes fell on Kiyo. "And a bodyguard?"

"A friend," I said sharply. "I don't need a bodyguard."

"Right." Enrique didn't sound like he believed that. He pointed us to some plush leather chairs while he sat in an even bigger one across from us. A huge cherry desk was situated between us. It gleamed deep red in the late afternoon light and didn't look like the kind of thing you'd find at IKEA.

I stared around at the rest of the office, still amazed at how it contrasted with the exterior. Books—ranging widely from *Moby Dick* to Arizona state law—lined shelves that matched the desk, and small pieces of art—paintings, statues, et cetera—adorned the room.

"So," began Enrique. "What's his name, and why do you think he's cheating on you?"

"I—huh?" I jerked my head from a sculpture that looked like some Mayan god and stared at Enrique in astonishment. "What are you talking about? Is that what Roland told you?"

"No, he didn't tell me anything. I just figured that's why you were here. That's usually what women come in for."

Kiyo made a small sound beside me that I think was a laugh. "That's ridiculous," I exclaimed, unsure if I should be offended or not. "I need you to investigate a murder."

Enrique arched an eyebrow. "That's what the police are for."

"They already investigated it. And actually, they declared it a suicide."

"And you need me because . . . ?"

"Because I don't think it was," I said. "I think it was a murder and that the victim's family might be in danger."

Enrique made no attempt to hide his skepticism. "Do you have any evidence to support this . . . theory?"

I took a deep breath, hoping Roland had been right about this guy. "The victim's, um, ghost said she didn't kill herself."

"Her ghost," he repeated. As though on cue, Deanna materialized in the room, though Enrique couldn't see her. Kiyo and I could with our Otherworldly senses, but neither of us gave any indication of her arrival.

I nodded. "Roland said you—"

"Yeah, yeah," said Enrique. "I know about that hocus pocus he deals with. I'm also guessing suicide might be so traumatic that afterward, maybe a ghost blocked out what she actually did."

"That's not true!" exclaimed Deanna.

I supposed it wasn't out of the realm of possibility, but I'd explore all other options first. "I don't think that's the case. I think she really was murdered. If that's true, we need to make sure no one else in her family gets hurt."

"If she was murdered," countered Enrique, "then statistics say someone in her family probably did it."

"That's not true either!"

I ignored Deanna's second outburst and stayed fixed on Enrique. "Well, one way or another, I need to know."

He leaned back in his chair, putting his feet up on his desk and crossing his arms behind his head. If he'd called me 'dame,' I wouldn't have been surprised. "The police take all this into consideration, you know. What makes you think I'd find something they haven't?"

"I thought guys like you were smarter than the police," said Kiyo. "Figured you had connections and channels above the law. That you didn't play by the same rules."

"That's true," said Enrique, seeming pleased at the compliment. I swore, he was also taking Kiyo more seriously than me. "I can look into it, I suppose. But it's not like I'll do it for free, just because you're cute." That was directed back at me.

I repressed a scowl. "I didn't expect you to. I can pay."

He considered this and finally gave a nod, straightening back up in his chair. "Okay. Tell me what you know, and I'll get to it when I can."

"What!" cried Deanna.

"This is kind of time sensitive," I said. Mostly because I wasn't sure how much more of Deanna I could handle.

Enrique gestured to a stack of folders on a table. "So are these. I'm drowning in paperwork. Can't keep half of these straight."

"We'll pay for you to expedite it," said Kiyo.

I shot him a look of astonishment, not thrilled that he'd speak for me—especially considering my income was lower than it used to be. Nonetheless, it got Enrique's attention. "Expediting it is, then."

I gave him all the details I'd recently learned from Deanna, and to his credit, Enrique diligently wrote them all down and asked pertinent questions that reaffirmed my faith in his legitimacy. The price he named didn't cheer me up as much, but there was nothing to be done for it.

When Kiyo and I finally got up to leave, I couldn't resist asking the obvious. "You seem to be doing pretty well . . . so why's your office in a dump like this?"

Enrique didn't look offended so much as scornful that I'd ask such a ridiculous question. "Do you know how much office rent is lately? I'm saving tons of money."

"Maybe you should put that surplus toward a secretary instead of statues," I pointed out, nodding toward the tower of folders.

"I don't trust anyone," he said bluntly. "Especially when ghost clients show up." He opened the door. "I'll be in touch."

"Charming," I said, once Kiyo and I were on the road again. "The only thing I'm convinced that guy can do is help in the regression of women's rights."

Kiyo tried to hide a smile and failed. "He was right about you being cute, though. And I don't know . . . something tells me that despite the attitude, he's pretty competent. Crappy building aside, he couldn't afford that office if he wasn't achieving results. Besides, Roland wouldn't recommend anyone incompetent."

"Unless he was trying to sabotage me."

Kiyo's smile faded. "Do you really think he'd do that to you?"

I stared out the passenger seat window. "No. He wouldn't."

"I'm sorry, you know. I really am. About Roland."

"I don't want to talk about it," I said. My mood plummeted each time Roland's name came up.

"Okay, then. You want to salvage this 'date' and get some lunch?"

I didn't have faith in the change of subject. I didn't think anything could really distract me, certainly not the crappy Mexican restaurant Kiyo took us to.

"Are you serious?" I asked. Felipe's Fiestaland was the cheesiest restaurant in town, figuratively speaking. In a place like Tucson, where you could get amazingly authentic southwestern cuisine, Felipe's was for tourists and suburbanites who didn't know any better.

"Are you saying a margarita wouldn't do you good?" he asked, getting out of the car.

"I would never say that. But there are better places with better margaritas."

"They still use tequila in theirs. Isn't that what really matters?"

"Fair point."

We were greeted by a hostess who sounded like she'd taken one semester of Spanish in high school. Piñatas hung from the ceiling, and bad mariachi music blasted from speakers. I scanned the drink menu as soon as we sat down and was ready when the waiter came by.

"I'll have your Double Platinum Extra Premium Margarita," I told him.

"*Grande* or super *grande?*" asked the waiter.

"Super."

Kiyo looked impressed. "I'll have the same." When we were alone, he asked, "What is that exactly?"

I propped an elbow on the table, resting my chin on my palm. "I'm not sure, but it sounded like it had the most alcohol in it. Places like this tend to drown their drinks in mixers."

"Spoken like a pro."

"Stating the obvious. You and I both know Roza's has the best margaritas."

Kiyo smiled at that, flashing me a warm and knowing look. I had a feeling he was thinking about a memory that had come to me too, back from when we'd dated. We'd gone out to Roza's—which really did have the best margaritas in town—and gotten so drunk that neither of us could drive home. So, we'd used the car for the only thing we could: sex. Twice.

The drinks arrived and were about the size of fishbowls. They were also about half-mixer, as suspected, but at least that still left a reasonable quantity of alcohol. I drank mine down quickly as we waited for our food. Alcohol numbed my shamanic powers a little bit and sometimes let me forget my problems. Not so much today.

"Do you think Enrique might be right?" I asked. "That Deanna did commit suicide and blocked it out?" The ghost had left us once we departed from the office.

"I don't know. I don't know if she'd believe it, even if he turned up a film or something."

I grimaced and downed more of the drink. "I hope not. It's nothing I'd want to watch. I'm tired of bloodshed."

"I know," he said gently. "And no matter what I said before . . . and how upset I was when this war started . . . well, I have to admit. You've handled it as best you could. Word gets around. I know you've made some tactical moves that minimized casualties—and not just for your own people."

"'Tactical.' 'Casualties.'" I shook my head, eyeing my low margarita. "Those are terms I never thought I'd use. And really, I don't have much to do with that planning. Rurik does."

"But you give the okay," Kiyo pointed out. "Not many rulers would. Most would do whatever it took to crush their enemies quickly."

"I've certainly wanted to." Dorian had as well, and the few disagreements we'd had during our wartime partnership had been over civilian collateral damage. "Can we talk about something not Otherworldly? And not about suicide?"

"Sure." Our waiter suddenly appeared with the plate of Mile High *Muy Bueno* Nachos we'd ordered. Kiyo flashed him a grin. "She'll have another margarita. Also, it's her birthday."

I shot Kiyo a look of horror as the waiter scurried off. "Are you out of your mind? You don't say something like that in a place like this!"

But it was too late. Because in a matter of minutes, the entire waitstaff of Felipe's Fiestaland had surrounded our table. Someone put a sombrero on my head and a candlelit piece of flan in front of me. The whole group then launched into an out-of-tune rendition of "*Cumpleaños Feliz,*" set to equally bad out-of-rhythm clapping. I stared at Kiyo the whole time and mouthed *I will kill you.* It only made his smile grow.

"You don't look a day older," he told me, once the mob had dispersed.

"I can't believe you did that." I jerked off the sombrero and dove into the new margarita. "Do you know how humiliating that is?"

"Hey, it got your mind off everything else, didn't it? Plus, check it out. Free flan."

I blew out the candle and hesitantly poked the gelatinous mass below it. "It looks like it's been sitting around a while."

"Don't worry," he said, dragging the plate over to his side of the table. "With all the preservatives in it, I'm sure it's fine."

"I'm going to get you back for this," I warned, narrowing my eyes.

The look he gave me was knowing. "I hope so," he said. "I certainly hope so."

I can only blame the margaritas for what happened next, because as soon as we'd paid our bill and were back in the car, we attacked each other.

"See?" he said, trying to pull my shirt over my head. "Who needs Roza's?"

"It was dark out then," I reminded him, my own hands fumbling for his pants.

"We're in the back of the lot," he argued. "And the sun's going down."

He had a point, and when he brought one of my nipples to his mouth, I kind of let the subject drop. We really were out of sight, and there were more important matters to take care of. We reclined and pushed the seat back as far as it would go, then finally managed to get each other's jeans off. I brought my hips down, taking him into me.

"See?" I gasped. "You're sorry now."

"Very," he managed to say.

Our awkward positioning kept my breasts pretty close to his face, and he was taking advantage of it with his hands and mouth. As for me, I was just thrilled at the feel of being on top of him. After always playing submissive with Dorian, I suddenly exalted in this sense of power—especially since Kiyo had definitely been the one in control the last time we had sex. Now, it was all me, and I took a fair amount of satisfaction in taunting him, alternately increasing the speed of my movement and then slowing down when he got close to coming.

"Eugenie," he begged at last. "Enough. Please . . . do it. . . ."

I leaned toward him like I might kiss him—and then pulled back when his lips sought mine. With a grin, I straightened up as much as I could and rode him hard, finally letting him have the release he'd begged for. His body bucked up as he came, his hands holding tightly to my hips as though I might leave before he finished.

After that, I guess we were kind of dating again. The next week or so passed in an easy pattern. I saw Kiyo almost every day, and we slipped back into our old routines. I started taking more jobs, much to Lara's relief, while Kiyo alternately worked at the vet clinic and checked in with the Otherworld. At night, he and I were always together, either at my place or his. My body began to remember what it was like being in a relationship, and slowly, my heart did as well.

I only crossed into the Otherworld once during that time, both from Thorn Land withdrawal and curiosity over the war proceedings. No progress was being made with Katrice. I was grateful for the lack of fighting, but the hoped-for peace talks still seemed a ways off. It was frustrating.

"She's being difficult," said Shaya, when I asked about it. Understandably, she looked weary. "These are delicate matters. They take time."

I left it at that, feeling impatient, but figuring she knew better than me. Back in Tucson, I also got sporadic updates of another sort: Enrique's. To his credit, he called almost every day to report what he'd done or investigated. At first his attitude remained the same, full of that cockiness and irritability that said this was a waste of his time. Then, one day, things changed.

"I think," he said. "You might be right."

I'm not sure who was more surprised by this: him or me. I'd honestly started to believe he wouldn't turn up anything at all as evidence of either a suicide or a murder. I gripped the phone tightly.

"What? That someone killed her?"

"Yeah . . . I found a couple things. Did you know her husband has a girlfriend?"

"Deanna told me. She seemed okay with his moving on." It had been a few months since her death, too soon to start dating in my book, but still a semi-respectable timeframe. According to Deanna, he'd begun seeing someone a few weeks ago.

"Yeah, well, he moved on before she was dead. The girlfriend? His alibi."

I frowned. "Seriously?" Deanna's husband had been removed from suspicion because he'd had a solid witness to his whereabouts when she'd been killed. He'd been at a real estate agent's office; the agent was helping him with a vacation home for their family. "Maybe their relationship started after Deanna died . . ."

"Not if a witness I found is reliable. I also might have a lead that proves Deanna wasn't the one who bought the gun."

"If that's true . . ." I couldn't finish right away. Deanna acquiring the gun that had killed her had been one of the most damning pieces of evidence for suicide. "If you can prove that, then it could reopen everything."

"Yes," said Enrique matter-of-factly. "Yes, it could. I'll be in touch."

We disconnected, and I suddenly wished he hadn't been quite so good at his job. If he was right about all this and turned up the evidence he needed . . . well, someone was going to have to break the news to Deanna that her husband had murdered her. And that someone would be me. She currently believed some crazed killer had done it, one that was after her family now. The thought of it all sickened me.

As I sat there in my room, an Otherworldly presence made my skin tingle. For half a second, I thought Deanna was appearing unsummoned— something I wasn't ready to deal with. I'd essentially given her a "don't call me, I'll call you" directive. But, no. It wasn't her. It was Volusian, his red eyes as malevolent as always. Lately, his appearance meant news from the Otherworld. I hoped it would be good.

"What's up?" I demanded.

"Shaya requests your presence immediately."

Something good at last. "The peace talks?"

"No. She needs you because the Oak King is at your castle, demanding to see you."

Chapter 15

I had two immediate reactions to this. One was that Dorian could wait around forever; he had no right to demand anything of me. My other reaction was outrage that he could come traipsing into my home when I was banned from his. Admittedly, that was my own fault. I hadn't put down any hospitality rules to keep him out. As such, he'd be welcomed like any other non-enemy monarch—particularly by my people. I considered simply sending Volusian to revoke hospitality but then tossed that idea aside. I'd take care of this myself.

I drove out to the gateway by my home as fast as I could without getting a ticket and then crossed over to the anchor inside my castle. Once there, I hurried through the halls, oblivious to servants' startled stares. I knew where Dorian would be. My people would have received him in the nicest chamber, the one befitting any visiting monarch.

Sure enough. Dorian sat inside the parlor, lounging in a central chair with Shaya, Rurik, and others sitting around him. He looked like he was holding court in his own castle. My anger doubled. Everyone except him jumped up at my sudden approach, giving hasty bows.

"Out," I snapped. "All of you. And shut the door."

My words left no question about who exactly I wanted out. Dorian didn't move, but the rest scurried to obey my orders. I saw Shaya and Rurik exchange looks with each other, no doubt worried what was going to happen with the two monarchs they loved.

Once we were alone, I turned on Dorian. "What the hell are you doing here?"

He regarded me coolly, face perfectly at ease. "Visiting, as is my right. There's nothing that says I can't. Unless you're revoking my hospitality?"

"I should," I said, stepping forward with fists clenched. "I should have my guards throw you out on your ass."

He snorted and absentmindedly smoothed a piece of his long hair. "Good luck with that. They'd throw you out first, if I gave the order."

"So that's why you're here? To start a rebellion in my own kingdom?"

"No. I'm here to remind you of your responsibilities to your kingdom—since you've clearly forgotten."

"Really?" I crossed my arms across my chest in an effort to stop myself from doing something stupid. "I think *you've* forgotten what I've done for my kingdom. Say, like, saving it from disaster. And risking my life for that fucking crown so that we could finally have peace."

"If memory serves, you caused that disaster

when you created an inhospitable desert." His voice was still damnably calm. "And that crown is doing you no good."

"Didn't you hear me? We have peace. The fighting's stopped."

"The fighting's temporarily stopped. Katrice is playing you, and you're letting her. She's dragging her feet, using this negotiation delay to figure out a way out of this. If you really want to end the war once and for all, you need to get involved and let her know you're serious. Wave the crown around. Dare her to call your bluff. Show her you're in control and stop all of this for real."

I gave a harsh laugh. "That's so typical of you. Attempting to pull the strings, as usual. You don't even have the crown, but you're telling me what to do with it."

Dorian shot up from the chair, smooth features breaking into annoyance. "*I* am remembering what it means to be a king. I'm not running away and letting others deal with things that seem too hard."

"Right," I said, keeping an eye on the distance between us. "Getting the crown was easy. Which is why, of course, you were right out there with me."

He narrowed his eyes. "You know I would have if I could. So I did the only thing I could: I got you out there after it."

"By lying!" I exclaimed. I tried to keep my voice strong, letting anger be the only emotion to slip, but grief cracked me a little. "By creating an elaborate set-up with Masthera in the hope I'd seize more land for us. Why do you not see how wrong that was?"

"Was it?" His volume was starting to match my own. I'd so rarely seen emotion seize him, and it was both terrible and beautiful. "Do you think our people think it's wrong? The ones whose homes are no longer in danger? The ones who are alive because of this? The crown bought that, and you're going to ruin it all if you don't force her into talks! Not only that, by not acting, you're letting what Leith did to you go unpunished."

"Oh, he got punished," I said.

"Yes," agreed Dorian coldly. "By *me*. Something you seem to have forgotten, now that you've jumped back into bed with that animal."

"Kiyo isn't part of this. And what you did isn't enough to obligate me to stay in a relationship with someone who constantly deceives me."

Dorian turned away, putting his back to me. Somehow, this was more insulting than all the glares in the world. "I can only assume this is human logic. Achieving peace by bending the truth is deceitful. The greatest sin in the world. But infidelity is moral and just."

"It's not! And I wasn't—I didn't cheat on you. As far as I was concerned, we were through. I was free to do whatever I wanted."

"Obviously."

I didn't want to show any weakness in front of him, but the thing was, part of me still questioned if having sex with Kiyo back in the forest had been right or not. I'd even felt conflicted at the time.

I'd let my impulses win out, using muddled logic to satisfy both my lust and need for revenge.

"Look," I said, trying to calm myself down. "I didn't mean to hurt your feelings—"

He spun around so sharply that my words dropped. I didn't fear Dorian, not with my power and in my home, but something in his eyes made me step back. "Queen Eugenie," he said formally. "Don't trouble yourself over my 'feelings.' Replacing you in my bed isn't that difficult. You have too high an opinion of yourself in that regard."

Those words slapped me in the face, despite all the reasonable parts of my brain screaming at me that it didn't matter. I had no reason to care what he did. No reason to care about him.

"So," I said, matching his tone. "Ysabel has a place to sell her skills again."

"Very good ones," he agreed. "The question now is if you're going to use yours. Put Katrice in her place. Get her to negotiate so that we can get the concessions we deserve. Stop acting like a human."

"I *am* human. You keep forgetting that."

He studied me up and down, giving me the opportunity to do the same to him. *You don't care, you don't care,* I told myself, trying to push aside how much I'd loved that gorgeous face.

"No," he said at last, contempt in his voice. "It's impossible to forget. You're acting like one now, refusing to do the right thing just because I've asked you to. You're being contrary out of spite." He strode toward the door. "If you don't act soon, you'll regret it."

I didn't like him being the one to end this

conversation. It was more of him always having the power. "Are you threatening me?"

Dorian put his hand on the door's handle and glanced at me over his shoulder. "No. I'm not the threat. Katrice is. And while you keep going on and on about how much I've wronged you and lied to you, I can say with absolute certainty that what I've just told you is the truth."

"Noted." Hastily, I made an attempt at acting like the queen around here. "You can go now. And don't come back."

That earned me a half-smile, though there wasn't much humor in it. "Are you revoking my hospitality?"

I hesitated. "No. I'm above that. I'll just assume you'll do the right thing and stay the hell away from me."

"Noted," he replied, imitating my earlier tone. He opened the door and walked away without another look. I stared at the empty space where he'd been, wondering who'd come out on top of that argument.

By the time I emerged and found Shaya, Dorian had already left my castle for his own lands. She asked nothing about what had transpired with him, but worry was written all over her face.

"How close are we?" I demanded. "How close are we to sitting down with Katrice and writing up a treaty?"

Shaya paled, and I realized I had turned my anger at Dorian on her. "Not as close as I'd like. She agreed . . . she agreed she'd come in person, but only if the talks were held in the Willow Land.

Queen Maiwenn has agreed, but Dor—King Dorian says that's unacceptable. He suggests the Linden Land or the Maple Land. Katrice refuses."

Linden and Maple. Kingdoms both staunchly neutral. Maiwenn theoretically was too. She'd always put on the pretense of friendship, and I was certain Kiyo would endorse her hospitality. But something about it made me uneasy. I didn't want to support Dorian . . . but then I realized that instinct came from exactly what he'd warned me of: wanting to oppose him just out of spite. Our personal mess aside, he was my ally. Neutral ground was best for us.

"Reiterate Dorian's stance," I said. "Linden or Maple. I'm going back to Tucson. Let me know what happens."

Shaya opened her mouth, to protest or beg for help, I couldn't say. Dorian's words came back to me. Get actively involved. "Wave the crown" and make Katrice agree to our terms. No. On that, I wouldn't agree with him. I wouldn't use that crown like he wanted me too, even as a threat.

"That'll be all," I told Shaya. She nodded, obedient as always.

The look on her face as I left made me feel a little guilty. Maybe I could make things easier for her. Maybe I could expedite all this. But for now, there was literally no harm being done. What could Katrice's stalling achieve? If she began hostilities again, she ran the risk of facing the crown she obviously feared. My people were safe. The waiting was frustrating, but it had to end soon. I'd told Dorian I was human, and that's what I intended to be. I would go home, start following up on jobs, and let the gentry deal with this red tape until I was absolutely needed.

And that was exactly what I did.

I returned to my old life. Kiyo and I continued dating, and being with him, reestablishing our old connection and sex life, went a long way toward blocking out images of beautiful, voluptuous Ysabel in Dorian's bed. My workload increased— as did my income—though my jobs tired me out more than I was used to. That scared me. It made me think about what it meant to be human and gentry. I'd fought to keep my human side dominant. Was the gentry part taking over? Stunting my shamanic abilities? No, I firmly decided. This was stress, pure and simple.

In the two weeks that followed, though, I had to concede to my gentry side occasionally. The Thorn Land called to me, so I continued my quick visits, keeping the land strong and—no matter how much I hated to admit it—strengthening myself. Unfortunately, I took little joy from that because no good news ever came from the Other- world. Katrice kept switching back and forth. Yes, she'd agree to the Maple Land—no, she'd changed her mind. Linden. But only if ambassa- dors went first, then the monarchs. No—she'd go. But it was back to the Willow Land. Or maybe some place altogether different? What about the Palm Land?

Dorian made no attempts at direct contact with me, but there was no need. When I went to bed each night, I could see his face. *Wave the crown, wave the crown.* Fortunately, my aggressive work-load tired me out enough to fall asleep quickly.

Good news of sorts finally came one day when Kiyo and I were out hiking. The temperature had shot up, heralding spring, and I'd welcomed the break from work. Traipsing through the wilder-ness was something Dorian would certainly never do—especially in the desert. But like me, Kiyo ap-preciated the rugged beauty and heat of the land. I'd missed these excursions with him.

His eyebrows rose when my cell phone rang. "You can get a signal out here?"

"Apparently."

I was as surprised as him. Looking at the ID, I saw Enrique's name pop up. His recent reports, after that brief surge of promising news, had been clipped and vague: simple reminders that he was still working on things.

I answered eagerly. "Please tell me you've found something."

"I have," he said. Enrique had that smug tone from when we'd met. It had been annoying then, but now, I found it encouraging. "I finally tracked down the gun dealer and—"

I didn't hear the rest because a sudden drop in the temperature and tingling in the air her-alded Volusian's arrival. Apparently, I could get an Otherworldly signal out here too. My minion's orders to report all urgent news trumped what-ever Enrique had to say.

"Hey," I interrupted. "I'll call you back."

"What the—"

I disconnected, not giving him a chance to finish his outrage. He probably wasn't used to being hung up on. I turned to Volusian, who waited patiently and silently for me. He was a spot of darkness on the sunny day; he seemed to suck away the light of the world.

"Please," I begged. "Please tell me Katrice has finally given in, so that we can talk."

Volusian stayed silent a few moments. I swear, it was for drama's sake, and I felt like choking him. "No," he said. "The Rowan Queen has not agreed to negotiations yet, although . . . she has acted."

Kiyo and I exchanged looks. There was no way this could be good. I was also pretty sure Volusian liked delivering this news.

"She's kidnapped your sister," he said. "And has a list of demands to be met, if you want to see Jasmine alive again."

Chapter 16

Kiyo asked no questions when I called Enrique back and told him I'd be out of town and out of contact for a while—but that I trusted him to carry on. Really, Kiyo said little at all as we hurried back to my house. Within minutes, I had a small satchel packed, and then we were off to the Otherworldly crossing. No matter what ups and downs had occurred in our relationship, he knew me well. He knew I had to act on this immediately.

The questions began once I reached my castle.

"How the hell," I began, "did this happen?"

I was in one of the receiving rooms, Kiyo by my side as I stared down Shaya and some of the soldiers who manned the grounds. Rurik was with them, which gave me mixed feelings. I was glad he was back from Dorian's. I trusted him more than any other military guy around here. That being said, there was a petty part of me that held him responsible. How could someone as capable as him have let this happen?

He grimaced, as though guessing my thoughts.

"A small group sneaked onto our grounds, overpowered her guards . . . and took her." He hesitated. "She only had two with her, Your Majesty. As you'll recall, her escort was lightened. Still. There is no excuse."

I hadn't witnessed this kind of diplomacy and respect from Rurik since . . . well, actually, I'd never really witnessed it. With Dorian? Yes. Not with me. Jasmine's abduction had really gotten to Rurik, no question. I was pretty sure he was taking it personally. But I'd also caught the slight meaning in his carefully worded comment about her lightened guard. That had been *my* call. I had done it in response to her good behavior and had let her outside more. I'd known it was a potential security risk—but not one that involved her leaving *against* her will.

"We're at war," I said. "Regardless of her guard, this whole place should have been under lockdown."

He nodded, face growing grimmer. "As I said, there's no excuse. I take full responsibility."

I waved a hand dismissively. "It's too late now. I know you're doing your job. Don't lay yourself out for the slaughter. Volusian said there was a note?"

Shaya handed me a piece of rolled parchment. Kiyo leaned over my shoulder as I read it silently to myself:

To Eugenie, Usurper Queen of the Thorn Land, Daughter of Tirigan Storm King:
    As you no doubt know by now, I have your sister within my custody. If you wish her returned

*to you alive, you and the Oak King will surrender
unconditionally to me. You will cease hostilities
immediately, withdraw your armies, and cede
your lands. Additionally, you will turn over the
Iron Crown to me.*

*If you do not comply with these terms, your sister
will be executed at noon, three days from the receipt
of this letter. For now, she is alive, and I have given
her into the keeping of my nephew Cassius.*

I await your response.

        Sincerely,
        Katrice, Queen of the Rowan Land,
        Beloved of the Gods

I looked up at the many watching eyes. "'Given
her into the keeping of my nephew Cassius.' Does
that mean what I think it does?"

Shaya grimaced. "That *is* the nephew she wanted
you to marry."

"Why execute Jasmine then?" I demanded.
"Why not marry her off to Cassius? Isn't that a
waste of one of Storm King's daughters?"

"Katrice hates you," said Kiyo softly. "At this
point, she probably doesn't even care about the
prophecy. She wants to get back at you, hurt you,
and if that means killing Jasmine, then it's probably an acceptable loss—especially if she tries to
then give you to Cassius after this 'surrender.'"

"So *I'd* get to live?"

Kiyo shrugged. "Longer suffering."

"Why choose her as a hostage though?" I didn't
know why I was arguing the logic here. None of it

mattered. Only the outcome did. "Everyone knows we don't get along."

"Everyone also probably knows that's been changing a little," said Kiyo. "You brought her to Dorian's."

"And," added Shaya, "a royal family member usually makes the best hostage in these situations."

These situations. For a moment, I nearly swayed on my feet, wanting to close my eyes and pass out. It had nothing to do with the heat. It was this. All of this. This situation always repeating itself. Me and Jasmine, cursed by our blood, always to be used and captured as possessions in a greater game. I'd hated Aeson, but at least he'd lured Jasmine into some pretense of love before taking advantage of her. But what about this Cassius? He'd make no attempts at kindness. This was all about punishment and revenge, after all. Had he already raped Jasmine? Was he doing it now? A sickening memory of Leith came to mind, one sharp and clear in spite of the drugged state I'd been in during my ordeal with him. Moments later, it was replaced by an image of this faceless Cassius lowering himself over a cowering Jasmine. . . .

I pushed my weakness aside, steadying myself and bringing the world back into focus. I turned to Rurik. "How far are our armies spread out? How soon could we get them together and march on her? I want to raze that bitch's lands and burn her castle to the ground! I want to have the fucking wrath of heaven rain down on her and—"

I cut myself off, as startled at my words as the

others were. Where had that rage come from? Well, the situation, obviously. I wouldn't want anyone thrown to Katrice's nephew before facing execution. But it occurred to me in that moment that my reaction was also . . . personal. Somewhere, in the ups and downs of our dysfunctional family, I'd come to care about Jasmine. My anger came from the loss of *her*.

"Easy, Eug," said Kiyo, resting a hand on my arm. There was a nervous note in his voice, mirrored by the others' expressions. I'd once been told that when I was angry, I resembled my father. I took a deep breath and pushed back any further outbursts.

"Leading a massive army in—while deserved— wouldn't be . . ." Rurik was still treading lightly, still choosing words carefully. "Well, Katrice was already in wartime mode, heavily guarded. After this? The lands outside her home probably have triple the guard they did before."

"But if our force was large enough . . ." I began.

Rurik nodded. "True. It's possible. Especially if . . . especially if my lord Dorian's armies were involved." He looked uneasy at mentioning Dorian, but I could see a considering look on Rurik's face. I had a feeling we shared the same puzzle. Would Dorian lend forces to help me? Possibly not, not if his anger overrode any devotion to me. On the other hand, Dorian *was* still in this war, and I knew him well enough to think he might welcome a full-out march on her castle. Rurik knew that too. "With his forces, it's possible," Rurik said at last. "But Katrice's would be defending. It would be bloody. It would be ugly."

He didn't sound opposed to that, per se. He was a military man; ugly battles were the way of the world. But we all knew that wasn't ideal.

My mind spun. Part of me wanted that large force to beat on Katrice because I thought she deserved it. This was about more than revenge, however. It was about Jasmine. I needed to go with the plan most likely to get her back, and an invading army wasn't it. It would take a smaller group, just as she'd no doubt sent here, one that could slip in. We were heavily guarded, but with the assorted petitioners and refugees always coming and going, it was no wonder Jasmine's kidnappers had slipped in. Katrice undoubtedly had a similar stream of people coming to her in these times, but she'd probably be on high alert with them too.

"Imanuelle," I said, realizing too many moments of silence had passed. "Can you get me Imanuelle?"

It was this, finally, that took the group's eyes off me—because they all exchanged astonished looks. Kiyo's face grew troubled.

"*That's* your plan?" Kiyo asked. "Assassinate Katrice? Eugenie, you're better than that." He'd apparently heard of Imanuelle.

"I am," I agreed. "And smarter. Get her for me." That was to Shaya, who nodded and then shot a look at a hovering servant. He gave a hasty bob of his head and darted out of the room.

"Ready to repeat history?" I asked Kiyo. "It'll be like raiding Aeson's all over again."

"You're going . . . No. Eugenie, you can't go there."

I gestured to Rurik and began moving for the exit. "You heard him. We can't get in with a large force—not easily."

"Yes, I get that," said Kiyo, following after me. "But *you* can't go."

"I *have* to go," I countered.

Rurik had hurried along after us. "He's right. Send someone else. I'll go. We'll sneak in and take her."

I came to an abrupt halt, nearly causing both men to run into me. "I'm going. This is my responsibility. Besides, who else around here can match me magically?" I peered back and forth between their faces, daring them to challenge me.

"Even so," said Rurik, "if you're discovered, you'll be outnumbered. And you're an enemy queen. In wartime. Walking right into your enemy's stronghold. I can't allow this."

"It's not your place to allow me to do anything!" I snapped. "*Or* you either." I turned to Kiyo for that, guessing his words. "We won't be discovered. Not if Imanuelle's as good as she claims." I was so tired of men telling me what I could and couldn't do.

I left them and stalked off down the hallway toward my bedroom. Neither followed me right away, but I just barely heard Rurik mutter to Kiyo, "Well, if she's caught, she *will* get a massive army descending on Katrice, at least. My lord Dorian wouldn't permit anything less."

The flaw in my plan, as it turned out, was waiting

on Imanuelle. After our last meeting, she'd left my kingdom, and finding her wasn't easy. You couldn't just openly summon a famed assassin. Girard was at my court, however, and apparently had secret ways of sending messages to his sister. I didn't ask any questions about his means, so long as she showed up.

Waiting for her gave us time to plan strategy. Once my advisors grudgingly accepted that I'd be going personally—and once Rurik accepted that he would not be accompanying me—they fell in line to pool their knowledge about Katrice's castle. I'd joked earlier to Kiyo about this being like our break-in to Aeson's . . . but really, it was true. This time, we had no guide personally to take us in. We had to rely on anecdotal knowledge from those who had been there and could make best guesses at where Jasmine might be held. And that was presuming Katrice was actually keeping her on-hand.

Perhaps the most surprising part of all of this was Kiyo's acquiescence. I'd expected protests about my safety or perhaps a diplomatic solution. But, no. He realized the importance of saving Jasmine. And he too knew this was probably our best shot—at least on such short notice.

"You should know," Rurik told us later, "that you aren't going to be able to bring Volusian." He, Kiyo, Shaya, and I were in my bedroom, which I'd made my makeshift war headquarters.

"Why not?" I asked. That was a surprise. I'd been counting on his muscle, something I had to admit I'd missed while fighting for the crown.

What was the point of an undead minion if I couldn't put him to good use? "He can go in with us invisibly."

Rurik shook his head. "Everyone knows about him. Katrice does. She'll have people on-hand who can sense him. She'll also probably have those with the power to banish him. Enough of them united together could."

"You have a lot of faith in her," I noted dryly. Volusian was hard to banish—I couldn't do it—but Rurik had a point. Get enough magic-users together, and they could eventually pull it off.

He gave me a twisted smile. "She's not stupid. And she has advisors. Not as good as yours, of course, but they would have thought everything over before kidnapping Jasmine."

A knock on the door interrupted any response I might have made, and after I called entry, a servant showed Imanuelle in.

"Finally," I said.

She swept in, clad in billowing red silk pants and a matching, midriff-showing top. The assassin arched an eyebrow and gave me an amused look as she put her hands on her hips. "I don't wait around on your every command, Thorn Queen. And last time we spoke, you made it pretty clear, you *didn't* want me around. Have you finally come to your senses? From what I hear, now's a pretty good time to get rid of Katrice." Imanuelle paused carefully. "Although, getting ridding of her before now would have been even better. Would have saved you and your sister a lot of trouble."

I bit off any snide remarks. "We can't have

Katrice killed. I'm pretty sure the instant her people found her dead, Jasmine would be next. I need you to sneak in and get Jasmine out of there."

Imanuelle's cocky smile dropped. "That's not what I do. I kill. I don't rescue."

"I'll do the rescuing. You need to get me and Kiyo in. Disguise us with this so-called power you keep bragging about. Or is masking more than one person out of your skill-set?"

"I can do it," she said, narrowing her eyes. "But it'll cost you."

"We can afford it," I said, trying to ignore the pained look crossing Shaya's face as she no doubt added up mental ledgers.

Imanuelle said nothing for several moments as she pondered it all. "Just you two?"

"Yes. And you, of course," I added.

"Do you have any idea where you're going in there?" she asked.

Kiyo and I exchanged looks. "Kind of," I said.

"Kind of." Imanuelle snorted. "Fine. I'll do it. But I'm only there to disguise you. I'm not fighting if you get caught."

"You don't have to," I assured her. "We'll protect you."

This brought another scoff and a haughty curl of her lip. "If they detect us, I can get myself out of there, believe me. *You'll* be on your own."

Chapter 17

We learned more about the full extent of Imanuelle's ability as Kiyo and I made our way with her on horseback to the Rowan Land. Her illusions were every bit as good as she'd demonstrated the first day, and I watched with grudging awe as she transformed Kiyo into Girard, Shaya, and—ack—Dorian. The illusions were perfect—and dangerous. I began to fully understand why she was such a good assassin. She really could be whomever she wanted, slipping into high security places without anyone knowing. I was a bit shocked when some part of my brain skipped right past employing her to detaining her. That part of my brain said getting rid of her would be safer for me in the future, and I immediately chastised myself for the idea. Imprisoning potential enemies was something Storm King would have done.

"It's not all-powerful," she said at one point. I think she was just making idle conversation now, having no clue of my concerns. We'd crossed into the Rowan Land now, and she'd dropped her tricks with Kiyo, settling on illusions of bedraggled peasants for all of us. "Doing it for three people takes more power. And even for myself, I can't hold up disguises forever." She made a small face. "If I could, I'd be a spy instead. A lot less messy."

I said nothing but exchanged brief glances with Kiyo behind her back. He too had to have analyzed the implications of her abilities. I was also thinking that when we'd first tried to rescue Jasmine from Aeson, our plan had failed because a spy had betrayed us. There was every possibility now that Imanuelle could do the same, and I wondered if I'd been too quick to trust such an unknown quantity. I could only hope love for her brother would keep her loyal to his employer.

Despite its name, the Rowan Land was dominated by cherry trees. Well, at least that was my impression whenever I crossed through it while journeying to other kingdoms. As we traveled further along roads that delved deeper into Katrice's kingdom, the cherry trees gave way to other plants and trees—including rowans. They were smaller than I'd expected and laden with berries of their own. This land was really quite nice, temperate and pleasantly warm, with beautiful green landscapes. It would be a shame if I did have to raze it to the ground.

We saw signs of Katrice's castle long before the castle itself. Other travelers joined us on the road, those whose towns had been caught in the crossfire of war and now sought out food and shelter from their monarch. Most were on foot, and we passed them quickly, for which I was glad. I needed no guilt on this journey.

We also began seeing soldiers, undoubtedly part of the increased security that Rurik had predicted. Some were traveling to and from the castle. Some were stationed along the way, carefully watching those of us who passed. I held my breath each time, waiting for Imanuelle's illusions to fail us. Along with acknowledging her power limits, she'd also told us some gentry were sensitive to her type of magic and could see through her spells. She'd told us this halfway through the journey. It was information that kind of would have been useful before setting out.

But, although we were scrutinized, the soldiers allowed us to pass, and before long, the castle itself came into view. I paused a moment, admiring it in spite of myself. Dorian and I both had dark, blocky stone castles, like Norman strongholds left on barren English countryside. Maiwenn's home was elegant and fanciful, always reminding me of a Disney movie. Katrice's castle, however, could have been straight out of a postcard from Bavaria. It had strong, straight rectangular lines, its sides white and covered with windows. That sturdy boxiness was offset by graceful turrets rising from the center, almost delicate looking with their pointed black roofs. The land had been rising as we traveled, so it wasn't a surprise to see the castle was situated high on one of the foothills leading off into pretty, snow-capped mountains. It had a sweeping view of the area we were approaching from, and a sturdy wall surrounded its immediate grounds.

Here we came to a stop along with the others seeking admission. We formed a long, clustered line, making me nervous.

"Why the backup? Are they refusing people?" I asked softly. "We don't usually have this many at our gates."

Kiyo peered ahead, his sharp eyes seeing what we couldn't. "No, they're letting them in, just doing a fair amount of questioning, which is slowing things down. And you're right—you never have this many because your lands haven't been attacked as much."

Good and bad, I thought. I'd kept my own people safe, but the war *I* was waging was devastating homes. It occurred to me I might not have to worry about Katrice. If these people discovered who was among them, I might very well be taken down by an angry mob.

"Easy," murmured Imanuelle. "Don't look nervous. I can't hide your expressions."

I schooled myself to neutrality, hoping I looked blank and exhausted. After almost an hour of restless waiting, our turn came. Four guards interrogated us, and we were quick with answers. For our cover story, we'd chosen a village that had been near a battle Dorian's armies had fought with Katrice's. Most of the residents had cleared out before the fighting, but a large part of the village had been destroyed.

"Our house was burned to the ground," Imanuelle said. She didn't even need the illusion of an older, rag-clad woman to be pathetic. Her demeanor and voice were filled with perfect, convincing despair. "Our crops were wiped out."

After a bit more questioning, they let us in, sending us toward what was essentially a gentry breadline. The inner grounds of Katrice's castle were packed with people—most soldiers—and we had to shoulder our way through the crowd to reach the corner where the poor and huddled masses were situated. Many appeared to have made this courtyard their temporary home. It looked like a well-used campground. Nonetheless, food was on hand, and I was relieved that these victims of war were being cared for.

We hovered near the food line so as not to raise suspicion, all the while assessing the area. In particular, our attention rested on the main gates to the castle itself. It was the most heavily guarded spot of all, and I knew then that an outright assault would have indeed been long and bloody. Other soldiers moved through the door with little questioning, which was what we'd hoped for. Finding a relatively obscured corner between a tall tent and the wall, we ducked out of sight and let Imanuelle work her next spell. She closed her eyes and took a deep breath. A tingle ran over me, and the world blurred. When I could focus on my companions again, I saw myself looking at the guards who had admitted us.

"Whoa, wait," I said, assuming I probably looked like one of the gate soldiers as well. "Don't you think we might have a few problems if we run into our clones? Why didn't you make us look like random unknowns?"

"Because if the other guards don't recognize us, we'll get questioned more," Imanuelle explained. She studied her hands critically, a small smile showing pride in her work. "I don't think the ones at the gate are leaving their posts anytime soon. We shouldn't run into them." She spoke confidently, but I had a feeling she was secretly thinking *I hope*.

Everyone was too concerned with his or her own affairs to realize that three peasants had ducked away, and three soldiers had emerged. When the refugees saw us, though, they stepped quickly out of our way. No pushing this time. None of us needed lessons on how to behave. Whereas our initial entry had been weak and bedraggled, we now walked with the confidence and strength of those who ran this place. We barely hesitated as we moved to the castle's entrance, and those on guard stepped aside without comment.

Being inside proved a bit more confusing. We'd received some information on the castle's layout, but we didn't know exactly where Jasmine was being held. We couldn't pause to deliberate, though. We had to keep moving like we had purpose or else attract attention. Soldiers and servants hurried around us, and we fell in step with some down a random hall. Kiyo, always fast-thinking, stopped a lone, young soldier.

"Hey," said Kiyo brusquely. "We've had reports

that someone might try to rescue the Thorn Queen's sister."

The soldier's blue eyes widened. "What? We should alert—"

"No, no," Kiyo interrupted. "Keep it to yourself. We don't want to raise suspicion. The outside guard already knows and is on watch. We need to know if she's been moved or not. There were rumors that she had been."

I tried not to bite my lip. Kiyo sounded like he knew what he was talking about, but this was a dangerous moment. As I'd worried before, Jasmine might not even be held here. There was also a chance that this guard didn't know her location, and we'd have to keep playing this game with others. The more people we talked to, the riskier our mission became.

"Not that I've heard," said the soldier. "She's still in the dungeon."

I breathed a sigh of relief. I'd half-expected him to say she was in Cassius's bedroom. The dungeons weren't great either, but well . . . it was no different than how I'd initially treated her. I waited for Kiyo to demand more details—how many guards were on her, where the dungeons were, et cetera. Instead he gave the soldier a curt nod and again warned him to be on alert but not to share his knowledge.

"We needed more info," I hissed to Kiyo as we continued walking down the hall. Whatever her faults, Katrice had good interior design sense. Floral paintings hung on the walls, and elaborate plants spilled out of vases. The beauty was lost on me, though. "Why'd you let him go?"

"Because real guards would already know anything else we wanted to ask," he replied. "Asking where the dungeons are would definitely be a tip-off that something was up."

"And I already know where they are," said Imanuelle.

Both Kiyo and I looked at her in surprise.

"Downstairs," she added.

"Dungeons are *always* downstairs," I pointed out.

"Have you been to them?" asked Kiyo.

She nodded and crooked us a grin. "Powerful leaders aren't the only ones with prices on their heads. Sometimes important prisoners need to disappear too."

I grimaced at her amusement but was grateful when she got us turned around. With a clear purpose, I grew more and more tense. This was it. What would we find? No one was giving us a second glance up here, but in the dungeons, we'd attract attention—especially when we busted out one of their prisoners.

Our castle façades might have been different, but Katrice and I possessed similar dungeons. Dark. Gloomy. Gray stone walls and torches. It was such a stereotype, but I supposed it helped dampen the hopes of any prisoners.

Imanuelle led us confidently down flights of stairs and into a long, wide corridor. Jasmine's cell was easy to spot because six guards stood outside it—again, reminiscent of her earlier conditions at my place.

"Good luck," said Imanuelle, falling behind us. She was apparently holding true to her word that this was all on us now. The guards on duty were sharp-eyed and naturally noticed our approach, but none of them reacted with wariness or alarm. A couple displayed curiosity, wondering perhaps if orders had changed, but that was it.

Kiyo and I had discussed several strategies on our journey and finally decided swift and surprising force would be the way to go. When we were still several feet away, I sent my magic out, pulling in the air like a deep breath and throwing it back at the guards in the form of a gale-worthy wind. It ruffled our hair and brushed our skin, but the blast literally threw the guards off their feet. There were cries of shock, and two went down right then and there from the impact of slamming against the corridor's end.

The other four were up on their feet, three drawing copper swords. Fire appeared in the hands of the fourth. I should have expected Katrice would put magic-users on Jasmine, along with brute force. There was no other time to ponder that, though, because the guy suddenly hurled a fireball at us. I instinctually drew on the surrounding air again, along with its moisture, disintegrating the fire with little effort. Kiyo surged forward then, attacking one of the guards. I ran forward as well, my attention focused on another guard as I created a vacuum around him, pulling all air away from him. His eyes widened as he gasped and clutched his throat, trying to draw an impossible breath.

I held the magic as one of his colleagues tried to attack me. I dodged the sword, largely because the iron dagger in my hand was making him keep his distance. The guy in the thralls of my magic finally passed out from the lack of oxygen, and I released him, letting him collapse unconscious to the floor. Before I could even deal with the other soldier by me, Kiyo leapt out and tackled him to the floor. I took this to mean Kiyo's first opponent was out of commission, leaving me with the magic user.

Not having learned anything the first time, he hurled another fireball at me. I admired his control; too much would have incinerated everyone in the hall. But with my magic, swatting the fire away was an afterthought for me. He had no weapon out, and I stepped forward, pushing my athame to his throat. He cried out at the sting of the iron, offering no fight as I began drawing away his oxygen too. A realization glinted in his eyes. Illusion or no, he must have figured out who would wield air and water so easily—and hold onto iron.

"Thorn Queen . . ." he gasped out, as the last of his air left him. I saw unconsciousness seizing him, but just before it did, he managed a weak flutter of his hand. No fire came, but I felt an intense wave of heat spread out. It didn't hurt me, but there was a physical power within it, one that rippled the air and made the walls tremble slightly just before he too collapsed to the floor.

Kiyo and I stood there among the bodies—dead or alive, I didn't know—and glanced at each

other and our surroundings carefully. Imanuelle
still stood back but looked impressed.

"What the hell was that?" I asked.

"I'm guessing an alarm," she said.

"Fuck."

I turned toward Jasmine's cell and saw her huddled in the farthest corner, regarding me with
large, wary eyes. Water was her true specialty; she
had only slight control over air. Nonetheless, she
would have felt the strength of the magic I'd used.
Like the guard, she knew there were few who
could do what I'd done—but her vision told her it
wasn't me standing there. I was still under Imanuelle's illusion.

Kiyo was already searching bodies and soon
found a key. We opened the cell, but Jasmine
didn't move. She didn't look too worse for the
wear, but I knew some of the most terrible behaviors rarely left a mark. There was a small tear in
her dress and a bruise on her arm that looked like
the signs of a struggle, probably during her initial
capture. I also noticed they'd left the fine iron
chains on her that Girard had created to stunt her
magic. My own safeguard had undoubtedly been
useful for her captors.

I gestured to the door, uneasy about what
Imanuelle had said about an alarm. "Jasmine,
come on. It's us. Me and Kiyo."

"And by me," said Kiyo, pointing in my direction, "she means Eugenie."

Jasmine hesitated, looking between our faces.
"How is that possible?"

Imanuelle, who'd been watching the hall's

entrance, turned hastily toward the cell. "How do you think? With magic. Look at yourself." Jasmine's features rippled, and soon, we were staring at another Rowan soldier. Jasmine studied her hands in astonishment. The illusion showed no chains, but she would still be able to feel them.

"Your iPod's playlist sucks," I said when she continued to hesitate. "Would a gentry guard say that?"

"Come *on*," urged Imanuelle. She'd been confident she could get herself out of any danger here, but those odds were better if she wasn't in a hall that could easily be blocked off if a regiment came tearing toward the entrance.

Jasmine must have decided this new development could be no worse than her present fate. She jumped up and left the cell, following as the rest of us made for the stairs. We reached the main floor without opposition, but once there, all was chaos. Soldiers were running in the direction we'd come from, and I wondered how long it'd take them to realize we were the only ones *not* going toward the dungeons.

Except . . . it turned out that wasn't the case. In the confusion, no one stopped us from exiting the front door, but the inner grounds were packed with soldiers. They were cramming terrified refugees into one well-guarded section, and the gates in the outer walls had been shut.

"Fuck," I said again. It still seemed like the only adequate way to sum up this situation.

"We could jump to the human world," said Kiyo. "Imanuelle can get out on her own."

I considered this. It was true. Imanuelle could

change into a peasant or whatever and escape detection until an opportunity for escape popped up. Kiyo's abilities allowed him to transition with relative ease through the worlds without a gate. I could do it—but not without difficulty. And I needed to use an anchor to draw me back. I had a couple back in my home, but Jasmine had nothing like that. She probably couldn't jump at random from the Otherworld. I wasn't even sure if she could with an anchor—and the iron chains made it worse. We could both end up doing serious damage to ourselves.

"We can't," I said. "We've just got to hide out." I turned to Imanuelle. "How are you doing? Can you turn us all to peasants again?"

She nodded. "We've got to get out of sight, though."

Her confidence was a small blessing, at least. Imanuelle was keeping up four illusions now, and her strength had been a concern in all this, that and someone who would be able to see through—

"It's her! It's the Thorn Queen!"

The shrieking voice that suddenly drew all eyes to us didn't come from the soldiers. It came from an old woman among the huddled refugees. She reminded me of Masthera, with white hair and wild eyes. She was pointing at us, and there was something in her gaze . . . some piercing quality that made me believe she could see straight through the illusions to us.

"Damn," said Imanuelle. There was both fear and hurt pride in her voice. Although this had been a possibility, I knew she'd secretly felt her powers were too strong for detection. Maybe the four of us had stretched her magic thin.

Honestly, I wouldn't have thought that one shout would be enough to pull attention to us, not in the chaos out there. Yet, the woman's voice brought silence to those nearby. They turned to stare at us, and soon, others who hadn't heard her noticed the reactions and fell quiet as well.

"Hush," snapped a guard, finally breaking the confused silence. He was one of the ones keeping the civilians out of the way. "We have no time for this."

The old woman shook her head adamantly. "Can't you see? Can't you see them? It's the Thorn Queen and her sister! They're right there!"

The guard's face darkened. "I told you, we—"

His jaw dropped because that was when the guards who'd been on gate duty earlier approached. They came to a standstill, staring at us in complete shock. If we hadn't panicked over the alarm, one of us probably would have thought to change the illusion so we looked like the unconscious soldiers, not the ones we would have to pass by again. It was a bad, bad oversight, and now everyone could see us and our mirror images.

The guard yelling at the old woman might not know what was going on, but he knew *something* was going on. "Seize them," he said. He glanced uneasily at his true colleagues and decided to cover his bases. "Seize them too."

Other soldiers moved toward us unquestioningly. I sized up the numbers. We were good, but

I didn't think Kiyo and I could take that many in melee. Jasmine came to that same conclusion.

"Blow them up," she said. "We can blow our way out of here."

By 'we,' she meant 'me,' and I knew she was talking about storms, not explosions. Some part of me had already known that was the answer. Barely even realizing it, I summoned all my magic, making the beautiful, sunny day in the Rowan Land quickly fade. Black and purple clouds tumbled across the sky at impossible speeds, lightning flashing so close to us that the ground trembled. Humidity and ozone filled the air, wind rising and falling.

It had come about in a matter of seconds, and the approaching soldiers halted. The old woman's crazy claim was no longer so crazy in light of that magic. They were all realizing that no matter what their eyes said, the possibility was now very good that Eugenie Markham truly stood before them. And I might be a wartime enemy, one they needed to capture, but I was also Storm King's daughter, and that was not a title taken lightly. They knew what I could do, and it was enough to freeze up years of training.

"Let us pass," I said. I began slowly moving toward the gate, my three companions following a moment later. "Let us pass, or I'll let this storm explode in here. It's already on the edge. One breath, and I can let it go." Thunder and lightning crackled above us, driving home my point. There were small screams from some of the crowd. "Do you know what that kind of storm will do in an area this small? To all of you?"

"It will kill them," a voice suddenly said. "Horribly."

I looked over toward the castle's entrance and saw Katrice herself standing there. Guards hurried to flank her, but she held up a hand to halt them. It had been a long time since I'd seen her. All of our antagonistic contact had been through messenger and letter. She looked like she had at our last meeting, black hair laced with silver and dark eyes that scrutinized everything around her. She was in full regal mode too, in silver-gray satin and a small jeweled tiara. But no . . . as I studied her, I saw a slight difference. She looked older than the last time we'd been together. Leith's death and this war had taken their toll.

I stared her straight in the eye, my adversary, the cause of so much recent grief in my life. I needed no storm around me because one was breaking out within, winds of fury and anger swirling around and around inside me.

"Drop the spell," I said to Imanuelle, without looking at her. I wanted to be face to face with Katrice, and honestly, it wasn't like my identity was a secret anymore. I felt another tingle, and a few gasps told me I wore my own form now. A small, tight smile crossed Katrice's lips.

"Yes," she continued, "you could unleash a storm here. You could destroy a large part of this wall, this castle. You could most certainly destroy all these people—which is what you're good at, right? You put on this lofty pose about protecting lives, yet somehow, death always follows you. You leave it in your wake, just as Tirigan did. But at least he had no delusions about what he was doing."

The comparison to my father increased the anger in me. The weather mirrored my reaction, the sky growing darker and the air pressure intensifying.

"Go ahead," said Katrice. "Show me your storm."

"You don't have to kill them," said Jasmine beside me, voice low. "Just her."

Was she right? Was that all it would take? I could kill Katrice, no question. One unexpected bolt of lightning, and she'd be gone. If memory served, her magic was similar to Shaya's: a connection and control with plant-life. As a queen, someone with the ability to conquer a land, Katrice possessed that power to levels that dwarfed Shaya's. It was probably why the trees and plants here were so beautiful. It was also probably why we hadn't been attacked yet. This inner courtyard around the castle was cleared land, hard-packed dirt that facilitated travel for guards, merchants, and other visitors. If we'd been outside the walls, I would have likely had a forest marching on me by now.

"You can do that too," said Katrice, still trying to bait me. I couldn't tell if she was simply attempting to prolong her life or trying to catch me off guard for some other attack. "Kill me in cold blood. Just like you did my son. It's in your nature."

"It's not cold blood in wartime," I growled. "And

your son deserved it. He was a weak, cowardly bastard who had to lie and drug women to get what he wanted."

This made her flinch slightly, but she didn't hesitate to return the arrow. "But he *did* get what he wanted. He got you. He couldn't have been that weak."

Those words stung, but before I could respond, a young man slipped into place beside her. His resemblance was so strong to her and Leith that there could be no question of his identity: Cassius, her nephew. The rage within me doubled. Seeing him reminded me of what he'd most likely done to Jasmine. My reason was slipping, replaced by pure fury.

"You should have let this go," I told Katrice, my voice perfectly level. "You should have accepted Leith's death as punishment for what he did. An even slate. Lives have been lost because of you. More will be now."

One bolt. One bolt, and she was dead. Hell, I could probably take out Cassius with it too.

"Eugenie," said Kiyo. "Don't. Don't do it."

"What else am I supposed to do?" I breathed, out of the others' earshot.

"I warned you before there would be consequences. Please listen to me this time," he begged. "There will be again."

"What do you expect me to do?" My voice was louder. I didn't care who heard. "This is wartime. I kill their leader. I win. Otherwise, I let hell loose in here, and these people die. Which do you want, Kiyo? Pick—or else find another way."

He didn't respond, but Katrice's tight smile grew at seeing dissent within my ranks. "No options but death. You *are* Tirigan's daughter. I'm glad now that Leith didn't get you with child. His plan seemed wise at first, but it's better my exalted bloodline isn't mingled with yours—though the gods know how much Leith tried. He told me about it. Often. Ah, well. I suppose we'll know soon how Cassius fared . . ."

Her gaze lingered slightly on Jasmine beside me. Imanuelle had dropped all our disguises.

"Eugenie—" Jasmine tried to speak, but I didn't want to listen.

"Are you trying to get yourself killed?" I demanded of Katrice. Each word was harsh, almost impossible to get out. I was changing my mind about the lightning. I was remembering how I'd killed Aeson, literally blowing him apart by ripping the water from his body. There were so many ways to kill her, so many ways to bring about humiliation.

Katrice gave a small shrug, and despite that smug attitude, I saw a pang of regret in her eyes. "I have a feeling I'll die one way or another today. I just want everyone to know the truth about you before I do."

I froze. I'd told Kiyo to give me another option, and he'd had none. But there was one other.

"The truth," I said slowly, reaching toward my backpack, "is that you aren't going to die today. But you'll wish you had."

I can only assume what happened next was born out of pure emotion, out of the anger and despair her words about me and Jasmine had evoked. Situational adrenaline probably played a role too, and . . . well, maybe there was something in my genes after all.

I pulled the Iron Crown from my backpack. Katrice turned white, all cockiness gone. Those who recognized the crown displayed similar fear, audible and visible. Others just stared curiously.

"No," she gasped. "No. Please don't."

I think until that moment, she hadn't truly believed I had the crown. I also think that had I demanded it, she would've named whatever terms of surrender I wanted. But I didn't want simple surrender. I wanted suffering. I wanted her to suffer, just as I had.

So many ways to bring about humiliation . . .

I placed the crown on my head, and somehow—maybe it was part of its magic—I knew exactly what to do. The iron athame was still in my hand, and I crouched down with it. Katrice dropped to her knees too, but it was in supplication.

"Please," she begged again, tears in her eyes. "Anything. I'll do anything you want."

"You're right," I said. "You will."

I slammed the blade down—and pierced the land's heart.

Chapter 18

It really felt like that, like I was killing a living thing. And in a way, I was. I was destroying the land's connection to Katrice. The land and its monarch are one. Kind of an esoteric concept . . . but, well, the truth. I'd certainly felt it in the Thorn Land. It was why I couldn't ever stay away from that kingdom for very long. It called to me. It was part of me.

And so, I was essentially cutting a living thing in two. White-hot power burned through me as I did, the crown's magic connecting with my own and pouring into the dirt below. I had little sense of my surroundings, save Katrice screaming. Below me, in a spiritual sort of way, I could feel the land resisting at first. It didn't want to break its ties. In the end, it had no choice. The crown's magic was too strong. Seconds, minutes, hours . . . I don't know how long it took, probably hardly any time at all. But suddenly, it was done. The crown's power faded from me, and the land lay there open and unclaimed. Raw and wounded.

As the magic's haze wore off, the rest of the world slowly shifted back into focus for me. I stared around at the gaping faces and at Katrice, huddled and sobbing. I thought she'd aged before, but it was nothing compared to now. Being ripped from the land had devastated her. Her dark hair was almost all gray now, her face gaunt and lined.

And all around . . . all around, the land was restless. I could feel its energy, calling out . . . reaching out . . . yearning for a new master. Hardly any of the people gathered showed any recognition of this. They were still watching the drama of me and Katrice. A few spectators had puzzled looks on their faces, as though they too could hear the land.

It was because they were powerful enough to take it, I realized. The land was already seeking those who possessed the strength to join with it, and looking up, I saw from Cassius's face that he could sense that. Katrice's son hadn't had the power to claim a kingdom, but her nephew did.

So, for my next impulsive act of the day, I stuck my free hand into the ground. Just like the last time, soil that started off hard and ungiving soon grew soft and warm. My hand sank into the earth, and I was welcomed, as though someone were clasping my hand in return. Warmth filled my body, a comforting warmth very different from the crown's searing heat. I closed my eyes, striving to stay with that connection, to show I was worthy. Part of me was already given over to the Thorn Land. I had to fight to claim this land as well.

Then, I felt it. . . . I felt the land accept me. And

as it did, the ground began to shake. At first, I thought it was just some aftereffect of the magic, but then I remembered what had happened when the Thorn Land had bound itself to me. The land took on the form that spoke to my soul, that was natural and right to me. Aeson's former kingdom had shaped itself into the Sonora Desert, the land of my birth. The Rowan Land was trying to do the same thing.

No, no! Not again. A semi-tropical kingdom transforming into a desert had wreaked havoc on its residents. We'd faced starvation, drought, poverty. . . . It was only recently that the kingdom had gotten on its feet again, becoming prosperous and self-sustaining. I wouldn't go through that again. Frantically, I tried to think of some other form. But what? I hardly ever left the southwestern United States. A quick image of the Catalina mountains flashed into my mind, the slopes snowy and pine-covered like the day Kiyo and I had fought the demon. I could feel the land start to grip that picture, and I yanked it away. This kingdom had some small mountains, but that was a tiny percentage of its terrain. I couldn't turn this place into Switzerland or Nepal.

Stay the same, stay the same, I begged the land. For the sake of its occupants, I needed the landscape to remain unchanged. It was difficult, though. The land wanted to bond to me, to what was ingrained within my soul. Thinking back to the journey here, I tried to picture the rows and rows of cherry trees along the road. I remembered the sun shining through other deciduous trees and flowers growing in clusters. I thought about the stretch of rowan trees. *Stay the same, stay the same.*

Gradually, the earth around me began to slow its shaking and finally stop—except for one spot. Not far from where I rested my hand, the ground cracked open and leaves and branches burst through. I scurried back, watching in as much awe as I had the first time a magical tree burst forth, growing and unfurling its leaves to full-size in seconds. I held my breath, wondering what it would be, this tree that dictated my new kingdom's nature.

It was . . . a rowan tree.

I wasn't the only one who thought this was weird. "Didn't you claim it?" asked Jasmine, puzzled. I rose to my feet beside her, brushing dust off of my jeans.

"I . . ." Had I? That was a rowan tree, making this—by all Otherworldly reasoning—the Rowan Land. Which is what it had been already. Maybe it hadn't worked. Maybe the crown hadn't done what I expected it too. Maybe Katrice had won it back somehow.

But, no. There it was. I *felt* it. The land. The earth. The rocks. Every leaf and flower. The scents, the colors . . . they were all sharper and more intense. If I opened myself up, I could feel every single piece of this land. It hummed. It buzzed. The energy was dizzying, and I forced myself to shut it out for a moment.

"No," I told Jasmine, wonderingly. "It's mine." I stared at the rowan tree, more perfect than any real one could be, its orange-colored berries bright against green leaves swaying in the breeze. I reached out and stroked one of the leaves, vaguely aware of Katrice still sobbing. A tingle of power ran through me. "It's still the Rowan Land . . . except, it's *my* Rowan Land."

Things were a little awkward after that.

The soldiers were no longer trying to imprison me, but they also weren't ready to jump at my every order. My companions were of little use. Imanuelle, per her nature, was content to sit back and watch the mess I'd stumbled into. Kiyo wore a disapproving look on his face, and I feared I'd have a lecture coming later. Jasmine still seemed to be in shock. The only time she came to life was when I debated what to do with Katrice and Cassius. Unsurprisingly, Jasmine's suggestion was to kill them.

"Confine them to her rooms," I ordered, hoping someone would obey me. "Guard them with . . ."

I was kind of at a loss. Theoretically, gentry knew how this worked. Whoever controlled the land ruled, but I wasn't entirely sure the guards around here would be so keen about imprisoning the woman who had ruled them ten minutes ago. *Volusian*, I thought. Now that I was in control, I could summon him without fear. Then, I realized I needed him for more important things. I looked pleadingly at Kiyo, needing no words.

He nodded. "I'll watch them." He turned

abruptly, urging the former royalty inside with a couple of guards who'd decided to get on board with me right away. Kiyo being on guard served two purposes. I could trust him to do a good job—and, the longer he did, the longer I was safe from his disapproval.

I then spoke the words to bring Volusian to me, the sight of him further frightening those who already watched me with terror. I'd let the storm dissipate, but darkness still seemed to wrap around my minion as his red eyes assessed me, the Iron Crown, and the tree.

"Unexpected," he said.

"Go to Rurik," I told him. "Explain what happened and have him bring an occupying force here immediately." I didn't know what that meant exactly, but I did know military control took precedence here if we were going to secure the land. Rurik would know what to do. Governing would come later. "And then . . ." Now I hesitated. "Have Shaya contact Dorian about what happened. Then return to me."

Volusian paused, waiting for anything else I might add. When nothing more came, he vanished, and the sun seemed to shine a little brighter. It was all a waiting game now, and I glanced around at the Rowan Land's still-stunned residents.

"Well . . . that's it. Carry on as usual. Guard the gates. No one leaves. And you . . . go get your soup or . . . whatever you're eating." That was for the civilians. When no one moved, I hardened my expression and repeated my orders more loudly.

Fear flashed across the Rowan citizens' faces, and they sprang into action.

This inner courtyard was huge, and I spotted an unoccupied spot near some carts that must have delivered supplies earlier. I walked over to them, Jasmine following, and sat on the ground. It was a weird spot for a queen, I supposed, but I wanted to rest while waiting for Rurik. Plus, it still let me keep an eye on this delicate and dangerous situation. The bulk of the guards were out here, and I didn't think mutiny was out of the question yet. People were moving after my commands, but it was mostly to gather in anxious clusters and discuss what had happened.

Jasmine sighed and leaned her head back against the wall. "I want to go home," she said.

"We will. As soon as Rurik gets here, we'll head back to the castle and let him deal with this."

"No." Her voice was small. "My other home. The human world."

I turned to her in astonishment, dragging my gaze from some peasants who were begging the guards to let them out. "What? But you hate that world. You always said this is where you fit in."

"It is," she agreed. "But I just want . . . I want to get away from all this for a little while. From magic. And castles. And . . . whatever. I want to watch TV. I maybe want to see Wil. I want to charge my iPod. And my playlist *doesn't* suck."

I couldn't help a laugh. "I kind of want all those things too. We'll go soon. We'll . . . we'll cut those chains. I-I'm sorry I don't have the key with me."

She shrugged. "It's fine."

"Kiyo's going to be upset about all this," I murmured, surprised to be confiding in her.

"You did the right thing," Jasmine said. "I mean, aside from not killing Katrice and Cassius. But you can still do that."

Any residual smile left on my lips vanished. "Cassius . . ."

"They were lying," she said bluntly. "He didn't do anything."

"Jasmine . . ."

"I'm serious." She looked at me, her blue-gray gaze level and steady. "He talked a lot of talk when he came to see me . . . touched me a little. But that was it. I think they just wanted to scare me."

She didn't elaborate on the touching. I didn't ask. I was just relieved she hadn't gone through what I had. "I'm sorry," I told her. "I'm sorry I didn't protect you better."

Now she smiled. "You did fine. And hey, you ended the war, right? You won."

I turned away, staring off into space. "I guess I did."

We didn't talk much after that. I was tired, exhausted from all the magic. Apparently, using an ancient, powerful artifact wasn't as easy as it seemed. Neither was proving your dominance over a large piece of land. I'd felt wiped out last time but had gotten out of the Thorn Land as quickly as possible. Now, sitting here, I was stuck in the Rowan Land, still acutely aware of its every sensation. That intensity would fade, just as it had with the Thorn Land, but for now, it was like a hammer banging inside my head, demanding attention.

I practically flew to the gate when Rurik arrived. Once admitted, he and the force behind him paused. Studying the situation, he had a reaction similar to Volusian's.

"Really?"

"Things happened kind of fast," I admitted.

"It was well done. Possessing this land was a much better idea than simply defeating Katrice in battle."

I scowled. "Well, can *you* possess it for now?"

He grinned. "Gladly."

Turning from me, he fixed a hard gaze on those gathered. "You're all now subjects of Queen Eugenie, daughter of Tirigan Storm King," he barked. "Kneel."

I looked on imperiously as they obeyed. I knew this was necessary to establish our control. No weakness, no hesitation. We were conquerors. I'd long since taken off the Iron Crown but wished I'd brought my normal one of authority. Oh, well. It wasn't like I could've foreseen this when packing.

Everyone in the keep fell to their knees, heads bowed. We let them stay like that for several seconds while my stomach sank. Finally, they were allowed to rise, and Rurik kicked into full martial law mode, demanding an assessment of all soldiers and issuing rules for servants and refugees. He had a few tasks for me—more actions that made me seem queenly—before finally declaring I could leave.

"I'll sort out the immediate problems," he told

me in a low voice. My own soldiers were now out
and about, establishing order. "We'll lock this
place down, start scouting the immediate area,
sifting out those who can be trusted." He paused
eloquently. "I'll probably have to throw a large
part of their military into the dungeon."

"Do what you have to do," I said. I had a feeling
he'd eventually want to talk executions but was
holding back for now. I imagined I looked as tired
as I felt.

"And you simply want to imprison the former
queen for now?" he asked.

"For now."

Jasmine scoffed beside me, and Rurik's expression showed he shared her opinion.

"Well, don't stay away long," he said. "You need
to make your presence felt. And you need to connect with the land."

"I know, I know," I grumbled. I'd avoided the
Thorn Land before, but it had kept calling me
back. "I know how this works."

He arched an eyebrow, that sardonic smile of
his returning. "Do you? Do you know what's happened?"

I threw my hands up, gesturing around. "I got
stuck with another kingdom."

"Do you know how many other monarchs control more than one kingdom?"

I shook my head, presuming whoever did must
live far from me.

"No one," said Rurik.

"I . . . What? No." Dorian had mentioned conquering more than one land, making me think it

must happen now and then. The Iron Crown's purpose suggested as much. "There must be someone else."

"No one," Rurik repeated. "You're the only one. The only one in ages . . . well, except for Storm King."

The world swayed around me again. I once more just wanted to go somewhere and lie down. My reaction brought a bigger smile to Rurik's face, but I swore there was a little sympathy in his eyes too.

"Congratulations," he said. "Congratulations, Eugenie—Queen of Rowan and Thorn."

Chapter 19

It took a while before Kiyo, Jasmine, and I could return to Tucson. We had to go to the Thorn Land, of course, where Shaya and the others asked me all sorts of questions about what had happened and what I wanted to do. Kiyo and even Jasmine provided most of the answers for me because honestly, I wasn't sure what I wanted now. The only thing I had the real sense to do was demand Jasmine's key and unlock her chains. She stared at her freed hands wonderingly, stroking her wrists. I nearly left the chains and key in the castle but soon reconsidered and took them with me to the human world.

She'd never seen my house before and regarded it with approval as we entered. All was quiet, and the empty driveway made me confident I wouldn't find Tim and Lara holed up in his bedroom again. Evidence of their 'love,' however, was still obvious.

"Damn them," I said, gingerly picking a red lace bra off of the couch and tossing it down the hall toward Tim's room. "I'm going to have to sanitize this thing. Probably every other piece of furniture too."

"You have Pop-Tarts!" Jasmine hadn't made it to the living room. She'd stopped in the kitchen, opening every drawer and cupboard she could find. "And Apple Jacks! Peanut butter, ranch dressing, saltines . . ."

I was surprised that last one excited her so much, but after a couple years eating gentry food, even the most mundane human cuisine was probably exciting.

"Oh!" she exclaimed. "Can I have one of your Milky Ways?"

"Sure. Have whatever you want."

Her eyes were wide as she tore into the package, and both Kiyo and I watched her with smiles on our faces, like proud parents on Christmas morning. Although they didn't sound good to me right now, Milky Ways were normally my candy bar of choice. From the way she was consuming hers, Jasmine appeared to share that family trait. She completed her sugar rush with a can of Coke and then made herself at home on the couch. Watching her reach eagerly for the remote control, I decided it was best not to mention the amorous activities that had likely occurred where she sat.

She flipped through the channels in continued amazement. It was evening—prime time entertainment—and the emotions on her face were transparent as she stumbled across old and new shows alike.

"You want me to see if I can find anything that

fits you?" I asked. She might have slipped back easily to human behaviors, but she still wore a long, flowing gentry-style gown.

"Sure," she said, not looking up from the screen.

Kiyo followed me into my bedroom. "You think she's safe out there?" he asked. "Alone?"

"Yeah, I do actually." Jasmine and I weren't the same size, but I found some drawstring shorts that would likely fit. "I don't know why . . . but I feel like I can trust her."

"Be careful," he warned, sitting on the bed's edge. "For all we know, she was happy to be captured and have Cassius throw himself at her."

"He didn't do anything." I found the smallest T-shirt I could; her frame was more slender than mine.

"So she says."

I sighed and faced him. "Kiyo, you've got to trust me. I can't explain it, but she's telling the truth. Is she going to turn into a normal teen and forget about her plans to have Storm King's heir? Unlikely. But for now, she's in shock and not dangerous."

"If you think so. Just be careful, Eug. You've been tricked by people you've trusted before."

"Surprise, surprise. A slam on Dorian." I crossed my arms, holding the clothes to my chest. "Soon to be followed by a lecture on seizing the Rowan Land." I'd been bracing myself since it all happened, but during the ensuing damage control, he'd held back. I appreciated that but still dreaded the inevitable.

"Actually," he said, "no."

"No?" I'd started to take a step toward the doorway and froze.

He laughed, though there wasn't much humor in it. "No."

"But I just thought . . . well, after last time . . . You weren't very happy about the Thorn Land . . ."

That small smile faded. "No. And it's not like I'm happy about this. But the truth is, you *did* find a—relatively—bloodless way to end all of this. When we were out there, you asked me what other solution could fix things. I didn't have an answer. You did. It's not great . . . but it didn't kill Katrice or those other people. It didn't get you captured." He shrugged. "Not ideal, no, but better than the alternatives."

I leaned back against the wall, still shocked at his reaction. "If it makes you feel better, it's not like I wanted this either. I wanted to sneak in and out and get Jasmine."

He nodded, but there was a sharp look in his eyes. "And yet, you brought the crown." I hadn't mentioned that to him when we first set out to the Rowan Land.

"Her note said she didn't believe I had it! I was hoping waving it around might do something to help us." He stayed quiet. "Don't look at me like that! You can't believe I planned to use it."

"I do believe you." He approached me and rested his hands on my shoulders. "And I'll help you in any way you need."

Something inside my chest released, and I leaned into him, taking comfort in his warmth and the security he offered. "Thank you. I'm definitely going to need you."

Kiyo pressed a kiss to my forehead. "I'm here."

I felt a small smile pull at my lips, though as with his earlier laughter, I didn't really find the situation funny. "I suppose if there is a silver lining here, maybe I can do a better job ruling the Rowan Land than she did. Some sort of greater good."

To my surprise, his hold on me stiffened, and he stepped back. The smile he offered me looked tight. "Maybe."

We went back out to Jasmine, who was still riveted to the TV. The only acknowledgment we got was when I handed her the clothes, and she examined them. "What's 'The Clash' mean?"

I ignored the blasphemy—and Kiyo's obvious amusement at my pain. "If you want to shower, everything you'll need is in the bathroom. Towels, shampoo."

That too got her attention. "A shower . . . oh, man. I've missed showers."

"Will you two be okay?" asked Kiyo, all signs of his earlier discomfort gone. "I need to take care of a few things."

I nodded. "We're fine. Will you be back soon?"

"As soon as I can." He kissed me again, this time on my lips. I must have worn another pained expression because he cupped my chin, his brown eyes full of love and compassion. "It's going to be okay, Eugenie. Everything will be okay."

I nodded once more and watched wistfully as he left. I wanted his arms around me again, to hold me and let me escape this mess. A small part of me wouldn't have minded Dorian's arms either. I sat beside Jasmine, whose attention was back on some reality show.

"He's running off to Maiwenn, you know." Her gaze didn't move. "Off to report on what happened."

My ire started to rise at her accusation, except . . . I had a feeling she was right. Even if there was no more romance between them, he was still devoted to her. The recent developments were going to rock the Otherworld, and she'd want the story straight from him. I wondered how she'd take it; she'd always feared my becoming like my father.

"Probably," I admitted. I rubbed my eyes. "God, I'm so exhausted. I feel like I could fall over."

This time Jasmine turned to me. There wasn't exactly sympathy in her face, but something surprisingly close. "No shit. You just stole a kingdom and took it over."

"It sounds so ugly when you phrase it that way."

She shrugged and looked back at the TV. "You'll probably do a better job." Her words echoed my earlier comment to Kiyo. "You know," she added conversationally, "everyone acts like our dad was such a bastard, like he just wanted more power. I mean, he did, but you know what Aeson told me? He said that Storm King was always talking about how he could do a better job too, that the other monarchs weren't as good. He said he was doing the people a favor."

I froze, unable to respond. That was why Kiyo had reacted the way he did earlier. He'd heard that about Storm King's "good intentions," I realized. I'd expressed exactly the same sentiment as my father.

Jasmine didn't notice the effect of her words and instead jumped subjects in that easy, short-attention-span way of hers. "Hey, do you think you could get Wil to come over? I want to see him."

"Sure," I murmured automatically. My mind was still lost in her earlier words. "Sure."

Wil was surprised to hear from me the next morning, more surprised still when I told him the reason I was calling. He said he'd be over in five minutes.

Jasmine had asked that he come alone after I'd mentioned he now had a girlfriend. Still, she'd been curious. "Seriously? What's she like?"

I thought back to my one meeting with Wil's ladylove. Once I'd banished the monsters living in their house, she hadn't shut up about conspiracy theories and assorted coverups. "Exactly like him," I'd replied to Jasmine.

The reunion between brother and sister was strange. They stood there awkwardly, both staring at each other and assessing all the ways they'd changed. Then, with no communication, they hugged each other. Jasmine's face was filled with legitimate emotion, and for once, Wil didn't seem like the crazy, paranoid guy he usually was.

"Are you okay?" he asked her, voice trembling. "I've missed you so much."

Jasmine swallowed, and I was pretty sure there were tears in her eyes. "I . . . I missed you too."

And it was the truth. She'd told me once she didn't care about this world—or about the half-brother who'd raised her. But she did. This whole time, despite her Otherworldly plans for domination, she'd always loved him.

Things grew increasingly bizarre when it became obvious the two weren't quite sure what to do with each other. Wil didn't chastise her for her absence, and at last, she simply asked if he wanted to hang out and watch TV. I think that was partly because it provided a concrete activity and partly because she'd become obsessed with making up for lost TV time.

I kept my distance but couldn't help a small, envious feeling as they sat on the couch. Jasmine leaned her head against her big brother's shoulder, and I became acutely aware of the emptiness in my own family life. I hadn't heard from my mom or Roland since getting the referral to Enrique. The closest I had to any familial connection was those goddamn kingdoms I ruled. Just as the Thorn Land had always called to me, the Rowan Land now did too, leaving such an ache within me that I practically felt nauseous. Rurik had been right. I wouldn't be able to stay away.

But first things first. Thinking of Enrique reminded me I was due for an update. Retreating to my bedroom, I dialed his number and hoped he was up this early.

"Miss Markham," he said after just one ring. Caller ID left no surprised anymore. "Always a delight."

"I'm sure. What are you doing with the case right now?"

"Nothing."

"Nothing?" I exclaimed. Irritation rose within me. I wasn't paying him to sit around, especially after he'd gotten so close.

"Nope," he said cheerfully. "It's out of my hands. I found what I needed, proved that Deanna Jones didn't buy the gun. From what I hear, the police are searching Cal Jones's house right now and questioning him. Far be it from me to get in the way of the fine men in blue."

Finally, some good news . . . well, at least as the case's progress went. It wouldn't be easy on Deanna to learn the truth about her husband. "And women," I said. "There are probably women in blue there too."

"If you say so."

"Thanks, Enrique. I really appreciate it. I honestly didn't think it could be done."

"Don't get all emotional," he said in that brisk way of his. "At least not until you see the bill."

We disconnected. Attitude or no, Enrique had been a good call on Roland's part . . . which once again brought about the sadness over the turn in my parental relationship. Well. Nothing to do for it at the moment, not with all my other problems. And anyway, I had a loose end that could now be wrapped up.

Taking out my wand, I closed my eyes and cast a minor summoning spell, calling to Deanna. I had no control over her but she'd responded to my call before—particularly since she was always on edge listening for it. After several minutes and no results, I gave up and sadly suspected she wasn't coming because she already knew the truth. As eager as she'd been to get answers, it wouldn't have surprised me if she'd been following Enrique around while he worked. She might have discovered for herself what her husband had done. If so, I hoped she'd now move on to the Underworld and seek peace, rather than staying restless and sad in this world. There was enough suffering here already.

I tried as hard as I could the next couple days to stay away from the Otherworld. Wil visited off and on, and Jasmine and I began doing mundane yet enjoyable activities, like seeing movies and shopping for clothes for her. Tim and Lara often appeared, still in the throes of their love, and Kiyo returned with reports about the Otherworld, reassuring me that my kingdom's control of the Rowan Land was progressing smoothly. And at night, he came to my bed, and I found the return of our fierce sex life went a long way toward taking my mind off my laundry list of problems.

But finally, I had to give in. The call to my lands was too strong, and even Kiyo admitted that with my new and fragile hold on the Rowan Land, I needed to visit and connect with it to reinforce our bond. By that point, I needed no urging. My own body was telling me as much. I still felt weak and drained, my dreams haunted by cacti and cherry trees.

I took Jasmine with me. Our relationship wasn't quite sound enough yet for me to leave her alone. She drew the line at going to the Rowan Land, however, insisting she would stay in the Thorn Land until my return. I had no problem with that, knowing she was secure there. Kiyo was still going with me, and Shaya caught us before we could leave.

"There's a few things you should probably know," she said uneasily. Her nervousness was likely due to the fact that I hated being troubled with the day-to-day running of a kingdom—in this case, kingdoms. Something about the fear in her eyes told me she also knew I wouldn't like what she had to say.

I sighed. "Go ahead."

"I . . . I've heard from King Dorian a number of times."

Kiyo shifted uncomfortably beside me, and I felt that familiar prickle of anger run down my spine. All the memories of Dorian's lying and betrayal came back to me. It stung all the worse because in the end, he'd gotten exactly what he wanted: the Iron Crown had done its job. He probably wanted me to take still more lands.

"What's he want?" I demanded. "The war's over. We're no longer in a partnership."

"Well, that's just it. Since you are—were—allies in the war, he says he deserves some of the spoils of your victory."

"He . . . what?" My fury increased. "He doesn't deserve anything. *I* was the one who won and used the crown."

She nodded, still looking like she wished she could be anywhere else. "Yes . . . but he argues that he was the one who sent you to get the crown. And that his armies lost as many lives as yours."

That last point silenced me. His soldiers had fought with mine. His people's families mourned those casualties as much as mine . . . and for what? To fight against a slight that had nothing to do with them, not really. I didn't owe Dorian anything, of that I was certain, but I was indebted to his subjects.

When I didn't respond, Shaya continued. "Some of his people are also helping hold the Rowan Land."

"Oh, are they?" Of course Dorian would have swooped in. "I never asked for that."

She shook her head. "Nonetheless, you need it. Many are still having trouble accepting your rule. There's a lot of seething resentment. No violence has broken out yet—but that's largely because of the sizeable presence Rurik sent to keep control. Dorian's helping with that."

I'd meditated with the Thorn Land as soon as I'd arrived, making me feel a little better, but the pressure and continued political complications were already draining me. I wasn't meant for this. "What's he want? Half the kingdom?"

"No. Trade. Tribute. The Rowan Land is a huge food producer, and he wants part of that."

"That doesn't sound so bad," I said tentatively.

"I'm guessing he wants it at low, low prices," said Kiyo, speaking up for the first time.

Shaya nodded. "He does. And he's entitled to it to a certain extent. But his current demands are extreme enough that it could endanger the Rowan

Land's economy. Maybe that's not an issue. It all depends on what you want for them."

I thought about the refugees at the gates. What did I want for those people? I wanted them to prosper. I wanted things to return to normal. "Can you negotiate with him to something in the middle?" I asked Shaya.

"Most likely."

"Then do it."

She bowed her head in acknowledgment, and I knew that's what she'd already known had to be done. She was simply giving me my dues as queen, going through the motions and reminding everyone that ultimately, I still held the authority around here.

When Kiyo and I finally made it to the Rowan Land, I felt the land's relief and welcome. Its energy burned into mine, strengthening me. At the castle, we saw little sign of the Rowan military but plenty of mine and Dorian's. They were stationed everywhere, keeping the order Shaya had told me about. They bowed low when they saw me, their actions mirrored by the kingdom's citizens. Only, Katrice's subjects didn't bow out of respect and deference. There was fear in their eyes, confusion in some, and an obvious show among a few that their actions were forced.

Rurik was still in residence, personally overseeing the occupation. I felt secure in his control and listened as he explained what needed to be done next. I understood it only a little better than the economics Shaya had pushed on me, the main point being I'd need a governing body here soon.

Picking that staff would be a problem. Shaya was one in a million, but even she couldn't be in two places at once. Seeing my dismay, Rurik hesitantly added that Dorian had offered to provide people for the job. My expression at those words gave Rurik all the answer he needed.

The Rowan Land's energy continued to flow into me when I set out to have my meditation session with it. The nature of the connection was similar to what I had with the Thorn Land, but the kingdom's feel was totally different. The Thorn Land was harsh—filled with life, yes, but life that fought fiercely against the elements for survival. The Rowan Land was softer, its life bursting forth easily and radiating through its many trees and plants.

"Eugenie," said Kiyo, following me out to a small garden behind the castle. "Look."

I paused and glanced behind me. Where I'd walked, flowers had blossomed, small red ones scattered throughout the grassy path. I knelt down, inhaling their heady scent. "Why's it happening?"

"You're its ruler. You're giving the land life and energy."

I thought about how being here had made me feel marginally better. "It's strengthening me too . . . but this doesn't happen in the Thorn Land. I don't have that kind of effect."

"Don't you?" he teased, a mischievous smile on his face. "You make it rain. . . ."

A memory came to me of when the Thorn Land had floundered in drought. While connecting with the land, I'd had sex with Kiyo, and the energy from that union had empowered the kingdom, breaking the dry spell and sending much-needed rain that made the people and plants flourish.

I smiled back at him. "Looks like we don't have to worry about that today. This land doesn't need as much help."

He slipped an arm around my waist and pulled me to him, voice husky. "But imagine the results if we did. Extra credit."

Leaning down, he brought his lips to mine, his tongue pushing into my mouth with a rough passion. I felt my body answer, and for a moment, the offer was tempting. I pictured what it would be like to make love among all this greenery, here in the sunshine. Would a bed of red flowers fill the ground below us? Again . . . I kind of wanted to find out, but I also wasn't comfortable in this kingdom yet. I didn't want to risk discovery of my sex life, even if it wouldn't be a big deal to the gentry. Reluctantly, I pulled away from him.

"Another time."

After a few more protests, he let me be. I sat on the ground while he waited, closing my eyes and opening myself to the world around me. *We are one,* I assured the land. *I am here.* I felt its answer, felt warmth spread through me and lost track of time. When I finished, I was startled at how far the sun had moved across the sky. Kiyo sat on the ground cross-legged, looking at ease as he watched me.

"Crap," I said, jumping up. "I'm sorry. I didn't mean to make you wait so long."

He stood as well. "It's no problem. You needed it.

You both needed it." I knew he was right. I was more energized, and the land felt strong and content.

After another check with Rurik, Kiyo and I headed back to the Thorn Land. Here, he parted from me, again to "take care of a few things." He assured me he'd be back in Tucson as soon as he could, but I saw the look Jasmine gave me when she overheard. I could guess her thoughts: more reports to Maiwenn.

Jasmine was impatient to go to Tucson, but before leaving, I impulsively set out alone to where I'd communed earlier with the Thorn Land. It had been on a distant part of the grounds, one of my favorite places, in the shade of a mesquite tree. Its perfume rivaled that of the Rowan flowers, and around it stood cactuses in all shapes and sizes, some of them small and squat and some tall and foreboding like sentries.

Almost all of them were blooming.

A chill ran down my spine as I stared at the flowers on the cacti. They formed a brilliantly colored perimeter, right around where I'd been meditating, the petals in all shapes and sizes. The flowers were beautiful. Exquisite.

And none of them had been there earlier.

Chapter 20

I didn't know what the flowers meant. Nothing like that had ever happened when I'd meditated in the Thorn Land. Over the next few days, I just kept thinking about what Rurik had said, that no other monarch save my father had ruled more than one kingdom in recent history. It had taken great power and magic for me to exert my dominance over the lands. . . . Were they feeding it back to me in return? I certainly felt stronger with them, but I'd never expected any sort of unconscious physical manifestation. What else was I capable of? What could I make the land do?

I didn't mention the matter to anyone, not even Kiyo. He'd seen the red flowers but brushed them off. If I told him about the Thorn Land, I feared he'd grow upset about the thought of my magic increasing. He grudgingly accepted what I already possessed but still feared it would turn me into my father, no heir needed.

And although I'd felt physically better in the Otherworld, I grew weak again after a day or so back in Tucson. I didn't mention this to Kiyo either, but Jasmine was around enough to pick up on it.

"Are they calling to you again?" she asked over breakfast one day. She was devouring Pop-Tarts, another love we apparently shared. I was too worried to have an appetite and simply watched. "You look like crap."

"I don't know," I said, drumming my fingers against a glass of water. "There's no precedent for this—at least not anymore. No one knows what to expect from me having two kingdoms."

"I bet Dorian would know."

I bet he would too, but I shook my head. "He's not all-knowing no matter how much he wants to be," I countered. "And I'm done with him."

"Okay." She didn't fight it. For a while, she'd kept telling me I'd made a mistake in breaking up with Dorian, but Kiyo had been growing on her. I still wasn't sure if she approved, but at least I didn't have to listen to teen advice about my love life anymore. "But you might just have to go back soon. I mean, think about it. You're bound to two lands in the Otherworld. Aren't the lands and the monarch one? Part of you's there. It makes sense you'd have to be there twice as much."

I winced at the idea, though it had been on my mind too. "If I were there any more, I'd be living there permanently."

She swallowed the last of some crust. "You may not have a choice."

Her flippant tone irritated me. "There's always a choice. I rule them. They don't rule me." I stood up abruptly and briefly became dizzy. It felt like the lands were mocking me. *Damn it,* I thought. *You will not call me back so quickly. I'm staying in this world for a while. I'll come and go when I please.* "I just need to stop thinking about it. I'm going to see if Lara's got a job."

"Yeah," said Jasmine dryly. "That'll fix everything."

Lara did have a job for me, several actually. Even though she was all but living with Tim—in my house—she still kept meticulous records and took all my calls. She looked disappointed that I only accepted one from her growing list of jobs, a small one at that: a simple haunting that would probably take about five minutes. She said nothing, but I knew that she worried if I didn't make any money, she wouldn't either. So, remembering Enrique's comment about needing help but not being able to trust anyone, I gave her his card with the suggestion she call about part-time work.

"Are you firing me?" she asked.

I smiled as I gathered up all my weapons. "No, but I want you to have a backup plan in case you get laid off." Her eyes widened in alarm at the joke. Or, I suddenly wondered, was it a joke?

I brought Jasmine with me to the job because I still felt uneasy about leaving her alone. Besides, she was finally getting her fill of the human world, and I had a feeling her insistence on me returning to the Otherworld was partly selfish.

Later, after I'd finished the job, I kind of regretted bringing a witness.

"Wow," she said, as we drove home. "You got your ass kicked."

"I did not."

"Did too."

So. This was what it was like having a sister.

"I banished it, didn't I? You saw it go to the Underworld."

"Yeah," she admitted, "but it sure did take a long time. I felt like I could have done it, and I've never banished anything before."

I gritted my teeth, refraining from commenting that I still had her chains. The troubling thing was, I had kind of sucked. I'd been in no real danger—not with a ghost that minor—but it had beaten me up more than it should have. I was off my game, a little slower, a little weaker. I'd walked away with some bruises and now noticed as we drove that my shoulder itched. For a moment, I thought the ghost must have hit me there, but there was no pain. The stitches. I'd nearly forgotten about them, now that they'd finally been able to heal. My skin had probably started to grow over the threads. I needed them out.

No one was at my house, much to my disappointment. I'd hoped Kiyo had stopped by and could remove the stitches. Trying to be optimistic, I decided he must be pulling a shift at the veterinary hospital and wasn't with Maiwenn. Thus far, I'd heard no official word from her about my new double-queen status. Other monarchs had weighed in, though. Some had responded by showering me with congratulatory gifts and groveling. Others had let me know—in an amiable way—about other monarchs they were pals with, monarchs with big armies. It turned out everyone did fear the Iron Crown.

I called my regular doctor, hoping to get an appointment this week as backup, in case Kiyo stayed absent. To my pleasant surprise, they'd had a cancellation that afternoon and could remove the stitches right away. It was good news for me but an annoyance for Jasmine, who'd just gotten comfortable on the couch.

"Oh, come *on*," she said, stretching out. "We just got home. Can't you please leave me here? I promise not to conquer the world or get pregnant while you're gone."

"You know," I said, "Lara and Tim had sex right where you're lying." She jumped up.

A half hour later, we arrived at my doctor's office.

I left Jasmine in the waiting room, deeming her safe enough with her iPod and magazines for the five minutes it would take to remove my stitches. Maybe she'd read some contraception pamphlets to pass the time.

"They did this in the ER?" the doctor asked when I was admitted to an examination room and had taken off my shirt.

I'd been seeing Dr. Moore for a couple years now. She was a pleasant, mid-fortyish woman who had eventually learned not to ask too many questions about my injuries. She thought I was a "contractor" who practiced martial arts on the side.

"Not exactly," I said. "I tore the ones the ER did, so my boyfriend had to redo them."

She took hold of tweezers and a tiny pair of scissors and leaned over. "Well, his work's neat, and it didn't get infected. If I'd seen you when this happened, I would have confined you to your bed. I would have known better than to assume you wouldn't promptly rip these out."

"Yeah, I really pulled one over on the other doctor."

She snorted a small laugh and proceeded to pull the stitches out. They stung where they tugged the skin, but honestly, it was nothing compared to my normal wear and tear.

"There you go," she said, stepping back. "You'll have a scar."

I put my shirt back on and faced her. "Battle trophy."

She rolled her eyes, leaning against the wall with crossed arms. "You shouldn't joke about that."

"Sorry." I picked up my purse, but her expression said we weren't done.

"Eugenie . . . I don't ask many questions, not any more than I need to treat you, but I'm worried about how often you come in with these kinds of injuries."

If only she knew how many I didn't come in for. "I—"

"No, no," she interrupted. "I don't need to know all the details of your life. I try not to judge—but *you* might need to. There are jobs out there that are physical in nature. That's life. But whatever you're doing . . . maybe you should reevaluate it. To be blunt, you look terrible today."

"Oh, that." Crap. I could hardly explain that it

was the residual aftereffects of a magical battle in the Otherworld, during which I'd fought for dominion of a fairy kingdom and become its new master, thus doubling my reign. "I'm just, uh, coming down with something. Just kind of tired, you know."

She arched her eyebrows.

Double crap.

"Then let's do some quick blood and urine tests," she said, straightening up. "Check your electrolytes, thyroid . . ."

I fumbled for an excuse. I'd never been comfortable with those kinds of tests since discovering I had gentry blood. I was pretty sure human medicine couldn't detect that sort of thing, but I didn't want to take any chances. "I don't have time. My sister's waiting for me in the lobby."

"I'm sure she'll be okay," said Dr. Moore. "This'll take five minutes."

"Fine." I sat back on the table, defeated. "But can you send someone to make sure she's still out there? She's the sullen one."

Dr. Moore's nurse returned to send me to the bathroom and then drew blood when I came back. She was in the middle of telling me they would send the tests out to a lab, when Dr. Moore herself stuck her head back in.

"Can we talk real for a moment?" she asked.

The nurse discreetly left, and once we were alone, I braced for another lecture about my lifestyle. "I really need to get back to my sister," I told her. "You don't know what she's capable of."

"Eugenie." Dr. Moore's voice was kind but firm.

"Most of those tests we have to wait on, but there are a few we do right here with urine."

"And?"

"And, you're pregnant."

I thought about this for a moment and then enlightened her.

"No. I'm not."

Those eyebrows rose again.

"Your test came back positive. Now, we can't tell how far just from a urine test, but based on—"

"Your test is wrong!" I sprang up from the table. My world was starting to reel again. "I can't be pregnant!"

To her credit, she took my outburst calmly, but that was probably part of her training. "The test is very accurate, and it would explain why you aren't feeling well."

"I *can't* be pregnant," I repeated adamantly. There was a mistake here. A terrible, terrible mistake, and she needed to understand that. Until she did, I refused even to process what she was claiming. "I take my birth control pills. Every day. Same time. Just like I'm supposed to. I'm not going to lie: I do other stupid shit all the time. But not with pills. I take them perfectly. I did with the antibiotics too. I'm careless with stitches but not prescriptions."

That calm expression shifted to surprise. "Antibiotics? When were you taking antibiotics?"

I pointed to my shoulder. "When I got this. The ER doctor gave a prescription." I frowned. "What? Why are you looking at me like that? I told you: I took them correctly, all of them."

"Antibiotics can negate birth control pills," she said. "Didn't you know that?"

"I . . . What? No. That's not . . . No." *A mistake. A terrible, terrible mistake.*

"Women taking both need to use some other form of contraception until the antibiotics have run their course."

A horrible, cold feeling began spreading over me. "How was I supposed to know that?" I asked in a small voice.

"Your pharmacist should have told you when you got the antibiotics. The interaction would have shown up in your records."

I thought back to that night, how my mom and I had stopped at the place closest to the hospital. "I didn't go to my usual pharmacy. . . ." And I had gotten out of there as fast as I could, not bothering to talk to the pharmacist because I'd taken antibiotics lots of times in my life. I certainly hadn't bothered with the enclosed pamphlets.

Dr. Moore seemed to think she'd gotten through to me. "Now, we can figure out how far along you are if you know when your last period—"

"*No*," I exclaimed. "No, no, no. I can't be pregnant! Don't you understand? I can't be. I can't have a baby. *I can't!*" I was shouting again and wondered if this place had security.

"Calm down," Dr. Moore said. "Everything will be all right."

No, no, it wouldn't. Everything wouldn't be all right. Nausea welled in me, nausea I'd felt for a few weeks or so—and that had nothing to do with inheriting the Rowan Land. After all this time,

after all the planning and lofty talk, after all my
fears about Jasmine . . . it was *me*. Human medicine had screwed me over. No, *I* had screwed me
over. I'd fucked up. My own carelessness had
brought this about. Everything anyone had ever
said about the Storm King prophecy began to run
through my mind. *Storm King's first grandson. An invasion of the human world. Led by his mother. Domination and blood.* And I, I was bringing it about. . . .
I was the instrument. . . .

"Eugenie!"

Dr. Moore was supporting me, and I had a feeling she'd said my name a few times. She glanced
at the door and opened her mouth, about to call
her nurse.

"No!" I clutched at her white coat. "Don't.
Listen to me." My voice was raspy and desperate.
"I can't. I can't have a baby. Don't you under-
stand?"

She peered at me through her glasses, regarding me knowingly. "Then you don't have to. There
are options—"

You can't have a boy, some voice inside me said.
What if it's a girl?

"Wait," I interrupted her. "When can you tell
the gender?"

That got a shocked look. "You'd base an abortion on gender?"

"I—no, wait." Fuck. I couldn't think. I was panicked and scared and confused. I needed to get
my head together. What did I do? I had to get rid
of this baby, pure and simple. People did it all the
time. It was easy in this day and age, right? "I

meant, how long until you can tell gender and if . . . if there's anything wrong." I groped for something reasonable, something that wouldn't make me seem like a heartless woman who'd kill her son. "You can do those tests, right? Like, genetic tests? I . . . I'm so afraid of having a baby and having there be something wrong. My family has a bad history. My cousins have had babies with birth defects, and I can't . . . I can't handle that. I have to know. I have to know . . . right away . . . as early as possible because otherwise I'll . . ." The lies rolled easily off my lips. Anything. Anything to know the gender.

Dr. Moore studied me again. I still sounded crazy and scattered, I knew, but a little less than before. "When was your last period?" she asked quietly.

I turned to her wall calendar. The numbers swam before me. I couldn't focus. How the hell could I remember that when the fate of the world was on the line? I remembered my last period and tried to link it to some event, something that would trigger a date.

"There." I pointed. "It started on the fifth."

She nodded, doing mental calculations. "Which lines up with the antibiotics. You're almost nine weeks along, as the reckoning goes, though technically only seven since conception."

Seven. Seven weeks . . .

"You're almost in the range for chorionic villus sampling," she said. Chorionic what? "They don't like to do it unless it's necessary, though. There are risks for the fetus. They almost never do it for someone your age, who's in good health. . . ."

"But it can tell me?" I said urgently. "It can tell me what I need to know?"

"It can tell you a lot. No test can tell you everything, but it can give you peace of mind . . . especially if you really do have a bad family history . . ."

Did I ever.

"I do," I said. "Please."

I held my breath, knowing she was wavering here. Finally, she turned to her filing cabinet, rifling through it until she found a carbon form. She scrawled something in doctor's handwriting on it and handed it over. "Here."

It was a referral to an OB-GYN's office nearby. The form had my name, some boxes checked, and a few illegible words. I did make out *CVS* and *emergency.*

"Emergency?" I asked. I mean, it was, but I was surprised she'd nailed it.

"It means you'll get scheduled in right away. Most of these tests are backed up—because they aren't done this early. Give it to my nurse when you leave." She was writing something else as she spoke. "She'll call them and schedule you—but you need to be aware they may refuse it when you're there, based on their judgment. I meant it: this isn't routine."

My next words were hesitant. "Then why are you doing it?"

"Because I believe that in pregnancy, the mother's health outweighs everything else."

Mother's health. I didn't like thinking of myself

as a mother. Fuck. This shouldn't even be an issue at all! We should be discussing abortions. Why did I care about gender? I didn't want a baby. I wasn't ready for a baby. Certainly not one who'd fulfill a world-conquering prophecy.

"In this case," said Dr. Moore. "Your mental health is especially concerning. Which is what this is for." She handed me the other piece of paper. It was a referral for a psychologist.

"I don't need—"

"Eugenie, shock over an unplanned pregnancy is normal. Expected. But it's clear . . . you have some very serious issues around this."

She had no idea.

"Have my nurse call for the test. Then schedule yourself a therapist appointment and a follow-up with me."

There was no way I could tell her I had no intention of going to therapy. I wasn't even sure about the follow-up. But I'd gotten away with something, and I knew it. I nodded meekly. "Thank you." I left before she could change her mind.

Jasmine's face was filled with irritation and impatience when I finally returned. "That took forever," she said, tossing a magazine aside. "How deep were those stitches?"

"Not that deep," I murmured. I walked toward my car on autopilot, still stunned. "She was worried about how tired I was, that's all."

"Well, you can fix that when we go back to the Otherworld."

I started the car, staring off into space for a few ponderous moments as numbers floated around in my head. Nine weeks, seven weeks. Two days. That was how long until my test. Two days.

I refocused on my surroundings so I wouldn't get us into an accident. "We aren't going to the Otherworld anytime soon," I replied.

Jasmine shot me a look that clearly expressed her feelings on that, but there must have been something in my own face that answered back because she didn't fight the issue anymore.

When we returned to my house, I put my purse and paperwork in my bedroom before sitting with Jasmine in her usual spot on the couch. Mindless TV suddenly seemed like a good idea . . . except, well, it didn't do a very good job of taking my mind off of my problems.

Pregnant. Conqueror of worlds. Storm King's heir.

Me. It was all on me: what had happened and what was to come.

We hadn't been home long when Kiyo showed up. He gave me a cheerful grin and wore his white coat from work, meaning he must not have been cozying up with Maiwenn. Small blessing. His smile was enough to make Jasmine smile in return, but I couldn't muster one. There was nothing to smile about right now. Nothing good in this world. Nothing good in either world. He joined us on the couch, sandwiching me in between him and Jasmine, and caught hold of my hand.

"Hey, how are you?" he asked. He peered at my face, even though I was pointedly not looking at him. "Are you okay?"

"Fine," I lied. "Tired."

Storm King's first grandson will conquer the human world.

"She's been like that all day," said Jasmine. "She needs to go back to the Otherworld but won't."

"Is that true?" he asked.

"I didn't think you'd have a problem with that," I said. "You've always wanted me to stay away."

"Yeah, but not if it's affecting you like this. You really look sick, Eug."

"She also got beat up by a ghost," Jasmine added helpfully.

"Hey!" I glared. "I did not!"

Kiyo chuckled and pulled me closer. "Stop playing tough. Go to the Otherworld tomorrow. I'll come with you, so it won't be as bad." He relaxed, and there was a finality in his voice that I didn't like. I didn't like his presumption. I also wasn't entirely sure I should be going to the Otherworld, in light of recent developments.

Flowers. Flowers everywhere, everywhere I step. I'm the land, and the land is me. Where I bring life, the land does too. . . .

Or death. I could bring death as well. It was my choice.

Over and over. The words in my head were all I heard. I didn't hear the TV, or Kiyo and Jasmine's occasional comments. I didn't really hear when Kiyo said he'd make dinner and went to drop off his overnight bag in my bedroom. But I *did* hear him when he came raging back to the living room, waving my CVS referral form in the air.

"Eugenie!" His voice was a roar, one that made

Jasmine cringe and widen her eyes. "What the *hell* is this?"

I stared up at him levelly, surprised I could be so calm in the face of that outrage, especially after the emotional upheaval I'd been through all day. My own despair and shock had never left, but now I was able to push it down and meet Kiyo's eyes, as I allowed myself to finally acknowledge the other thought that had been bouncing around in my mind. Because along with the choices I had and the consequences I faced, there was one other matter to consider.

I'd looked at the numbers, at the calendar. I'd factored in the dates, the antibiotics, what had been done—or, perhaps most importantly, what hadn't been done. It was all very clear. There was no soap opera here. No talk show-worthy mystery.

"Congratulations," I told Kiyo. "You're going to be a father. Again."

Chapter 21

For a few moments, we were frozen in time. It was Jasmine who finally got things moving again.

"Oh," she said. "Wow."

Kiyo's grip on the form tightened, and for a second, I feared he'd crumple or rip it. Instead, he let it fall to the ground and strode toward me as swiftly and fiercely as his predatory alter ego. I felt Jasmine shift—not away, but closer to me.

"Are you sure?" he asked, in a low, deadly voice.

"About which part?" I snapped. "That I'm pregnant? Or that it's yours?"

"Both."

I felt my eyes narrow as I continued feeling angry and defensive. "Yes. Both."

Silence fell. Then:

"When are you getting rid of it?" he asked.

"Christ. You get right to the point."

"You know the point!" he exclaimed. "You know what it's always been! You're *sure*? You're really sure you're pregnant?"

I'd had the same questions for Dr. Moore and

found myself repeating her answer. "Yes. The tests are very accurate. Besides, why else do you think they'd schedule me for that?" I pointed to the referral lying on the floor. He might work with animals, but he'd still know what a CVS was.

Jasmine, however, did not. She slipped away, gave him a wide berth, and retrieved the paper. "What's a . . . chorionic . . . vil-vil—"

"It's a test to detect defects," I said. I gave Kiyo a pointed look. "*And* gender."

"It's a waste of time," he argued. He swallowed and attempted a kinder, more reasonable course with me. "Eugenie, you know the danger. You can't waste another day. If anyone finds out—if anyone in the Otherworld—"

"I know, I know! Do you think I'm stupid? Do you think I somehow missed the constant rape attempts—and actual rape—based on that prophecy? Damn it, I know better than you what it means! But I can't—I can't get an abortion until I know what it is. If it's a girl or a boy."

"And then what?" he asked. "You'll keep it if it's a girl? You always said you weren't sure you wanted to have kids."

"I'm still not," I admitted, my voice trembling. A baby—world conqueror or not—had never been on my agenda. "But I have to know."

His expression darkened, the coaxing gone. "It's better if you don't. It's better to keep it all anonymous, better not to think of it as a person. Stay ignorant. Just have the abortion and be done."

Jasmine hadn't moved from her spot, her eyes going back and forth as she watched my verbal volley with Kiyo. "Geez," she said. "You don't seem too upset about killing your own kid." I had been thinking the same thing. His cold detachment shocked me.

He flinched and gritted his teeth. "I never said I'm not upset."

"But you're not just upset about what this means for the prophecy," I pointed out. I studied him carefully, realization dawning. "You don't entirely believe it's yours anyway."

"Do you blame me?" he asked.

"It's yours," I said adamantly. The last time I'd been with Dorian, we'd had kinky oral sex. Maybe I hadn't known about antibiotics interacting with birth control pills, but I knew where a guy had to come to make you pregnant. "I know without a doubt."

This gave Kiyo pause, as though he really were truly pondering the reality of losing his child. "I told you: I never said I'm not upset about this. But it's got to be dealt with. How could you have let this happen?"

"Oh, nice," I said. "It's my fault. If you're so into caution, maybe you shouldn't have fucked me in that grotto."

Jasmine's eyes widened.

"Okay, forget it," he said tightly. "And forget your CVS. Just get the abortion while it's still easy. You can't be that far along."

I shot up. "While it's still *easy*? Like you know! You're not the one who has to go through it!"

"Why are you fighting me on this?" he exclaimed in disbelief. "You always said you'd do this. Do you *want* the prophecy to come true? Do you *want* to have a son who leads armies here from the Otherworld to conquer and enslave?"

"Of course not! You know that."

"Then stop wasting time! Look, if you're scared about getting it done . . . you don't have to do it here."

"Oh? I can check in at the Otherworld's Planned Parenthood clinic?"

"No," he said wearily. "But there are potions. Maiwenn could help. Along with healing, she can work all sorts of other medical magic."

"I'm sure she can." I couldn't hide the bitterness in my voice. "And I'm sure she'd be more than happy to."

"Eugenie—"

"Look," I interrupted. "Here's how it is. I don't like your attitude. I don't like you dictating this to me like I'm stupid or something. I know the consequences, okay? And you know where I stand on the prophecy. But I just have to know what exactly is in me first. Two days. We just wait two days for the test."

"And then how long until the results?" he asked. "More time passes. Every day is dangerous."

"But what if it's a girl?" This came from Jasmine. Both Kiyo and I turned to her. "What if Eugenie can have it? You're always going on and on about how awesome Luisa is. Wouldn't you want another one—especially with, like, your actual—sort of—girlfriend?"

"It's not—" Kiyo bit off his words and turned back to me. Those dark eyes studied me, and I felt my anger diffuse as they softened. I felt his love and knew all of this was coming from panic, his fears about the prophecy finally coming true. "Two days," he said at last.

"Two days," I repeated. "And then I'll do the right thing." I wasn't exactly sure what the 'right thing' would be if I was having a girl, seeing as motherhood still didn't really jump out at me. But that didn't matter right now. What mattered was that I had the choice.

Then, abruptly and without warning, Kiyo wrapped his arms around me, crushing me to his chest. "I love you," he said, voice shaking. It was the first time he'd spoken those words since we'd gotten back together, and they tore something inside of me. "But I'm just afraid."

"I am too," I said, feeling tears spring into my eyes. Fucking hormones. "Everything'll be okay."

When he released me, I finally really comprehended that Jasmine had witnessed all of this. The dramatic factor had probably trumped anything she could find on TV. Her face was a blank mask now, which made me uneasy. What was she thinking about all this? For so long, she'd wanted to be the one to have the heir. I supposed she should be all for an abortion. Yet . . . maybe she was so keen on our father's prophecy that she didn't care who had his grandson, so long as she could ride the power with us.

"I need you to stay with Jasmine tomorrow," I told Kiyo later, when we were lying in bed. "I wish she hadn't found out about this. Maybe I'm over-reacting, but I'm worried she'll do something with the information. I could have Volusian watch her like he is now . . ." I usually summoned my minion for night watches. ". . . But I'd feel better with you there."

Kiyo drew the covers up around us. "Where are you going?"

"Where do you think?"

He groaned. "Eugenie, you can't go back there until this mess is settled. If they find out—if anyone finds out—well. All hell will break loose, from those who are for the prophecy *and* those who are against it."

"I have to," I said. "I realize now that most of my being sick is because . . . well, you know. But being apart from those lands is affecting me too. I just need to check in." No more full-fledged meditation sessions, though. I couldn't risk any more telltale signs of my pregnancy from that intense communion. I'd just do the bare minimum required. "And not just with the lands' magic. I need to keep an eye on the Rowan Land's transition."

I feared his reaction, particularly after his earlier outburst. Instead, he brushed a kiss to my lips. "Be careful. Be quick."

"I will." I pushed my lips back, kissing him harder. I moved my body closer to his, wrapping our legs together. I was terrified of what was happening, terrified of what I might be carrying. But now, with Kiyo on my side, I felt safe. We would get through this together, and I suddenly wanted to connect with him and feel his love around me.

He responded instantly to the kiss, one of his hands tipping my head back in order to consume more of my lips. His other hand gripped my upper arm, nails lightly scratching my skin as animal lust began to take over. Then, abruptly, he stopped and pulled away.

"What's wrong?" I asked. I started to say he didn't have to worry about getting me pregnant, but that joke seemed kind of inappropriate.

"Nothing . . . I'm just . . . I'm just tired." He kissed me again, but this time it was on my cheek. "It's been a long day. Just not up for it tonight . . . even though you're as sexy as always."

The lightness in those last words seemed forced, and I was glad he couldn't see my frown in the darkness. I had just been rejected because . . . because why? Having sex during pregnancy wasn't harmful, I knew that much. Was I repulsive? Was the thought that I was carrying Storm King's heir putting him off? Whatever the reason, I didn't buy that he "wasn't up for it." We'd been pressed hip to hip moments ago, and his body had most certainly been up for it.

A sexless night was the least of my problems, and although neither of us spoke, I knew he slept as badly as I did. We tossed and turned, our movements as disturbing to each other as our individual worries. We both had bloodshot eyes when we woke.

I headed off to the Otherworld as soon as I could after breakfast—well, after what passed as breakfast for me. My appetite was still low. Jasmine wasn't happy when I denied her request to come with me, but Kiyo and Volusian's presence was too daunting for her to put up much of a fight.

I felt the Thorn Land's welcoming energy when I crossed over, but thankfully, it revealed nothing about my maternal state. My staff was equally happy to see me, particularly Shaya, who looked like she'd thought I wasn't ever going to return. It wasn't an entirely unwarranted fear. She and I sat alone in one of the parlors while she updated me on the situation.

"Rurik feels the Rowan Land is stable enough to move in a governing body. There's still some unrest, and he'll stay on for a while, but most have accepted your rule. It's the way things go. He's also culled the Rowan military and feels you can trust who's left."

I tried not to grimace at that, wondering what his "culling" had entailed. "And Katrice and Cassius?"

She shrugged. "Still imprisoned. Awaiting your verdict."

"I don't really want to do anything with them," I admitted. "I don't know what to do with them."

"Honestly? With Katrice? You could set her free, and it wouldn't matter. Stripping the land from her stripped most of her magic. Her reason to live. She's harmless. Without hope. But Cassius . . ." Shaya frowned. "He's dangerous. He can't wrestle the land from you, but he's got enough power to make trouble. Dorian's already written and advised execution."

I scoffed. "I'm sure he has."

"Dorian's also provided a list of people he'd like to see installed in the Rowan Land. We settled the resources split, but he feels he deserves a controlling interest in your rule there."

"A 'controlling interest?' This isn't a corporation!" I exclaimed. "Write him and make it very, very clear that his help isn't needed over there. It isn't wanted. He has no right to it. Tell him all of that."

Shaya hesitated, fretfully toying with one of her black braids. "No matter how diplomatically I word that . . . well, the antagonism will still come through. It'll anger him."

"Good," I retorted. Dorian was a safe target for my churning emotions at the moment, and God knew I needed some sort of outlet. "Let him be angry or pout or whatever. I'm pretty sure he isn't going to declare war on me."

It was something I'd figured out recently. Dorian had been an advocate of using the Iron Crown to scare other monarchs, but the thing was, now that we weren't together anymore, he had to realize it could be used against him too. I actually hadn't had to give in to his "spoils of war" demands. That had been a kindness on my part, and he knew it. I didn't have to fear Dorian. I no longer needed him.

"Very well," Shaya replied. Her tone was obedient, but I knew she dreaded that letter. She'd never lost her devotion to him, and I was forcing her to split her loyalties. "But we do need someone to manage the Rowan Land . . . unless you're going to do it personally."

"No," I said swiftly, not that I needed to. She'd

already known I had no interest in it. "Do you have someone in mind?"

"Yes. . . . Me."

I wasn't exactly surprised that she'd step up to the task. I was surprised, however, that she didn't look particularly upset about it. Maybe she relished the challenge.

"I'm cool with that," I said. "Hell, after what you did around here, I know you can get Rowan into shape. But . . . who's going to run things here?"

"I was thinking Nia could."

"Nia?" I asked, startled. "My hair stylist?"

Shaya crooked me a grin. "What do you think she does when you're not around? She's been helping me and learning. . . . I think she'd do very well. There'd be others to assist her, and, of course, she could always contact me."

It was still an unexpected choice, but Shaya seemed confident. And, I supposed, we'd gotten the Thorn Land into good enough shape that it now functioned pretty smoothly.

"Okay," I said at last. "Let's make it happen. When do you plan on moving?"

"Today," she said. "I'll go when you go. My things are packed."

I couldn't help laughing. "You knew I'd agree. And you knew I'd refuse Dorian."

Shaya put on her primmest look, but her eyes sparkled. "Yes, Your Majesty."

I walked the Thorn Land before leaving, long enough to reassure the land I was there and boost the morale of the soldiers guarding my keep. Not that they needed it. We were victorious, and they were still celebrating. I'd donned my gold crown for the trip to the Rowan Land, and my men regarded me with adoration, calling out cheers for their brave, all-powerful queen. *What would they do if they knew?* I wondered. *What would they do if they knew I was carrying a potential warlord?* Somehow, it wasn't much of a mystery. They would cheer more. They would worship me and revel in the chance to extend our rule.

It made me eager to go to the Rowan Land, where I was feared rather than adored. Of course, I didn't know if that was any better. If those people knew I was carrying Storm King's grandchild, it would simply intensify their fear and convince them more than ever that they were under the control of a tyrant queen. Kiyo was right, I realized. No one in the Otherworld could know about my pregnancy. Any reaction it drew would be a powerful one. The sooner I could leave, the better.

Borrowed soldiers from the Thorn Land still made up the bulk of the guard at Katrice's former castle, and their expressions mirrored those of their colleagues back home. I played the part, smiling and walking among them confidently, not daring to show the fear and uncertainty I felt. Like the Thorn Land's, the Rowan Land's energy buzzed around me. Only I felt it, of course, but once, when I paused and talked to a guard for several minutes, I saw a small red flower growing where I'd stood. No one noticed, and I hastily headed for the castle, figuring nothing would sprout out of stone walls.

Rurik greeted us happily, having already known about Shaya's new position. As we all converged, I saw something flash between them, something that surprised me. Affection. More than friendly affection. It was then that I also noticed a bracelet Shaya wore, made of emeralds and pearls. I'd seen it before. Girard had been working on it when I first met Imanuelle. It was the piece Rurik had commissioned. I tried not to gape as the truth hit me. Shaya and Rurik. They had a relationship going on, some romance, probably one that had been building right before me that I'd been too oblivious to notice. That was why she hadn't minded taking on stewardship of a kingdom conquered through unorthodox means.

No one else seemed to notice—or maybe everyone already knew about them—but as I stood there and listened to more debriefings, I felt a pang in my chest. It was like Tim and Lara—and not because both couples were so bizarrely matched. No, the similarities came in that it was so easy for all of them. Just fall in love and go with it. No political machinations and motives. No world-altering prophecies to muck things up. I'd untangled myself from Dorian's scheming—and not without a fair amount of heartache—but things with Kiyo now were irrevocably altered. No matter how my pregnancy panned out, even if it had as happy an ending as it could, I knew things between him and me would never be the same. I would never have an easy relationship.

Queasiness welled up in me, and I didn't bother trying to figure out which of the myriad reasons could be causing it. I leaned against the wall as Rurik continued speaking about troop placement. Even though it wasn't part of the land, the wall and castle's foundation touched the land, and I felt that magic warm and comfort me. I took a deep breath. I could do this. Everything would be all right, just as I'd told Kiyo. I'd know my child's gender soon. Then I'd know what to do.

My intention had been to stay around longer and make sure Shaya was settled in, but I soon decided I needed to get back. The others looked like they would have liked me to stay a little longer too, but they were also used to my weird—or as they considered them, "human"—ways. I assured them all that I had the utmost faith in them, reminded Shaya to rebuke Dorian, and then headed back to Tucson as soon as I could.

When I arrived home and analyzed how I'd been feeling today, it occurred to me that the transitions from world to world were making me sick. Transitioning wasn't an easy feat in general; some couldn't even do it. I'd grown adept at it, but now, it took its toll, even with the help of a gateway. I understood enough about pregnancy to know these annoying symptoms only lasted for a short time, but that didn't negate their annoyance. I didn't want anything slowing me down. I didn't want to be hampered. My body was turning against me, and Kiyo's urging just to end the pregnancy began to seem like a better and better idea. What did gender matter? I wasn't ready for this.

He was relieved to see me back early and wrapped

me up in another big embrace. "Everything's okay?" he asked in a low voice. "Nobody found out?"

I shook my head. "No. And I'm not going back until . . . until this is settled. I'm also starting to think . . ."

"What?" he prompted.

"That you were right. That gender doesn't matter. The test is so close, though . . . I'll still do it. But. Well. Like I said, it doesn't matter."

Relief flooded his features. "I'm glad, Eug. It's the right thing to do." He hugged me again, and the hug was filled with more intensity. "You can always cancel the test."

"No, I'll do it. Especially after the fit I threw with my poor doctor."

"I wish I could go with you," he said wistfully. "But I'm not sure I can. I'm taking a couple of work shifts."

Are you? Or are you running off to Maiwenn?

"It's fine," I said. "You wouldn't be able to find out anything that day anyway."

"But you'll let me know the moment you know?" he asked, staring at me hard.

"The very moment."

Kiyo might not have been able to go with me . . . but Jasmine did.

Ostensibly, I told myself it was because she couldn't be left by herself. Yet, deep inside, when I really looked at my heart, I knew the truth. I didn't want to go through this alone. I knew what the test entailed, and even if we got no answers today, it was still one step closer to what could be a huge event.

"You can do it, you know," Jasmine told me.

I'd let her come into the exam room with me. It was dimly lit for the ultrasound equipment, and the doctor and tech had stepped out so I could change. Undressing in front of Jasmine felt weird, so I kept my back to her as I put on the hospital gown.

"Do what? This test?"

"No. I mean, yeah, whatever, you'll be fine. But I mean, have the baby. Whatever it is. Even a boy. You can fulfill our father's prophecy." There was a zeal in her voice I hadn't heard in a while—one I'd hoped had gone away.

Gowned, I turned around. "No. That's out of the question. If it's a boy . . . well, I can't have it. End of story. A girl . . . I don't know. I'm probably not doing that either." I couldn't help adding, "Besides, I thought *you* wanted to be the heir's mother."

Her face was deadly earnest as she considered my words. "I did. But maybe I'm not meant to."

The staff returned and situated me on the examining table while Jasmine retreated to a corner. They introduced themselves: Dr. Sartori and Veronica the tech. They explained the procedure to me, though I'd already read up on it several times. The doctor was going to—ack—stick a giant needle in me to collect cells and would use ultrasound to guide him. He made sure I understood the risk of such a test. A small percentage of women miscarried. Dryly, I told him I was willing to accept that.

Veronica raised the gown to bare my stomach. As she rubbed gel on it, I stared down wonderingly. Honestly? It looked no different than in the past. I'd always been skinny, and with my lack of appetite, I probably wasn't putting on much weight. If not for my symptoms and Dr. Moore's "very accurate" test, I never would have guessed what was inside me. And what *was* inside me? My stomach took on a strange, sinister countenance. Again, I had that feeling of my body's betrayal. It was doing things out of my control.

"Okay," said Veronica, moving the paddle to my stomach. "Let's take a look."

Both she and Dr. Sartori watched a black monitor that had my name, birthday, and a few other stats at the bottom of the screen. When the paddle made contact, the screen flared to life, showing the indecipherable gray and white confusion I'd always seen when people had ultrasounds on TV. I could make no sense of it nor see anything resembling a baby, but sound immediately accompanied the images, repetitive swishing noises, kind of like waves. I at least knew what that meant.

"That's the heartbeat, isn't it?" I asked, a strange feeling crawling over me. Heartbeat. Another creature's heart inside of me.

Neither practitioner answered right away. Dr. Sartori frowned curiously, and Veronica shifted the paddle around to get more views.

"Huh," said the doctor.

"What?" I exclaimed. Two immediate possibilities

sprang to mind. One was that my gentry blood mixing with Kiyo's kitsune blood had created some sort of monster. The other thought—one that suddenly offered a world of safety—was that there had been a mistake. The test wasn't accurate, and I actually wasn't pregnant. "Isn't that the heartbeat?"

Dr. Sartori's gaze fell on me, a small smile on his lips. "That's the heart*beats*. You have twins."

Chapter 22

No one had to tell me the ways in which that exponentially complicated things. Jasmine's gasp confirmed my many realizations.

"Two placentas," said Veronica, pausing and typing something one-handed while still keeping hold of the paddle.

"What . . . what's that mean?" I asked.

"It means they could be identical or fraternal," said Dr. Sartori. "One placenta would be identical for sure."

I swallowed. The noise, that wave-like sound . . . It was drowning me. My heartbeat, another heartbeat, and another still . . . How was it possible? How could there be so much life in one body?

"Can you still do the test?" I stammered out.

Dr. Sartori was holding the needle but made no moves as his eyes flicked back to the monitor. "I can . . . but it's not recommended in this situation. With twins, the risks are increased."

"I don't care," I said firmly. "I still want it. I have to know. With my family history . . ."

I prayed he wouldn't demand too many details beyond what Dr. Moore had sent over. He and Veronica discussed a few things, using medical language I couldn't follow. She used the paddle to check every angle, taking measurements on her computer as he occasionally pointed details out. Finally, after another warning against the procedure, he agreed to do it.

It hurt as much as you'd expect from a giant needle being stuck into you. His hands were superhumanly steady, as his eyes held firm to the monitor so he could watch the needle's progress. I still couldn't make out much in the images but knew the challenge was to get to the placenta without touching a fetus. Placentas, in this case. They had to get another test kit, using another needle in order to sample from both babies.

Babies.

I still couldn't believe it. They helped me when they finished the test, loading Jasmine and me up with post-care instructions to reduce both self-injury and the risk of miscarriage.

Does it matter? I thought bleakly. A miscarriage would take the decision away from me. It'd be out of my hands.

For now, one tiny problem did present itself: getting home. I was sore and didn't feel like driving. In fact, I'd been advised not to. Jasmine helpfully offered to.

"I know for a fact you don't have a license," I told her. I was leaning against my car, baking in welcome sunshine.

"No, but I can drive. Come on, it's not that far.

And *you* certainly can't. What do you want to do? Call Tim and let him know what's going on?" she challenged.

I wanted my mom, I realized. I wanted my mom to come and drive me home—to her home. I wanted her to take care of me and talk to me like she used to. I wanted her to fix all this.

I blinked rapidly and turned my head, not wanting Jasmine to see me tear up.

"Fine." I held out the keys. "If we get pulled over, the ticket's coming out of your allowance."

To her credit, she drove responsibly, and she was right—it wasn't far. I tilted my seat back slightly, wanting to sleep for the next few days or however long it would take to get back my results. I didn't want to endure the waiting. I *couldn't* endure the waiting. The car's silence and rhythm nearly took me under until Jasmine spoke.

"So," she said matter-of-factly. "If they're boys, you get an abortion. If they're girls . . ."

"Then I don't." I hadn't realized I'd made my decision until that moment. When I'd heard those heartbeats . . . well, it didn't matter if motherhood and drastic body changes scared the hell out of me. If I had two daughters, daughters unconnected to any prophecy, I would have them. I'd figure parenting out. "If they're girls, I'll keep them."

She nodded and said nothing more until we were turning down my street. Honestly, I was surprised she waited that long because I'd already known what else she was dying to ask.

"Eugenie?"

"Yes, Jasmine?"

"What are you going to do if one's a boy and one's a girl?"

I stared ahead at my house. I suddenly didn't want to sleep just for the next few days. I wanted to sleep for the next nine months. Or seven months. Or whatever. I didn't answer her question.

"I can't have a son," I said at last. "You know that. That's all there is to it."

Chapter 23

I decided it would be best not to mention the twins thing to Kiyo. As it was, I was having a hard enough time processing it.

Twins.

Twins?

This was the ultimate 'when it rains, it pours' cliché. I'd gotten pregnant through an idiotic slip, putting me right in the line of the prophecy I'd tried to avoid for so long. And now, just when I'd managed to coax an early test so I could nip this situation in the bud, I was faced with a potential situation that I never, never could have foreseen.

Kiyo had been right. I should have terminated the pregnancy the instant I found out, before I knew more about it. It was becoming real now. Every detail I learned made it more substantial, giving more life to what I carried within me. *It's not too late. You don't have to wait for the results. Maybe it's better if you don't.*

I'd boldly told Jasmine that I'd keep the twins if they were girls, but the reality of that was harsh.

How would I raise two children? I didn't know if I could handle one. How could I manage motherhood when half my life was spent in another world? How could I even keep working? Would I get a nanny—or force my kids onto someone like Tim or my mom? That latter seemed pretty unlikely. And then, of course, I was faced with the most mundane problem of all.

Money.

"You're going to be in serious trouble if you don't start working again soon," Lara told me the day after I'd seen the doctor. She'd spent the night again and was sitting at my kitchen table with me. In front of her, a laptop showed an array of spreadsheets. "You're still okay . . . but it won't last. Part of your money goes into the business's account—the one I'm paid from. The other profits go to your savings. The first one's running pretty low . . . and if it goes empty . . ."

"We go into my savings," I finished.

She nodded. Her face was grim, a far cry from the giddiness she'd shown when she and Tim had stumbled out of bed this morning. A bitter part of me thought maybe I could pick up extra cash by charging her rent. I dismissed that, of course. None of this was her fault.

"I know there's . . . stuff . . . going on, Eugenie, but why can't you start taking more jobs? You cut the workload before, and we still did okay, but now . . . there's next to nothing. Your savings can't hold out that long. And what on earth did Enrique do that got us such a large bill?"

I ignored that and simply stared at the numbers

on the screen, my heart sinking. "I've got a lot of equity in the house."

"What?" Her jaw nearly dropped. "You'd risk your house instead of just taking on more work?"

A terrible image came to my mind: me, trapped in some small apartment with two screaming babies. *End it, just end it.*

"It's just an option," I pointed out. "A safety net. And speaking of which . . . Did you talk to Enrique?"

Lara nodded. "I did. I'm going to do a little administrative work for him on the side."

"Good." One less thing to feel guilty about. "You'll be okay then."

"This isn't about me! I don't understand. Why can't you just take a couple of jobs? I've got reams of requests! There are easy ones, like that ghost the other day."

I tried to hide my dismay at that. "I haven't been feeling well, that's all. And this is kind of a physical line of work."

Lara's blue eyes scrutinized me for several seconds. "Then maybe *you're* the one who needs to be looking for another job."

"No!" I exclaimed. "This is what I do. It's the only thing I do."

"But if you're sick—"

"I'm fine. I'm seeing the doctor tomorrow and then . . ." I faltered. And then what? "And then I'll be fine. Back to work. My appointment's at noon, so hell, you could schedule something later that afternoon. Find me a troll or a banshee."

She sighed. "I didn't mean to upset you."

"I'm not upset." But it was a lie. My volume had increased without my realizing it, and I felt flushed.

Lara rose, shutting the laptop and picking up her plate. "Just get yourself better. We can figure this out then. Do you need a ride or anything tomorrow?"

"I'm not *that* sick," I told her. And, of course, I could always have my unlicensed teenage sister drive me. "We'll be back in business again soon, you'll see."

Lara gave me a tight smile, trying to hide concern but failing. She wandered off to Tim's bedroom, and Jasmine sat up on the couch, where she'd overheard everything. "That's a good idea, you know," she said. "Sell this place. Just move to the Otherworld with the kids."

I started to rebuke her but paused. It was an option. I'd have plenty of daycare there—a whole castle of babysitters. My daughters would be raised like royalty. They *were* royalty. But raising them there meant they'd probably lose whatever humanity was in them. They would be gentry for all intents and purposes. Was that what I wanted? It was already happening to *me*.

"They may be boys," I reminded Jasmine. "Then it's back to work."

Kiyo called that night, wanting to know if I'd heard anything. I told him it was too soon for the results but that I'd let him know when the doctor called. It was a small lie. As I'd slipped to Lara, I was actually going back to the office for the results. Twins had popped me into a high-risk category, apparently, and along with delivering the results in person, they'd wanted to do another ultrasound. I didn't want Kiyo around for that, obviously, but I wouldn't have minded him coming over that night. I wanted the contact, the love. Most importantly, I wanted to feel like he wasn't repulsed by me in my current state.

When noon came the next day, I went like someone going to her own funeral. My mind was blank, unable to focus on anything, and Jasmine probably would have been a safer driver. She'd come along; there'd been no discussion. Neither of us spoke on the drive over, and I could see she was wound just as tightly with tension. Whatever happened, it was going to be big.

"Soon," I murmured as we walked in. "Soon this'll be over, one way or another."

Or not so soon.

The office was running behind, and it was like the continuation of some cosmic joke. I'd been counting down the seconds until this moment, and now the wait was indefinite while Dr. Sartori caught up with his schedule. Admittedly, I'd never felt angry at doctors who fell behind. I figured it just meant they were giving needed time and care to their patients. Maybe he was tied up because some other woman had discovered she was having a world-conquering monster.

"Eugenie?" The sound of my name made me flinch. A nurse smiled serenely at me. "We're ready for you."

It was a repeat of before, changing into a gown and getting on the examination table. *This is it, this is it.* Dr. Sartori was back, but a different tech worked today. Her name was Ruth, and she had a kindly, almost grandmotherly air that felt reassuring. Like she could maybe fix all this.

Dr. Sartori had a file of papers he began flipping through as Ruth lubed up my stomach. Again, I stared it, still having a hard time believing there were *two* living beings in there.

"Well," he said. "I have good news."

Jasmine made a sound that almost sounded like a laugh. A bitter one, that is. Like me, she knew there was little that was going to be good here. In fact, things soon got worse.

A knock sounded at the door, and the nurse I'd seen earlier stuck her head in. "I'm sorry to interrupt you," she said. Her eyes fell on me. "There's a man here who says he's your boyfriend and that he was running late for the exam."

My mouth went dry. "Kiyo?" I managed.

"That's him. I'll go get him."

She'd taken my ID of Kiyo as confirmation and acceptance. I opened my mouth to protest, but she was gone. I started to tell one of the others to go stop her, but by that point, Ruth's paddle had made contact. The screen again showed shadowy forms, and the sound of those rapid heartbeats filled the room.

"There they are," said Dr. Sartori. "We can wait for your boyfriend before getting to the results."

"No, we—"

The nurse returned with Kiyo, who was all charm and smiles as he introduced himself. "Sorry I'm late. I had the time wrong. Lara corrected me." That last part was to me, and despite the pleasant expression on his face, I saw a hard look in his eyes. He didn't like the deception. I had kept this from him, lying about when I'd get the results.

How had he found me? Lara had known the time but not the place. For a moment, I thought Jasmine might be playing a game, but her face showed shock and wariness at his arrival. She was as surprised as me. The referral, I realized. He'd read it before and knew which doctor I was seeing.

"Well, then," continued Dr. Sartori. "Now that we're all here, we can go over everything. You can rest easy about your family history. No trace of anything abnormal in either one. Both of the fetuses' genetic tests came back fine."

It was a sign of Kiyo's self-control that he said nothing because I could have sworn the word *both?* was on his lips. His only reaction was another sharp look at me, his expression growing darker as he realized what I'd been hiding. The doctor and tech were watching the monitor, so they didn't see what Jasmine and I did.

"And you know . . . you know the gender?" I asked.

Dr. Sartori nodded. "You can't actually see it on the ultrasound now, but the one Ruth's got a close-up of now . . . that's a girl." I exhaled in relief, and yet . . . somehow, I knew what his next words would be as Ruth shifted to the other amorphous blob. "And this one's a boy."

Silence so cold and so heavy fell that I couldn't

believe neither of the office's staff noticed the lack of joy this news was receiving.

"A girl," said Kiyo. "And a boy."

Dr. Sartori nodded, flipping through a few more pages. "Based on what you've told us and what we can see, we're putting your due date around the end of October. Although, with twins, you're at a higher risk for early delivery, so we'll be seeing you more often than in a normal pregnancy. And while this test gives us a lot of info, it doesn't tell everything, so you'll have others soon. You haven't had any pain since the CVS, have you? Any reactions?"

"No," I said flatly. My eyes were on those images, my world dominated by those heartbeats.

"Good. You'll still want to take it easy to avoid any miscarriage risk."

He went over a few more issues, told me when to come back, and then asked if we had any questions. I half-expected Kiyo to ask for an abortion then and there, but he was still biting back his words. It was going to be a *for later* conversation, I knew.

Ruth cleaned me up and then retreated with the doctor. They gestured Kiyo along with them. "It's crowded," said Dr. Sartori good-naturedly. "You can meet up in the waiting room to schedule your next appointment."

"Yes," said Kiyo, eyes boring into me. "We'll talk out there."

I forced a pained smile, and Jasmine turned anxiously toward me the second the door shut. "He is *pissed*," she said.

"I know. You don't have to tell me."

I pulled on my clothes, my limbs feeling leaden. "Oh God. I can't believe this is happening. Why? Why did I defy the odds? It was a one in three chance. One in three!" My voice was turning hysterical, as I begged this teen girl for answers. "All girls. All boys. Either was more likely than this. Why couldn't it have been one of those? Why couldn't we have had an easy fix?"

Jasmine's face was solemn. "But you do. You said if one was a boy, you'd still have an abortion. You said you'd do it." There was a challenge in her voice.

I finished putting on my shoes and looked away from her. The monitor was black, the room silent, but I could still hear the heartbeats in my head. If I had an abortion to ensure the prophecy wasn't fulfilled, I'd be taking an innocent life. My daughter—that concept was still crazy to me— had no part in this. It wasn't her fault her brother was destined for blood and destruction. Really, was it even his fault? There was hardly anything to him yet. Just a shadow. And a heartbeat. How could you dictate the future of someone not even born? How could you know what he would turn into? Was anyone's potential really set in stone?

And how could *I* be the one to kill that potential?

How could *I* silence that heartbeat?

Either of them.

"Eugenie?" Jasmine's voice was puzzled. "You're going to do it, right?"

I lifted my eyes from my feet. "I—I don't know."

"You have to."

A new voice spoke in the room. My skin tingled, and suddenly, Deanna materialized before us. I jumped. In light of everything else that had been happening in my life, she'd kind of gone off my radar. I'd left her in Enrique's hands and assumed that everything was settled with her when she hadn't answered my summoning.

"What the hell?" I demanded. "What are you doing here?" So much for her moving on.

Deanna looked like she always did, wearing that desolate look ghosts so often had.

"You have to," she repeated, ignoring my questions. Her expression grew bleaker. "If you don't get rid of your children, Kiyo will kill you."

Chapter 24

"What?" exclaimed Jasmine.

I didn't share her concern. "Damn it. I should have banished you the first time I saw you. I don't have time for this, not with everything else. You should be in the Underworld by now. Kiyo isn't going to kill me."

"I'm serious!" said Deanna, as frantic as a ghost could get. "You're in danger!"

I shook my head. "Look, I'm sorry about your husband . . . really, I am. But not every guy is homicidal. Don't transfer this to me."

"I'm not! This is real. I was going to move on after . . . after . . . well, after my husband was arrested. . . ." There was a mournful pause. Her story had come to a close, but it hadn't had a happy ending. "I wanted to say good-bye formally and went looking for you . . . but found Kiyo instead . . ."

I put my hands on my hips, wishing I'd brought my wand. I did *not* need a delusional ghost, not with everything else right now. "And then he said he was going to kill me?"

"No. He told that other queen he would."

That cut off my snark, leaving me speechless for a moment.

"What other queen?" demanded Jasmine.

"The blond one. The Willow Queen."

Jasmine and I exchanged looks. Suddenly, Deanna's crazy statements had become slightly less crazy.

"What exactly did you overhear?" I asked quietly.

"He told her you were pregnant and that you'd have an abortion if it was a boy . . . but that he was concerned. He was worried because you hadn't just done it already." Deanna looked back and forth between our faces, desperate for either of us to believe her. "He said it was probably just shock and that you'd 'do the right thing,' but that if you didn't . . . well, Maiwenn said they'd have to make you lose the baby. Or . . . if that didn't work . . . that Kiyo would kill you."

"That's insane," I said. "Kiyo wouldn't kill me."

"Kiyo doesn't want the prophecy to come true," said Jasmine. "It's not that insane."

I turned on her. "He *loves* me. This whole idea . . . it's ridiculous."

"Why would I lie?" said Deanna. "You helped me. I'm helping you by warning you before I move on to the next world. I'm telling you, I *heard* them. Kiyo swore he'd make sure the prophecy couldn't be fulfilled."

"Kiyo. Loves. Me."

"Dorian loves you too," pointed out Jasmine.

"And look what he did. When you think about it, Kiyo's the type who'd think one tragic loss of life was worth saving many. Or something stupid like that."

"He would." Admitting it surprised me, and yet . . . as the meaning of Deanna's words sank deeper and deeper, I remembered my first meeting with Kiyo. He'd found me on Maiwenn's orders. They hadn't known what kind of person I was, if I'd wanted to fulfill the prophecy or not. He'd never said so explicitly, but my impression had been that both were willing to go to extreme means to stop Storm King's heir from being born. Our relationship had obviously changed since then, but maybe . . . maybe some things hadn't. . . .

"But he wouldn't go *that* far," I finished.

"Do you want to take that chance?" asked Jasmine softly. "Maybe he wouldn't really kill you, but you heard what he said about Maiwenn's 'magic' abortion."

What had Deanna claimed? That Kiyo and Maiwenn had planned to *make* me terminate the pregnancy if I wouldn't willingly?

"We just need to talk," I said, hoping I sounded convincing. My next words gave me away. "Somewhere I know I'm safe."

"Kiyo's in the waiting room," said Jasmine, seeing that I was finally taking this seriously. "Is this a safe place?"

"Probably not." I had finished getting dressed. "There must be a back door. There's *always* a back door. We'll go . . . we'll go home. I'll get my weapons, and then we'll go to the Otherworld. He and I can talk about this reasonably in the Thorn Land. I'll be safe there."

"You'll never make it there," said Deanna. I'd practically forgotten about her. "He can follow you. As soon as you leave here, he'll know and come after you."

"How could he—"

I lightly touched my upper arm, the spot where Kiyo's nails had barely dug in the other night. I took a deep, shaking breath. "He marked me," I said. He'd scratched me the first night we'd met too, leaving a long-healing wound that allowed him to track me wherever I went. This one was smaller but would work just as well.

Jasmine was already moving toward the door, so full of tension and purpose that she seemed much older. "We'll just go straight to the Otherworld then. You'll be safe there. Where's the nearest gateway?"

I racked my brain, thinking of our location. "By Morriswood Park. Farther than I'd like."

"Well, we have to go soon. If we stay here any longer, the doctor'll come ask what's wrong," said Jasmine. "And we can't let Kiyo find us in the parking lot."

"You'll never make it to the park in time," wailed Deanna. I scowled, but she was right. Jasmine looked at me questioningly. For a moment, I considered calling Volusian, but he might happily kill Kiyo and claim it was in my defense. I wasn't ready for that.

"I know where we can go," I said. "Come on."

We left the exam room, stepping out into the hallway. I turned with purpose, opposite the direction of the waiting room we'd entered from. This took us deeper into the clinic, past more examining rooms and their lab. A couple staff members passed us, but we walked confidently enough that no one stopped us. They probably assumed we'd been directed somewhere. Meanwhile, my eyes were searching for an exit sign. There *had* to be a back door. Surely hypocritical health professionals had to go somewhere to smoke.

"There."

I nodded toward an exit sign, praying it didn't lead to a fire door, which would be of no use to us. Nope. It was just an ordinary door, one probably used for maintenance or shipments. Someone did notice us then and start to ask what we were doing, but by then, we were outside and behind the building.

"Eugenie, where are we going?" asked Jasmine anxiously. Deanna had faded away, perhaps now finally leaving this world after fulfilling what she believed to be her last duty. As we walked briskly toward my car, some part of me kept wanting to think she'd lied. But why? As she'd said, she had no reason. She'd held true to me before.

And with every passing second, I grew more and more conflicted, wondering what I should believe. Kiyo loved me. He'd gone out of his way to win me back . . . but he was firmly set on protecting the human world. At any cost? We'd see. Deanna was mistaken; she had to be. My worst fate was probably going to be Kiyo's talking me to death.

We got in the car, and I did briefly consider

trying to make a break for Morriswood Park and its Otherworldly gate. After all, what was Kiyo going to do? Get in a high speed chase with us? The thing was, with that mark, he would be able to track me. He could probably feel me moving away now. If we headed anywhere near the park he'd figure it out. He'd either try to beat us there or just catch up with us on the other side. No, I had to go somewhere else. Somewhere with protection. Somewhere I could be sure I was safe until all of this madness was settled.

Jasmine's face grew increasingly troubled as we drove away from the doctor's office. She kept glancing back, as though expecting to see Kiyo right on our bumper. When we turned into a suburban neighborhood, her worry shifted to confusion.

"What is this?"

"Home," I replied, pulling into the driveway of a well-kept house surrounded by trees and flowers. A fence surrounded the backyard but couldn't hide the efforts someone had made to turn a Tucson backyard into something lush and green.

The gate in the fence was unlocked as I'd known it would be. The yard was unoccupied, save for birds and insects. The house's patio door had its glass open, covered only by a screen that let in the afternoon air. It too would be unlocked.

"Kiyo won't really do it," I muttered, as I jerked the door open. "Maybe he's upset . . . but we can talk this out. Deanna overreacted. *We're* overreacting."

We stepped into a small breakfast nook, and in the adjacent kitchen, a man spun around. My heart leapt when I saw him. The familiar, kind face. The graying hair. The tattoos of whorls and fishes. It felt like a lifetime since our last meeting.

Roland.

I'd gone to my parents' house.

Roland's reactions were those of a man who'd spent years fighting and training, but even that didn't prepare him for the sight of us. Astonishment filled his features, quickly giving way to outrage.

"Eugenie! What are you—"

"Get your weapons," I ordered, casting an uneasy glance behind me. Jasmine followed as I strode toward him. "Whatever you've got in the house."

He didn't move. "You know you're not—"

"Get them!" I exclaimed. "We don't have time for this!"

I don't know what look I wore on my face, but it was enough to pierce the walls of hurt and anger he'd built between us since learning of my involvement in the Otherworld. I'd taken a risk coming here, a gamble that no matter what happened, Roland would protect me. And I was right. He transformed before my eyes, suddenly the concerned and caring stepfather I'd grown up with.

"What's—"

Before he could finish, the screen door flew open. Kiyo stood there, face dark and stormy.

"What the hell are you doing?" he demanded. "Why did you take off?"

"You first," I said, taking a step back toward Roland. "What are *you* doing?" Jasmine moved to my other side. My eyes were on Kiyo, but I could sense Roland bracing for battle. Maybe he didn't know what was going on, but anyone could have seen how dangerous Kiyo was.

"I wanted to talk to you, and you disappeared!" Kiyo moved forward a little but stopped, recognizing the united front that Roland and I—and yes, even Jasmine—presented.

"Talk? Is that all you wanted to do?"

"Yes. Of course." Kiyo glanced between all of us. "You promised, Eugenie. You promised if it was a boy, you'd get rid of it."

"There's a girl too!" I exclaimed. "You can't get rid of one without the other."

"It doesn't matter," he said. "The consequences are too big."

"I can't kill an innocent. She hasn't done anything."

"Not directly. Letting her live means *he* lives. And there's nothing innocent there. He can't live. Eugenie, you know that. I'm not trying to be cruel. Please. Do what's right."

Jasmine and Roland remained silent as this drama played out. Meanwhile, I realized how sickened the language of this whole matter continued to make me. *Get rid of it. He can't live.*

"You're so quick to kill your own children," I said in disbelief, echoing what Jasmine had said a few days before. "Don't you feel *any* remorse? You know better than me what it's like to be a parent!"

"Yes," he said, clenching his fists. "I do know.

And it's amazing. I wish you could know what it's like. . . ."

"But I can't? I can't have the same chance you and Maiwenn had?"

Kiyo shook his head. "You aren't the same as Maiwenn. You can't ever be."

It was like a gut-punch. I was stunned into silence, and a bit of his fierceness eased. I think he read my reaction as acceptance.

"Look, I don't get this," he said. "I don't get why you're resisting all of this after what you've always said! You never wanted a baby—any baby. If you've changed your mind, then . . . well, try again. You just can't have these."

"And what then? I just keep having abortions until a girl comes along? What kind of a sick bastard are you?" I moved forward without realizing it, my anger exploding. Roland put a hand on my arm, keeping me back. It wasn't affection. It was a warning. It was defensive strategy, keeping us together.

"I'm trying to protect the human world," Kiyo said. He hadn't come any closer, but he was as ready as we were, his reflexes even faster. "And you should be too."

"And what happens if I don't do what you want?" I asked quietly. Here it was, the moment of truth.

He sighed. "I don't want it to come to that."

"To what?" My voice rose sharply, the anguish in me ready to explode. *What will you do?*

"I'll take you to Maiwenn—by force. And then . . . and then she'll take care of it."

"The hell you will," I said. Goddamnit, I wished

I had a weapon. I almost always traveled with them—but not to the doctor's office. Out of the corner of my eye, I saw Roland's hand rest on the counter and wrap around something. A wand. He'd had his wand in the kitchen. But of course he would. Unlike me, he hadn't become careless. "I'll never let that happen. You guys aren't going to experiment on me!"

Kiyo's face displayed a mix of emotions. There was sorrow and disappointment. He did care. He didn't want this fight between us—but he also believed in his greater good. He believed he had to do anything to stop the prophecy, and I knew then that Deanna had spoken the truth. Ideally, he just wanted the pregnancy to end. If that wasn't possible, then I was what needed to be eliminated.

"How can you do this?" he asked, his voice both a threat and a plea. "How can you risk all this—just to save one life?"

It was only in that moment, as the words left my lips, that I learned the truth about myself, what I'd been holding deep inside. The girl and boy thing didn't matter. Only the heartbeats did—those tiny, rapid heartbeats pounding in my ears . . .

"I'm not," I told him. "I'm saving two lives."

I sealed my fate with that. Kiyo moved so fast that I wasn't prepared for the attack. He sprang toward me, shape-shifting as he did into his giant fox form, fangs out, snarling. A blast of wind slowed—but didn't stop—his leap, providing enough time for Roland to jerk me out of the way. The wind magic hadn't come from me. It had been Jasmine, which was why the power hadn't packed much of a punch. The unaccustomed magic left her gasping, but it had been enough to buy us a brief escape.

Roland pulled me out of the kitchen, out to where we had more space to maneuver in the living room. Kiyo followed without hesitation, all brute strength and speed.

"He can be banished," I gasped out to Roland. "The same as a gentry."

Roland gave a brisk nod of acknowledgment. He already knew this, but in the sudden flurry, he didn't have the necessary pause to do a full banishing. Kiyo reached us, throwing himself on me and pushing me away from Roland. I fell hard to the ground, Kiyo's weight pinning me there. As quickly as he'd turned fox, he transformed back into a man. Still displaying amazing speed, he pulled me up by the arm. I didn't know if his intentions were simply to cart me out of the house or to attempt a world-jump then and there, but I didn't give him the chance. I'd recovered my senses and took hold of my magic. The air grew thick, and a hurricane-worthy gust blasted him away—along with a substantial part of my parents' furniture.

Kiyo grimaced as he regained his footing and agonizingly took one step at a time toward me.

"Damn it!" he yelled over the roar of the wind. "Stop this!"

"*You* stop this!" I shouted back. The magic burned in my blood, and no matter how annoyingly weak the pregnancy had made me, my power hadn't diminished too much. "We don't even know that this prophecy's real! I've already

met one fake seeress. It could all be for nothing."
Roland and my mother had once told me that
prophecies were a dime a dozen in the Otherworld, and I'd seen that to a certain extent. Until
now, I'd never wanted to take the chance that
mine wouldn't come true.

"But we don't know!" Kiyo countered. I could
see the irritation on his face. I was keeping a
storm raging around me, one that held him at bay
while hopefully Roland began a banishing. "We
can't risk it. *Please*. Please come back with me to
Maiwenn. We'll fix this."

I didn't answer and instead kept the storm
going. My gaze stayed on Kiyo, but I felt the tingle
of shamanic magic—human magic—beginning to
glimmer. Roland was indeed performing a banishing spell.

Kiyo transformed into a fox again, and with that
extra strength, he managed to push through the
storm-shield around me and knock me to the
ground again. He stayed as a fox this time, holding
onto that strength. His teeth bit into my shirt,
through to my shoulder, and I yelled out in pain. My
magic wavered, and to my astonishment, he began
dragging me—slowly—across the living room.

His progress was halted when a small end table
slammed into his back. I tell you, those things are
lethal. Instinctively, he reared up against his at-
tacker: Jasmine. He shoved her away, and she stumbled back. Snarling, Kiyo returned to me, and I had
the uneasy feeling my odds were getting worse as to
whether he'd cart me away or just kill me. He could
hold on to human thoughts in fox form, but they

became increasingly influenced by animal reactions the longer he stayed transformed.

He suddenly looked away from me, gold eyes on Roland, who stood planted firmly across the room with his wand extended. I'd sensed the banishing earlier because of my training. Now, with the spell in full force, Kiyo could feel it too. Abandoning me for the new threat, Kiyo raced toward Roland. I screamed as all that animal power slammed into my stepfather, pinning him against the wall. The wand flew from Roland's hand. The banishing spell disintegrated.

Kiyo shifted to human form again, still trapping Roland. Roland was strong but couldn't match Kiyo's strength. Struggling was useless.

"Stop it," cried Kiyo. "Both of you."

His arm pressed against Roland's neck. Roland managed a gasp as the grip cut off his air. Immediately, I let the storm magic around me drop. As I did, I felt that Jasmine had been lending her strength to me without me even realizing it. She too ceased her wielding and struggled up from where she'd been knocked down, coming to stand with me once again. The room fell eerily still.

"Let him go," I growled, moving slightly forward. I knew I couldn't win against Kiyo in a physical fight, but I also couldn't let him harm Roland. "This isn't about him. Don't hurt him."

"Believe me," said Kiyo, "I don't want to." His eyes were dark and human again, but there was still some feral glint in there. "Come with me, and I'll release him."

"Come with you," I said flatly. "To Maiwenn's?"

"You'll thank me later," said Kiyo.

My mind raced frantically. Roland was struggling for breath. How much longer did he have? Would Kiyo really kill him? I wondered if I could get off another blast of magic. Another attack of wind? Lightning? I could create a controlled bolt indoors, but it'd probably kill both men. And if I went with Kiyo . . . let him take me to Maiwenn . . . well. There'd be no getting out of that, no escape.

Roland looked ready to pass out. His blue eyes were fixed on me, and then, quickly, he glanced toward my feet. I thought it was him about to lose consciousness, but then I saw the purpose in his eyes. His wand was near my feet, within easy reach. I didn't let on to Kiyo that I'd noticed. Roland's eyes returned to me, some message there.

"Please," I begged, wondering frantically what Roland wanted me to do. "Let him go." I couldn't pull off a banishing spell. There wasn't enough time. Kiyo would release Roland, true, but then I'd be the one attacked again. I honestly didn't know how long Kiyo would play it safe. He was attempting "reasonable" solutions: force me to go to Maiwenn, blackmail with Roland, et cetera. Sooner or later, if he truly believed the prophecy's threat, he would simply eliminate me.

Roland was still staring at me, still wanting me to do something he thought would save us. He'd trained me. Surely I could figure it out. I *had* to. What could a wand do? It cast spells. It banished creatures, sending them out of this world. . . .

I felt my eyes widen. I knew what he was telling me to do. Doing it would save him, I was certain, because Kiyo would release him and come after me . . . into the Otherworld. Roland wanted me to open a gateway for myself. I could do it. It was a fast spell, one I had the power for. Forcing another being through was what took so much time and effort. But opening the gate and stepping through? That could be done quickly.

If it could be done. Getting in was easy. Passing through the worlds unassisted was hard, and I'd even had trouble going through fixed, physical gates lately in my weakened state. Making a blind, unaided transition might not even be possible for me. I'd done it once before, and it had required a lot of power. And dear God, had it hurt. If I could do it, though . . . I'd get away from Kiyo, and Kiyo would let Roland go in order to chase me down. This could buy me the time to flee to safety.

The only thing that might make it possible was that I had anchors in the Otherworld to help pull me in. If I jumped with no solid destination, I could end up trapped between the worlds, my essence disintegrated. Hell, that might still happen, but an anchor would reduce the likelihood. I didn't know where I was in relation to the Otherworld's layout, but the closest anchor would pull me in if this worked.

Time to find out.

With speed that rivaled Kiyo's, I reached for the wand and then grabbed hold of Jasmine's hand. Bringing her only made my task more difficult, but I wouldn't leave her to Kiyo. With the wand, I summoned the necessary magic and ripped open a gate to the Otherworld. Kiyo realized what was happening and released Roland, trying to reach me—but it was too late. I threw myself into the opening, clinging to Jasmine, and knew it would shut immediately behind us, simply because I couldn't hold open a personal gate for long.

It felt just as painful as last time, like I was crashing through the floors in a building. Down, down, down. Smash, smash, smash. Each layer was more agonizing than the last, and with each blow, I felt like I was being torn apart. It was likely I was, and I would destroy Jasmine with me, ripping our souls from our bodies.

Then, I sensed a tug. My soul turned toward it, and I felt my fractured self coalesce and become whole, even as that falling, excruciating sensation continued. Then—there was only one impact left: a real one. Jasmine and I slammed into a hard stone floor. My body cried out at the pain. True, physical pain. I had already been hurting from the fight with Kiyo, and now, crashing through the worlds had taken that pain to new levels.

Nausea welled up in me, and I fought hard not to throw up. I could hear Jasmine whimpering, but the sights around us were a blur as my disoriented mind tried to get a hold of itself. Finally, the world came into focus, the colors and lines growing sharp once more. A faint hum of magic in the air, one that was always present, told me I'd made it intact to the Otherworld.

And Dorian was looking down at me.

Chapter 25

"Ow."

I squeezed my eyes shut as another wave of nausea rolled through me. *Control, control.* A few deep breaths later, I opened my eyes and met Dorian's gaze.

"Unexpected," he said in that dry way of his. "And unwelcome."

I sat at the base of his throne in the banquet hall, which was packed. It must have been mealtime, but no one was paying attention to the food. They were all on their feet, staring at the evening entertainment that had literally dropped into their midst. I peered around, wondering how I'd been drawn to this spot and then found it—the Slinky I'd left here as my anchor. It had once had its own little room, but now sat on a table beside Dorian's throne, one he kept small treasures and knickknacks on to amuse him when holding court. Odd placement.

There was no time to ponder that, though. I turned to Jasmine who looked as disoriented and sick as I felt but didn't seem to have suffered any permanent damage. Her body and soul were intact, which was what counted. I looked back at Dorian and tried to stand up, but my legs gave way beneath me. I started to fall and clutched his robe instinctively. Jasmine, with surprising speed, moved in to catch my arm and steady me.

"Hospitality," I gasped out. "Please."

Dorian's *unwelcome* comment had been a reminder that I currently didn't have hospitality and that I was technically trespassing and fully vulnerable to attack within his walls. Yet, the fact that I hadn't already been removed was a good sign, and though his expression more or less remained unchanged, there was a spark of curiosity in his eyes. He couldn't ignore me on my knees, begging him for protection. Not yet. No matter how angry he was at me, this kind of novelty was too irresistible for his nature.

He started to speak, undoubtedly ready with some witty quip, but was interrupted when Jasmine clutched at him and added her pleas to mine. "Please. Give us your protection. Hurry!"

Dorian frowned, no longer able to hide his curiosity and surprise. "The daughters of Storm King, begging me for help after one made it *quite* clear she didn't ever want to see me again. Do tell me why I shouldn't have you thrown out or imprisoned." He paused thoughtfully. "Or ransomed back to your own people. Quite a profit there, I imagine."

"Dorian—" I began.

Suddenly, there was a commotion at the hall's

entrance. A cluster of Dorian's guards appeared—
with Kiyo between them. I wasn't surprised he'd
showed up so quickly. My mark would have led
him right to me, and while he couldn't jump directly into Dorian's castle, he'd probably crossed
over right in front of the gates.

"Sire," said one of the guards. "He seeks
entrance—"

Kiyo wore that fierce, raging expression, and no
one in that room could have any doubt that he
was there ready for battle. Dorian's guards certainly had picked up on it, and they closed ranks
as he strode forward. I had a feeling Kiyo wanted
to fight right through them, but reason and self-
control held him at bay—for now.

Meanwhile, at the sight of him, I managed to
make my legs work again and scrambled to my
feet. Jasmine grasped my hand, helping me rise,
and as one, we backed up slightly so that we stood
in line with Dorian. The world reeled a little, but
I refused to show my weakness. I would not faint.

"Get rid of him," I said, trying not to sound hysterical. "Deny him hospitality and throw him out."

"She's an outcast here," growled Kiyo, fists
clenched. "And this has nothing to do with you.
Send her away."

Tension and silence filled the space between all
of us, and all eyes swiveled to Dorian. Neither Kiyo
nor I—nor Jasmine, for that matter—had hospitality and protection within Dorian's household at
the moment. We had no guarantees of safety.
Hell, if Kiyo decided to attack me right now, no
one had to intervene. We would be a great dinner

show. I wondered how good a defense Jasmine and I could put up, if it would be enough to give us a chance to escape to my own land if Dorian wouldn't help us.

I could guess Dorian's thoughts—or rather, his confusion. That Kiyo would be on the verge of killing me made no sense. Asking why would go against Dorian's natural, all-knowing façade. Plus, Kiyo and I weren't his favorite people right now. Giving in to either of us meant a concession Dorian didn't want to make.

"Hail to you!"

An unexpected, raspy voice made me jump, and even Dorian flinched a little. From the crowd, Masthera had emerged, her white hair streaming behind her and eyes as wide as ever. She came forward with purpose and—to my total astonishment—fell onto her knees before me. She stared up at me, and I expected that usual scattered and crazy look. Instead, I saw awe and rapture. Worship, even.

"Hail to you, Queen of Rowan and Thorn. Hail to you, bringer of life, bringer of life. I see it—I see the life growing within you, the mother who will fulfill the prophecy!"

She reached a skeletal hand toward my stomach, and I jerked away from her grasp. "Don't touch me!" I exclaimed.

"I see it," she cried. "You shine, Queen of Rowan and Thorn. You carry the heir. You shine with it."

"Dorian!" exclaimed Kiyo, drawing our attention back. His expression had grown dark at Masthera's words. Full disclosure was the last thing he wanted. "Give her to me! Stay out of this!"

I again looked pleadingly at Dorian. "He's going to try to kill me," I said. "If you throw me out, he and Maiwenn will come after me. Please give us your hospitality."

Dorian—like most everyone in the hall—had been left dumbstruck by Masthera's proclamation. Dorian forcibly schooled his face back to neutrality, but the gaze he turned on me was so heavy and penetrating that I was nearly knocked to my knees again.

"Is it true?" he asked in a low voice that probably only Jasmine heard. "Are you pregnant?"

There was no point in lying or pretending. I gave a swift nod.

His next question nearly broke my heart. He tried so hard to keep his voice level and strong, but I heard the break in it, the longing and desperation. "Is it—is there any chance—is it—"

He couldn't finish but didn't need to. He wanted to know if he was the father. A million thoughts raced through my head. Would things have been different if we'd actually had intercourse the last time we were together? Would I have gotten pregnant with his child, instead of Kiyo's? Maybe. Maybe not. Sex didn't always lead to pregnancy, especially with the gentry. I could still have ended up with Kiyo's babies or been left with a talk show-worthy paternity dispute. If Dorian had been the one to get me pregnant, my future would have been signed and sealed. He would have moved heaven and earth to keep me

safe. As it was, I probably could have lied now. The
gentry had no paternity tests. That would have
simplified things—but I couldn't do it.

"No," I said softly.

Dorian's features stilled, and a surprising wave
of regret and sorrow filled me in response to the
cavalcade of emotions that had to be going
through him as well. He had no reason to help me,
not after what he saw as my betrayal. And certainly
not with me carrying another man's children.

"Please," said Jasmine. Her blue-gray eyes were
large and desperate. I'd never seen her so humble
and meek. And I'd certainly never expected to see
it on my behalf. "Please help us. Please give us
your hospitality. Your Majesty."

My eyes were still locked with Dorian's, my
heart still breaking over the hurt I'd caused him.
Off to the side, I heard Kiyo warn Dorian again,
"This is between Eugenie and me. Give her to me,
and this ends. If you don't, Maiwenn and God
knows who else will get involved."

"I'm sorry," I said to Dorian, my voice barely
audible. "I'm so sorry."

"Please," Jasmine repeated, nearly on the verge
of tears now. "Hospitality."

The whole world hinged on Dorian. No one
breathed. Then, abruptly, he turned away from me.

"Granted," he said crisply. "The daughters of
Storm King are under my protection. Remove the
kitsune, and do not allow him entrance again."

The guards were in motion almost before
Dorian finished speaking. More had slipped into
the room in the last minute or so, and it was a good

thing too. Kiyo fought against all of them as they laid hands on him and began dragging him backwards. They made little progress, so great were his struggles He was strong, so insanely strong, and it scared me to think what would have happened if I'd been left to him in my weakened state.

"Dorian!" roared Kiyo, still fighting against the guards' grip. "Don't do this! You'll regret it!"

Dorian had returned to his normal laconic persona. "You will address me as 'King Dorian' or 'Your Majesty,'" he replied. "And you will *not* disobey my orders within my home."

The floor trembled, and I heard a gasp from those gathered. Uneasily, I remembered an idle comment Dorian had once made, about how he could bring the castle down around us if he wanted to. The walls stayed intact, however, but a large section of the stone floor ripped up, eliciting more cries of fear. Before my eyes, the slab of stone morphed and stretched, then flew through the air toward Kiyo. It wrapped itself around his torso, enclosing his arms in a sort of magical straightjacket. Kiyo, unsurprisingly, stopped struggling, but his shouts didn't cease.

"Eugenie! You don't know what you're doing! This isn't over! *Eugenie!*"

"Get him out," said Dorian coldly. "Now. If he resists again or changes form, kill him."

The guards hurried to obey while Kiyo continued yelling his outrage at me, Dorian, and the world. I hoped they moved fast because Dorian had had a point. If Kiyo transformed into a fox, he'd slip out of his stone prison. Of course, he'd have to transform into a small fox, which would do little harm, but still. It would be a lot better for all of us once Kiyo was outside the walls.

The guards must have succeeded because no more commotion followed. Jasmine turned to Dorian.

"You should have killed him anyway," she said flatly. Her standard response.

The ghost of a smile flickered across Dorian's lips, though his eyes were still hard. "You're nearly as delightful as your sister," he observed. "No matter how displeased I am at the two of you right now, I admit, things will certainly be entertaining with you around. And they will become *very* entertaining soon." That was directed at me. "If you think you brought a war down before, you haven't seen anything yet, my dear. You've caused me quite a bit of trouble."

I barely heard him. The adrenaline was fast fading from my body, and all the pain from fighting with Kiyo and then doing the forced transition began returning. I felt sick, and my surroundings were spinning once again.

"Sorry," I managed to say to Dorian, just before collapsing.

Chapter 26

"So, let me make sure I'm following this correctly."

I sighed and shifted on the bed, knowing Dorian was repeating this conversation mostly because he liked seeing my discomfort.

"Your 'technology' can tell you you're having a boy and a girl, when they're due, and allow you to hear their heartbeats," he continued. "But some medicine inexplicably totally counteracted the other one you take to prevent pregnancy."

"*Took*," I muttered. "Seeing as it's kind of pointless now."

Dorian leaned back in a plush armchair, face expressing overly dramatic pondering. After fainting, I'd been given a guest room befitting my status, a good sign since 'hospitality' simply meant protection and in no way related to one's accommodations. It wasn't quite as nice as Dorian's room, of course, but the mattress was thick and fluffy, and the green velvet canopy coordinated with the heavy brocaded bedding. As sick as I'd felt, I honestly would have been content to curl up on the floor somewhere. I'd been awake for about an hour now, alone in the vast room save for Dorian.

"What a fascinatingly bizarre turn of events," he mused, stroking his chin. "If you thought the Iron Crown scared people, just wait until this news spreads. Which, of course, it already has."

I draped a hand over my forehead. "Isn't it bad enough that I'm carrying a world-conquering prophecy child? Why all the political fallout?"

"Because you're carrying a world-conquering prophecy child," he responded. "It's the type of thing people tend to have strong feelings about."

"I thought almost everyone wanted to conquer the human world."

"Most," he agreed. "But not all. Especially those who—after observing your record thus far— might fear you'll conquer this world first."

I rolled over to my side, giving me a better view of him. Since the earlier spectacle, Dorian had masked whatever personal feelings he had about my pregnancy, switching into cunning ruler mode. "But not you," I said. "You've always been in favor of this—fulfilling the prophecy."

"I've never made a secret of that," he agreed. "From the moment we met."

That was true, at least. He'd sat on that desire while we were involved, but I'd always known it lurked. "You've just kept other secrets instead," I blurted out.

He didn't answer me right away, but those

green-gold eyes weighed me thoughtfully. "Yes. Yes, I have. Secrets I now regret."

That silenced me for several moments. I hadn't expected any kind of apology. Something in me softened toward him. "Really?"

"If I hadn't deceived you about the Iron Crown," he explained, "we would still be together."

I could only stare. The piece of me that had never stopped loving him tentatively reared its head. It was hard to believe he was here confessing his feelings, admitting that what we'd had had been more important than his scheming. It gave me a new insight into him, one that astonished . . . yet pleased me.

"And if we'd stayed together," he continued, "*I* would have been the lucky beneficiary of this medicinal slip."

So much for new insight.

I groaned and turned away. "Of course. Of course that's the real source of your regret. You don't get to lead the revolution."

I heard him get up and sit on the bed beside me. A few seconds later, he actually had the audacity to lie down. I wiggled over to make room.

"It's more than revolution," he said. "I *also* told you the first time we met that I'd have a child with you, regardless of any prophecy."

"I'm not convinced that the 'with me' part was so relevant."

Dorian touched my cheek and turned my face toward his. "Do you really believe that? Do you really believe my feelings for you were so small that your being the mother of my child wouldn't have meant the world to me?"

I started to snarkily correct him with *worlds*, but it seemed petty. "I don't know what I believe," I said honestly. "I don't even know if I have the energy or motivation to analyze our relationship when I have *this* going on." I rested my hand on my stomach. Dorian's eyes followed that motion, utterly captivated.

"Despite your foolish fathering choices, this . . ." He reached toward my stomach as well, then pulled back. "This is a miracle. This is a prophecy fulfilled. This is life. And really, Kiyo is no longer relevant. He's given up any claims to these children. They are yours and yours alone now."

My fingers tightened on my stomach, not painfully, but more in a possessive type of way. My gaze grew unfocused. "I still can't believe that. I can't believe that he'd dismiss his own children so easily. That he'd dismiss *me* so easily . . ."

"I doubt it was easy. You aren't that easy to get over." A small note of bitterness there. "But his opposition to the prophecy was too great. Just as my support is great enough to take you in— despite your betrayal—and embark in the madness to come."

Betrayal? I started to tell him he was the last one who should accuse anyone of that—but held back. "Will people think you're crazy to do it?"

"Hardly," he snorted. "Most will think they're my children anyway, ironically enough." No one except Jasmine had heard my brief paternity exchange with Dorian in the hall.

I frowned. "I think sometimes Kiyo does too."

"They can be."

My first reaction was that this was some sort of joke of his, but all humor had disappeared from his face. "I don't think you fully understand genetics."

"I understand that parenting is more than just blood," he said, still deadly earnest. "And as I said: he's relinquished any claims. You are in control, and if even he and others question the children's parentage, then so much the better. Simply declare me the father. Have it recorded, and by our laws, the children will be mine for all intents and purposes."

Something about that set off my alarms. "What do you mean 'intents and purposes'?"

He shrugged—a bit too casually. "Titles. Prestige. Protection. Inheritance—if either is strong enough to hold my kingdom. Which, according to the prophecy, your son should be."

"I don't know," I said. There might be some safety benefits to this sort of gentry 'adoption,' but I had a feeling that Dorian wasn't telling me all of them—particularly things that benefited him alone. He was still upset with me. He didn't like Kiyo. There was no reason that I could see for this. "I have to think about it."

"Think fast," Dorian said. "Things will be in motion soon, particularly once we get you back to your own lands."

"Why?" I asked. "Why would you want to claim someone else's children? I mean, I get your wanting to see the prophecy come true, but you don't have to take that extra step."

"Maybe someone else's children are better than no children at all," he said.

It was another odd statement from him, a surprising one. Both philosophical and touching. Yet, I still believed there was a deception here. This wasn't out of love for me. Not anymore. His hand moved toward my stomach again and he didn't pull it away this time, though he made sure to keep away from my hand.

"Let me ask you a question," he said when I made no response. "Why did *you* choose to keep these children? Do you fear the unholy procedure your people use to end life? Were you unable to live with your daughter's blood on your hands?"

My mind rewound back to that day at the doctor's. That day? Hell. It had only been earlier today. So much had happened since then that weeks might have gone by. My horrible ordeal with Kiyo had blurred the memories, but now, the ultrasound came back to me, the sights and sounds as real and vivid as though I were experiencing them all over again.

"I heard their heartbeats," I said at last. "And I saw them." Well, kind of. Those blurs still didn't look like much to me, but the point was irrelevant. "And when I did . . ." I groped to explain my feelings. "I just . . . I just wanted them. Both of them. None of the rest mattered."

A slow, strange smile spread across Dorian's face. "That," he declared, "is the most gentry thing I've ever heard you say."

Normally, I would have mocked him for using 'gentry' instead of 'shining ones.' It was a slip he sometimes made around me. His words' content, however, was of more importance. "That's ridiculous."

"Not so. Humans overthink things. They throw away life heedlessly. Honestly, after all this time, I was beginning to think you were more human than shining one."

"I hate to tell you, but I am," I said.

Dorian made himself more comfortable, and the hand on my stomach moved so that his arm lay over me, almost—but not quite—an embrace. It was possessive, like I was a prize that had fallen into his lap. "Are you, my dear? You're expressing philosophies very like my own. You're carrying a child that will allegedly conquer the human world—a world you can't go back to for a while, seeing as it would give the kitsune an edge. You're safer here in this world where, I'd like to add, you rule not one but *two* kingdoms. That," he declared triumphantly, "makes you, by my reckoning, more like a gentry than a human."

I looked away, not meeting his eyes—because I had a crazy feeling he was right.

NEW YORK TIMES BESTSELLING AUTHOR

RICHELLE MEAD

DARK SWAN

Graphic Novel
COMING 2011